REC the ORD
KEEPER

BY AGNES GOMILLION AND AVAILABLE FROM TITAN BOOKS

The Record Keeper
The Seed of Cain (June 2020)

RECORD the KEEPER

AGNES GOMILLION

TITAN BOOKS

The Record Keeper
Print edition ISBN: 9781789091151
E-book edition ISBN: 9781789091168

Published by Titan Books
A division of Titan Publishing Group Ltd
144 Southwark Street, London SE1 0UP
www.titanbooks.com

First edition: June 2019
10 9 8 7 6 5 4 3 2 1

A CIP catalogue record for this title is available from the British Library.

Printed and bound in the United States.

To Herron always, and Lana. More, to the birds
and the Byrds, especially Bill and Connie.

RECORD OF THE LIFE

OF

ARIKA COBANE

AN

AMERICAN SLAVE

WRITTEN BY HERSELF

"To make a contented slave, you must make a thoughtless one. It is necessary to darken his moral and mental vision, and, as far as possible, to annihilate his power of reason. He must be able to detect no inconsistencies in slavery ... If there be one crevice through which a single drop can fall, it will certainly rust off the slave's chain."

FREDERICK DOUGLASS

EDITED BY M. LARK PARADISE
SOUTH CAROLINA COLONY
c.1739 A.D.

PREFACE

Dear Reader,

The following record is no fiction. I am aware that many of my adventures will seem incredible to you. And yet, they are true. I have not concealed names or places that you might substantiate the facts as they come to pass. I cannot know where or when you are. If you are Kongo or friends of the English. Will you keep my words or toss them away? I cannot know. And yet, like any good Kongo, I hope my story, faithfully told, will persist. I will speak it out onto these pages so, even when I die, my story will live on. And even when these pages die, breaking into dust, my story will live. Now in a book, now in a letter, now on a breath. Now in a song, now in a dance, now in the sea. Now, I cannot imagine. Such things are best left to the one true God, Soltice.

Arika Cobane

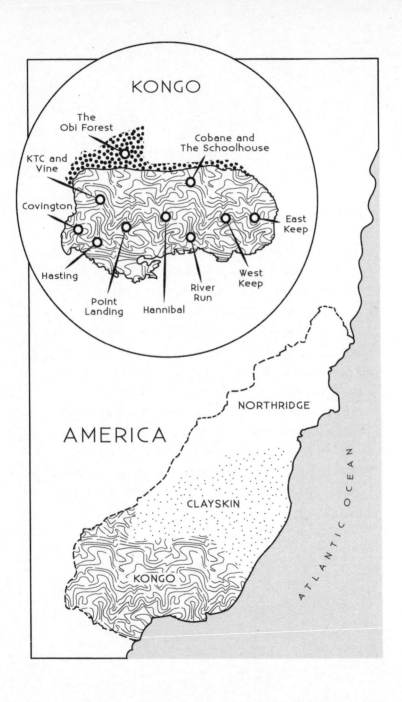

PART ONE

THE
SCHOOL
HOUSE

THE REBEL

I sang a song as I sprang from the womb—which is not unusual. After nine months many Kongos come like baby birds—crying and craning. What's strange is that I remember being in my mother's womb. The heat of the birthing channel, the thickness of the fetal fluid, the embrace of my enemy— *Funiculus umbilicalis.* It wrapped around my neck before I realized. I opened my unborn eyes to see it reared up over me, and I caught the snake by the throat. I tossed it over my shoulder like a braided scarf. Thus, I was delivered. Embattled and calling like a canary.

I recall the shock of the cold world on my skin, and the hands that caught my slippery form. I can't forget my mother's face—because I never saw it. It was hidden from me, and I from her, in accordance with the law. The laws, back then, were many. And this one applied only to us, the darkest race in the southernmost territory—the Kongo.

They say my voice resounded that day. A victorious refrain, although I don't personally recall the song. Years later, my papa sang it to me again and again, until I remembered:

I am Arika of House Cobane.

Do not swaddle me.

I dare you.

I dare you.

•

In keeping with full disclosure, I'll share my reservations. Men, as you know, are not permitted in birthing rooms in any American territory, except the Northridge, where male doctors attend. How, then, my papa came to hear my first song, from his hut, where he would have been obliged to wait, I cannot know. All I can say, without trampling on his memory, is this: for seventeen years, before I met him and he sang it to me in buttery baritone, that song he could not have heard clung to the back of my throat like coal.

Shortly after my birth, I was settled in the Cobane nursery, with every other baby born in the village that year. They called us brothers and sisters and we suckled from the same handful of heavy-breasted attendants. I milked one ripe coconut, touching toes with my sister, who fed off the other. Across the room, our brothers fed in much the same way. We were not related by blood, but we were closer than family; we were comrades! So close, the lines between us blurred. I was me, and them, and us—and we were comrades!

Instead of one mother, we had many. And every Kongo man was our father. On Sunday afternoons after work in the field, mother would come en masse, forming a line so long it curved like a hazel rainbow. I remember hearing her slough off the week as she waited to mother us, pulling her neck from side to side so it popped.

I remember the day she ran late. I cried incessantly, so a

nursery attendant offered me her dry breast. I sucked in a mouthful of sour milk, retched and pushed it away—only to have her pull me back and pin me by the neck. She was new, and didn't know any better.

I broke free, of course. I reared back and sent out a cry to my comrades. *Hurrah!* They rallied at once. *Hurrah!* Waking from their naps, slapping their own tits away. With me at the helm, we bawled—*Hurrah!*—until our cries reached the fields of Cobane. Our mother came at once—as I knew they would. I saw their face in the nursery door, like dawn, and I gave the okay. We settled down, cooing like kittens. We had won.

In the old world, where they studied the stars for signs, they'd say I was born on a cusp. Part bull, part twin, double-minded and stubborn, practical and adventurous. The old world had many strange beliefs. This one seemed true that day, as I curled in our mother's lap. In my ignorance, I supposed my bullishness had won the day. I knew not the law of the land, the Niagara Compromise. I had not heard of its omnipotence. Nevertheless, it hemmed us *all* in, *every* day.

The next morning, I was classified as a Record Keeper. I woke early, as a pair of dark hands lifted me from our crib. His dark lips kissed my forehead as he carried me out of the nursery and across the meadow to the big white house serviced by the Cobane village. I was one year old that morning.

A Teacher with a pale face received me. She took me to a small crib where, alone for the first time, I cried. I cried and cried, growing weak and sick. I imagined my nursery family waiting, just beyond the ecru cage of bars, and I called to us— *Comrades*—but we did not come. That was the first night of the first phase of my training, *Separation*.

The second night was the same, as was the third. I resisted for seven times longer than any initiate before or since. As a result, I was held back from my class and spent the next phase of my training, *Ingraining*, in my dormitory—alone—with three exceptions. I heard conversations through the power-fan grates, though I never spoke back. Second, a trio of nervous Clayskin maids, diplomats from the Clayskin Territory, alternated bringing my meals.

My third companion was one of three dozen diplomats from the Northridge, where the English people dwell. These diplomats handpicked us from our village nurseries and lived with us in the Schoolhouse. I never learned this particular woman's name. I called her Teacher.

"The Niagara Compromise, Article 4, Section 3, Kongo Classification." She paced before me, wan-faced, as she lectured. "We, the Committee of Representatives, have observed two brothers of men, each as dark as the other. The first has a narrow nose and ample intellect."

She stopped, turned and thumped my nose.

"His hair grows in the thick bush fashion, and his mouth is finely drawn." She waved a hand at my cap of dark brown hair, declining to touch it. Then her eyes skimmed my mouth, leveling on the small black dot just above it. I ducked my head, hiding the mole from her sight.

She slid a glossy drawing of a Kongo man onto my desk, pointing out his features with a bony finger. "The Second Brother has a heavy nostril," she said, tapping his nose. "He is brutish in mind and sparsely furred. His mouth is like his spirit, coarse and low. Both men are Kongo, each as dark as the other. But the First Brother, the Record Keeper, shall rule the Second."

I studied the picture, then blinked up at her. We'd gone over this before, hundreds of times.

Her lip curled. "You, girl, are classified as a Record Keeper. Your role, under the Compromise, is to manage the Second Brothers of your race—the workers. See to it that they know their place is in the field. You are better than them and you must conduct yourself accordingly. Now, repeat after me: no yelling, no running, no jumping—for the greater good."

"No yelling, no running, no jumping," I said.

Her eyes, the color of overcooked broccoli, narrowed. "Do you enjoy solitude, girl?"

I glanced at my dormitory window. There *were* other students in the Schoolhouse. Each morning, they filed out for exercise. They were stiff-backed, even as they played for an hour, then filed back in. Only then was *I* let out for exercise, a walk with Teacher close beside me. "No, Teacher. I would play with the others," I said.

"Then, for both our sakes, *be* assimilated! No yelling, no running, no jumping for the greater good."

I didn't know what *be assimilated* meant; I decided it meant *be quiet*. I stiffened my back, like the students at play, and whispered, "No yelling, no running, no jumping—*for the greater good.*"

She nodded. "Now again."

For five years, I learned the hallmarks of my classification— reading and writing. And, in time, I *assimilated*—or, at least, I appeared to. In truth, my spirit lay dormant. When Teacher wasn't looking, I imagined myself complete with wings arching from my back. And in my head, where she couldn't follow, I flew on those wings to my family.

I was seven when I got approval to join my peers in the next phase of training: *Primary School*. On the first day, I scurried along the Schoolhouse halls until I found the primary classroom door. I grasped the knob and stepped inside with a sigh. *Finally!* There, in stiff chairs, with their hair braided back too tight, was the skin of my skin, my family. And, just like that, my spirit awoke. My assimilation fell away.

"Comrades!" I cried, swelling with love. I hiked up my skirt and took the helm, jumping onto the nearest desk. It was occupied, but I didn't care.

"Comrades! It is I!" I dipped my knees and threw up a fist. "To me!"

Slowly, they turned, pupil after pupil, eyes narrowed and intelligent. But they didn't move. I frowned.

Suddenly, the classroom door opened behind me. Heels clicked, coming my way. *It must be the rules*, I thought. *No yelling, no running, no jumping.* They'd been quieted. I shouted again to wake them up, "Comrades, it is I! To me!" Leaping onto another desk, and another, I pleaded, buying time for them to rally. How long did it take me to realize that they wouldn't?

When it finally struck me, like lightning square in the heart, I slipped and fell. My nose cracked against the ground and spurted blood.

Above me, the other students jittered nervously as the heels at the door clicked closer. They whispered a name I didn't recognize. "Jones," they choked. "Jones!"

A gray skirt stopped beside me. Pointed boots protruded from beneath. The toes, fortified with steel, were black as rat snakes. A drop of blood shivered on the tip of my nose, as one toe began to tap. *Tap. Tap...*

THE PIT

The tapping stopped as a voice spoke from above. "Do you know what happens to children that won't learn their lesson?"

My eyes peeled from the boots and rolled up the skirt. I shivered, meeting her eyes. Ice blue and colder than her voice.

"Primary Cobane, I asked you a question." Her eyes sparked. "Answer me!"

My fear ripened and my teeth chattered in my head, sounding an alarm—*run!* I obeyed without thinking. Taking her by surprise, I jumped to my feet, and sprinted through the classroom door.

I didn't look back, but a pinch in the back of my throat told me she followed.

I sped up, racing down the hall, pumping as fast as my hobbled skirt would allow. My heart beat like a bird as I looked for escape. Suddenly, I found it, a window at the end of the wood-paneled hall. I lowered my head, ripping my skirt as I ran.

For years, I'd watched the workers from my dormitory window. In *bambi* cloth britches, they swayed with their labor, in the heat of the Kongo sun. They were hundreds of yards away. I couldn't hear their song. But I learned it from the rhythm of their work: swinging the sickle, catching the wheat, tossing the wheat, swinging the sickle.

I imagined I toiled along with them as I ran. *Swinging the sickle, catching the wheat, tossing the wheat, swinging the sickle.* The song became my breath, in and out. *Swinging the sickle, catching the wheat, tossing the wheat, swinging the sickle.* I lengthened my stride, and leapt up from the ground as my back began to tingle. I imagined I felt something sprouting there—my wings! They would lift me! Into the air, into the trees, where the wind breathed. *Swinging the sickle, catching the wheat, tossing the wheat, swinging the sickle.* I was close now. I'd dive through the window, fly to the village, rally my comrades there—only, *would they rally?*

I was at the window, about to leap, when I faltered. I pivoted, looking for another route. There wasn't one, and she was right behind me. I was cornered. I squared my shoulders and turned to face her.

"Primary Cobane," she said, delight in her eyes. "Students must not run in the Schoolhouse."

Before she could say more, I threw up a fist and charged at her middle. *"Hurrah!"*

Her hand darted out like a viper, opening and snapping shut, barely missing my throat.

I reared back, rallied, and charged again. *"Hurra—"*

Her fist drove into my ribs. I flew back, cracking my head on the pane. The last thing I saw was her nametag etched in gold, pinned to a cold, hard breast—Headmistress Jones.

•

A garbled sound woke me. A whisper crackling in and out—and there it was again! A girl chirping in the pitch black, but I couldn't make sense of her words. My eyes strained to see her.

I tried to shift, turn my head, but I couldn't move. I was locked in a space so tight, I barely fit. I was seated upright, my arms around my knees and my chin jammed between.

I was certainly alone, so what was that voice? *A ghost?* And where was I? *A tomb?* Suddenly, I remembered. The wan-faced Teacher had warned me of a dungeon in the Schoolhouse basement. This was not a tomb, but the Pit. Panicked, I arched my back and gasped for breath, bruising the knobs of my spine as, all around, the indistinct harping continued.

My only concept of time came each day, when Jones opened the iron grate above. Over my heart's refrain—*hold on, hold on, hold on*—I'd hear her ask the question. The same one, every day: do you need more? When I didn't answer, she'd give me a swallow of water, then slide the grate shut for another day.

Day three—the dark is complete. It sucks my bones to the marrow. Do you need more?

Day six—my grip on reality frays. My memories wobble. What is real? Did I only imagine my birth—my mother, my comrades? Were we all, like wings, merely figments?

Day eight—I am disappearing. *Hold on Hold on Hold on.* My nails grip the flesh of my arms, carving crescent moons in my biceps. My mind unravels. Do you need more?

Day ten—I am gone, lost in a dream, when the grate opens above me. Clean air rushes in and I drink it, as quick as I can. Suddenly, a hand grasps my arm and lifts me out of the Pit.

Blood needled through my limbs as she—Jones—dragged me from the dungeon. Bright light scorched my eyes. And, oh, the thirst! The thirst made me delirious. She pulled me up the stairs and down corridors until we came to the window from whence I'd attempted escape.

"Open your eyes," she commanded.

I did, seeing nothing but frightful shadows. Her gigantic form, a massive fist raised like a thundercloud.

"You will learn your lesson, girl. You will learn your lesson now."

The thundercloud zoomed and clapped. My nose broke. Fluid spewed. My neck snapped left and right. And still, the fist came. Relentless, whaling. *Whumph*, a tooth cracked. *Whumph*. My thirst paled as my head swam with pain. I dove and dodged—no good. The blows were methodical, falling again and again. I had to think. There had to be a way out. I twisted wildly. She caught me in the temple—once, my ears rang—twice, I went limp.

A sound woke me sometime later. A garbled whisper. The same voice from the tomb! Only now, the harping made sense. Broken exchanges I'd heard through the power-fan grates and whispers of pure fear. *She'll beat you like nothing for this. More, 'cause you've made her wait. Listen to me! Fall down with the first blow, okay? And don't scream. It'll make her mad. Don't plead; roll over and grovel. Play dumb. She'll like that. She likes to see the marks. So turn your face up, okay? Can you hear me?*

I opened one eye just as the shadow fist fell again. I angled my chin up, *crack*, it drove into my jaw. Again, again. Her hands, slick with blood and sweat, lost their grip. I slid to the floor. Fear whispered in my ear.

Whatever you do, stay far back from her feet. She'll kick like a donkey.

I curled into a ball, just in time. Her heavy foot drove the air from my lungs. I heaved with two more blows. *Umph umph*. My lips puckered and blood pooled in my mouth. Her leg swung back once more. My dread mounted. Back—up, up—for the blow, it swung. It would finish me. It would strike and I'd be done.

Don't plead! Roll over and grovel. Play dumb. She likes that.

Instinctively, I obeyed. My shoulders convulsed. I lay down on my belly and turned my face up, a humble swollen thing.

She grimaced, unsatisfied.

If you can, drool and roll your eyes. She likes that.

My neck stiffened and my gut resisted one final time—*No! I will not. I will*—Oh, but the pain was bad. And her leg was swung back for the kill. I hung my head, rolled my eyes and let my lip hang. Drool trickled down my chin.

For a heavy second, her leg hung there, suspended with my fate. Then, finally, she stepped back, shaking life into her dominant hand.

I collapsed.

She cracked her joints. "For a First Brother, you're a stupid mule, aren't you?"

Make sure you agree with everything she says, but stay quiet.

With my cheek flush to the ground, I nodded vigorously.

"Now, let's see if ten days in the Pit taught you anything." She bent, grabbed me by the neck and breathed into my ear, "Do you need more?"

When she came for me, I'd been dreaming of my papa, judicious with his affection, but fierce. He would look me over from a distance, with his hands tucked in at the waist, until he found something familiar in my face—a crooked tooth, an attached lobe. Then, he would smile. His song was always the same, and he sang it over and over, until I repeated.

Say Papa.

Say Papa!
Come now, say Papa.
Say Papa.
Say Papa!
Come now, say Papa.

A tear joined the mess on my face as I looked up at Headmistress Jones. Silver fish eyes, yellow hair, a thin line of lip. "Please, no more," I said. "Enough."

She straightened and pulled me upright.

My nose ran, tracing jowls on my cheeks.

"Very well. Now, stand up and follow me."

Her gaze sat upon me as I struggled to my feet, clutching the windowsill for balance. There was a thin line creeping up from the center of the pane. Once it reached the top, the glass would break in two. I froze.

If you jump now, the glass will oblige.

I looked out at the workers dotting the field like black ants. Their heads bowed, so I couldn't see their faces. I craned my neck to look down. We were quite high. I'd never make it. Biting my swollen lip, I turned from the window and limped after Jones.

Even after this incident, I struggled. During long lectures, my chair became a thousand pointed quills beneath me and my legs would riot, itching to jump and run. On especially bad days, I would slide one hand beneath my desk and pull my *bambi* skirt up, inch by inch, so the power fan—with its chill *hush*—cooled the rebellion in my limbs. It was months before I, finally, quieted completely. My wings, the run, the wood panels, the sun were one by one forgotten.

THE STUDENT

Ten years later, two days before I completed my training at the Schoolhouse, I began to remember. I was seventeen that winter, the year of the Great Drought, and my ambitions consumed me. I'd risen from last in the class to teacher's pet— Jones' favorite. I was valedictorian of the seven of us set to graduate—two from Cobane and West Keep, one each from East Keep, Covington and Hannibal. On that particular day, the day it all began, I arrived to class hours before dawn in search of the meeting.

I let myself in and surveyed each corner of the moonlit room. Seeing I was alone, I shut the door carefully behind me—wishing I could lock it. I settled for a firm tug, then, as if in a trance, I moved across the wood floor to the classroom's only window.

It was small and square, overlooking the village beyond the Schoolhouse gates. As I gazed out, letting my eyes detangle the nappy mat of streets, Jones' voice warned me. *Don't tarry! Find a seat and read, girl.* I grimaced; as always, she was right. But, for once, I ignored her.

Twenty minutes passed. Then, suddenly, a flash of light in the east end of the village caught my eye. I looked quickly, but it was gone. A candle snuffed out, no doubt, to avoid detection. I curled my lips into my mouth and bit down, concentrating on the place the light had flickered a moment before.

Slowly, my eye adjusted, and I saw them. A dozen human shapes, standing in a circle around a central figure as dark as the night. A cluster impossible to detect, unless one knew to look for it. And, as far as I could tell, *I* was the only one who knew. I'd discovered the pre-dawn meetings last week by pure chance.

I'd been organizing Teacher Saxon's office when a newspaper cartoon shifted into view: a Kongo man with a tattooed head, a thick nose and fleshy lips—all the marks of a worker. Dark eyes glared from his black face, covered in white paint. His huge fist, raised above his head, gripped a bloody dagger.

I glanced at the caption: *A White-Face Rebel Attacks!* Next to the image, a headline in bold font: *Voltaire's Rebel Army Ravages the South*. Wide-eyed, I skimmed the article. Late January—Rebels at Hannibal House—a handful of Record Keepers injured. A month later, a raid at River Run—fifteen dead. All organized by the Rebel, Voltaire, the leader of the White-Face Army. Trembling, I shoved the clipping under a stack of exams. I hadn't looked at it again. I told myself the danger would never reach Cobane. Our village was known all over the Kongo for our loyal, peaceful workers.

Even so, I couldn't sleep that night; I'd gone to the senior classroom to study. I happened to look from the window—and there they'd been, across the meadow, in the isolated east end of the village. Twelve dark moons around a black nucleus. All that morning I'd searched for a legitimate reason a group of workers would meet in the middle of the night. I couldn't find one. Troubled, I woke to watch them the next night, and the next.

On this, the seventh night, I pressed my nose against the

classroom window, determined to identify the attendees. No doubt they were Rebels—Second Brothers who refused to take the Rebirth. But were they White-Face Rebels, members of Voltaire's Army? Plotting an attack? I squinted, searching for a smear of white paint on their faraway faces. I didn't see any paint, but the distance between us was great and I couldn't be sure.

When it was time for class I gave up my vigil. Exhausted, I made my way to my desk to start my morning routine. It was always the same. Opening my pack, I set my ink at the top right corner and two quills beside it. At the top left, I lined up my required readers. I placed a dictionary, a notebook and my extra reading material on top of that pile. Taking a deep breath, I sat as, over the next hour, my classmates arrived in gossiping pairs.

Covington, tall and thin with a stork-like neck, bumped into my desk as she entered, spilling my ink. "Oops, sorry," she said lightly. "I wouldn't want to upset the *valedictorian*."

My hand shot out to right the ink. I glowered. The lip of the glass jar was cracked. "Of course you'd love to upset me," I said, smiling tightly. "But, since you study half as much as I, I'm not worried."

"Half as much," she agreed, showing her teeth. "And yet, I'm *right* behind you. If you don't get the highest score on the Final Exam—you can bet, I won't."

I turned my head so Covington could see me roll my eyes. She was talking to her usual cohort, East Keep, and didn't acknowledge me. Something hot bubbled in my gut.

In truth, she was right. I was on top, but the race was tight. I could stomach losing if we were only competing for valedictorian. After all, even the last in our class—the West Keep twins—would move on to Hasting House, home to all the Record Keepers. However, we weren't just competing for top marks at the Schoolhouse—more was at stake. The governing body of America, the American Assembly, was in flux.

Two days ago, the Assembly politicians had successfully voted to remove a Kongo representative. This meant one Senatorial seat that, by law, had to be filled by a Record Keeper, was up for grabs. On that same day, the Director had ordained by special decree that the senior who scored the highest on the Final Exam, the entrance exam to Hasting, would replace the ousted Senator and infuse the Assembly with fresh ideas.

Disobedient students could be sent back to the field. Ordinary Record Keepers were vulnerable too. At the whim of a vindictive Teacher or Dana Kumar, the Director of the Kongo, we could all be reclassified as workers. Senators, however, were above reclassification.

None of my peers knew of the open seat. I'd learned of it directly from Teacher Saxon, who favored me. More, only *I* knew that Rebels were meeting in Cobane. With Voltaire's Army gaining traction, the safest place in the Kongo would be in the Assembly. If I was going to land that seat, I had to beat Covington.

Just then she laughed, throatily. My eyes skewered her. Beside her, East Keep smirked at the drops of ink on my desk. Lifting my chin, I turned my back on them. I ripped out a sheet of paper and began sopping the spilled ink. *A student's desk should be neat and tidy.* I scrubbed vigorously until the desk was warm and polished beneath my hand. *Cleanliness reflects the ideals of the Niagara Compromise.* I opened my notebook to a fresh page. I chose a quill, and kept busy, writing the preamble to the Niagara Compromise from memory.

We, the human remnant, in order to form a more perfect species…

I was bent over my desk when Jones arrived. I set my quill down and began checking my page for errors. It wasn't until Jones' words penetrated my studious fog that I realized something was amiss.

"Class, say hello and welcome to a new student, Hosea Khan Vine."

Stunned, I looked up.

Teacher Jones, a big woman, cleared her throat. *Ahem.*

I jumped and spoke with the rest of the class. "Hello and welcome."

She nodded. "Hosea will sit in on lecture for our final two days."

She turned to address the new kid privately, and I felt something poke my shoulder. To my right, Jetson Cobane, my house brother, had jabbed me with his quill. He was the one chosen to take my place at the Schoolhouse when they thought I would die from crying that first week. When I did, eventually, recover, they had consulted the Compromise and kept us both. Jetson reminded me ceaselessly that my stubbornness had saved him from life in the field.

"*Psst.* Do you know anything about this?"

I shook my head and shrugged, facing forward again, just in time. Teacher Jones was frowning at me as she spoke.

"A volunteer, please. Hosea is in need of a tutor for the next two days. He'll need notes and an introduction to our Schoolhouse customs. The tutor must have a work-up of the Final Exam structure, as he'll be taking it with you next month."

Another shocked silence. Behind me, I felt my classmates exchanging curious looks. I could even guess their thoughts.

A new kid, a worker from the look of him.

Did I hear correctly? Is he really from the Vine House?

There hasn't been a Vine Keeper in years!

For good reason, Vine workers are rotten. All they do is drink liquor and smoke hash.

Nothing good comes from the Vine.

I brushed the end of my quill along my chin and mulled. So long as Covington remained distracted with her social schedule, I had a fair chance of beating her. But what of this new kid? *Had he trained privately? Would he ace the Final Exam? Was he eligible for the Senator seat?* I worried my lip. Jones was tricky when it came to questions. Too few would garnish more homework. Too many would land you in the Pit. Cautiously, I raised my hand.

Jetson spoke out of turn. "Teacher, forgive me, but how is that possible?"

Jones sniffed. Under her gray uniform, she was covered all over with heavy slabs of visceral fat, as hard as muscle. Her voice tended to pound from her throat in a bark—especially when she smelled defiance. "How?" she replied.

Surreptitiously, I lowered my hand.

Jetson ventured on. "Yes, how? How is he going to pass a test in three weeks that we've been preparing for our whole lives? It's impossible."

She lowered her gaze to Jetson. "Mister Cobane, you're not to speak on this matter again. Hosea's presence here is a matter for *us all to accept*. Is that understood, *Mister* Cobane?"

In the Kongo, the titles *Mister* and *Miss* were customarily reserved for workers.

Jetson bowed his head. "Yes, Teacher."

Jones turned back to the new kid.

I wilted at my desk. I'd gone ten years without a rebuke from any Teacher, especially Teacher Jones. I had to be careful not to ruin my record in these last days. Teacher Jones called my name, and I immediately composed myself.

"Yes, Teacher," I said.

At this, Jones smiled, the solid pudge of her cheeks swallowing her eyes. "Very good. Girls, move back a row. Hosea, take the desk beside your new tutor. Arika, introduce yourself."

My jaw dropped. Surely not! I'd not *volunteered* to be the Vine Keeper's tutor—had I? Teacher Jones gestured toward me. A commotion began to my left. The West Keep twins were vacating their double desk. Their eyes, black and beady, exchanged a stony look of annoyance as they repositioned themselves at my back.

I stared stupidly at their empty seats. They already despised me, and now this!

The new student, I couldn't remember his name, paused before me on his way to sit. I felt his attention settling on me, like dust.

"Arika?" Teacher Jones prodded.

Steeling myself, I glanced up and got my first look at Hosea Khan. It passed in a blink of the eye. I looked up at him, over at Jones, and back down at my notes. It was a flutter almost too fleeting to remember, and yet, in it, I know now, the whole world changed.

Jones called me to task—*Ahem*.

I composed myself. "Hello," I said. I saw the new student's mouth twitch with amusement. I huffed and swallowed my welcome.

Jones sniffed aggressively. "Arika, you must *welcome* our new student."

Fixing my eyes on the chalkboard over Jones' shoulder, I jerked out a stiff smile. "Hello and welcome. My name is Arika Cobane."

I don't know whether he continued to smirk or acknowledged my introduction. He remained silent, however, taking the seat assigned to him.

Jones seemed oblivious to the tension that gripped the room. Wanting no more trouble, I picked up my quill and pretended to write as I studied the new student. Was he special, more advanced? I couldn't guess.

"Arika," Jones said. "Shift over and share your reader with our new student."

My nostrils flared. *Why did the valedictorian have to sit with the new kid?* Reluctantly, I scooted my desk over half an inch. I thought I heard him chuckle.

With a loud *screech*, he slid his desk the rest of the way. It collided with mine.

Stiff-necked, but conscious of Jones' attention, I angled my reader a quarter inch so he could read along—if he strained.

Jones began to lecture, pacing back and forth. As Record Keepers in training, we studied everything about the seven continents of the old world as well as the solar-powered new world. We'd been over this material time and again. Even so, I took copious notes, lifting a shoulder so that the new kid, whoever he was, wouldn't benefit from my work.

An hour later, Jones paused to retrieve a new box of chalk from her desk. I set down my quill to massage my palm. She moved back, front and center, to write a question on the board. I glanced at it and recited the answer in my head. I was about to signal for her attention when she called on Jetson for the third time in a row. He stuttered a reply. I winced—*wrong again!* I glanced covertly at the new kid then sat back, revealing the top page of my notes:

* Return Library book
* Finish model Crystalight assignment for Teacher Saxon.

Hastily, I added a third task to my daily to do list: *Reconsider friendship with Jetson.* He was nice enough, but how useful would *nice* be when I was a Senator at Hasting? When he failed, for the fourth time, to answer correctly, Jones picked up her ruler and strode to his desk.

"What chapter are we on, Mr Cobane?"

"Chapter five," Jetson guessed.

Obi, wrong again! I froze, forgetting to hide my notes from the new kid. It made no difference. His eyes were glued to the steel edge of Jones' ruler. I followed his gaze. Nearly everyone boasted marks from it, dark lines along their forearms and wrists. No one but Jetson had these scars on their face.

The ruler flashed, opening a gash on Jetson's cheek. "Arika!"

I dropped my quill. "Yes, Teacher?"

She glared at Jetson as she barked at me, "What chapter are we on?"

My eyes flew, like magnets, to Jetson's bright green gaze. His full mouth was pressed thin. I didn't like his study habits—but I did not wish him pain. In the corner of my eye, Covington passed a note to East Keep, who snickered and passed it somewhere behind me—no doubt to the West Keep twins. Jetson's cheek oozed. The twins put their heads together and chippered.

My chest throbbed. Jones wanted an answer and I was running out of time.

Just then, she turned slightly, showing me her profile. Time was up.

I opened my mouth to answer. Then, for some reason, I glanced at the new kid. His hand was fisted on our joined desks, veins popping. Jones tapped the ruler on her thigh, *snap snap—snap!* There was a reason that ruler had *never* marked me.

I cleared my throat. "We're technically covering chapter thirty-one, the last in our reader," I said. "But, when Hannibal questioned our use of the Joust as a deterrent to Kongo aggression, you introduced the current segment. We're to move back on track this afternoon."

"Excellent, Arika. *Mister* Cobane can learn from your example." She turned and brought the ruler down—*snap*—on Jetson's face. Satisfied, she returned to her lecture.

I huddled over, scribbling furiously. The power fan kicked on with a noisy buzz. Even so, I heard the talk going on behind my back. Some was about the Vine Keeper, but most was about me, punctuated with an ugly word—a word I hated.

I lifted my chin and ground away at my notes, reminding myself that fielding jealousy was part of being valedictorian. I felt a jab in my shoulder—East Keep. I kept writing, determined to keep busy. Jab *jab*—that one hurt. I ducked my head, writing nonsense words now—bits and pieces of memorized text, squiggles and punctuations. The sharp tip of the quill ripped through the page. I dipped ink and kept writing.

Finally, East Keep forced the issue. She wrote the word down and passed it to the twins. They folded it and tossed it over my shoulder. It opened, ugly on my desk—***TRAITOR!***

THE LAST WAR

In the fall before I met Hosea Khan, I accepted the Silver Medal Award in old-world history. In my winning essay, I outlined the events leading up to the Last War, the war that destroyed the old world, save a sliver of the east coast of old North America.

Every Record Keeper knows the paramount forces behind that catastrophe, as they validate our aversion to electro-technology. The conclusion I drew in my essay, however, was extraordinary. I argued that the fate of the old world could be traced to a single instant.

I had many unfortunate moments to choose from. For example, in a last-minute decision, the Director of the Omega Project, the final brainchild of the bankrupt SETI group, decided to cut costs by using the Allen Telescope Array in place of more sophisticated models proposed for the Project. It was an important decision since the Allen elements linked directly to the Internet and left the whole world vulnerable to attack.

If not that moment, I might have pinpointed the minute Steve Kalowitz, a manager on the Project, relinquished control of the monitor room to Henry Burns, an overworked intern. Leaving an intern unsupervised was against protocol, but that night was the last of the year, and Kalowitz was eager to celebrate with his wife and triplet toddlers—all of whom died eight days later when the first heavy bomb, dubbed "the Volcano Maker," landed. I could have chosen the moment one of the radio telescopes transmitted a signal to the undermanned control room, a process that took less than a second. Or the moment Burns, in receipt of the signal, comprehended its significance.

The Allen telescopes were designed to scan the sky for artificial radio waves. A synthetic signal, such as the one transmitted that night, *could* have come from an extraterrestrial society, with superhuman transmitters. Or, more likely, the signal was a hoax—a human hacker fishing for dramatic entry into the worldwide network he intended to destroy.

Regardless, the telescopes collected the signal and fed it into imaging software. A moment later, the Project monitor displayed the software's yield—a sheet of music! Staffs, a treble clef, time signature and waves of black notes.

In my essay, I wondered why Burns, presented with this chillingly sophisticated image, did not immediately send for Kalowitz, who would have called the Project Director, who would have alerted the American President, who might have saved the world. But I found no satisfying answer. Instead, Burns downloaded the signal and processed it into sound: a long overture of static, a series of beeps and drones, a moment of silence, a tune.

Listening, Burns sighed. By no coincidence, we think, the tune was one his grandmother Burns had sung to him in the crib. Her sweet face came to his eyes that night, and her breath to his nose. The chorus crested, and his heart melted— in an instant.

And I shall hear, though soft you tread upon me
And all my grave will warmer, sweeter be

For you will bend, and tell me that you love me
And I shall sleep in peace until you come to me.

Lulled by the familiar ballad, Mr Burns relaxed his ordinarily cautious nature. He emailed the song to his mother, Patricia, who sent it to her brother, Jonah, who forwarded it to his entire address catalog.

A recipient of Jonah's email had a premonition of danger and marked the attachment as potentially hazardous spam—too late. The virus had learned to propagate itself. It infiltrated every computer that came within range of an Internet signal, even momentarily. At 98.9 percent saturation, the virus began to feed. Confusion, blackout, global meltdown. Whoever launched the Volcano Maker, United Korea we think, triggered the Last War—the end of an age. The United States responded, along with the Pax-Putinia, violating the Upper-East Treaty. When that treaty fell, all the old allegiances and grudges resurfaced in total war.

On account of the blackout, aerial navigation was imprecise. Bombs exploded hundreds of miles off target, shattering alliances and bolstering animosity. As the lines between nations dissolved, mad men took over each of the seven continents, and bombing continued, destabilizing the crust of the Earth. The ten-year Continent Conflict ended when a parasitic organism rose up, we think, from the magma layer and killed millions before it was contained. Crashing seas of molten lava, unpredictable quaking, and boiling geysers that sprayed strange bacteria and disease left most of the world uninhabitable.

Hungry herds of refugees sought shelter, strength and

new world order. Eventually they found it, on a stable island that was old North America. They organized into tribes and managed a few years of peace before fighting broke out again, a six-year race war. When the three remaining armies—the Dark Kongos, the Brown Clayskins and the Whites, called English—finally agreed to end it, they met in the north country, near Niagara, and hashed out a compromise.

THE QUEEN BEE

At last, the bell chimed for break. I snatched my reader from our joined desks and headed for the classroom door. I wasn't running from my classmates, or their note, I assured myself. I opened the door and yanked it shut behind me, smoldering.

None of them knew what it took to be the best—complete focus. While I pulled extra study sessions, they watched old-world television in the Reel Room. While I squeezed in hours at the library, they smoked hash in the gardens. They had inside jokes and illicit meetings with the Clayskin merchants, and I had the ear of the Teachers.

They called me traitor now, but someday soon they would wish they had done the same. My time was coming. Stooped over, with busy little strides, I increased the distance between me and the senior class.

"Arika!"

Ducking my head, I hurried on.

"Arika, wait! Arika!"

With a sigh, I turned to see Jetson, Covington and East Keep gaining on me. Jetson was waving me down. He stopped me with a hand on my shoulder.

"Jetson," I said. My eyes avoided his cheek.

Covington snorted. "I think what Jetson meant to say is— Arika, what are you doing out of the library?"

East Keep snickered. "I hardly recognize you without a book under your nose." She wrinkled her own nose, which was short and stout.

I looked between them dispassionately.

"Leave off," Jetson said. "She bagged the Silver Award, didn't she?"

"She won the award last year," Covington pointed out. "So, what's her excuse now? We've barely laid eyes on her in weeks."

"Not that we want to," East Keep added. "I don't know how you stomach her."

"Graduate Assessments are this week, or did you forget?" I said to Covington.

Her cheekbones were set at a sly angle. She looked down her nose at me. "I remember the Assessment; I'm just not dwelling."

I clutched my books. I'd spent many anxious nights speculating on the Assessment. If even one Teacher objected, I'd be reclassified, despite acing the Final Exam.

"Besides," Covington added, "everyone knows that Teachers only object out of spite. If you've put them off that badly, you're vexed regardless."

My eyes cut to her. "So I should, what—hang out in the Rec Room drinking punch and varnishing my nails?"

Covington's eyes lit. Jetson stepped between us. He looped an arm around my neck and spoke in my ear. "At least you can take a break and come to the gathering East Keep is hosting tomorrow."

On cue, East Keep brandished a pink, elaborately decorated invitation. She tried to hand it to me. It reeked of flowers.

"No thanks." I ducked from under his arm.

"Come on. It'll be fun," Jetson wheedled. He quirked one brow. "I'll be there."

"*You're* going to a nail party?" As the only boy in our class, he generally avoided them.

"It's not a party!" East Keep said, flapping the invite. Cloying waves of perfume advanced against me.

Taking it from her, Jetson set it on top of my books. His buffed nails gleamed. "At least read it before you say no. We called a preliminary Planning Committee meeting. All you have to do is show up."

"And don't wear that blouse," Covington said, arching a brow.

I looked down at my dress to see a large dark blotch across the front. My notebook, cradled with my reader against my chest, was also smeared with ink.

East Keep took a step back, covering the rest of her invites protectively. "*Obi*, Arika! Did your ink explode or something?"

In my haste to make the door after class, I had forgotten about the cracked ink container. I dabbed anxiously at the blotch with a handkerchief—Jones had a keen eye for messiness.

"Or maybe you're trading fashion advice with the new kid," Covington said, jerking her chin back toward the Vine Keeper. He was ambling our way, deep in thought.

"*Obi*, look at him. Straight from an old-world jungle," East Keep said.

Everyone laughed, except me. I frowned sympathetically. Toward the end of class, Jones asked him to comment on a simple issue. In response, he'd sat silent as a mute as we all drew the same conclusion—he was even dumber than he looked. It wasn't his fault. The Rebirth pills were known to backfire sporadically. Instead of scrambling memories as intended, they made lesions in the brain, causing terrible mental side effects.

"He's twenty at least," East Keep said. "That's old enough for thirteen Rebirths, *and* thirteen misfires. He must be completely feral."

"All that bulk and a spoiled mind," Jetson added, shrugging. "If he can follow simple orders, he'd make a fine Guardsman."

My eyes roved over the boy's taut muscles. Every year, the most robust male workers were selected for specialized erasures and trained to police the three territories. Jetson was right. Ferals made excellent Guardsmen, but terrible students. He was *no* competition for Senator.

Covington grimaced. "Don't be cruel, Jetson. Only field hands have to *protect* their feet. The Captain of the Guard is an English gentleman. He wouldn't stomach those shoes. I bet the Supply Room Merchants won't even sell them."

They laughed again as Jetson struck a gentlemanly pose, showing off his belted tunic. His leather sandals laced up his ankles and legs.

I shifted my books to cover the stain on my shirt. The Vine Keeper had a silver medallion around his neck, but it was dull and needed polishing. If he entered the Main Hall like that, he would be done for—socially crucified.

Before I thought, my mouth opened. "And how do you know the Captain of the Guard, Covington?" I said. "Or, for that matter, since when do you *talk* to Clayskin merchants? From what I hear you do everything *but* talk."

Her eyes narrowed. "What have you heard?"

"They say a jeweled cuff for a kiss is the going rate. A spool of thread for—*more*. It's no wonder you wear such finery."

She snapped. "Hush up, Arika!"

"Leave off him."

"Why should I?"

I was already regretting my intervention. "Because—I'm his tutor," I stammered.

Her mouth dropped open. "You're seriously considering tutoring him?"

"*Obi*, you're such a nut," East Keep said.

I clinched my books. *Why hadn't I just kept my mouth shut?* Covington was the definitive queen of the class. More than that, I did not want to tutor the new kid.

"Arika, don't do it," Jetson warned. "You said yourself, you don't have the time."

I lifted my chin. "Don't tell me what to do."

With animated disgust, East Keep pinched the fat bridge of her nose and tipped at her pudgy waist, pretending to gag.

I ignored her. He was feet from us now. With his height and weight, he might have cut through the crowd. Instead, he flowed along with easy, efficient motions.

I stepped in his path.

He stopped, waited a beat, and looked up. "Excuse me— Arika. You are Arika, right?"

Surprise. His voice was smooth and cultured. "Uh, yeah," I managed.

Hannibal and the West Keep twins, dressed identically in draped sheets of cloth called *auras*, had joined Jetson and the others, which meant the entire senior class was present as he surveyed each of us. His eyes settled on me.

"Didn't you volunteer to share notes with me?"

I dropped his gaze, unnerved. In rough tunic and britches, he appeared so pathetic. I'd assumed he'd speak accordingly— *'scuse me Ma'am*, with a thick field-hand accent.

44

"No," I said, finally, flatly. I stepped out of his way.

After a second, he strode past.

Covington and East Keep guffawed.

"So much for friendship!"

"And here I thought you'd be nice for once—guess not! *Obi*, Arika, that was mean."

I ignored them, turning to follow him with my gaze. His skin was medium brown, like my own; and his dark hair, twisted in Keeper style, was tied back with a *bambi* thong. He held his back straight and his head high. Before he turned the corner, he looked back at me, his expression tense with curiosity.

Jetson tapped my temple playfully. "*Helloo*—Arika?"

"Arika!" Covington squawked.

Tearing my gaze from the new kid, I glanced briefly at her. "Huh?"

"Like I said, I want to make sure you're coming to the meeting."

I waved a hand as if swatting a mosquito. "I'm busy."

"But it's for the Committee."

"The what?"

"The Joust Planning Committee! Ever heard of it? You *are* the Secretary."

I checked my list. "Meetings don't start until Saturday. The first day of Break, right?" I turned fully to her, finally, for confirmation.

The West Keep twins pursed their lips. They were a thin-faced, squirrely pair, and each tended to finish the other's thoughts in breathy bouts.

"I think that's why she called it a preliminary meeting,"

said one, leaving her twin to explain. "It's a pre-meeting meeting to go over Director Kumar's proposal."

"A pre-meeting meeting?" I repeated, scathingly.

"To discuss Dana Kumar's proposal!" Covington insisted. "It's no small thing, you know. He wants the Joust to be a fight to the death."

She was right. The annual Joust was a mock battle between twelve Champions, one each from the twelve Houses of the Kongo. Drink and hash flowed freely at the annual event, which prepared the workers to partake of the Rebirth the next day. Dana Kumar's plan would leave eleven Kongos dead, which, according to the proposal, would provide an outlet for the tensions brought on by Rebel violence and drought.

"Is the meeting mandatory?" I asked, thinking of the cartoon of the bloody dagger.

Twin one chimed in. "It's mandatory for the Secretary."

"Fine—I'll be there." I turned to Covington. "What time?"

"Seven, right after supper," she said.

"And what time can I leave?"

She crossed her arms. "*Obi*, does it matter? School's over tomorrow!"

"School isn't over until after the Final Exam," I corrected. "During Break, we have to write our final essays."

"Oh, well *pardón!*" She threw her hands up dramatically. "I thought the three weeks of Break would be sufficient, even for you."

"Not three weeks," I retorted, tightly. "Apparently, I have to spend at least one night at your party."

Her eyes lit, and Jetson stepped between us. "Come on, Arika, I'm sure you have a little time."

I hesitated, looking around at them, a well-groomed flock of vultures.

"If it's mandatory, I'll be there," I muttered.

Covington sneered. "You'd better." She turned on her heel and stalked away. The West Keep twins and East Keep followed immediately. Hannibal cast a long look at Jetson, who remained by my side. Then she walked away too.

THE LIBRARIAN

When they were out of earshot, Jetson turned to me. "Where are you off to?"

"The library," I said. "I have to—"

"Study?"

I nodded ruefully. He was different when he wasn't with the rest of them.

"Can I join?"

I pursed my lips. "What about noon meal? Covington will be expecting you."

He smiled sheepishly, showing the white ridge of his teeth. "I ate a big breakfast."

He considered me as we walked, an irritating habit he'd developed in the past year. Self-conscious, I tugged the folds of my blouse closer together and remembered the stain there. *Obi Solomon!* I would have to fix that first thing. I took the next right, the long way to the library, but we would pass by a water fountain where I could keep the ink from drying into a permanent stain.

Jetson rounded the corner with me, his eyes searching my face. "You've lost weight. Does Robin still make you take-away meals when you skip?"

I ignored the question. "How many times do I have to ask you not to mention her in public?" My friendship with Robin had started before I knew better than to befriend workers, and had persisted, despite my better judgment.

Jetson glanced around the empty hall. "You call this public?"

"Students should assume that Teachers are always listening," I quoted.

"But don't you and she talk?" he asked, puzzled. "They could overhear that."

"We rarely talk, and only in secret," I said. "We're very careful." It was true. She hid her treats for me inside my top drawer. And when I bought an orange scarf for her birth month last year, I'd made a show of buying it for myself then giving it to her as charity.

He shrugged. "So then, where's your secret take-away meal? Did the two of you fight or something?" He opened a dividing door and I walked through.

This wing of the Schoolhouse, a late addition to the basic structure, was regal, with arched openings and soaring sandstone ceilings. I kept my eyes on the lava tile flooring as I answered him. "No, we didn't fight. Not exactly."

"Then what's the vex?" he prodded. He wasn't going to let it go.

I sighed. "If you must know, she hasn't been around for days."

"How many days?"

"Six," I admitted. I frowned, realizing she'd disappeared on the same day I'd discovered the newspaper clipping—and the nightly Rebel meetings. I shook my head. "I'm sure she's fine. Besides, I'm too busy to worry."

I stopped at the fountain and wet a handkerchief from my pocket, dabbing at my *aura*. Jetson rested back against the wall and stared at me, his brow a rigid cliff of condemnation. Finally, I snapped. "*Obi Solomon!* Will you stop staring? I have no clue where Robin is."

He didn't let up.

My hand shook, smearing the ink. I sighed. "Fine. I have *one* clue."

He uncrossed his arms. "What is it?"

I stuffed the handkerchief into my pocket. "It happened last week, when I was leaving the library. You have to promise not to tell anyone."

"Promise."

I glanced around. We were alone. "I was on my way from the library, in the girls' hall, when someone waved at me," I said. "At first, I thought it was a shadow, but then I saw a kitchen maid. She was waiting for me."

Jetson's brows lifted in surprise.

I lowered my voice to a whisper.

•

I stopped with one hand on the knob and studied the little black maid. Her dress was standard issue. Dirt brown, unhemmed, sewn from half of a grain sack. With her shorn hair, the dress was all that distinguished her from the little boy workers, who went around bare-chested in sack pants that ballooned around their legs. The whites of her eyes were pure alabaster around pecan-colored irises. Her lashes curled lavishly, as if to make up for her hair.

"Is this official business?" I said shortly. If not, I would *have* to report her for insolence; the rules required it. She stared too boldly for a kitchen girl.

"Come quick," she said. "She needs you."

"Who needs me?"

"Robin, Miss. She sent for you."

"Not Miss, girl!" I glanced around. "Refer to me as Ma'am or Mistress—not Miss."

She bobbed a choppy curtsy. "Yes, Ma'am."

I considered her appeal. I'd assumed Robin's absence of late meant she understood the way of the Kongo. When I took my place at Hasting, I couldn't have ties to a kitchen worker.

"What exactly does she need?" I asked.

"I don't know."

I huffed. "Well, is she hurt?"

Without answering, the girl turned and hurried down the hall, beckoning me to follow. Reluctantly, I caught up with her. She waited, one hand on the wood-paneled wall. She pushed and the wall slid back, revealing a set of stone steps. I hesitated. The secret passages of the Schoolhouse were for servants only. This particular passage, I figured, emptied into the kitchen where the hands prepared our meals. *Students must not enter the kitchen.*

"This is the way, Mistress," she urged.

I shook my head slowly. "I can't. Tell her—tell her I just can't." I turned and hurried away.

•

Jetson slipped his hands in his pockets. "And the maid never said what was wrong?"

I shook my head. "I dared to ask a worker the next morning, but she shunned me." I resented this, and it showed.

He chuckled. "Can you blame her?"

"Yes, I blame her! Robin and I are—somewhat close," I admitted.

"Well, you're also close to Jones."

"Jones is the Headmistress."

He put up both hands, defensively. "I know—she's in charge. Just don't let her tell you who your friends are." He glanced at me, pointedly.

I looked away from the cut on his cheek. "You know you vex Jones on purpose. If you studied more and showed her respect, she wouldn't treat you badly. You should know what chapter we're on. It's not my fault I do!" Fumbling in my pocket, I shoved the crumpled handkerchief toward him. It was damp and black with ink. "Take it; you're bleeding."

He stared at me, holding the cloth to his face. "Jones hates me more than the rest of you. I don't know why. But, the way I see it, she's going to hate me no matter what I do. So, I might as well do what I want."

"Students must follow the rules," I quoted.

"*Obi*, don't you think I've tried? For a month last year, I was nearly perfect."

"And?"

"And she hit me with her damn ring, *whop!* Right under the chin, out of nowhere." He pointed to a scar.

I looked skeptically. "Why would she hit you for doing what she wants? It's illogical."

"Not everything is logical, Arika." He grinned, suddenly. "The twins say she's smitten."

I rolled my eyes. "Oh, Jetson."

"Hear me out! It's starting to make sense. Last week, she made me polish all of her English trophies. I felt her eyes

52

crawling over me the whole time." He laughed.

I smiled, reluctantly. "Well, maybe consider returning her affection. It'd be less painful."

"Kissing Jones—less painful? I doubt it."

I laughed. "Oh, come on."

"No chance. Besides, my heart is already taken." He caught my eye. His mouth tilted up at the corner.

I looked away. "Enough talk. I've got to study." I started down the hall.

"Hey, not so fast." He caught up.

"I'm busy, Jetson."

"I have one more question."

I groaned impatiently, but slowed down.

"What do you think of the new student?"

I shrugged; I was trying not to think of him at all.

"Come on," Jetson urged. "You must think something."

I pictured the new kid. His burnished skin and wild brow, the look he leveled on me from across the hall. I swallowed. "I think what everyone thinks, that he doesn't belong here."

"Covington was talking about him after class."

"Get to the point, Jetson. I don't care what Covington talks about."

He scowled. "Don't tell me you're on his side. I saw how he tried to embarrass you, brushing up on you in class and nearly trampling you in the hall."

"I'm not on his side," I said. "I want to know why he's here too. On the other hand, Jones has her reason for secrecy. As her legal subordinate, I respect her reasons. So should you!"

"Well, I don't. I want to know how they expect him to pass the Keeper test. He's basically a feral, don't you think?"

I nodded, knowing that was what he expected. Privately, I thought there was more to the Vine Keeper than met the eye. It wasn't just his accent. He had a self-assuredness unheard of in workers. Also—his eyes. Where had I seen that particular shade of brown before?

"I mean, is it even fair to pit him against us at this juncture?" Jetson went on.

"Fair to whom?"

"To us, of course. I don't care about him."

We were at the library door and I stopped, impatient.

"Do you?" he said.

"Do I what?"

"Do you care?"

"About the Vine Keeper? Why would I?"

"For whatever reason you decided to tutor him when, lately, you won't even stop to eat. You're losing weight, Arika."

"I'm not hungry."

"You have to eat."

I lifted my chin. "Now you *will* excuse me—"

The library door opened behind us. Surprised, I spun around.

Teacher Purnell, the head librarian, stepped into the hall. She was a crabby woman given to blunt conversation. For years I courted her trust and, in return, she let me work late in the old section of the library. Just after the Compromise, the Tri-territory historical society had stocked the library with books that had survived the Last War. Later, when the library was transferred to the Headmistress' purview, many of the original books were removed. The old section held what remained. As far as I could tell, I was the only student studious enough to use the old books to supplement my schoolwork. Teacher Purnell was mostly harmless, a stickler about one thing—speaking above a whisper.

"Teacher Purnell," I said brightly.

She lowered her glasses. "*You* are supposed to be at noon meal."

I smoothed a hand over my hair. "I—that is, I'm not hungry."

"Stop shouting girl. Why aren't you in the Main Hall?"

I lowered my voice. "I came to study in the library, alone." I stepped away from Jetson.

She frowned.

"I have time," I went on. "Perhaps we can discuss old-world transportation." The subject fascinated her. She secretly spent hours constructing model trains.

"Are you an idiot?" she said, flatly. "Your kind need to feed in order to work."

I looked down at my sandals. The stain on my blouse would be unbearable in the Main Hall. With the way I'd shown up Jetson in class, the others would be relentless. Even so, I nodded. "You're right, Teacher. I wasn't thinking."

Her chin wobbled righteously. "Your kind are hot-blooded. I'll be in the Hall later to check your clean plate." She turned to leave.

"Teacher," I said, impulsively stopping her. "I need to change my *aura*. If I go to my dorm before the Main Hall, I could miss lunch."

She studied the ink blotch spreading on my shirt.

Jetson looked too.

I flushed.

She replaced her glasses. "Your kind are vain and bawdy,"

she declared. "You'll go as you are and be grateful. If you feed well, I'll grant a pass to the Supply Room. Students must be trained up in cleanliness," she quoted. The library door shut soundlessly behind her.

I stared at my feet.

"Well, whatever happens," Jetson said, "you'll have a clean plate to show. I'm hungry enough for two."

I swallowed hard, reminding myself that there were only two days left.

"And a pass," Jetson added, prodding me down the hall. "You don't get those every day." He smiled good-naturedly and maintained an optimistic monolog for the rest of our walk. Just before we entered the Hall, his voice faded mid-sentence. He stopped me with a hand on my arm.

"Here," he said. He unpinned his *pallium* and threw the short cape over my shoulders, hiding the stain on my shirt. Capeless, his arms were bare, which was against the rules. I opened my mouth to protest. Before I could, he gave me a shove through the doors.

•

At the meal line, Jetson handed me a tray and took one for himself. He waggled one posh brow at the girl plating the stew. "My dear Miss Windy, tell me. What hath your hand prepared today?"

I snorted. Our meals were served by female workers who were privileged in that they avoided fieldwork. They didn't have the tired look of the rougher field hands and Jetson practiced wooing them. In his spare time, he memorized bits of the old-world poetry book he stored in his back pocket.

"Pork and potatoes," Windy whispered. She turned her face and coughed into her shoulder. Her smile thinned to a grimace.

I frowned. She seemed to be in pain.

"Any pork left?" Jetson asked, eyeing the pot.

She nodded weakly. "I saved some for you, Master."

"Hardout, my girl! Miss Windy of the south wind, you are my favorite." He passed over our plates, which Windy filled generously, a sweet expression lighting her bloodshot eyes.

I glanced back at her as we took napkins and moved on.

"I, for one, am not looking forward to meals at Hasting," Jetson declared.

I picked up utensils and inspected my plate. Meals were, at best, reliable. Breakfast was cereal with yogurt. Noon meal, like supper, was stewed meat and potatoes, greens, and nuts. On occasion, there were fluffy cinnamon muffins or pudding. "Well, *I* am," I said. "At Hasting, we can decide for ourselves whether we're hungry and what it is we want to eat."

He grinned. "*Obi*, Arika. Your stomach growled all morning. And now, you're vexed you're eating?"

I jumped to my own defense. "I need to study! Graduate Assessments—"

Jetson laughed. "You're a nut," he concluded. "You quote rules incessantly. And yet, you hate taking orders—even if they're in your best interest."

Unable to deny this, I lifted my chin.

We joined the other senior students at our assigned table. A wooden chair had been added to accommodate the Vine Keeper, who was nowhere in sight. The senior girls were huddled together whispering and didn't notice our approach.

"What we need to know," Covington said, "is exactly which

Senators voted against the New Seed Bill. If possible, we must contact Director Kumar and—"

Jetson coughed. She glanced up, saw me at his side, and fell silent.

I looked between them. She snatched a book from the table—but not before I recognized it. It had been required reading in Teacher Rowan's New World Government elective. On its cover, Director Kumar wore a military uniform. Instead of a sword, the sheath that hung from his waist held a rolled copy of the Compromise; evidence that, despite his garb, the Director was not a military leader.

The last military leader of the Kongo had been General Obi Solomon. Upon Obi's death, the Assembly had dissolved the military, expanded the diplomat program and created the Directorship, tapping an English man to assume the first life tenure. When Kumar had assumed power over twenty years ago, he'd caused a scandal. Being half Clayskin, Kumar was the first Director in fifty-three years who was not full-blooded English.

Covington glared at me and adjusted her beaded arm cuff. "What are you doing here?"

I stared curiously. She was trying to distract me. Why did she have the reader now, months after Rowan's class? And why was she whispering about the Senate? *Did she know of the open seat?* My heart drummed.

"You're nutty if you think you're sitting here," she said, fiddling with a gold earring.

Jetson set our trays down. "Now, Covington, be nice. Where else would she sit?"

"Why not with the Teachers, where her loyalties lie?"

I slid my tray to the far end of the table. "Gossip all you want. I care nothing about French braids, manicures, or anything else you care to discuss."

I sat down, anticipating Covington's retort.

Instead, Hannibal replied. "We weren't talking about nail varnish, Arika."

I paused, the spoon at my lips.

Hannibal rarely spoke and never to reprimand. She was nothing but gentle. I recognized her keen intelligence from the start. Up on the desk on that first day of school, when I'd cried out—*Comrades*—there'd been a query in her eyes, burning to be answered. She looked undecided, even as I fell from my summit. Later I thought that perhaps she wanted to join me. That, given answers, she would have. Over the years, however, I kept to myself and she fell in with Covington.

I searched Hannibal's kind eyes. In their reflection I saw the political cartoon, *the dagger dripping blood*. It was on the tip of my tongue to warn her, but I hesitated. There was one open Senate seat, not two—and the last thing I needed was more competition.

Before I could answer Hannibal, a drumbeat blasted—bold and loud. We all jumped. My spoon dropped, splashing broth everywhere. A set of trumpets joined the drums and I covered my ears.

Jetson shouted in my ear. "To the window! They must be making an arrest!"

I barely heard him over the racket: drumbeats, trumpets, chairs screeching back, and a hundred feet clamoring to the Hall windows.

Jetson pulled me through the chaos. He shoved open a space

by the nearest window. It overlooked the village. We pressed our faces to the glass, straining to see.

In theory, we knew what was coming. The drums meant that a fugitive was on the run. The culprit's name would pass by word of mouth, spreading like wildfire beneath the shriek of the trumpets which would stop once the workers took up the cry. We knew in theory, but there hadn't been an arrest in Cobane for ten years. This arrest, no doubt, had something to do with the secret Rebel meetings.

Jetson put his mouth to my ear. "*Obi*, the New Seed can't come soon enough. The workers have become unmanageable since Voltaire's latest raid."

I blinked. That was the second time I'd caught wind of this *New Seed* business. It was, somehow, related to Voltaire's rebellion. The ruckus rose, drawing my attention outside.

Workers—hooting, grunting, slapping their hands—overtook the drums and trumpets. The ritual was primeval. The Guards sent forth the field hands, like bloodhounds to the chase. They searched every nook and cranny, calling the fugitive by name.

"Can you hear his name?" I asked, suddenly.

"Not from here," Jetson said. "Why do you care?"

"I don't. I just—"

"Look, there he is!" Jetson shouted.

I followed his finger. A fleet-footed man sprinted across the field closest to the Schoolhouse. We had an unimpeded view.

"*Obi*, he's fast! Look at him go!"

The fugitive headed toward the edge of Cobane territory. If he crossed it, the chase would not follow him out. He'd be left to the bounty hunters, discharged Kongo Guardsmen that roamed the verboten land between Houses.

Most students, in favor of law and order, shouted encouragement to the Guard. I remained silent, biting my lip. The fugitive was fast, but a barrier of workers closed in on either side. They would meet in the middle and trap him.

"I wonder what his crime was," I said.

"Who cares? They're going to get him!" Jetson shouted excitedly. "He'll never make it past that last line of defense!"

The noise reached a fever pitch. Along the window, I traced the fugitive's progress with my finger. Soon he would accept capture. He would stop on a quid, slip back, fall down. His head would pivot as he looked for a way out. Just then, it happened as I predicted. He slipped and fell.

"The mob is vexed! They won't bother waiting for the Guard. They'll tear him apart!" Jetson shouted.

I squinted to see the fugitive's face. He was like a turtle on his back, openly afraid. Suddenly, his head snapped right. He'd heard something. Before I could guess what it was, he hurdled upright and ran, taking another angle—east! Toward another line of workers at the far perimeter! I shook my head—*nooo!* The line was solid; he would never break through. He galloped toward them.

"Damn, he's going to run right into them!" Jetson cried.

I screamed to release the tension. The firm black line was steady. The fugitive came abreast of it and—suddenly—it faltered. From one split second to the next, the workers shifted, broke hands and allowed the man to pass. In a flash, he crossed the perimeter. His path was clear as far as the eye could see. There were no fences in Cobane, they were considered barbaric. A properly trained worker respected the law—or, at least, he used to.

Stunned, I looked back at the men who had let the fugitive go free. Their hands were still clasped, twelve in all, one man short of a cluster. I gasped knowing, instinctually, that these were indeed the Rebels that gathered at night in the heart of the village.

A mob had formed around them. A black sea of workers, pointing and shouting their confusion. This was Cobane, after all. The House known for nurturing the most honorable workers in the Kongo. Our workers were strict Loyalists—happy to partake in the Rebirth. So loyal, the Guard here had dwindled to a handful of soldiers who didn't bother to patrol the village at night.

I spotted the red head of the Overseer. Beside him, the English Captain of the Guard shouted orders. I shivered. I didn't have to hear his words to know them. By aiding their cohort, the remaining Rebels had forfeited their lives. Each one would be hanged on the spot and burned in the village pyre. The Schoolhouse, and all of Cobane, was the Headmistress' domain. Even now Jones would be en route to the village to pass judgment.

•

The crowd of chattering students thinned as the workers set about constructing a triangular gallows in the village square. Teachers bustled about, ordering us to return to our meals.

"What in Obi's name just happened?" Jetson asked, directing his question to the circle of senior students.

I tore my gaze from the window. "They let him go free," I said.

The twins' black eyes darted to Covington. "But that's

impossible, right? There was a line of workers. Why would a line of workers let a fugitive go free?"

"Isn't it obvious?" East Keep asked. "They're Rebels."

The twins jabbered nervously. "*Obi Solomon!* Rebels—here?!"

"Cool it, West Keep," Covington said. "For now, we know nothing."

"But they'll murder us in our sleep!"

"I said cool it!" Covington looked hard at them. Identical hands moved over their mouths. "We'll talk later. For now, let's get out of here."

I watched them leave. *Rebel!* Given their half-choked whispers, the twins might have been saying "devil." They had looked just as terrified that first day, when I jumped onto the desk, shouting—*It is I, comrades.* Their vapid expressions had melted into matching masks of fright and their hands had moved to cover the small shells of their ears, simultaneously, as if tied together by invisible puppet strings.

Hannibal touched my shoulder, making me jump. "Are you coming?"

"Where are you going?" I asked.

"Sometimes, when we need to talk privately, we meet in the Reel Room and watch a movie." The heavy fringe of her lashes, in her otherwise plain face, made her eyes seem impossibly large—as she winked.

I frowned.

"If you want to join us in the Reel Room for a *nail party*, feel free." She winked again.

The Assembly selected a handful of old-world movies to debut in the Reel Room each month. I watched my share, though not as many as Covington and her clique, who went nearly every day. They were obviously up to something.

"You should come," Jetson said solemnly. "We could use your insight. The New Seed Bill—"

I held up my hand, warning him not to say anything more about this *New Seed*. "I don't want to know. Besides, I have to stay in the Main Hall."

"Why?" Hannibal asked.

"Teacher Purnell—"

Jetson scoffed. "Are you talking about that clean plate nonsense?"

"It was a direct order," I said.

"Come on, she's probably forgotten already. And this matter is urgent! If the White-Face Rebel Army has infiltrated Cobane, we're not safe anymore—you included." He softened his tone and fingered his cheek, which had finally stopped bleeding. "Besides, the cuts heal."

Lifting one hand, I rubbed the crescent moon scars I bore on my upper arm. They were a constant reminder of the Pit. Jetson and the others pulled small pranks and, accordingly, none of them had seen the Schoolhouse dungeon. They merely feared the hell that I *knew*. I shook my head. "Wrong," I said. "Not all scars heal, Jetson."

He opened his mouth to argue and I snapped. "Maybe *you've* forgotten, Mister Cobane. Political talk is forbidden to students. If I hear it again, as the valedictorian, I'll report you!"

He looked hurt.

I bit my lip and looked at my sandals. "Jetson—" My voice died. There was nothing to say. I took off his *pallium*, tossed it to him and turned my back.

•

I ate my meal alone at the senior table, shoveling food into my mouth mechanically. In my mind, I watched Jetson leave again, shoulder to shoulder with Hannibal. The vision turned the food in my mouth to dust.

As I chewed, my mind wandered to the fugitive who had escaped. According to the murmuring crowd, he'd been convicted of distributing illegal paraphernalia. I'd read once of a convict living for months in the Kongo desert on nothing but subterranean lizards and ants. If he could avoid bounty hunters, survival *was* possible. Only, this was a poor year for any fugitive to attempt it.

The drought had turned the desert into a deathtrap. Without water, the fugitive would join his coconspirators in mere days— *unless.* A thought tickled the back of my mind, a chapter from a supplementary reader. Slowly, the details came back to me.

The Kongo was situated on a network of underground waterways that surfaced at random, and pooled before running dry. As a water source, these pools were unreliable, which is why man-made hydroplanes nurtured the farmlands of the Kongo Houses. However, for the months they lasted, the pools sustained all sorts of plants and animals. An ecosystem—even a temporary one—could save the fugitive's life.

There were only a few of these oases in the Kongo, and their locations weren't marked on maps. More, they were likely overrun with outlaws. Still, if the escapee was lucky he would be *free* and live. Something inside me quickened at the notion.

•

After lunch, I hurried to the Supply Room with the pink passes Purnell had given me upon inspecting my plate. Stationed there was a colossal Guard trained to attack, on sight, anyone foolish enough to enter without a pass. We called him the *Chalk-Hand Guard*, on account of his dry fingers, which were dusted with a layer of ash-white skin. I held my pink passes high in the air for him to see.

Inside the Supply Room, I handed my slips to Teacher Barrett, catching a nose full of her peculiar scent—like boiled cabbage.

"What do you want?" she said, looking closely at the slips. She was a miserly woman, known to reject requests because of spelling errors.

"I need more ink and a new blouse," I said, holding my breath. "And, if you would, some notebooks for my personal use."

She picked up a wood-handled stamp, plopped it on an inkpad and slapped it in the middle of each slip. "Black ink only, until Sunday."

I glowered. She had ink every color of the rainbow—for her favorite students. When they did her bidding, she doled out choice supplies, like treats.

"Blouses in back," she went on. "No notebook without a third pass. You know the rules." She blew her hot vegetable breath on the stamp mark then placed my slips on top of a small stack of voided passes.

I collected my items from the towering shelves that lined the warehouse. As I walked to afternoon class, I imagined my welcoming at Hasting. Senator Osprey, the chief of Senators, would single me out. *Senator Cobane*, she'd say, *take your place in the Assembly.*

THE REBIRTH

During The Last War, torrential bombing corroded the lithosphere layer, deep within the Earth. Shifting tectonic plates resulted in disaster—earthquakes, volcanoes, tsunamis, and a permanently altered surface terrain. A concurrent shift in weather patterns left most of the only inhabitable slice of land, on which sat America, malnourished and dry.

The freezing tundra in the Northridge territory was unworkable as were the rocky Clayskin plains of middle America. The Kongo alone, and only with the aid of sophisticated irrigation machines, called hydroplanes, could be farmed. We Kongos had volunteered to cultivate it for the greater good of all humanity.

It was excruciating labor. So hard, the Framers of the Niagara Compromise had instituted the Rebirth as a means of relief. It was not illegal for a worker to refuse to take the pill. But, the majority lined up patriotically to swallow it and forget their misery. Those Rebels who refused the Rebirth were universally shunned.

As Record Keepers our task was to record the history of the Kongo race. Once we graduated, we had the power to grant storytelling privileges to any non-Rebel worker we deemed worthy. We'd listen as the worker detailed any bits of his life that he remembered. Later, the worker's story was stored in the Sun Room, at Hasting, to be remembered for all eternity.

THE ROOSTER

The new kid strolled into class just after the late bell. Jones' gaze followed him from door to desk. He had not bothered to garner school supplies during the two-hour break.

I rolled my eyes, anticipating Jones' reprimand. *Wrong dress, unprepared, arriving after the bell*—all punishable offenses. I waited.

After a tense silence, she began class. "A volunteer to remind us where we are in today's discussion."

My jaw dropped. Behind me, the others rustled uneasily. Had Jones—Teacher Jones—been lenient? From the corner of my eye, I saw the new kid yawn lazily and scratch the dark hint of beard beneath his skin. Catching my gaze, he smiled wolfishly as his ugly silver medallion winked at his neck.

Abruptly, I faced forward again. I took out my quill and opened my reader.

Covington volunteered. "Before break, we started the last chapter. You posed a question to—him." Her eyes ferreted to the new kid. "But he couldn't answer."

"And what was the question?" Jones said, ignoring her smirk.

Covington read from a page on her desk. "I believe it was— what is the ultimate goal of the Rebirth?"

Jones nodded. "Yes, Article 3, Section 1 of the Niagara

Compromise, justifying the Rebirth. Open your readers. Let's take a closer look."

She wrote on the chalkboard in her furious manner. "Having observed the benefits of the *Animus Rasa*, we establish the annual Rebirth to further American peace and prosperity." She turned back to us. "Operative words?"

Jetson signaled. "Peace"

She underlined the word peace. "Very good."

Covington signaled. "Prosperity."

She underlined that too.

East Keep signaled. "*Animus Rasa.*"

"Excellent." She underlined this word twice. "*Animus Rasa.* What does it mean?"

One of the West Keep twins sat forward, her eyes fixed on Jones' expression. Watching Jones' face, we all knew, was the best way to gauge for an unpleasant reaction. West Keep cleared her throat. "In light of our discussion, I suppose it means altering the memories?"

Teacher Jones wrinkled her nose; indicating West Keep's answer was wrong.

The other twin spoke up, eager to get a good comment in early. "Could it mean something about forgetting your troubles?"

Another nose wrinkle. "Anyone else?"

From my left, the Vine Keeper's voice. "It means 'spirit scraping.'"

I shivered. His tone reeked of defiance.

The room fell silent.

Jones shifted her girth, and barked. "What was that?"

The Vine Keeper maintained his tone and volume. "*Animus*

means mind, spirit, consciousness, courage. *Rasa* means scraped."

Her gaze fixed on him. Then, suddenly, she smiled, her eyes hard above the balls of her cheeks. "Correct, Master Vine. The bare Latin is as you say. Now, perhaps someone will interpret the phrase for our purpose. Arika?"

I floundered, unprepared. I looked down and grabbed the last note I scribbled. "The section's operative words are peace and prosperity."

Jones' face remained clear, but expectant.

I went on, improvising. "So a scraped spirit, while seemingly harsh, is actually beneficial for the workers."

To my relief, Jones nodded. "Thank you, Arika. How?" She scanned the room.

Jetson signaled. "How is the scraping beneficial?"

She nodded again.

He continued. "Perhaps the benefit has something to do with the limited nature of their minds. If their minds can only hold so much information, then clearing their memory makes room for more useful ideas."

"Is that all?" His answer was not satisfactory.

He thought. "Over the years, thousands of memories are lost entirely due to misfire. So, I guess, the pill has the benefit of unsettling any negative memories, along with the good."

"Yes, yes, go on." She eyed him, greedily.

"Which means the workers forget things that, perhaps, we don't want them to recall."

"Like what?"

Jetson shrugged.

Covington signaled and chose to provide an academic

challenge, a wise move as Jones encouraged debate—so long as she had the final say. "Is it even true that the workers' minds are physically more limited than ours? I thought that hypothesis was unproven."

East Keep signaled, supplying a predictable counterpoint. "The Compromise says the Second Brother has a brutish heart, which indicates that the true difference between us and them lies in the spirit. They lack ambition. Their hearts are content to be farmers while we want more." She looked around as the class nodded agreement. "We *must* rule them, because they can only go so far without our guidance."

"True, but that doesn't answer the question," Covington said. "Are their minds limited?"

Hannibal spoke up, her voice soft. "A man with a brutish heart is not, necessarily, less intelligent."

We looked to Teacher Jones for the final word.

"Jetson has the right of it," she said. "Their minds are limited, severely so, which effects how they comprehend and maintain information."

Covington touched her chin. "Let's say they aren't as smart as us. Even so, does that justify exposing them to misfires?"

"She's right," Hannibal said. "If they truly are Second Brothers, shouldn't they *want* to be field hands, even if they aren't scrambled?"

"I agree," Jetson said. "From the moment of conception, their limited minds, their brutish bodies," he glanced at the new kid, "everything in them should want to work in the field."

Teacher Jones frowned. We'd gone too far, asked too many questions. She slid her chalk beneath the word "peace." It screeched, making us all jump. "This is where I want the conversation to go," she barked. "Tell me how the Rebirth keeps peace."

I signaled. "Like Jetson mentioned," I said. "Scrambling their minds relieves them of unpleasant memories. So, they won't remember any animosity they might harbor against the laws of America. So content, they'll be invulnerable to the Turner-style violence that plagued the old world."

Teacher Jones flung a finger my way. "Arika, once again."

I reworded my answer. "If they can't remember their history, they won't remember their grievances. And, so bereft, they won't resist the law. Thus, peace in America is accomplished."

I sat back, satisfied. I'd get extra points for berating that old-world Nat Turner Massacre—a tidbit from my personal study. Jones relished that sort of talk. She wrote my answer on the board and directed the eight of us to repeat it.

Into the silence that followed, the Vine Keeper spoke without signaling. "You say we will attain peace for all America. But what good is peace, if innocent Kongos must be disabled to achieve it?"

The class froze, staring at the Vine Keeper. *What good is peace?* The concept was axiomatic. After two hundred years, Earth was not recovered from the Last War. And he questioned the value of peace?

When no one responded he doubled down on his statement. "Can none of you answer?"

My shock hardened into anger. This kid truly deserved the field, but it was not our place to answer him. Jones would put him down.

"No one?" His voice was close.

I glanced up. His eyes were on me, looking to me for an answer!

"So, what?" His gaze bore into mine.

My back stiffened. "Peace matters because war would destroy us all, that's what!"

He pondered this. "So the workers must lose themselves for northerners they don't even know? Why not leave the union and start our own nation?"

"If you read the Compromise," I snapped. "If you can read at all, you'd know that the Second Brother doesn't lose himself in the Rebirth. He becomes himself."

"He loses his mind."

"He begins anew."

"Without a spirit."

"Without the bitterness and hate that ruled the old world."

"Better bitter than docile. Hating hateful things is part of being alive. And what do we get in exchange?"

"We get peace for the Kongo!"

"You saw the arrest today. Is that peace?"

His words smacked me, cold in the face. I stared. How had he known? The arrest had not invigorated me, as it had the others. There had been no contest, no hunt. Just a caged animal. The whole show had made me sick. It was lawful but it had felt—*wrong*. A bolt of lightning shot through my legs, forcing me to my feet. "Any harm done in pursuit of peace is necessarily justified by it!"

The Vine Keeper stared up. "It's justified, you say, even when you *know*, in here, it's wrong?" He tapped his chest, once, twice, just over his heart.

I breathed. He'd spoken softly but his words, that motion,

resounded inside me—like a rooster's call.

"Yes," Jetson said, making me jump. "Arika is right. Peace is justification."

"Always." The twins spoke together.

"Besides, they aren't merely northerners," Covington said. "They're our countrymen."

"Yes," several voices agreed.

The Vine Keeper eyed them all, but settled on me. "You contend for the North so convincingly. I wonder, have you been there? Does the North contend for you?"

He knew the answer. The Obi Forest separated the Kongo from the northern territories, and travel into the Obi Forest was verboten.

"It's forbidden," I said.

He shook his head, amused by my logic. "Of course it is."

I had a retort—*I did!*—founded on years of education. But, for some reason, it lodged in my throat. I just stood there, staring.

"Arika, sit down," Jones said.

I tore my eyes from the new kid to glance at Jones, braced against her desk. Her face was shiny red. I shifted unsteadily, scratching at my legs that itched and twitched beneath the skirt of my *aura*. No field for him, I thought, with queer satisfaction. And no ruler either. Open defiance was no childish prank. Jones was on the brink of true violence. I sat— waiting for her to drag him to the Pit.

Only, she didn't. After a long while, her shoulders squared. She pressed a hand against the line of buttons on her gray uniform. "Arika has the right of it," she said, gruffly. She wrote on the board—*Any harm done in pursuit of peace is necessarily justified by it.* "We must never forget the horror of war," she concluded. She faced the class. "Another volunteer."

I held my breath, certain something more would happen, but Jones continued on with class. *That was it?* Stunned, my mind scurried over the facts.

Aside from being the greatest military strategist to ever live, the Kongo General Obi Solomon had been a wise civic leader. So, when the English General suggested the Kongo, the Clayskin, and the English armies—the three armies left fighting the Last War—attempt a compromise, Obi convinced his people to lay down their arms. Each group sent two delegates to the North—a representative, and an alternate— forming a committee of six Framers.

They debated for months. Talks broke down and the committee scattered, only to reconvene again. One thing was certain—after years of fighting, the people were sick of war. In the end, the Compromise was geared toward maintaining harmony between the three races of America. The basic principles were simple, but ingenious: divide the work and conquer it, separate but equal races, each with spheres of influence, all for the greater good.

The English were agricultural engineers, researching ways to make Earth hospitable to life. The Clayskin people were household servants, manufacturers and merchants. In exchange for the privilege of occupying the largest territory, the Kongo diplomats agreed to work their land and provided food for the others. It was difficult labor, but we did it for the greater good, for the human race, under penalty of death. We students, in particular, answered to Jones. She was harsh, but impeccable in her adherence to law and order—until now.

I took out paper and grasped my quill, but my hand shook

too badly to write. Around me, the class discussed the pros and cons of the new tournament proposal, approved by the Assembly earlier that day. For once, Covington's haughty eyes were lowered and East Keep wasn't doodling. Instead, she worried her lip, as silent as the twins—who were never silent. Not a whisper or giggle among them. Even Jetson was studiously taking notes.

I sat straight in my chair, clenching my quill in a fist. *The Vine Keeper!* It was plain to see he'd made them all doubt. His question lingered in the air like a foul odor. And Jones' acquiescence added insult to injury—*why had she capitulated?*

The new kid's rough whisper assaulted me. "Enough."

Startled, I looked to my left.

"Enough," he said, again.

I followed his pointed look to the blood dripping from my clenched fist. I had buried the sharp point of my quill into my thumb. Seeing it, I suddenly felt the pain. I removed the quill and brought the wound to my lips. I looked over, meeting his eyes.

"Stop it!" I hissed. "Look away!"

"Take it out of your mouth. You're making it worse." His low voice forced me to read his lips.

"It's none of your business," I whispered.

Ignoring me, he pulled my hand from my mouth and laid it across his lap. He pressed the sleeve of his tunic against my thumb. The cloth was rough and warm from his skin. It felt strange. I forgot to protest. Jones droned somewhere in the distance. He pressed hard for a while then carefully removed the dressing. I looked down. It had stopped bleeding. He deposited my hand onto my desk.

"Don't use that hand for an hour. Can you write with your other?"

A moment passed. I shook my head.

Reaching across me, he took a notebook from my desk along with my ink.

"Remember, you owe me," he said. His eyes flashed and, all at once, I remembered where I'd seen their color—a mix of gray and brown. They were the exact shade of the thatch roofs on the Cobane village huts.

THE KEEPER FACTION

After lecture, I waited hopefully at the classroom door. Maybe, in an unprecedented bout of generosity, Jones hadn't wanted to undress the new kid publicly on his first day. Maybe, when the two were alone, Jones would answer his insolence.

I watched as he took his time stretching and stood. His desk creaked, relieved of his weight. I heard his footsteps pause by Jones' desk. I leaned in to watch. He passed by. She didn't look up.

Before the new kid reached the door, I slipped around the nearest corner and wilted against the wall.

"What did she say to him?"

My eyes popped open. The senior class, minus the Vine Keeper, surrounded me in a half circle. They'd been waiting. Slowing my breath, I addressed Covington's question. "Nothing."

Covington edged closer. "This isn't the time to keep secrets, Arika. Whether you know it or not, we all have a stake in the New Seed."

My mouth twisted. There was that phrase again—the New Seed. "What do you mean we have a stake in it?" I asked.

Covington waved aside my question. "Just tell us what Jones said to the Vine Keeper!"

"I told you, nothing. She said nothing." I didn't believe the truth myself. "She just let him go." I flattened my palms against my face, trying to wrap my mind around it.

"That's impossible. Jetson, talk to her."

Jetson huddled closer. "Arika, please, be honest. She must have said something."

I uncovered my face to stare him down. "She let him go."

"And you swear, you swear to me, you know nothing about why he's here?"

I shook my head. "I told you before—no."

He rubbed his chin. "Do you think it has anything to do with the Assembly?"

"What about the Assembly?"

"Don't play the nut," Covington said. She crossed her arms. The twins flanked her sides. "We know Saxon spouts off about politics, and we know you're angling for the open Senate seat."

I lifted my chin, covering my distress. *Obi*, I'd hoped to keep my secret for a few more days. Now that Covington knew about the open seat, she'd want it. "How did you find out about the ousted Senator?" I said. I glanced at Jetson—he was always following me. Had he somehow overheard?

"Jetson didn't tell us, if that's what you're thinking," East Keep said. "We found out because—"

Covington broke in, her eyes hooded. "We have our ways, just like you. Only we know there's more at stake than our own hides, and we're trying to do something about it."

Jetson broke in. "The point is, do you think the new kid's presence has something to do with the open seat?"

I shrugged. "I don't see how they're related."

"Well, it's certainly not a coincidence," Jetson said. "For the second time this month, The Assembly comes to a tie regarding the New Seed Bill. And now, a new student appears just in time to take the Final Exam and join the Assembly?"

I groaned, feeling dizzy. His words made little sense to me. If I asked, he would explain, opening a chasm of secrets. Part of me wanted to run to the library. Another part was desperate to learn more. If this New Seed had something to do with my Senate seat, I needed to know. "What—what's the New Seed?" I said.

Covington looked surprised. She glanced at Jetson.

"I thought you knew," he said. "When I mentioned Voltaire during the arrest earlier today, you didn't seem surprised."

I shook my head. "I've heard of Voltaire. I don't know much, but I've seen the name and I read about the uprising in Hannibal," I admitted. "But what does that have to do with the Seed you keep mentioning?"

"The *New* Seed," he corrected, "and, if you really don't know, it started early last year. A genetic engineering firm, a private company in the Northridge, published a paper. I'm not clear on all the science but, basically, they genetically altered a soybean plant so that it grew with much less effort. After publishing, they got funding to alter all sorts of plants. They're stockpiling the modified seeds for use in the Kongo."

I frowned. "You say these New Seeds grow with less effort? What do you mean?"

"Less effort," Jetson said, staring expectantly. "Less water, less fertilizer, less light, less tending by humans."

I inhaled. "You mean the field hands."

He nodded. "With this New Seed, the Second Brothers could work half of the time and produce just as much food."

I pictured the backbreaking work. From my window, the people were small. Just brightly colored hair scarves in the outfield. "With this New Seed, they could rest," I said. An unexpected desire bloomed inside me. "This New Seed sounds like a gift from Obi Solomon himself," I said. "So, what's the problem?"

"They can't plant the Seed without Assembly approval."

"Right." I knew this from my studies. "Is someone blocking the approval?"

"Yes and no," he said. "A conservative faction of Senators, led by the English, don't want change. The last two votes on the Seed were tied."

"I don't understand, why would anyone be against agricultural progress, especially the English?"

"Think about it, Arika."

I shrugged. "The English are supposed to engage in agricultural engineering."

In fact, from my personal research—aided by Teacher Saxon's private library—I knew that the North was crowded with mega-laboratories, skyscrapers staffed with research assistants conducting thousands of studies.

I thought out loud. "Why would a Northridge Senator be against the Kongo producing food more efficiently. From the birthing control laws, to the laws against waste, the Compromise prizes efficiency. Opposing the Seed should be treason!"

"Yes—which is exactly what the New Seed Party claims," Jetson said. "That's the political faction that supports the New Seed. Director Kumar is the head. He sponsored the Mind-Lab Bill that provided Assembly funding that expanded the technology beyond the soybean."

Covington stepped forward. "Look, I don't have all night to wait while your boyfriend here fills you in."

Heat burned my cheeks.

"What we need to know now is whether Jones is in support of the New Seed."

"How do you know she's chosen a side?"

"This is the central issue facing America today. *Everyone* has chosen a side."

"I haven't. I only just now learned of the Seed."

She snorted. "Pardón, what I meant to say is, everyone who lives in the real world, and not some fantasy Schoolhouse land, has chosen a side."

I pursed my lips. "I haven't heard anything," I said, finally.

"Are you sure?"

Hannibal stepped forward, a sympathetic look on her plain face. "The problem, Arika, is that sometimes you, well, we all tend to close our ears and eyes to things we're afraid to acknowledge."

"What they're trying to say is, you've probably heard something," East Keep said. "So take some time and think about it. We have the meeting tomorrow night, don't forget."

Reluctantly, I nodded. "What does all this have to do with the new kid?" I asked.

Covington answered. "Well, judging from her behavior today, it looks like Jones is with him, whatever side he's on. Given her position at the Schoolhouse, he's probably going to win the Senate seat."

I gasped. "He'll join the Assembly and tip the balance one way or the other."

"Well, you're no genius, but you got it—eventually," Covington said. "The thing is, if he's on the right side, we want him to go to the Assembly. If not, we need to warn the right person."

"Who's the right person?" I asked.

She rolled her eyes and moaned, "Director Kumar, the leader of the New Seed Party!"

"We're all New Seeders, Arika," Jetson said, gently.

"I see," I said. I thought for a moment. There was still one missing piece. I met Jetson's eye. "Earlier, during the arrest, you said that the New Seed couldn't come soon enough because the workers have been unmanageable since Voltaire's last raid," I said. "But you haven't told me what the New Seed has to do with Voltaire's Army."

Jetson glanced at the others before answering. "You said you'd read about the uprising in Hannibal, right?"

I nodded.

"Do you remember reading who was killed?"

I thought back. "The White-Face soldiers killed a handful of Record Keepers." I frowned. Jetson's expression was grim. "I take it that wasn't a coincidence," I said.

"No, Arika, it wasn't. Voltaire is a dangerous Rebel. The army he leads targets Record Keepers as well as the Loyalist workers who support the Record Keeper's role under the Compromise."

"Why would they want to harm us?" I asked.

"Jealousy. The White-Face zealots in Voltaire's Army want power in the Kongo. They're after our seats in the Assembly. They're riling up the good workers and turning them against Hasting. Our plan—" he paused and looked at Covington, who nodded, encouraging him to continue.

"Our plan," he began again, "is to persuade the workers to continue supporting the First Brother Record Keepers, by winning the New Seed battle. If the New Seed Bill passes the Assembly, the Second Brothers' work will be cut in half. We'll win back their favor and Voltaire's rebellion will die a natural death. On the other hand, if Hasting can't get Voltaire's Army under control, the Assembly will eventually have to step in and create order. If that happens, Obi Solomon knows how the balance of power will shift, and what will happen to us and our Senate seats."

"I see," I said.

"So you understand how important it is that we know whose side the new kid is on?" Covington asked.

I nodded.

"And you'll help us?" she added.

I hesitated, regretting my curiosity. I surveyed the circle around me. Except for Jetson, what did I know about them? From class, I knew they were well-read. From private conversation, I knew they were vain and sometimes cruel. I didn't trust them, and they certainly didn't trust me.

My eyes settled on Covington, the ringleader. Her face hadn't changed much in ten years. When I bounded onto her desk that first day of school, her close-set eyes were the only pair to spark as I called out—*Hurrah!* A fire lit behind them only to extinguish when she looked around and saw she was the only one poised to follow.

"Make a decision Arika, are you with us?" Covington snapped. She crossed her arms and lifted her stork-like nose.

Hurrah! Comrades, to me!

Slowly, I shook my head. I had no proof with which to corroborate their story. If Hasting was in danger, surely Jones would have told us. Knowing Covington, this could all be a ruse to distract me from the Final Exam. "No, I'm not with you," I said, finally.

"Why not?!" Covington demanded. "Are we breaking too many rules for little Ms. Perfect?"

I bristled. "Yes, you are. You're way past the line and tampering with policies you can't understand. All you have is gossip and political rumors, both of which are forbidden to students."

She crossed her arms. "At least we're doing something for the workers. They work too hard. As First Brothers, we're supposed to take care of them."

I pushed away from the wall. "I'm doing my part by fulfilling my role under the Compromise!"

"Arika!" Jetson said.

I avoided his gaze. "If I don't make the meeting tomorrow night, Jetson, you can be my proxy." I turned on my heel, my reader clutched to my chest.

THE KITCHEN MAID

That evening in my room, I stared at the colored ink I used to cross-reference my notes, counting the seven pots again and again. Colored ink was precious. Yet, it sat open on my desk, drying in the Kongo heat. I looked down at my notebook. Between counting, I'd read and reread the first page of my notes a dozen times.

Forcing a burst of energy, I sat straighter and dipped my quill in a bright violet color. I wrote the date in the upper right-hand margin—then stalled. I bit my lip and looked at the ink jars. *One two three four five six seven*. I glanced at the clock, another minute had passed.

My gaze shifted to the to-do list I made that morning. There were tiny, black checkmarks beside every task except the third: *Reconsider friendship with Jetson*. A trickle of sweat rolled from my hairline. I slapped it away. *Reconsider friendship with Jetson*. He was frightfully mischievous, but—

I slid my hand beneath the page and ripped it out. I crumpled the list and threw it in the trash. I drew in a deep breath and sighed. I couldn't abandon Jetson. He would need someone to watch over him at Hasting. That done, I bent over my notebook and began reading. I skimmed several bullet points and made a few notations.

Halfway through the page, I stiffened. A new script had

replaced mine. The letters were small and neat. It was *his* writing. I was squinting down, trying to ignore the penmanship, when a pair of gray-brown eyes appeared over the words. I blinked twice. Now his face was there! His wild hair and ridged brow, his neck and the plane of his back—unmistakable. The Vine Keeper! I stared as his visage changed shape, morphing into a golden beast. I'd seen this creature in pictures. Big cats had ruled the jungles of Africa, the continent of dark men in the old world. Before there was a Kongo territory, or even a Kongo army, there was—"The Pan-African Nation," I whispered. The lion, with his furious mane, had been the king of the cats. I slammed the notebook shut.

The problem—the real problem—was Jones' leniency with that boy. Even if Covington had convinced Jetson to lie to me to get the Senate seat, they could not have influenced Jones. Her tolerance simply did not fit. It was impossible to conceive of a Schoolhouse—a world—in which Jones was not willing to punish open rebellion.

I slammed my hand over my ears where the new kid's question clattered. *Why not leave the union and start our own nation?* The answer was obvious! We needed the North and they needed us! That's how the world worked—that is, according to the *old* Jones.

Covington assumed that Jones' leniency meant that she agreed with the new kid, but I wasn't so sure. Jones herself had provided a clue to the contrary. I tapped the quill against my chin as I thought. Just after Jones delivered her set down to Jetson that morning, she'd said, *"we must all* accept the Vine Keeper's presence."

My nails tapped faster. The quill brushed back and forth.

We must all. Not just the students, but Teachers as well. Pure instinct told me Jones and the Vine Keeper—with his village eyes—were not on the same side. So, who was he and why was he at the Schoolhouse?

I nibbled my thumbnail, as I left my desk and lay down fully dressed. My stomach growled, demanding attention. Once again, I had eaten only a few bites of supper. The meal had been poorly prepared. According to gossip, the kitchen had been understaffed for days. One of those missing, I knew, was Robin.

My insides growled and tumbled anew, forcing me to confront the problem bubbling inside it. Robin and I were the same age. We nursed in the same nursery. Yet, here I was, part of the elite. And Robin—*where was she?*

I rose from my bed and paced. A few minutes later, without acknowledging my destination, I left my dorm. I reached the kitchen without trouble. The youngest maids, who spent part of their day learning in the village Academy, slept separately from the older Schoolhouse workers. Squinting, I identified the girl Robin had trusted to fetch me. She was curled up asleep by a smoking hearth.

"Pssst!"

She sat up. Her eyes, as large and soft as I remembered, fluttered awake. I spoke immediately, not wanting her to talk loudly and bring unwanted attention.

"It's me, Arika," I said.

"I see you, Mistress," she said. She rubbed her eyes. "You've come to see Robin."

"Yes."

"I will show you the way." She stood and slid her feet into slippers. The stove's glow shone through her simple brown shift, making her appear spectral. Her eyes were clear and intelligent and I guessed she was no more than six, which meant her mind was as sound as it would ever be.

"We have to hurry; dawn is coming," I said, avoiding her eyes. When she took the Rebirth, at seven, it would rearrange and scatter her memories. Some would disappear altogether. Her gaze would acquire the blank, unfocused look that most of the workers had.

She led me past the hall, where the older maids slept, and stopped at an open storage closet. Robin was curled on her side beside a full cup of water.

"How long has she been like this?" I asked.

"Many days, Mistress," the girl said. "She cannot go on much longer."

"What's wrong with her?"

"She's sad."

Sad? I looked again. She appeared to be sleeping. I turned to ask the little maid for an explanation, but she'd disappeared.

"Robin, are you hurt?" I called.

At my voice, she shifted, exposing a gleam of metal in the darkness—a knife! I hurried to her side.

"Robin, what is it?" I hesitated to grab the knife, not daring to start a struggle. I wrung my hands. "Robin, please. Tell me. What is it?"

She lifted her head, showing me her face, hollow-cheeked and wet, her eyes staring blindly into the dark grief that encompassed her.

"Robin!" I called. She didn't respond. "Robin, are you there? Can you hear me?"

She jerked. Her hand tightened on the knife. She lifted it,

suddenly, so the sharp edge bit the pulse racing in her wrist.

I grabbed the hilt, wrapping my hand around hers. "Robin, please! You'll hurt yourself." I pulled her head against my shoulder. "Robin, it's Arika. It's Arika, Robin. It's me, Arika."

Again and again, I sent my voice into the black space that surrounded her. I said my name, chanted hers, and whispered comforting nonsense words until, finally, she went limp. I held her even closer, letting her feel my heart. She began to sob.

I looked down at her face again.

Tears swelled in steady waves, but the darkness had diminished.

I sighed. "That's it, Robin. Cry—cry it out."

"Arika?"

"Yes, Robin. Arika."

"I thought you wouldn't come. The rules say—"

"Shh." I needed no reminder of the rules. The Kongo birthing control laws specifically dissolved blood relations among us. My presence in the kitchen tonight was exactly why friendships with workers were discouraged. I took a deep breath. "I came. I'm here," I said. "Now, tell me what is wrong."

"Oh, Arika. I want to die. Please help me. I can't do it." She offered me the knife.

Appalled, I whispered harshly, "Robin, don't talk like that. I could never do that. Never!"

She closed her eyes. The darkness descended again and I searched for something to ward it off. I said the first thing that came to mind. "Do you remember the day we met, Robin? Do you remember? It was a beautiful day in the Kongo."

We'd met thirteen months before her first Rebirth, which meant the encounter was one of her safest memories. A faulty pill could erase it but, so far, Robin had been lucky. Her alterations had progressed as intended. For a decade, at the end of each year, her memories were scrambled in preparation for the coming year.

"Arika?" She sounded like a lost child.

I bent closer, placing my cheek against hers. "I'm here. Robin, do you remember that day—the day we met?"

Her trembling stilled. "I remember," she said. "I was seven."

"That's right, we were both seven," I said. "Do you remember what happened?"

She swallowed. "I'd dropped Mistress Covington's reader in wash water."

"You ruined it," I added. "And then you came to my room, crying."

"I couldn't help it," Robin said, her voice gaining strength. "I was bound for the field, I just knew it. But then—" She took a deep breath and let it out on a long sigh. "But then you saved me," she finished.

"I gave you my reader as a replacement," I said, shrugging. "It was identical to Covington's. I figured she'd never know the difference."

"I was so scared," Robin said.

"So was I." I hugged her close. "But when I saw your tears, I couldn't help myself." I didn't tell her how I'd regretted interfering the next morning, and most days since. Terrified Jones would discover the switch, I'd determined to ignore Robin from then on, to treat her like the maid she was. Only—by then it was too late. Our friendship had taken root. I managed to keep it hidden, most of time. But over the years it blossomed, despite the dark.

Holding her gaze, I reached for the knife.

She let it go.

•

After a while I brushed a tear from her cheek. "What is it this time?" I said. "Tell me and I will help."

She shook her head. "You can't help me. No one can give life. Not even a Record Keeper." Suddenly, she bent over as if an invisible knife twisted in her gut.

I held on, trying to decipher her wail.

"My baby, my baby. My baby. Where is my baby?"

Finally, I understood. As a Record Keeper, I received medicine to prevent my flow. Robin got no such courtesy. At sixteen, any Second Brother with desirable genes is required to produce life. Those who don't have partners at the time are paired up and mated. Workers who cannot conceive are put to work early along with other undesirables—the physically disabled, the weak and, of course, Rebels. This unfortunate contingent were given the most dangerous tasks and, generally, died young.

Robin had grown big with child until, for a week two months ago, she went to the birthing hut. Though she never spoke of it, Robin was a birth mother. I knew they suffered after labor, developing an affection for the child, though every precaution is taken to prevent attachment. In the rare case where a birth mother identifies her birth baby despite her facemask, she's recommended for intermittent erasure by the nursery attendants.

Robin cleared her throat. "The worst part is the Rebirth. It's three weeks away."

I frowned. Logic dictated she should be happy the Rebirth was nigh, as it would force her to forget her grief.

Instead of sounding relieved, however, Robin began to pant. "What if I don't remember her after the Rebirth?" she gasped. "It will be like she never lived." Wrapping her arms around herself, she howled. "My baby!"

I fought to hold her still. "Robin, you must stop. Listen to reason. The children are in the nursery. Go there; you can see as many babies as you like."

She drew back and gaped at me. "No."

"Yes—yes, there are dozens of them." Thinking she had forgotten, I explained. "Go hold one and you won't even know the difference."

Robin covered my mouth. "Arika, I would know it is not my baby."

I sat back, confused.

"I would know because—" She broke off and swallowed. "Because my baby is dead."

"No. It—"

"Dead, Arika!"

I stopped. Her flat look convinced me. Such knowledge was highly illegal and I wanted no part of it. But, somehow, she knew her birth child.

"Don't say any more," I said.

She ignored me. "She was sick. I took her to the medicine man, but he was no good. The sickness was in her chest."

I covered my ears.

"She died in his arms. She coughed and coughed. There was blood in her eyes—blood everywhere."

"No."

"Mark my words, a terrible thing has come to Cobane—a black plague!"

"No! No!"

"Would I lie, Arika? Would I lie?"

I stood, scrambling for a bit of memorized text. "Fever is foreign to the Kongo. They are a healthy and hearty lot, immune to the frailties of the North. The male grows seven feet tall and the female as much as six." I stopped to look at her. "That's word for word from my reader, Robin."

"But you yourself were sick this year. I brought tea and soup."

"Yes, sick with a passing cold. But a plague in the Kongo? Impossible."

Robin shuddered, unable to explain.

"Perhaps you've forgotten," I argued. "I'm a favorite of Teacher Jones. She would have warned us of a plague. Perhaps, well—the pill can damage your mind."

"I gave birth to my little girl in March. How could I forget? She was sick, I tell you. She would not eat. Her cry became raspy. I went to the nursery but I did not recognize her, so small and shriveled. She had pain, here, and it changed her song." She touched the hollow of her neck where her hot tears pooled. "When she came, she chippered like a wren— like a wren!"

Doggedly, I shook off her words, determined to make her see reason. "There were complaints at supper tonight, Robin. The kitchen is understaffed. I came to warn you. You have to go back to work. Jones will start asking questions. And then—"

Robin held up a hand. "How can I work, Arika? How can I work when a black plague—"

"There is no plague."

She went on as if I hadn't spoken. "I think to myself, if only—if only I had kept her with me, out of the nursery, I could have made her well. I could have stolen a hovercraft from the stables and fled."

"Fled where?" I asked her.

Her mouth trembled. Her eyes fluttered back and forth. "I could have tried," she finished.

Her tears were flowing again, scalding my heart. I offered the only comfort I could. "The child-rearing laws are set in place by the Compromise—approved by Obi himself. Such laws are good, Robin, even when we don't understand them."

"I'll never understand. Why would Obi Solomon want to keep my Wren from me?"

I hesitated. It boiled down to a single clause: *Care shall be taken to ensure the Second Brother develops a nature conducive to the life he is fated to live.* As the legislative notes explain: *When a child is nurtured as an individual, he values himself. When he's nurtured as part of a class, he values the group. Rooted collectively, the Second Brother grows to accept their place in life, for the greater good.*

I stroked Robin's hair and recited the prescribed answer. "The nursery helps produce honorable workers. It's all done for the good, Robin. You'll see, eventually."

I held her as she cried and cried. After a long while, she stopped. She was no better, but her tears dried up like an old well. She gazed at me. "You are my secret friend, Arika."

It wasn't a question, but I nodded anyway. "I am your secret friend."

She looked down and up again. "And you're sure? Are you sure the law is good?"

I hesitated. There was more to say, but *education is known to engender discontent.*

"Arika?" she prodded.

"I'm here, Robin, and I'm sure. I'm sure this is all for the good."

Grimly, she took my hand and we sat for a long time, in silence.

"I want to remember her song," Robin said, finally.

I hesitated only a moment. Then I took a deep breath and lied. "You will remember her song," I said. "You'll remember it, right here." I touched her chest, where her heart beat like a hummingbird. "You'll remember because the Rebirth has no power over the soul."

She swallowed. "But children forget their mothers and fathers."

"That's because a child's soul is undeveloped," I lied, again.

"People forget they are housemates."

"As they should. The lust that a man suffers for his housemate is not pure. It is not real love, and so it cannot last," I said. "Not like love of country."

She thought for a moment. "I believe in romantic love," she said.

I sighed. We'd been through this before. Having refused to choose a sire for her child, Robin had been bred with a near stranger. She told me, secretly, she had been waiting for love. "Did you love the man who you mated with?"

"He wasn't—rough."

"But did you love him?" I pressed.

"No."

"Do you see? You joined with him over and over for weeks

and you don't have a single tender feeling for him? I tell you, romantic love is not real."

"Then why does the medicine man condone it? He performs the fastening ceremony between couples every day."

I scoffed. "He ties their feet together and sprinkles water on their heads. Does that sound everlasting?"

Unlike Robin, I knew the Assembly developed the ritual a few years after the first Rebirth. The pill had been even more imperfect back then, and workers had only partially forgotten their romantic attachments, which had led to thousands of disputes. The fastening, offered in place of marriage, had brought about peace.

Under the fastening laws, couples entered into a relationship knowing it could not endure longer than a year. All romantic involvements were automatically dissolved with the Rebirth. Each man was free to take a hut with a new woman, and vice versa.

Fresh tears wet Robin's eyes. "They say romantic love is like a warm bath that never gets cold."

"Who says that?"

She shrugged. "People. My sister knew a woman whose grandmother loved a man. The grandmother said their love survived seventy-seven times seven Rebirths."

"*Obi*, Robin. Seventy-seven times seven is over five hundred years. Even if they were Framers, their love would last until 500 A.E. That's three hundred years from now."

"How romantic."

I gave up reasoning. If Jones heard this sort of talk, Robin would be recommended for intermittent erasure. Two erasures in one year—twice the risk of misfire. I leaned forward and took hold of her shoulders. "Listen to me. Your notions of marriage are fantastical. More, they're contrary to the law."

"Maybe I hate the law."

My hand flew to muzzle her mouth. "Robin! You don't mean that. You're just upset about the child."

"Wren. Her name was Wren," Robin said, her voice muffled. Her eyes welled and overflowed onto my hands.

Stung, I yanked my hand back. I wiped it on my skirt. "Yes, her," I said. I couldn't bring myself to say her name. It stuck in my throat and hung in the air between us.

Robin took a deep breath. "Wren," she said, again. Amazingly, the word seemed to comfort her. She wrapped her arms around her waist and I sat, uncomfortable, as she said it again. "Wren."

•

When we parted a few minutes later, Robin was subdued, but safe. She had agreed to return to work in the morning. So why did I feel so bad? I stopped outside the kitchen, my back pressed to the stone wall. A cramp tightened my empty stomach. Slowly, my knees bent.

As the lie goes, a soul cannot forget and cannot be erased. If the deceased was truly the object of another's soul-deep love, they would be remembered in their lover's story and, thus, receive a place in eternity. The workers themselves developed the lie, we think, to ease the pain of premature death. We First Brothers merely incorporated their falsehood into the web of contentment we wove around the village for the greater good.

In truth, the pill altered the synaptic structures in the brain's temporal lobe. They were designed to obstruct the most recent neural networks. After taking the pill, the worker's episodic autobiography was depressed to the point of erasure. So even though Robin loved her baby with all of her soul, she would not be able to repeat her child's song after erasure. In two weeks, when Robin was scrambled, her memory of the child would be so fragmented, it would seem like a dream that never existed.

I stared into the darkness of the Main Hall, seeing Jetson's mouth spiraling before me. It opened and spat silently—*Traitor!* I jammed my hands into my hair and clenched my fist. Robin's eyes, awash with tears, blinked before me—*Liar!* My stomach twisted. I could no longer ignore that the feeling churning there was guilt. Why did it feel so wrong?

Lost in thought, I didn't hear the footsteps coming down the hall. They stopped in front of me. Suddenly aware, my breath caught. *Students must not leave their dorms after dark.* Slowly, I raised my head. A black heel, a heavy skirt, a wide torso, a hard bosom. The back of my neck creased as I lifted my chin, exposing the tender skin of my throat.

THE ASSIGNMENT

I suffered from nightmares until my eighth year. Each dream began in the same place—the wood-paneled hall in front of the cracked window. As I walked the hall, a hole opened beneath me; there was no time to react. I fell several floors to land in another hall, in a dream world beneath the Schoolhouse. In my dream, I shouted as I hit a stone floor, facedown. I pushed myself aright and looked up. The hole I'd fallen through scraped shut. At the same time, another grate opened to my left, revealing a circle of light.

I jumped up and hurried toward the opening, eager to get back to the real world. In my haste, it took me a moment to see her—a girl, strangely familiar, illuminated in the circle beneath the grate. She crouched uncomfortably despite the wide hall. Her legs folded against her chest, her arms crossed over, her fingers burrowed in the dark flesh of her arms. I came to a skidding halt as I recognized her. She, the girl, was *me*, as I'd been in the Pit.

Suddenly, a voice—Jones' voice—came down from the open grate. "Do you need more?"

Obediently, I rushed forward. "Enough, enough!" I cried out, but I was too late. Jones shut the grate and I was alone with myself—digging crescent moons.

I reached the girl just as the light above her was snuffed out.

"No!" I fell to my knees, beside her. "Look what you've done? She won't be back for a day," I sneered, furious. "You're making it harder on yourself."

She didn't respond by word or deed. I watched her profile in the darkness.

"You are a fool," I announced. "The longer you stay in here, the more afraid you'll be."

Suddenly, the grate opened above us. I jumped. Only five minutes had passed. I squinted up into the opening.

Jones' voice called down. "Do you need more?"

"No more!" I shouted. Only, something about this dream world was wrong. Jones couldn't hear me. She waited a few seconds.

Desperate, I turned to the little girl. "You have to answer," I said, ignoring her distress. The little moons on her arms had begun to drip blood. Her mouth moved unintelligibly. Five minutes had passed for me and yet, for her, in the Pit, it had been a day.

The grate groaned shut above us.

"You can't do this!" I shouted at my younger self. "Do you have any idea what she'll turn you into?" The drooling, the mewling. I put my mouth to her ear and screamed aggressively, "Do you hear me?"

She didn't. She mouthed her silent words and trembled, but she did not hear.

Five minutes passed. The grate opened.

I tensed, expecting to hear Jones' question. Instead, her thick hand groped down into the darkness, searching for a grip. It was day ten, I realized. She was here to pull me out of the Pit and teach me my lesson by the window.

"Oh no, you're out of time." My voice shook with fear for

her—for us. "She'll beat you like nothing for this. More 'cause you've made her wait."

Jones' hand gripped her arm—my arm. No time to spare. The girl I'd been was stubborn. I had to convince her, right now! "Listen to me, fall down with the first blow, okay? And don't scream. It makes her mad. Don't plead. Roll over and grovel. Play dumb. She likes that. Whatever you do, stay far back from her feet. She kicks like a donkey. Oh, and drool and roll your eyes! And never forget—she likes to see the marks. So turn your face up, okay? Can you hear me?"

The grate closed over my head and I was alone.

•

I visited the dream Pit nightly for months. Each time I awoke with the grind of the grate in my ears. Shameful visions would plague me as I dressed for class: her—myself—as I'd been by that cracked window, mewling and drooling.

I'd see myself up close, mouthing as the blows fell. From above, twisting in agony. And I hated her—myself—more each day. I'd picture her face and work to be better than her, spurring myself on with shame. Study in the morning, study at night, study at noon. Escape the Pit.

On the last day of that year, Jones interrupted class to announce I'd earned perfect marks. I was on my way to becoming a proper First Brother. That night, I did not dream of the Pit or *her* by the window. She was firmly in my past—or so I thought.

Outside of the kitchen, Jones' hand snaked down to grip me, high on the arm, just above my crescent scars. "Come with me." She jerked me to my feet, testing my joints.

The years of safety fell away in a flash. A falling sensation, a dark hall, and there—below the circle of light—I saw *her* rocking and mouthing.

No! I shook my head to clear it as I hurried to keep up with Jones. We rounded the dining room, mounted the stairs. I stumbled. Jones didn't stop, yanking my arm nearly out of its socket.

Pain, garbled whispers. *Don't plead. Roll over and grovel. Play dumb. She likes that. Turn your face up, okay? Can you hear me?*

No! No! I squeezed my eyes shut. We rounded the dormitory wing.

Jones shoved open the door to my room and pushed me inside.

I fell to the ground.

"Stand up, girl!"

I jumped up, disoriented, wincing at the pain in my shoulder.

She bent forward into the hall and looked around. Satisfied that we were not followed, she closed the door. She turned, flayed me with her eyes.

I trembled out of control.

Finally, she spoke. "The Teachers gathered for the Graduate Assessment last night. Can you guess what was said about you?"

"Wha—I—" I shook my head to clear it. *Obi!* I had forgotten about the Assessment.

She moved to my desk chair and sat down. She beckoned me closer. "Come now, don't be modest. Give a guess."

I took a shaking step forward, searching for what she wanted me to say, what would keep me safe? I cleared my throat. "I hope I passed with the rest of my class, Teacher."

"You did pass, although not with the rest of them. That would make you mediocre. And, from every report, you're quite the opposite. You never speak out of turn, you rarely speak above a whisper. You never run or curse. You don't stay awake past lights out without permission. Or linger in the garden when you should be in your room. In fact, you're rarely out of the library. According to Teacher Saxon, you are a perfect student." She rubbed a knuckle along her chin. "And I almost agree with her."

I ducked my head. *What was she getting at?*

"Do you know why I say almost, Arika?"

I shook my head.

"Speak!"

I jumped. "No, Teacher."

"I say almost, Arika, because last night Master Vine was not in his room and this morning I found you out of yours."

She snatched my hand from my side and squeezed. I gasped with pain. "What are you and Master Vine plotting?"

She twisted her wrist and I heard my own *pop*. I fell to my knees. *Oh no. Oh no, no, no!*

"Speak!"

"Nothing," I gritted.

"Tell me."

"Nothing!"

"If you tell me now, you won't be punished."

I scrambled for the right answer. I had to think—*think!* "There's nothing to tell."

She pushed me away.

I caught myself on my sore wrist.

"Why did you leave your room?"

"I couldn't sleep."

"Liar."

"It's true. I was up late last night. I couldn't sleep. I went to the kitchen to find my maid."

She sat back, resting one thick arm along the solid wood of my desk chair. She shifted one heavy leg as she eyed me.

Remember, she kicks like a donkey.

Quickly, I slid out of range of her black boot. I dared to glance at her face. *Surprise*—it was not contorted with anger, but stiff with calculation. She truly believed I'd conspired with the new kid.

"Did someone warn you to volunteer for the tutoring position?" she asked.

"I'm sorry?"

"Did one of the other *Teachers*," she sneered the word *Teachers*, as if the other Teachers were not Teachers at all, merely imposters, "tell you to volunteer to tutor Master Vine? Did Teacher Rowan get to you?"

"No, no one."

"Then why did you volunteer?"

"I—didn't mean to," I was confused by her line of questioning. What was she getting at?

Her nose quirked. "Look at me."

I did.

"Have you had any private conversations with Master Vine? Any at all."

"No."

"What about conversations with those who've spoken directly to Master Vine."

I thought about my conversation with Jetson. "I don't think so."

"You don't *think* so?"

I gulped. "I spoke with Jetson this morning and we talked about him a little."

"What was said? Speak up, girl!"

"Jetson asked what I thought of Master Vine. He said Master Vine doesn't fit in here."

She squinted at me. "Is that all?"

"Yes."

"Nothing about Director Kumar?"

I shook my head. What would Jetson have to tell me about the Director? "Nothing at all, except what I've already told you."

"Fine. If Master Vine does talk to you, remember what he says and report it to me as soon as possible, is that understood?"

I hesitated.

"Arika!"

"Yes, Teacher. I understand," I said.

"Good."

"Teacher?"

She raised a brow, and I hesitated, not wanting to raise her ire. Only, I needed to understand—if only to avoid more trouble. I wet my lips.

"Do you have something to say, Arika? If you do, say it."

I cleared my throat. "Forgive me, but I want to understand."

"Understand what?"

I had so many questions; I hardly knew where to start. Jones was a doctrinaire when it came to the law. If I presented her with evidence that the Vine Keeper's presence at the Schoolhouse was unlawful, surely she would explain it to me. As a Teacher of the law, she would have to. I cleared my throat. "I want to understand why this new kid is here at all. Why is he posing as a Record Keeper when he looks like a field hand? Also," I added, pushing past my fear, "does his presence have anything to do with the—the New Seed?" The phrase burned my tongue, but I had to know if Covington and the others had been telling the truth. Jetson's words floated through my mind.

If Hasting can't get Voltaire's Army under control... the balance of power will shift, and who knows what will happen to us and our Senate seats.

Jones rubbed her bottom lip and smiled, unpleasantly. "Keeper Cobane, you've been gossiping."

"No," I said. My face felt hot and my heart revved like a hovercraft in my chest, but I didn't take back my query.

"You've been listening to political talk," she went on.

"Political talk is forbidden to students," I quoted.

"As are political opinions," she said.

I hung my head. She was right. *Only...* "Teacher?" I said.

She inclined her head impatiently.

I plowed on. I *had* to know if Jetson was right. My place in the Senate, my safety, depended on the veracity of his claim. "I was wondering—how is the Vine Keeper allowed to take the Final Exam without the proper training?"

She remained silent for so long, I thought my chest would explode.

I stammered to cover my nerves. "That is, the Niagara Compromise clearly states that the Record Keepers are to be set apart as infants. They are to be trained up as caretakers," I quoted.

"What's your point, girl?"

"Only that, he hasn't received the proper training. The training he, by law, has to receive to maintain First Brother classification." It was a neat argument, and I made it well. Still, I held my breath.

She sniffed. "You needn't be concerned about such a small aspect of the law at this juncture," she said.

I frowned. "But—it's the *law*," I managed. "The Compromise. No aspect is beneath our concern. That is what you've said— before." I looked up. Our eyes clashed for the briefest moment.

Her unpleasant smile was gone, her mouth flat. "You're quite the little student aren't you, Miss Cobane?"

My gaze found the floor.

"Rest assured," she said, "Master Vine will get exactly what he deserves under the law. More than that is none of your concern. I'll keep you informed as the need arises."

Despite myself, I wanted to argue with her, to tell her that the need had arisen the moment he'd opened his mouth and rebelled without repercussion. My insides shouted for answers, but I bit my tongue. She did not want to explain. Asking again could prove dangerous.

I lifted my chin. There was only one safe route. I would avoid everything political. I would shelter in the library. If I had to, I would ignore the others entirely—even Jetson. If the New Seed did, indeed, exist, *then maybe as a Senator I could help*—I shook my head. First things first. I had to stay out of it.

Teacher Jones stood, but she did not move to leave. Instead, she took a small black journal from her pocket and placed it on my desktop.

I flinched. I didn't know what the book was and I did not want to find out.

She nodded for me to pick it up.

My breath caught. "Teacher, I—"

"Don't speak, girl. Pick it up."

I wobbled forward and picked up the book with two fingers. "What is it?"

"Think of it as a gift." Her voice was low. "Open it."

Biting my lip, I flipped it open. I glanced at the top of the page. Jones had written Monday's date, three days hence. "I don't understand," I said.

"You spoke of the New Seed," she said, casually.

"Yes, but I know nothing. I—"

"Be quiet!"

I shut my mouth.

"I'm interested in the upcoming Assembly vote regarding the Seed," she said. "I'm interested in Director Kumar and the New Seed Party."

My jaw clenched. With every word, she confirmed Covington's story.

Jones touched her chin. "If Master Vine discusses a topic that you think would interest me, I want to know. Write it down for safekeeping. Be precise, mind you. Nothing lost in translation."

I set the book down, glad to get it out of my hands. "I don't need a notebook for that. Can't I just tell you?"

"No, you cannot just tell me," she growled. She snatched up the book, pried open my hand and slammed the book into my palm. "Use your head, girl. Today is the last day of class before Break."

"Oh, yes." The purpose of Break was to give the senior class time in which to complete the essay portion of the Final

Exam. It counted for fifty percent of our final score and the Teachers graded it blindly, so as not to show favoritism. To ensure accurate results, senior students were given complete autonomy from Teachers during Break. With the Senatorial seat open, autonomy this year would be more important than ever.

I bit my lip, considering Jones' request. I would spend the next few weeks in my room. Robin could fetch food for me, now that she was better. *Robin, better?* a quiet voice asked. I swallowed hard against it. There was no room for doubt. If I was to avoid the Vine Keeper and political entanglement, I'd have to shelter in my room. I met Jones' eye. "So you want me to record any conversations I have with the Vine Keeper and communicate them to you via this journal."

She nodded. "And Arika?"

"Yes?"

"See that he *does* converse with you."

I tensed. "You want me to—"

"I want you to welcome our new student."

I swallowed. There it was. I was to engage the Vine Keeper, pretend to be his friend, and betray whatever he said to Jones. With such an assignment, I could not avoid the intrigue. Briefly, I imagined what the others would say if they knew I spied on one of us for Jones.

"Doesn't the non-communication rule include written communications?" I asked, looking for a way out.

"Not if we don't want it to." Her eyes gleamed.

But the law is the law. We are to uphold it, bar none, for the greater good. I bit my lip, tasting blood. And, for a moment, my guilt overcame my fright.

"Can't you pick someone else?" I whispered. "Maybe a secondary student not subject to the non-communication rule?"

"No."

"But what if one of the other Teachers finds out? Autonomy is vital."

She sniffed. "Arika, are you arguing with me?"

I stepped away. "No, Teacher."

"Then kindly do not inform me of facts I already know."

I slumped. "Yes, Teacher."

She smiled knowingly. "No, you never do argue, do you? Not since the Pit." She cracked the knuckles of her right hand. "Which is why you've been given this assignment. I assure you, it comes straight from the top."

I glanced up. "You mean, from Director Kumar?" I asked.

She pressed her lips together. "What I mean, Arika, is that your future is in your hands as we speak."

My hand clenched around the little black book. She was right. What choice did I have? I could not hope to maintain my classification if I stood in opposition to both Jones and the Director. Ducking my head, I stuffed the little black notebook deep into the folds of my *aura*.

•

Hours later, my last block of classes at the Schoolhouse began. Jones towered at the front of the room. "We've got important information to cover. But, before we get to the material—take out your dictation notebooks."

To my right, Jetson sighed. We all disliked dictation, but he despised it.

Jones moved to her desk, took out a solar-powered metronome and started it. It produced a regular ticking sound that helped us stay on pace as we wrote. Two hundred words a minute was the goal. At my best, I produced two hundred and twenty-five. I opened to a clean page in my notebook.

"We'll be transcribing the Compromise," Jones said. "Whose turn is it to read?"

Covington raised her hand. "I believe it's my turn, Teacher."

"Fine." Jones glanced down, checking her notes. "Begin with the preamble."

As Covington read, I dipped ink and started writing.

Traaaitor.

I dropped my quill. The whisper had been as clear as a bell. When I looked around, however, no one appeared guilty. To my left, the Vine Keeper hadn't moved. I turned to glare at Covington. Reciting, she didn't look up. The twins were bent over their desks keeping pace with Covington's sentences. East Keep, a wiz at dictation, looked bored. That left Jetson, who would never deride me—not on purpose.

Liar.

I jerked and shook my head. The voice hung in the air like sour breath.

Traaitoor. Liar!

Robin's ravaged face flashed into my mind. The image caught fire and curled on the edge. I jammed a fist against the knot in my stomach. The black book in my pocket burned my thigh. I regained my quill and, as Covington droned on, my hand moved over my notebook of its own accord. After a moment, I looked down. In the middle of the blank page, I'd written a name—*Senator Cobane*. Biting my lip, I wrote it again in bold black letters. I underlined it twice, drawing wings above and beneath it. I dipped ink and wrote it again and again and again. I don't know how long the dictation exercise lasted and I did not hear Jones transition to the next part of class. When the last bell rang, however, the pages of my dictation notebook were full.

I dropped my quill and sat back, breathing heavily. My writing hand was smudged with blood where my callouses had rubbed away. Looking down at my palm, I clenched my fist. It should have hurt, but I felt nothing. I touched my face. It was numb too, like an icy wind had blown in to freeze it in place.

From my seat, I watched the new kid leave. Covington and East Keep followed him out. At the door, they turned and shot me hateful glares. Mechanically, I packed my bag.

What did I owe the Vine Keeper or the others, anyway? What had they ever given me? I had to take care of myself.

Jones stopped me on my way out. "Arika, a word."

A glance told me we were alone in the room.

"You're to return the materials I lent you to my inbox no later than midnight Monday. Is that clear?"

I heard myself answer. "Yes, Teacher."

"Make sure no one sees you."

I tried to nod, but my neck felt stiff.

"Speak up."

My mouth moved and I heard my voice say, "Yes, Teacher."

She said more, but I didn't hear. My gaze drifted over her shoulder to the panel of wood that framed the chalkboard. Engraved on the panel were three words. They seared my eyes like a bright light in a dark room. Even when I looked away, as I left the senior classroom for the last time, the words hovered in my view like a holograph. *Ad Maius Bonum*: for the greater good.

THE SPY

That night, an argument broke out in the supper line. I tilted my head for a better look.

Two secondary students gestured angrily at the Vine Keeper, who was holding up the queue. His mouth was set in a firm line as he stared with great interest at one of the kitchen maids. The other conversations in the Hall stalled as the argument grew louder.

I huffed and looked around. Teacher Rowan sat at a table with Teacher Saxon a few feet away from the ruckus; neither seemed inclined to interfere. I stopped short as, across the room, Teacher Jones caught my eye. Her gaze shifted to the scene of the argument, then back to me—pointedly.

This was my opportunity. Mouth dry, I strode to the front of the line. The two secondary students talked over each other in their effort to accost the Vine Keeper.

I raised my voice, undercutting their rant. "You two, you're holding up the line."

They stopped warily. They knew I had the Teachers' ear. I fixed my mouth in my best impression of Jones' scowl. "What are you waiting for? Move," I said.

One student pointed at the Vine Keeper. "He's the one holding up the line," she accused.

I crossed my arms. "He's a senior student, and deserves your respect. Now, to the back of the line, and hurry." My tone left no room for argument.

They looked at each other, shrugged, and retreated.

I watched them take their places then glanced at the Vine Keeper. I rolled my eyes. He wasn't paying attention to me. Instead, he continued to stare at the kitchen worker, Windy.

She tried again to hand him a plate. When he wouldn't take it, she pressed the tray into my hands. It was piled high with meat and fruit.

"Thank you," I said, still assessing the Vine Keeper.

"Yes, Mistress." She spoke quietly with her chin tucked in.

Suddenly, the Vine Keeper came to life. He took the next tray she filled and moved on.

I caught up to him. "What was that about?" I asked.

He ignored me and strode away.

I got a glass of water then followed him to the dining tables, intending to eat beside him and strike up a conversation. As he sat down, however, I jerked to a stop. I looked at the empty seat across from him, then back at Jones. Taking a deep breath, I bent my knees to sit. A split second later, I popped upright and stayed there, frozen with indecision.

Finally, he looked up. "What's your problem, Cobane?"

"At the Schoolhouse, the several Houses of the Kongo must become one, united in purpose," I quoted.

He took a bite of food and eyed me. "So?"

"So, we're not allowed to sit here. We sit by class to force mingling. That way, the students from each House won't just stick together." I saw he wasn't listening. I huffed. "You know, you'll have to make some effort if you want to fit in here."

He took a bite of apple. "What, like you?"

"I fit in as much as I want to!"

He shrugged, "So do I."

I picked up my spoon and we ate in silence for a while—me, standing up.

Eventually, he spoke around a large bite. "Do you know that girl?"

I nodded, balancing a spoon of carrots as I reached for a wedge of potato. "I know both of them; they're a few years behind me in school." I faltered, remembering he, too, was a senior. "I mean *us*, they're behind *us* in school."

"Not the students," he said. "The one serving—the worker."

I followed his gaze. "Oh, you mean Windy."

"Is that her name—Windy?"

"Yes, I think so." I waited for him to continue. He finished his apple in a few gigantic bites and stood to leave.

I started. "But—supper isn't over."

He gave me a dry look and picked up his tray. When he reached the bottom of the staircase, I sprang into action.

I caught up with him halfway to the second floor. "Why did you want to know her name?"

He picked up his pace.

"Hey."

He took the steps three at a time. I trotted after him, like a dog annoying his heels.

"Hey—did you hear me?" I knew he had. "Hey, Vine Keeper!" I barked summarily, forgetting my assignment.

He glanced down at me. "I thought supper wasn't over."

"Why did you want her name?"

"Why do you care?"

"Because she's my friend, and if you're going to complain

about her, I'd like to warn her first." It was a lie, but I told it well. This was just the sort of suspicious activity Jones wanted to know about. If I got her information tonight, I could spend the rest of the weekend in the library.

He turned right, toward the male sleeping quarters, where I wasn't allowed.

I sensed that he was testing me. If I wanted his trust, I would have to go along and explain to Jones later. "So?" I prodded, staying at his flank.

He walked a while longer, and I hurried to keep up. He stopped abruptly in front of a dormitory. I nearly ran into his back. He turned. He looked me up and down.

"Do you know my name?" he said.

I blinked, stalling for time. "What does that matter?"

"I'll answer anything you want, if you can tell me my name."

His eyes seared mine, looking directly into my pupils and through them, to my ill intention. He had not been fooled, I realized. Not at all. My temper flared. "I know you're rude and disruptive."

His mouth tilted, humorlessly. "I figured you weren't friends with her. Your kind never are."

He opened the dormitory door and shut it in my face.

•

After a minute, I took a deep breath. I grabbed the door handle and let myself in. The Vine Keeper was taking a thick mound of cloths from his pocket. He unrolled the mound and laid it flat on his desk beside a neat pile of white gloves. The rolled cloths, I realized, were medical masks. I'd seen the nurses wearing them along with white gloves in the Schoolhouse infirmary. Ignoring me, the Vine Keeper picked up a book and sat down at his desk to read.

I marched up to him, demanding attention. "Okay, fine. I should know your name, and I don't," I conceded. "I was rude yesterday in the hall. And you have every right to mistrust me."

He looked up, his face stony.

"I'm trying to apologize."

He shrugged. "Apology accepted."

He looked down at his book, but he didn't order me to leave.

His room was a standard-issue single except he had several bookshelves, all packed with books. His window was larger than mine, and a dozen pots of soil sat on the sill. A few boasted tiny green seedlings.

"Are these all yours?" I said. I moved to the bookshelves. There were several thick volumes, pamphlets, treatises and anthologies.

He took a while to answer. "Yes."

I knelt by his desk, where a tall stack wavered. "May I?"

He sighed, but nodded. I ran my hand along the spines. *Basic Botany, Botanical Gardens, The Secret World of Trees, Herbs and Roots.* "I don't get it. Are these for your garden?" I nodded to his potted plants.

"You ask a lot of questions, Cobane."

I scanned a pile by his feet. *Einstein's Physics, Human Maladies, The Complete Anatomy Reference Book, Advanced Organisms.* A book at the bottom of the stack caught my attention. "*Weapons of Combat*?" I asked. I opened the book and flipped through the first few pages. An inscription caught my eye. Before I read it, he took the book from my hands and placed it on another pile—right on top.

"Forget you saw that one," he said.

"Was that published here?" We were specifically forbidden books published outside of our territory. A special publishing house, managed by Clayskin diplomats, operated at Hannibal for the sole purpose of providing us with approved literature.

"It was published in the Northridge several years ago. I received it as a gift. Now, if you don't mind, I'm trying to study."

I ignored his hint that I should leave. Pausing for a moment, I pasted a Covington-like smirk on my mouth and attempted a new tactic. "*Obi!* Don't tell me you're going to study all night?"

He ignored me.

I kept one eye on the book he was so protective of and tried again. "Well, there's a party later on—if you're interested."

He said nothing.

"Oh, come on… you." I winced, I still didn't know his name. "No one is working tonight."

He flipped a page. "Wrong again, Cobane. While your kind are on Break, Windy and her kind are working. No weekends, no parties, no Breaks."

I opened my mouth to argue—then I shut it. He was right. My gut jerked guiltily, making my supper rise in my throat. I found his wastebasket just in time to empty my stomach. *No weekends, no parties, no Breaks.* My mind conjured a picture of Robin and her baby. I couldn't bring myself to think of the child's name.

The Vine Keeper's gaze burned the side of my face as I cleared my mouth into the trash. I wiped a hand across my cheek. "Stop it! You're staring."

He opened a drawer of his desk and handed me a skin of water. I eyed it suspiciously—then took it. I gulped it down.

"Easy, or you'll make yourself sick again."

I finished the water in smaller sips.

"Do you need to lie down?"

I shook my head, but grimaced. "My mouth tastes awful."

He opened his desk drawer and took out a trio of ridged leaves. "Chew this."

"What is it?"

"Eat them, Cobane."

I looked at the leaves, sensing he was testing me again. If I ate them, I trusted him and he could trust me. I ate the leaves. A sweet mint flavor burst in my mouth. "They're delicious."

He nodded.

I took my time chewing. "You weren't going to complain about Windy, were you?"

He shook his head. "I was going to diagnose her." He picked up the book he'd been reading and sat beside me on the floor. He set half of the volume in my lap, and flipped to a page he'd marked. He tapped at a paragraph in the middle. "Read it," he said.

I tripped over the unfamiliar words. "The typical symptoms of Blood Fever include pustular tonsillitis, pneumonia, pleural effusion, acute pharyngitis and acute rhinitis. If left untreated, survival is grim with death occurring within eight days of the incubation period in forty percent of the known cases."

Frowning, I read it again. "I don't understand."

"Her nose," he said. "Didn't you notice the sores around it?"

I thought back. "I didn't see her nose. She had her face turned down."

"Retropharyngeal abscess." He jabbed a finger at another point on the page.

I held up a hand. "Wait, what's that?"

"It's an infection in the back of the throat that makes the neck painful to move. Which is why Windy was looking down."

"And what did you say about her nose?"

"Her nostrils and upper lip were scaled with scabs, indicating rhinitis, or stuffy nose."

I verified that rhinitis was one of the symptoms. "And what do these other symptoms mean?"

He pointed to each word as he explained. "Swollen and pussy tonsils, inflamed lungs filled with liquid, swollen throat and swollen nasal passages. The victim usually dies of suffocation. They struggle to inhale air, and when they do, their inflamed lungs can't use it."

"And you think Windy has this Blood Fever?"

"I can't be sure, but I've seen it before."

"Where?"

"At the Vine House last year, and Point Landing just a few days ago. It's killed about a hundred people already. All Kongos."

I shoved his book away. "You're a liar."

"Suit yourself. But, if you're in the habit of sneaking off to the village, don't. The fever has spread here. The first case appeared one week ago. I'd bet on it."

"Going to the village is against the rules."

He shrugged. "I'm not concerned with rules."

"You should be," I retorted. I sounded smug, even to myself. "Rules are what make the work we do in the Kongo bearable."

He smiled. "Are you suggesting that Record Keepers work?"

I scowled. "Everyone has a role. We might not toil in the field but that doesn't mean we don't work. The Compromise—"

He held up a hand. "I've heard about as much as I can stomach about the Compromise."

"What, are you a White-Face Rebel? Part of Voltaire's Army? What do you know about the New Seed?"

I was hoping to catch him off guard. And, for a moment, he looked confused. Then he laughed.

I hated being laughed at.

He laughed harder. "*Obi,* Cobane. You're really hoping I'll answer—aren't you? Just like that?"

I glowered. "It's fine. Don't answer. I can see for myself. You're nothing but a lying feral," I spat.

Still grinning, he leaned back and crossed his arms over his chest. "You know, there's an easy way to resolve this. Talk to Windy, ask her if she's sick."

"I will," I lied.

His smile faded. "Well, do it today. Tomorrow will be too late."

I stiffened. His tone, his eyes—they left no room for doubt. True or not, he believed every word he said. I shot to my feet. "Possessed of a particularly sound countenance," I quoted, "the Kongo race—"

He made a face and moved to his desk.

I followed him. "The Kongo race is well suited to physical labor. We rarely get sick."

He sat. "Look Cobane, believe what you want. I'm not sure who sent you to spy on me, but please—get out."

My gut clenched and I turned to leave. I'd failed. Jones would be disappointed. And worse, for some reason, was the look in the Vine Keeper's eyes when he'd told me to go—something akin to pity. My back straightened. Suddenly, I whipped around, catching him by surprise. In a flash, I lunged for the book I'd seen earlier, the one he didn't want me to read.

He got to his feet.

I had it. I stumbled a few steps and flipped open the cover, bracing myself. He reached around my back, seized the edge and tugged, thinking I would let go.

I didn't.

The spine wrenched as it tore in two. He came away with the bigger piece, but I had what I needed. While he stood, too appalled to move, I didn't waste a second. I turned to the dedication page and found what I'd only glimpsed before—a brief scrawl followed by a signature that I recognized.

HK,
Go to House Cobane. And there, may you find the gift in death.
Your father, Dana Kumar.

He was upon me, snatching the pages from my palms, slack with shock. *Father?* My mind raced. If he was kin to Director Dana Kumar, here on the Director's behalf, *why would Jones order me to spy on him?* The answer came like a punch. Jones was not collecting information for Director Kumar; she was defying him—a violation punishable by death. And, with the black book in my pocket, I was helping her do it.

In a trance, I looked up at the new kid. His eyes were angry, more gray than brown. And, just like that, I remembered his name. It rose up, dividing the stream of my subconscious, to surface like coconut oil. *Hosea Khan, the Vine Keeper.* Just then, a sharp pain slammed into the base of my skull. Before I could cry out, everything went dark.

THE GIANT

I woke to the Vine Keeper's voice. "That was unnecessary."

I opened my eyes to darkness. I blinked. The blow to my head had knocked me facedown. I struggled to roll over, but pain forestalled me.

"I had it under control," he said.

I couldn't see him but he sounded close.

Another voice, one I didn't recognize, answered him. "She one of them. Not safe." It was heavily accented and paced, as if each word was a struggle to recall. It belonged to a Kongo feral.

"She may be a Keeper, but that doesn't mean we can murder her," the Vine Keeper said.

Murder? Very slowly, I rolled my head in their direction and opened one eye. Hosea Khan and, beside him, a giant with a crude club gripped in his hand.

"I assume you're Crane, the one who sent for me," Hosea continued.

The giant shook his head. "Not Crane."

"I was summoned here by the Cobane Champion, Crane Cobane, a man nearly eight feet tall with legs like tree trunks and a birthmark low on his left cheek. How many men in Cobane could fit that description?"

"I sent the message you say, but," the giant went on, "I do not have the name Crane Cobane. I am that no more."

Hosea hesitated. "Then what should I call you?"

The giant straightened, growing another half inch. "I am William Whittle. I do not live by the club."

"Alright, William Whittle," Hosea agreed.

"And you? Robin says you is Kha."

Robin—my Robin? My heart began to pound. Suddenly, I recalled where I'd heard the name Crane Cobane. It belonged to the Champion who had won the last seven Jousts. He was a god among the Kongo people, a living legend.

"I am Kha," the Vine Keeper answered.

"Good. You come," said the giant. "Quick, no time to waste. The people need you."

"I will come. But first, I have to help my friend. You hit her hard."

"No time to help," the giant protested.

Hosea Khan didn't respond. A moment later, his arms lifted me from the ground. I shut my eyes quickly as pain consumed me. The cold circle of his silver necklace pressed against my cheek as he laid me on his bed. As the pain ebbed, I opened my eyes again. His face was a shadow.

"Good, you're awake," he said.

I moaned.

"Don't try to talk. You took a bad blow. No more than you deserve. Haven't you school brats heard of privacy?"

He probed the back and sides of my head with tender fingers. He left for a moment and returned with a white bag.

"You need ice, but you'll live."

He pressed the bag against the worst part of the ache and my vision darkened again. I fought it. So many questions. Who was this field hand? Why had he hit me, and why had the new kid answered to the name, Kha? He was Hosea.

"How many are ill?" the Vine Keeper said, returning his attention to the giant.

"Many sick people. Babies, old men. Many—many sick people."

"Has anyone died?"

"One baby is gone."

"Windy is also very ill," the Vine Keeper said. "Why was she in the kitchen line? She needs rest, not work."

"The quota needs be done—they say." There was a shrug in the giant's tone.

Hosea opened and closed drawers, pulling out small vials and leather bags. Each slammed drawer rang in my head.

"Time is gone. We must go now," the giant said.

"We'll go in due time. First, we have to put her to sleep." He nodded in my direction.

I jerked, wanting to protest. I was so weak.

"I put to sleep," the giant said. His towering shadow stepped forward, weapon raised.

"William—no." Hosea blocked the giant's path, his hand at his hip. My eyes narrowed. A tube hung in a holster slung low around his waist. It hadn't been there during supper. The tube was silver and one-tenth the size of the giant's club. From the defensive way he touched it, I sensed it was a weapon. "Put that away," he said, nodding at the giant's club. "It's done for today."

The giant tightened his grip on his weapon. "She scream. Bring Guard running. Stop Kha. No good. Kha must go to village. Many sick people."

"She won't scream unless you hit her again. Or scare her.

Then neither one of us will go to the village. Let me put her to sleep instead. Besides, I thought you didn't live by the club."

The giant lowered his arm. "At times, I must," he explained. "For the people—many sick people—I pick up the club to fight."

Hosea took a vial from a sack at his side, knelt by his bed.

"Don't." I tried to turn my head.

"I have no choice," he said. "If I leave you awake, you'll raise an alarm."

"I won't tell."

"Liar." He dropped a pinch of powder into the vial and swirled it around.

"You're his son," I whispered. "I saw in the book. It said, *father.*"

He shrugged. "You can tell Jones. I assure you, she already knows."

"But—"

"Don't say any more. This will put you to sleep until tomorrow morning. When you wake, you'll be confused. Just ring for the nurse and she'll put you right."

He pressed the liquid to my lips. I twisted away.

"Don't be difficult. I'm the only thing standing between you and him."

The giant spoke as if on cue. "Kha come now."

I opened my mouth. The brew tasted awful and my upset stomach rejected it. Hosea helped me to my side and I vomited into the wastebasket.

"I think enough of it stayed down," he said to the giant. "We'll know in a minute."

Suddenly, my eyes grew heavy, my limbs weak. I sank boneless into the bed. Hosea lifted the covers over my body.

They smelled like mint. Lulled, I barely heard his parting words to me.

"If I don't see you again, Cobane, know this: you're not trapped here in America, there are other lands under the sun. You must question everything—and go west."

PART TWO

THE
VILLAGE

THE MEMORY

The work was nuanced, and I'd been at it for hours, skipping breakfast, eating noon meal behind a mountain of dusty texts. The small of my back ached, despite Teacher Saxon's cushioned desk chair. I sighed, set my quill down and checked the hour. Five minutes until supper. If I skipped it, I would finish before tomorrow's contest deadline. Then, if my luck held, I would be the next Silver Award recipient.

With renewed energy, I regained my quill as the door to the study opened. Eager to honor the trust Teacher Saxon had shown by allowing me to continue my research in her office as she attended a faculty meeting, I bent over my work, assuming a dependable air.

Two pairs of shoes scuffled into the room. I heard the door shut. When they failed to note my presence, I realized the crag of research material blocked their view of me. Before I could call out, a voice began speaking in the midst of conversation. It was Teacher Rowan.

"Are you with us?" she said.

Teacher Saxon responded shakily. "Oh, I don't know, maybe we should go to Alice with what we know now."

Alice, I knew, was Teacher Jones' given name. I shrank in

the chair, now desperate to remain concealed.

"Go to her for what?" Rowan said. "She will never question him."

"If we present this new evidence, she'll have to. She'll have no choice."

"Come now, Polly. She has plenty of evidence to oppose Dana Kumar right now. You said so yourself. There's the letter from my contact about his affair, the lack of transparency, the missing hydroplanes. We've been over the facts a dozen times. Do you need to hear them again?"

"Okay, the affair with the Kongo girl was wrong—despicable even. She was so young. And I heard that she bore him a child. But it's not proof of a divide in the Party. We're all for the Seed, and we have to stick together if we're going to withstand political challenge. I'm sure if we think it through—"

Rowan huffed, cutting her off. "It seems you *do* need to review. Fine. What about his lack of transparency?" Rowan asked.

"What about it?" Saxon countered. "Dana Kumar recruited *us* to the Party! He's not required to defend himself against ludicrous accusations."

"Far from ludicrous," Rowan declared.

"Not far at all! Dana sponsored the Mind-Lab Bill," Saxon said. "The bill that provided the funding to expand the Soybean Project. Why, then, would he try to have the Seed banned? It's nonsensical."

"And the missing planes?" Rowan asked. "Explain that!"

"How many did your contact say are missing?" Saxon said.

"Four, at least, according to her last letter. The Kongo Technology Center doesn't keep an inventory of planes that are out of commission."

"Then how can she know four are missing?" Saxon asked.

"At least four! And she knows because she's a staff engineer at the KTC, she knows what's missing. And besides the planes, let's not forget there are other issues." She paused, then whispered, "Kumar's project. Were you able to track down its authorization papers?"

"Well, no," Saxon said.

"No government authorization, and yet he's utilizing government funds. It's evidence of a secret project. The question is not how many planes are missing, but what *possible* purpose the Director could have for misdirecting them?"

Behind my tower of books, I stifled a sneeze. Even I could answer that question. The hydroplanes were an English invention, an irrigation solution to the scorched earth we were left with after the War. Around the clock, the solar-powered water planes shuttled between the Atlantic Ocean and the Kongo, desalinating and transporting millions of gallons of water a day. Along with the solar reflectors, that regulated the temperature of the Earth, hydroplanes made it possible for the workers to harvest all year round. They had only one purpose. If the Director was appropriating planes from the KTC, the reason was undoubtedly to rehydrate unauthorized land so that it might support life.

Teacher Saxon began a ticking sound with her tongue, a sure sign she felt overwhelmed.

Teacher Rowan's tone was soothing. "Forget all I'm telling you," she said. "I want you to focus on what you know—firsthand."

The ticking stopped. "About the textbooks, you mean?" Saxon said.

"Yes."

"I've asked Director Kumar countless times for more but he said the Assembly Senators wouldn't approve funding."

"According to him," Rowan purred.

Teacher Saxon went on. "I asked to use the KTC communication unit, so that I might address the Assembly myself."

"And? Did he let you use the comm-unit?"

"You know he didn't!"

"I do know!" Rowan agreed, stoking Saxon's indignation. "That's one reason why Teacher Alberta and I are against him. With the comm-unit, you could have broadcasted your plea by holograph and reached the entire American Assembly in an instant." She snapped her fingers. "But he wouldn't let you near it—why?"

"Well, he said it would create unrest in the workers."

"Perhaps, if you projected the image in the outfields. But you wouldn't have done that."

"He said it was unseemly for an English Teacher to be so involved with Kongo children."

Rowan scoffed.

"He said an audience with the Assembly would only be granted in important cases."

"Is a textbook not important at a Schoolhouse?" Rowan asked. "I say it is!"

I imagined Teacher Saxon nodding. Her loose red curls bouncing around her head.

"He acts as if he alone knows what's best," she said, resigned. "I've even heard him second-guess the Senators."

"Ah-ha!" Teacher Rowan hissed. "Treason."

"*Something* doesn't seem right," Saxon admitted.

"So join us—Alberta and I have started a petition."

"What about Alice?"

"Teacher Jones has made her choice. She's with Director Kumar, whatever comes."

"And where is it that you and Teacher Alberta stand, exactly? If I'm to join you, I want to be clear."

"We stand with the Party and against any force that hinders the Seed!"

Behind the desk, I shivered. There was something dark in her tone.

"We don't know what Director Dana Kumar is plotting," she went on, "but it's clear that he is no longer with us. And so, by proxy, neither is Teacher Jones."

THE AWAKENING

8 MONTHS LATER...

An urgent knock at the door roused me. I sat up, tipping the covers, Hosea's covers, to my waist. The knock sounded again.

"Arika, if you're in there, say something."

My befuddled mind registered Jetson's voice at the door.

"Hosea, I swear on my life, you'd better not have touched her," Jetson said.

I glanced around. The room was empty.

The door flew open. Jetson rushed in. "Arika, are you okay?"

I swallowed. "I'm fine, I think."

He knelt beside me. "Where is he? I want to see his smug face before I punch him. Where is he?"

"I don't know." I was only half listening. In my head I replayed the faint whisper of Hosea's last words to me—"You're not trapped here in America—go west." *West*, I thought. *But there's nothing west of America except the boiling seas.*

"What do you mean you don't know?" Jetson railed, interrupting my thoughts. "You're in his bed!"

"Leave off, Jetson!" I snapped. I looked around. The room was dark. I had slept for hours. "He gave me something to make me sleep," I said. "He said it would confuse me." Had his advice to go west been merely a dream? I lay back, trying to orient myself.

What I did remember firmly was his conversation with the giant field hand, William, the Cobane Champion. My mind flashed again and I remembered the dream I had about Rowan and Saxon. I'd overheard their conversation months ago, but the memory, freed from my subconscious, was now distressingly fresh. Unbeknownst to me at the time, the two had been discussing the New Seed. Both of them were loyal members of the Party, and both of them doubted whether Jones and Director Kumar were to be trusted.

Jetson took my shoulders. "Can you sit up?"

"I think I need a nurse." Hosea had said as much. "Will you ring for one?"

A few minutes later, the Clayskin school nurse met us in my room and inspected my head. She left me with a liquid bandage as well as medication for pain.

"You can also request a hash treatment," she said at the door. "It will relieve you quicker than anything I have. If you want, I can send up a Supply Room pass."

"Yes, I'd like that," I said.

She closed the door, leaving Jetson and me alone.

He eyed me. "Since when do you smoke hash?"

I curled away from him, drawing my knees to my chest. "It's not against the rules if it's for medicinal purposes," I said. "I've seen you do it."

"Yes, and you lectured me about it for an hour."

"Don't exaggerate."

"You soaked my entire stash in water, and now you're smoking it?"

He was right. Smoking hash was unlike me. Then again, Rebels in Cobane; Jones' order to spy; a split between her and the other Teachers. The fabric of my existence was unraveling.

I pressed my fingers to my temples, wanting to crush the questions marching like ants across my mind. But how could I? How could I erase the inscription in Hosea's book? If he was Dana Kumar's son, then Kumar, the Director of the Kongo, had broken the Kongo mating laws by fornicating with a worker.

How could I forget Rowan's words of a political coup? She had assumed that Jones was working with the Director. However, the black book, even now in my pocket, was proof that Jones had some other allegiance. She was not with the Director, but carrying out a deception against him. For what purpose, I could not guess. I did not *want* to guess!

"Arika, talk to me."

"There's nothing to say."

"Dammit, enough lies! I know something is wrong. Hosea interrupted the Committee meeting to tell me you were unconscious in his room. Covington is livid you missed the meeting, by the way. Of course I knew Hosea lied, but I checked to make sure. And there you were, in his room, just as he said."

I started to speak, but he held up a hand.

"You told us yesterday that you hadn't heard a word about the New Seed vote despite being with the Teachers day and night. And I believed you. I defended you when the others scoffed. But no more, not when I find you lifeless in his bed. You can't tell me you're innocent!"

I pushed him away and uncurled slightly, trying to wrap my mind around the nuances, to tease from the tangle of information what to do, now that I'd been dragged, kicking and screaming, into the middle of the mess.

"Arika?"

"I'm thinking, Jetson. I'm thinking."

I chewed on my lip. Talking with him was out of the question. He would undoubtedly update Covington, who would use whatever I said to her advantage. No, the safest bet for now was to side with the Teachers, until I graduated from the Schoolhouse. Only, which Teacher?

Saxon was an old ally, but Jones was the Headmistress. She'd given me the black book, which coiled—even now—like a snake in my pocket. Something primal told me to stick with her until I was out of her grasp. Then, I would see to placating the Director. I bit my lip. With a great deal of luck, I'd be out of his reach too—safe in the Assembly.

I turned to Jetson. "I need something from you."

His brows drew together. "What is it?"

"Don't ask me any more questions until the Committee meeting tomorrow afternoon."

"The meeting is tomorrow evening," he corrected.

"Fine, I'll be there. I swear."

"Why can't you explain it to me now?"

I answered honestly. "Because right now, I don't know who to trust."

Jetson frowned. "Arika, what are you planning?"

I ignored him. "Oh, and one more thing. I need your key to the Schoolhouse gate."

He balked.

"No more questions," I reminded him. "And don't deny that you have a key. I know you've snuck out with the others."

"You're nutty if you think you're going alone. I'll come with you."

I thought for a moment. "You can't come. I need to move in

141

secret. With two of us gone, someone is bound to find out." *Three of us*, I added to myself. Hosea had gone too.

"If I can't go, you're staying put. No one will give you a key now, they're vexed."

"Jetson, I must go!"

"No! It's dangerous out there." He lowered his voice. "Another attack happened last night, at Point Landing. Four Keepers were lodged at the Overseer's mansion when Voltaire's White-Face men broke into their room."

I clutched my throat. "Are they—?"

Jetson nodded. "Dead. And the riots aren't over. Workers are fighting the Guard. Dozens have been arrested. The Overseer is threatening to abandon the House entirely."

Moaning, I rubbed my aching temple. Behind my lids I saw the cartoon of the Kongo man, his eyes shining from a white-painted face, a bloody dagger lifted over his head.

I shivered and opened my eyes. The giant had held his crude club just like that, when he'd offered to put me to sleep. Was he one of them? I couldn't guess—but I needed answers. The Kongo leadership was splintering. Soon, we'd all be scampering like rats for a burrow. If I was to survive, I needed to be invaluable to the people in power—to Jones. I needed information.

I met Jetson's concerned green gaze and my stomach twisted with guilt, even as I plotted to deceive him. I touched a limp hand to my head.

He responded immediately. "Does your head hurt?"

I nodded, feebly.

He pulled the blanket up to my chin and tucked me in. "It must have been a nasty fall."

I blinked. "Excuse me?"

"Your fall. Hosea said you slipped and fell on the staircase down to the Main Hall."

"Oh right. I can hardly remember."

He brushed a hand along my forehead, then rested it against my cheek.

For once, I didn't push it away. "Jetson. You know I'm a stickler for rules."

"Yes, you are," he said, his gaze soft.

"Well, boys aren't allowed in the girls' dorms. I *want* you to stay, but…" My voice trailed off.

"I understand. I'll go." He took my hand. "Can I get you pain medication before I leave?"

"Yes, please," I said.

He poured a generous amount of medication into a goblet and watched as I took a mouthful. At the door, he looked back at me. "That should put you to sleep for some time," he said. "I'll see you in the morning."

As the door shut, I spat the mixture back into the goblet. I needed to be alert in the village, not addled with drugs. I tilted my head, listening for Jetson's footsteps in the hall. When they disappeared down another long corridor, I threw my cover back and raced to get dressed.

•

A quarter-hour later, I peeked into the hall, more nervous than I'd been in ten years. Going to the village was against the most fundamental of rules. If I was caught, my punishment would be severe. Jones herself would be lenient. She had ordered me to spy on Hosea, and Hosea was in the village. But if another Teacher discovered me, I would have no excuse.

I pushed back the hood of my *pallium* as I looked left and right. In a moment of inspiration, I'd chosen a heavy cloak over clothing more appropriate to the mild weather. Its dark color would blend in with the night and serve as cover—I hoped. I stepped into the corridor and waited, listening. The hinge of my door creaked loudly and Covington, across the hall, was a light sleeper. *One heartbeat—two.* She snored softly.

I gripped the strap of my schoolbag as I traveled along the girls' quarters to the main stairs. I descended the stairs to the Main Hall and past the corridor that led to the kitchen. High above me, the solar-powered crystalights hovered like diamonds in the darkness. I hurried through the front door, across the porch and around the side of the house, to the backyard, nearly an acre wide. Wrapped around the yard was a locked picket fence.

Jetson had refused me his key. But what he didn't know, what no one knew, was that the fence was not always properly maintained. Once, from my dorm room window, I'd seen a kitchen maid escape a beating by shoveling beneath a loose slate. If my luck held, I'd find a loose slate of my own.

I set about tapping each fence post as I walked alongside it. After several minutes one of the posts moved beneath my hand. I looked over my shoulder, across the wide yard and up at the Schoolhouse. Seeing no one, I pushed at the fence in earnest, loosening it more. I dug around its base until I had made a hole big enough for my frame to wiggle through. Finally, I struggled to the other side.

The meadow beyond the fence brimmed with grass high enough to irritate my neck and ears. I swatted it aside, pushed the hood of my cloak back and set off to the village.

My stomach tightened against a flood of nostalgia as I crossed the village perimeter for the first time in seventeen years. A wave broke loose, despite me, conjuring an image of the nursery. Lined with cribs, packed with half-naked babies. I'd sucked my own thumb or my brother's as he nibbled our sister's toe.

"It was all the same to us," I whispered, then pressed a fist to my mouth. I had to control myself. Shaking off the memory, I quickened my step, and turned down the first street I came to.

There were *Wanted* signs everywhere. Dark faces stared back at me from posters scattered along the ground and nailed to the wooden walls of the huts I passed. Below each *Wanted* criminal's face was a dollar sign signifying a monetary reward for their capture. I continued to walk.

There were no quaint cottages or chorusing workers milling the streets, as I'd imagined as a child. But, up close, it was even worse than I'd seen from my Schoolhouse window. Most of the shelters were in sad repair. Limp doors on rusted hinges, ripped wax-paper windows, and broken shutters. The dilapidation was distressing and I averted my eyes. I had an assignment to complete.

I wasn't worried about detection by the Guard. Even after the arrest yesterday, I doubted they were patrolling the streets. And the Cobane Overseer diplomat quarters were deep in the outfield. At this hour, the village would be empty, save the workers and, somewhere, Hosea Khan.

Before leaving my room, I'd seen a light flickering in the village square and I was headed there to investigate. I paused for a moment to orient myself, then took the most direct path, squeezing sideways down a narrow opening between two huts.

The fit was tight. Splintered slates scraped skin from my cheek. Iron nails twined in my hair. A *Wanted* sign dislodged and drifted away in my wake. My sandal sank into the ground, and a putrid wetness gushed between my toes. Yelping, I leapt forward into the next clearing. I inspected my foot. The feathered remains of a fowl stuck there, dank in the moonlight. As I scraped it away, a nasty feeling poked at my stomach. Cautiously, I walked on.

The light I'd seen from my dorm was a well-lit warehouse at the end of the next street. The structure bustled with movement. Shadows, cast through a large open window, skipped along the ground. I moved closer until, finally, I crept onto the front porch and peeked in.

Hosea Khan was bent low over a figure draped in sheets. Through the white medical mask that covered his nose and mouth, he was issuing orders. "Take those bleeding pans away! And make sure the room is clear of purge. I could murder you for this, old man! Bleeding and purging? You might as well administer poison."

I frowned: *bleeding?*

He turned his face, aiming another rebuke over his shoulder at a withered man with feathers decorating the neck of his *bambi* robes. The man cowered in the face of Hosea's rage.

"Don't hurt Potoo," he said. "I told 'em and told 'em. I don't never seen this spirit afore. Bad blood we got here. But do they hear—no! *Kha*, they cry, like little bird for help. 'Potoo. Help us, Potoo.'" His voice whined weakly.

Hosea's brow furrowed above his mask.

Potoo, I thought, must be the village medicine man. He was

a spiritualist, a faith healer rather than a medic. He instructed the village children in song and dance. He told them stories and made up myths meant to comfort. If ever the medicine man ordered a remedy, it was one of three prescriptions: hash, liquor, or a spoonful of salt.

A woman wearing a white mask appeared to do Hosea's bidding. I recognized the painted scarf wrapped around her head at once. I'd run my hands along it not two days ago, as she'd wept in my lap. Robin had a stack of wooden pans balanced in one gloved hand as she bent low to collect another from the bedside of a patient. I glowered at her through the window. Here she was, ignoring my good advice and breaking the law, again. She came closer to get a pan. She turned to pour its contents into a large bucket. A wash of red liquid *sloshed* into the pail.

I gasped. I backed away, tripped and cried out as I fell, hard. I shook my head and scrambled from the scene, but it was too late—I'd seen! *That bucket was filled with blood! Sick, bleeding Kongos?! No minor cold, but something much worse. Impossible!* The Compromise was clear on the matter. I shook my head again, resisting the image of that bright red waterfall.

"No, it's not possible," I whispered. "Jones would have told us."

Hosea called from the house. "What was that?"

"I don't know. I'll see," Robin said.

"Whatever it is, keep it away. We don't need anyone else getting sick until we can get a handle on this mess."

I have to hide. My mind fired orders to my limbs, but I couldn't move. I sat there, numb, staring into the past.

In their hushed conversation, the giant had spoken of an illness. *Many are sick*, he'd said. I'd dismissed Robin's concerns in the kitchen, she had been mad with grief. And later, I'd ignored Hosea's warning, as he was bent on deception. But what of the giant? What cause had he to lie? I covered my mouth. *Don't answer that!* I covered my ears and eyes, but the answer charged forth. He had no reason. He did not lie. A plague had come to Cobane.

Robin appeared in the open window. "Arika!"

In a flash, Hosea appeared behind her. "What are *you* doing here?"

He didn't wait for an answer. He propelled himself onto the porch and grabbed my arm. His hands and clothes were wet. He smelled of the antiseptic fluid the Clayskin nurses at the Schoolhouse used to cleanse superficial wounds.

"Let me go, you feral!" I twisted my arm.

He dragged me back in the direction I'd come from—back to the Schoolhouse.

Suddenly, I remembered my assignment. "Hosea, wait." I dug in my heels, dropped my weight to the ground. "I said wait! Please, be reasonable! I came because—" I stopped short; I couldn't tell him the truth.

"Because you're a nosy little brat who won't take no for an answer," he finished. "I knew I should have let William have you. How did you get out?"

I lifted my chin. "How did *you* get out? And where did you get that mask? Did you steal it from the infirmary?"

Growling, he dragged me along. "I don't have time for this. We have work to do, Cobane. Real work! Can't you see that?"

"I *do* have eyes," I sneered, keeping up with him. "Maybe I want to nurse!" My heart lurched at the prospect. Nursing was out of the question. I had to get Jones her information and get back to the Schoolhouse before anyone discovered I'd left.

He squeezed my arm. "I'd like to see that. A First Brother nursing a dying worker."

That threw me. *Dying?* I looked back at the warehouse. Sick, yes. I had to admit that. But surely not *dying.* Only, there *had* been blood. I could hear them coughing, even now. I winced at the sound. A thought occurred to me. I jerked at Hosea, demanding his attention. "Windy," I said. "You told me she was sick."

"She was."

"Was? Then she's better?"

He marched on. "What do you care?"

"I care," I grumbled. "Windy is sweet, always smiling at everyone."

He hesitated, looking over his shoulder. "I told you. The fever runs its course in days. Windy isn't better, Cobane. Windy is dead."

I froze, forcing him to stop or drag me down. "Impossible!"

He scoffed.

I opened my mouth to berate him then, suddenly, I thought of Robin. *If Windy is dead then—* "What about the baby?" I asked.

"What baby?"

"The giant said one baby had died."

"Yes, one child died. I never met it."

"Her—she was a girl," I whispered. My blood went cold at the admission. "Did he tell you her name?"

"What does it matter?"

Heat stung the back of my eyes. "Her—her name was—" I stopped. I couldn't say it. My love for Robin collided with my duty to uphold the Compromise. An arrow of grief split my temple and my hands found either side of my head, holding it together. My knees buckled and I fell to the ground rocking back and forth.

He looked down on me for a moment, then knelt. He pulled the white mask down so it hung from his neck. "You should have stayed where I told you," he said, softly. "Go back to your room. Go to sleep, and tomorrow it will be like none of this ever happened." He took my arm. "Come on, let's get you home."

Slowly, his words penetrated the fog surrounding me. He was right; I needed sleep. I would start on Jones' assignment tomorrow, after I'd rested. Only, something about that word, *home*, sapped my strength. I could still hear them coughing—and that blood. I looked down at my wrist, my veins—*our blood*. I shoved a fist against my mouth, stifling the thought.

He tugged. "Come *on*, Cobane. You're *going home*."

I glared up at him, yanking my arm away. "No!"

He shook his head. "Okay, I've had enough—William!"

I jumped to my feet. "Hosea, wait! I'm sorry—" He wasn't listening. I had to stop him. I spoke before I could think. "Hosea, I need to help!" I shouted. I cringed; I hadn't meant to say that out loud.

He pointed a finger at my nose. "See how you cringe? You don't want to be here."

"No, I don't!" I snapped.

He faced me, lifting one brow.

"I don't want to be here," I said again. "But I *am*, and—I *have* to help." I was shocking myself, but it was all true. Something inside me wouldn't let me go back to the Schoolhouse and study. I couldn't deny that terrible coughing, or the blood—not anymore.

He crossed his arms. "And Jones—what will she say?"

I looked down, biting my lip. He thought he had me, and maybe he did. She'd sent me here to spy. If I stayed and helped care for the sick, my cover would be forfeit. She would punish me harshly. *Unless*—I found out exactly what Hosea and the Director were up to regarding the New Seed vote. In that case, she might forgive anything. *That was it!* I would stay and help the sick and, at the same time, get information—premium information—for Jones.

"I'm going to stay," I said, straightening my shoulders. "You can drag me to my room, but I'll just sneak out again. You know I will."

Robin appeared beside us. In her hand was the pair of gloves Hosea had discarded when he'd come after me. "Hosea, come quick," Robin said.

"I'm coming too," I announced.

Hosea took the gloves from Robin, slipped them on and pointed a finger at me. "We'll talk about this later. For now, you don't move." He hurried toward the warehouse.

I leapt after him, only to jerk to a halt, midair. Something had caught the back of my *pallium*, tearing it from my shoulders. I fell to the ground and looked up, dirt-faced, to see William, the giant, looming over me, his club slung in a holster at his waist. I scrambled away just as his hand closed around my neck.

"You stay here," he said.

"No!" I twisted free. I managed to run a few feet before he caught me again, steely fingers fastening on the back of my *aura*.

"You stay here," he said.

He tightened his fist and lifted me from the ground to dangle three feet in the air. I was eye level with him for several seconds as he inspected me, taking in every feature. Suddenly, the fabric of my old dress gave way and I came loose.

My head slammed against the ground. I felt the night air on my back where my clothes were torn. My knee was bruised and my ribs stung. As soon as I was able, I rolled to my side, ignoring my ripped dress. On my hands and knees, I scurried away.

I glanced back to check his progress.

Surprise. He wasn't following me. He stood there like a statue of himself, fist raised, a patch of my dress still clutched in his hand.

I hurried on. When I didn't hear his pounding feet, I stopped again and turned, still on my hands and knees. He stared, frozen. In the darkness, the whites of his eyes were bright as they bore down on me.

What was he about? I blinked and squinted up at his expression. If I didn't know better, I would guess the emotion there was—guilt.

Suddenly, he moved. "You stay here," he said. He walked away.

Confused, I stayed put.

A second later, he was back at my side with my *pallium*. Up close, his guilt was unmistakable. He grunted and thrust the cloth toward me.

Quickly, I took my cloak and threw it around my shoulders, hiding my torn dress. I looked back at him. Something had changed, but what? He held out his hand. I hesitated then, slowly, let him pull me aright. We stood for a while, facing each other.

He was dark-skinned and older than I'd first imagined, in his forties. He was broad, and extremely tall. His arms were heavy with muscle. He stepped forward, lifting one large hand. I jerked back.

"Shh," he said, coming closer.

He was so big. I closed my eyes, trembling.

"Shh." He plucked gently at my hair. "You hair," he said.

I opened my eyes. His black and orange fingers threw aside a dry leaf. He picked out another.

"You hair," he said, again. He showed me the new leaf and let it fall, harmless, to the ground. He thumbed his chest. "I am William."

He had a small mark above his mouth and my eyes narrowed on it. It wasn't much, just a pitch-black circle, one millimeter wide, above his mouth and off to the right. A birthmark.

"I not hurt you, Arika."

Slowly, I nodded, not daring to remind him how to properly address his betters. His guilt at tearing my dress had softened him toward me—and that was enough for now. Besides, there were important matters to attend to. I pointed to the sick room. "Can you help me get into that warehouse?"

His expression was unreadable. He raised a brow. "You medicine man?"

Rueful, I shook my head. He made a good point. I could read and write hundreds of words per minute. I could dictate, memorize and recite several of the thickest volumes in the library along with the Niagara Compromise, annotated. However, I had no medical knowledge to speak of. "No. I'm not a medicine man," I admitted.

"Then how you help?"

From inside the sick room, Hosea Khan shouted an order. "*Tourniquet!*" Feet pounded, rushing to obey.

"I don't know how," I said, hurrying to the warehouse and mounting the porch. Someone had pulled the shutters on the large window. Against the candlelight from the room, their slats formed bars across my body. My eyes a bright stripe, my mouth a dark line, my chest a ripple of ribs. "I don't know, but," I whispered, "I *will* help." I looked back at him. "I have to."

William's mouth softened. Without a word, he disappeared inside.

After several minutes, an idea struck me. I turned and ran back down the porch steps. I was several yards away when the warehouse door opened behind me.

"Hey, Cobane," Hosea called, contemptuously. "Leaving already?"

I turned. "I'm not leaving," I said. "I'm retrieving supplies, so I can help." I indicated my schoolbag, which lay in the street covered with dust.

"Is that right?" He thought I was deluding myself.

"Yes," I hissed. I bent, snatched up my bag and stomped back to the porch. All those years of studying—*why, oh why have I not read a single book on healing?*

He stepped out of the warehouse and down two steps, stopping just above me. "Listen, I don't want you here, but William makes a good point. If he has to guard you outside all night, we'll be shorthanded." I held my breath, sensing he was about to relent.

"You're to wear gloves and a mask at all times. Robin will give you a bottle of antiseptic. You're to use it liberally."

I frowned, suddenly realizing that whatever the sickness was, Hosea believed it to be contagious.

"William is *your* master now, until I say otherwise," he went on. "You don't leave his side."

William came forward to stand over me like a shadow.

"Cobane," Hosea said, regaining my attention. "Are we clear?"

"Yes," I managed. "Wear the mask, follow William, stay in sight."

THE SICK ROOM

I strained to see around William's bulk as he led me into the sick room. The space was large but, somehow, it felt small. A low-pitched roof and a dirt floor. Tables of every size and splinter, laid with dark mounds, smooth shapes under blankets, which stank. I sniffed, trying to place the smell through my mask. Fleshy and salty, I decided, like wet fish.

Of course, I was wrong, as I was about everything back then. Entering the sick room was like leaving for breakfast with Teacher Purnell after studying all night. The library was the only room in the Schoolhouse without windows. In its false light, the pages of my reader glowed pale yellow, rather than white. And, over time, I would lose perspective. The false light became the sun, and their yellow lumination seemed bright, and white ceased to exist. Confronted with the glare of morning, I would fumble around for the senior table at breakfast. My eyes would eventually adjust. But, up until that moment of reconciliation, I was effectively blind.

That is how the sick room was for me. My mind, unable to reconcile with the horror of reality, simply ignored it. Looking back, I realize this impairment was my mind's way of shielding me from what I might have done, had I grasped the wretchedness before me. I would have known the fever was more than I could hope to cope with. I would have seen, from the start, how the next few days would go. And filled with fear, I might have turned back.

"I need a desk," I said, turning to William. "And a chair. Some place off to the side, where the storytellers can sit."

"What you do?" he asked, not moving.

"I'm going to take their stories," I said proudly. "Article 14."

He blinked.

"It's a section of the Compromise," I went on, briskly—feeling superior. "It's hotly debated, but, interpreted broadly, it just might anticipate untimely death, which would authorize a Record Keeper to take stories without the customary protocol."

"You bring medicine?"

I blinked. "Uh, no, nothing like that."

"You medicine man?"

"No, I told you. They don't train us in medicine. It would be a waste of time. Kongos are possessed of a particularly good countenance," I quoted. "We don't get sick." I cleared my throat, self-consciously. "That is, in theory. This is some sort of anomaly."

He gave me a blank look.

My voice trailed off. "Look, William, I can't heal their bodies, but I can give them new life after death. I can take their stories."

"You take people, go to Hasting." I could see he hoped there was medicine at Hasting.

"Well, we can't actually go there. For that, one of the Record Keepers would have to issue an invitation." I raised my quill. "But, with this, I'll bring Hasting to them."

He bent, pulled down his white mask, and sniffed the tip.

"Metaphorically," I added.

He frowned.

"Just trust me. Clear off a table and set it in that corner."

He straightened, replaced his mask and shook his head. "No table."

"Of course there are tables." I stepped to the nearest one, and lifted the dark blanket away. The man beneath was dead. I jumped back, knocking over a wooden pail. A clammy liquid that I refused to name oozed over my foot. I kicked the pail away, watching as it rolled a few feet to collide with the leg of another blanketed table.

A cold draft swept down my neck as I looked around the room again, noticing details about the black mounds that I hadn't before. Big thick mounds beside small ones, a bare foot sticking from the end, a dark crown too tall for the sheet. No two mounds were alike. *Shrouds*, I realized. The tables were makeshift coffins. The blankets served as shrouds. Dead men lined the room from wall to wall.

The bustling shadows I'd seen from the street came from the corner, where Hosea and Robin toiled over a few dozen restless bodies, not yet covered. My concern for formalities vanished.

"No table," I agreed, swallowing. "I'll take his story first." I pointed toward Hosea, where a bull of a man with waxy black skin lay. His arm was banded above a gaping wound on his forearm. A tourniquet, I realized. "Quickly, there's no time to waste."

As if on cue, the man rolled to his side, and erupted in a fit of coughs. His mouth was sealed behind a black scarf, but his cough deployed in blasts, like a cannon.

I stumbled, surprised anything human could make such a noise. "*Obi Solomon*," I whispered.

He gripped the table's edge. The cords of his arms strained

to hold his body steady as he launched another barrage.

"They need cough," William said, nudging me forward. "The poison in the chest needs come out. Some not so lucky, eh?" He lifted his chin to the right, where a bareheaded woman jerked rhythmically. Her face was uncovered and the pathetic sound of her cough was lost in the harsh boom of the cannon. Unlike the young man, her efforts merely underscored her weakness. At that rate, it was clear, she would never free her lungs of the poison.

"You're right. We must go there first," I said, drawn to the woman. I checked the close fit of my mask and hurried over.

THE AUNTIE, SKY

Everything about her was round and dark. A new moon face with half-moon eyes, no lashes. Her mouth perched between shiny bulbous cheeks. Her cotton shift frayed on the oak slab where she lay, covered in yellow wax cloth. She had no visible marks or tattoos—odd for a worker. Her toes, as bare as her head, were short—ten plump acorns. She opened her mouth to cough again, revealing beautiful white teeth.

"William," I said over my shoulder. "Her throat is dry; she needs water."

When he returned, I offered it to her. She drank thirstily, set the wooden cup to the side and beckoned me closer.

"Daughter?" she asked. She was out of breath and harrumphed forcibly, before asking again. "Daughter—is that you?"

Her question stumped me. I was not a Second Brother and, under the law, she was not my mother. After years of study, I knew this. And yet, her face was familiar.

Summer in the nursery: the attendants let their cantaloupes swing free between feedings and they stripped us down, except for our nappies. Near the double window by our crib, I counted the suns before she came. A sweaty wedge in the morning, a hot melon at noon, an open yolk in the evening. And then, like a late blossom, our mother came. The heat had been unavoidable, even at dusk. But her laughter, as we'd performed our tricks, our fists and kicks, had blown over us like a breeze.

I blinked. "Mother," I said. *Not my mother, but ours.*

She pulled me by the wrist, so her cheek rested on mine.

"I dying." She coughed, squeezing my hand.

I wiped her chin with a cloth William handed me. "No, not dying." I smoothed her forehead, as if she was the child. "You are going to rest soon—in a beautiful place prepared for you. No more work, no more sorrow, no more death."

"Soltice," she whispered. "With Obi."

"Yes." I was well versed in worker mythology. The Great Obi Solomon's heroic deeds on Earth had earned him a seat by the workers' God in the workers' paradise; both were called Soltice. "You will stroll her streets of fur. No dirt will touch your feet. Your family will walk with you."

"My sisters, my daughters," her voice cracked, "my sons."

I nodded, a lump in my throat. "They will all be there to welcome you home."

We clasped hands for a long while in silence, her tears wetting my cheek. Finally, she rested back. I took a deep breath. I saw my story comforted her and I knew what she would ask next.

"How do I get there? I do not know the way."

"*You* know," I said, indulgently. I held up my quill and pad.

"*You?*"

I nodded. "I am a Record Keeper," I confessed. A pride such as I'd never felt before settled in my heart. *This*, I thought suddenly, *this is what it means to be a First Brother.*

With a grunt the woman pushed herself up onto her elbows. A flame of hope lit her eyes as she determined to use the last of her strength to tell her story.

Blinking rapidly, I took ink from my bag and prepared to write.

•

"I was born under the stars," she began melodically. I could tell she'd practiced. "I slipped from the womb to hoot at the moon like an owl when a storm is nigh. And, you know, a storm did come. For three days and three nights, the workers picked in the mud."

I nodded, keeping pace with her. She spoke in the broken English of a half-feral, but I translated her words easily, in accordance with my training.

"Our mother had fine eyes," she mused. "Close your eyes midday and look up at the sun. That was their color. Orange, red, black—very fine."

She was quiet for a moment, then she took my hand and tugged me close, examining me.

"You have fine eyes," she said.

"Thank you," I said, though I wasn't allowed to talk during her story.

"My eyes, what color are they?" she asked.

I looked. "Black."

"Anything else?"

I looked again. They were the exact color of spilled ink. "Just black," I said.

She sighed and wiped a tear from her cheek. "Would you believe me if I told you they changed? When I went to work in the field, my eyes changed."

I said nothing, continuing to transcribe. I didn't believe her, but it was unkind to tell her so.

"You doubt me, but it's true. My eyes changed from the color of the sky to the color of the earth in one cycle—and they ain't gone back."

I finished writing that sentence, and looked back at her. "Why did they change?"

"This is the question I have thought about every cycle since," she said. "Real long and hard. *Real* long and *real* hard. All the time I'm in the field and when I'm bathing. Even when I sleep, I think about this one thing—*why?*"

She stopped talking, taking a sip of water.

"Did you find an answer?"

"I did."

I sat forward, mildly curious.

"They changed," she said, "because I toiled in the field."

I frowned. "But, didn't you always work in the field?"

"Not like this. In that cycle, we had a mean foreman and I was afraid to die. I forgot everything but the toil. I set my eyes on the dirt and produced three times the quota. Do you see?"

I didn't.

"I set my eyes on the dirt," she repeated. "On the dirt. On the dirt. Don-it hurt!"

Beads of sweat bubbled along her forehead as she chanted this rhythmically for a while.

"Set your eyes on the trees," she rasped, "your eyes evergreen. Set your eyes on the dirt, don-it hurt!"

I patted her down with a cool cloth, as an old man within earshot wheezed with laughter. When his coughing fit subsided, he rolled onto one side. "That old hoot owl at it again, eh?" he said.

The woman crossed her arms, as if his jeering was nothing new.

"What color your eyes now?" he mocked. He began to cough again.

Ignoring him, she went on. "When I was a babe, I would crawl to the edge of the crib to look up at the sky. Every shade of blue there is, I seen. Bright, fire, water, berry, midnight, new."

I stopped her. "What is new blue?" I said.

"Mmm, a blueberry before it ripens."

I pictured it.

"But, when I started in the field," she went on, "I got no time—no time. I stop looking up." She lowered her voice and leaned forward. "This is all very strange, but how else can I explain it?"

"Maybe you inherited your eyes from your sire," I offered.

She shook her head vehemently, drawing her hand back from mine, as if my words were contagious. "You believe that?" she asked. She sounded incredulous, as if she couldn't fathom why I didn't know better. "And why do you think the Kongo got dark skin?" she asked. She answered her own question, pointing a convinced finger into the air. "This skin is our toil." She slapped the table beneath her. "We got this skin working this earth. We put our whole head in the dirt. Our whole body. We got it all over, real bad, see?" She held up her forearm for my observation. "We been bent to toil so long; it be a fence, and we 'bout can't get out."

She was half sitting with consternation, and I patted her hand with my gloved palm to calm her.

"Listen to me, daughter," she said, urgently. "Write this down."

I positioned my quill to let her know I was ready.

"You don't belong to that skin. You got to look up."

Saddened by her confusion, I nodded.

"You remember that," she warned. "You still got time. Not like me. I dying."

"Don't say that."

She placed a hand on mine, as if *I* was the one in need of comfort. She rubbed the fine bones of my hand and closed her eyes.

"Arika."

I glanced up at William, then back at the woman. She was sleeping peacefully. "What is her name? I forgot to ask."

"We call her Sky."

I nodded and wrote her name above her story in elaborate cursive, letting the tail of the last letter wing out to the edge of the page.

"Come, Arika. We must do more."

He nudged me on to the next table.

THE UNCLE, KIWI

My first impression was of the hair that grew like a jungle all over his body. Snow-white, lush, overgrown. It crawled along his neck and chin, and shielded the vital parts of him—his chest especially. It stopped in a mowed line at his jaw. Above that, every inch of skin was weathered. I counted four creases in his forehead, one more when he frowned. There were two beams around his mouth, long parentheticals that told parts of the story he couldn't.

"They call me Kiwi."

I nodded, writing that down.

"They call me Kiwi 'cause account of my hair. I was born with hair all over, see?"

"I see. And, what do you have to say, Kiwi?"

"Oh, I don't know."

"You can say anything. Something you've learned that you want to pass on. Something that explains you."

"Ain't much *to* me, I suppose."

"Is there anything you find interesting, or odd?"

He scratched his chin, digging between the white wires. "Well, I never miss work—not ever. That's odd."

"How so?"

"I smoke that pipe thrice a day. Should be sleep, eh?" He gave a wet cough of laughter. "You're a little thing? You ever work?"

"Not in the field," I said.

"That's alright. Don't suppose you'd like it. It's bad work, 'til you get an understanding." He grinned mischievously, stretching his sun-scorched lips. "I'll pass you this. If you plow her right, she'll give up her secrets." He winked at me, his bottom lip oozing blood.

I ran a tongue across my own mouth. "The secrets—of the field?" I asked.

"The secrets of the whole Earth, girl. I'll pass you this." He beckoned me closer.

"This here the first secret. Remember it! The Earth gonna do what she want."

I waited for him to go on.

"That's it!"

"Oh." I sat back, mystified.

"You *hear* me?"

I nodded.

"That right there the first secret. Remember it, eh?" He repeated. "Forty men and forty ox can't make an ear grow, if Earth don't wanna grow."

"But, there are grain quotas—on corn in particular. We meet them every year. So, you—the workers—must have some control."

He looked at me hard with one yellowed eye, refusing to repeat himself.

"Okay," I said. I drew a large question mark beside the first secret.

"Hear me out now. We do our part—don't hear me wrong. We tend to the harvest, see? And we coax a little, do what we can. She like when we make music." He shrugged. "Sometime, she want more. Seen brothers drop dead—working. Do she care? No. We all just go on working. Used to call it, 'begging the field.'"

"What happens to the man that dies?"

He shrugged. "I don't be looking that way. I suppose she drink him up. She plenty thirsty. Drink him up and spit him out—if she want," he added.

"That's—so cruel."

He was quiet for a moment. "Mmm, don't think about that part. Don't look 'round. You just put your back to the begging plow. Earth gonna do what she want. Sun gonna beat-cha."

"You don't have very much free time, do you? Is that difficult?"

He grinned painfully. "Listen at you—difficult. It's plenty hard, pass you that. We get along though. One stripe need a picking, next need a planting, next need ploo-wing." He wiggled his brows and began to pat his leg rhythmically. "So on and so on, stripe after stripe, for day, for month, for year." He ended with a deep cough, his smile intact. However, I could see his strength was waning.

"Is that one of the songs you sing?" I asked.

He nodded. "Over 'n over. That Earth never say quit." He shrugged. "But don't think about that part."

"Then what *do* you think about?"

He thought. "Sometime, when the work way out on the farm, I get a mule and tent. Sleep out under the stars. *Boy-o!*"

I grinned. "And you like that?"

"Mmm, yes. Make you think."

"What do you think about?"

"Mmm, 'bout the Earth, I suppose—that black boss."

"And what do you think about the Earth?"

"Oh hell, listen at you. I don't know. Don't matter I suppose. Earth—"

"Gonna do what she wants," I finished.

He grinned widely.

"So, why not just take a hovercraft?"

"Huh?"

"A hovercraft," I repeated. "If the distance is so far, you have to sleep out overnight, why travel by mule? A hovercraft will get you there in half the time."

He looked at me as if I'd lost my mind. "You take a hovercraft, girl, you got to wash that craft off real good. We got the harvest to tend to. Got the quota and the foreman. Got no time for washing."

"Wash the hovercraft off—your body?"

"Oh, yes! Potoo say: lard soap three times, then dry." He gave me a hard look.

"Is that because you're afraid of technology? You're afraid it will infect you?" I knew this was the case. The workers were superstitious about technology. I was curious to hear one speak on the fear directly.

"Listen at you! You smart, but not too smart, eh? Don't you know it was electricity that mostly killed us?"

"In the Last War," I offered.

"Yes, girl. It's what started the whole thing. Don't you know that? You so smart. Man got the computer, got that electricity. And what? What!?"

I started. "I—don't know."

"And he forgot Earth—that black boss." He struggled to lift his hands and clap them in front of my face. "She turn on him." *Clap*. "Write this down, girl."

I scrambled to fill my quill.

"Ain't nothing good come from the Devil!"

"And the Devil is technology."

"Technology!" he agreed.

In truth, Kiwi had no choice; the stable master would not have let him access a hovercraft without a proper pass from the Overseer. The stable of solar-powered machines housed at Cobane were for the exclusive use of the English Diplomats. Still, I wrote down Kiwi's testimony without contradiction.

I'd been trained not to release the workers from their superstitions, no matter how far-fetched. I didn't tell him that he used technology every day, that there was no way to avoid it. He didn't know about the hydroplanes. Camouflaged by solar-powered cryptic coloration, the planes were indistinguishable from the sky. They came and went silently. And the solar reflectors, according to the workers, were benevolent windmills to prevent overheating.

"You write that down, girl?"

I nodded. He eased back. It was on the tip of my tongue to say to him that he was not as helpless as he supposed. That Mother Earth was not the boss, for we, humans, had mastered her long ago. We harnessed her power to strengthen our own. We commanded her to grow, and she did as we wanted, not the other way around. All this was on the tip of my tongue, but I swallowed it.

Even if I had time to explain the differences between the supercomputers of the past and the solar-powered modern world, doing so was against the law. And besides, there were tales, rumors of workers—enlightened by well-meaning superiors—going mad upon hearing the truth. Losing what was left of their minds, and for what? Knowledge they would never use, not in their line of work. Kiwi, sheltered beneath his white rug and fear, was better off.

I leaned forward, gazing into his face, crossed with wrinkles like dry riverbeds. *Not much to him, he supposed.* An acute sadness overwhelmed me. I leaned closer and whispered in his ear, "Thank you for never missing a day of work."

His lips, entirely inelastic, split as he smiled up at me.

The sadness pooled in my chest and caught fire. "I want you to know, Kiwi, that the work you do matters," I said, pressing a hand to my sternum. "I want you to know that everything you do has been noted and planned, for the greater good."

I told myself to stop, leave well enough alone. But heat inside me rose up like a tantrum. "Also, you don't have to subject yourself to any boss. You are part of America. We survived the Last War, and we are rebuilding the Earth piece by piece, as *we* see fit. You may not feel it, but you—we all—are part of something powerful."

I sat back breathing heavily; my lips tingled with danger. It was risky to empower the workers. I looked around to assure myself that no one but the old man and William had heard. My eyes landed on the old man's face, scrunched up in puzzlement. He scratched a chafed spot on his forehead.

"Are you alright?" I said, suddenly nervous. Would he go mad right here and now?

He was looking at me like I'd grown a third eye. "Are you?" he asked. He began to cough.

"You should rest," I said.

He shook his head. "No. No time to rest."

I gestured for William to get water. The old man stopped

coughing, but his chest continued to wheeze.

"I just reckoned what it is I got to say. What it is I've learned," he said, weakly.

"Okay, I'm listening," I assured him.

"Back long time ago, workers think the Earth was flat." He paused, catching his breath. "But we know now that she ain't flat, see? She fat. She been eating up all the people from all the years, see?" He reached down to scoop up an imaginary handful of soil and rubbed it between his fingers. "All the stories go down her gullet, and that how she grow." He waved his hand, spreading his fingers out from his palm, like sprouting plants. "Corn, wheat, sycamore, cattail—Kongo. They all the old folks come back. We all go down and we all come back." His digits closed over his palm, then sprouted again. "See?"

"No," I said. "I don't. What does all that mean?"

"It mean, we *be* her, so we got to trust her. See?" He flexed his hand open and closed, open and closed. Sprouting and re-sprouting his imaginary plants. "We come up from the earth and go back and come up again. You got to trust that boss girl, not no computer. No telling where that computer come from. They come from Her? No. Where they come from? What they made of? Where they going?"

I shook my head. "I don't know—nowhere."

"*See?*" He drew the word out as if he'd made a brilliant point. And, for a brief moment, I thought I did see. Then he broke into convulsions of coughing so hard, blood and spit ran down his chin. I jumped up, calling for Robin. She came with a black scarf and tied it around the lower half of Kiwi's face.

William took my arm. "Come, Arika."

"But he needs—"

"He no talk more," William interrupted.

Seeing that he was right, that there was nothing I could do, I put the lid on my ink and let William pull me away. In my mind's eye, I couldn't shake the image of Kiwi, his furred chest, and his hand flexing at his side.

•

The young man's terrible cannon cough started again from the far side of the room, causing everyone to tense. It went on, rattling and blasting. Robin finished with Kiwi, and produced a wooden pan for the young man to use as a spittoon.

"He tell story next," William said.

"Okay." As he pulled me to stand beside Robin, I wondered if he also sensed the young man's strength would not last long.

Hosea came to join us.

"Maybe we should give him the draft," Robin said.

"Not yet," Hosea answered.

"What's the draft?" I asked.

"It puts them to sleep," Robin said.

I looked hard at Hosea. "Why not give it to him? He needs rest." *And his cough is unbearable to hear.*

Hosea ignored me. "If he starts producing blood, let me know." He said this to Robin and turned away.

I followed him.

Sensing my presence, he warned me over his shoulder, "Remember our agreement. You're not here to interfere." He crouched over a case filled with labeled jars and riffled through them with barely leashed contempt. I knew, somehow, it was directed at me.

I stepped closer. "It's too late. I'm involved now," I said.

He didn't respond. His movements remained jerky.

"I can do more than take stories, you know."

His jaw tightened.

"What's wrong? I'm offering my help."

He ignored me.

"Hey," I said, annoyed. "Answer me."

"Or what—you'll report me to Jones?" He glared at me.

I stepped back.

"Do you really want to help, Cobane?"

"I'm here, aren't I?"

His eyes flashed. "Start by putting your quill away. No one here has a *story* to tell you. They're too busy surviving."

"Sky and Kiwi found plenty to say."

He shot to his feet, and took my arm. "And why is that? Did you tell them about Soltice?"

"They already knew."

"Did you tell them about the streets of fur?" He was in my face now, gripping my arm.

"I made them feel better—gave them peace."

"Did you tell them that none of it is true? That it's all made up so that they'll work harder and produce more food for brats like you? *You* are a liar!" He pushed me aside, not violently, but I tripped and fell, still holding his gaze. The disgust in his thatch-roof eyes was unmistakable. He hated everything I stood for. He turned on his heel and walked away.

William came to my side and lifted my cloak to examine the arm I'd landed on. I barely felt his touch.

I jumped up to follow Hosea, hearing William call my name.

"Hosea," I said.

He ignored me. I quickened my pace, colliding with his

back when he stopped at another bedside.

"Hello, sister," he said. His voice was gentle.

A young woman answered him. Her skin, as fair as Jetson's, was gray with the dusk of the fever. Silent, I moved to the opposite side of her bed. She glanced at me curiously.

My appearance was strange indeed. My long braid stuck out in the room of shorn-haired workers. Had she seen the clothes beneath my cloak, a hobbled *aura* wrapped over a fine *bambi* blouse, she'd know I was a student. After Hosea's contempt, I needed to justify my privileged life. We Keepers were *not* useless, and we did care.

I addressed the woman. "Hello there. I am a friend," I declared. "A First Brother, Record Keeper. I have come to heal you." I held out my hand benevolently. She didn't take it to her cheek, as Sky had. In fact, she paid me no attention at all. She watched Hosea.

He struggled to apply ointment to her chest as she twisted away.

She seized his wrist. "My baby," she whispered. "Will it hurt my baby?"

Surprised, I looked down, seeing that her stomach bulged with child beneath her blanket.

Hosea shook off her hold. "It won't hurt. I promise." His tone was tense.

He's tired, I thought. *He's being rough.*

With impersonal hands he unlaced the ties of her tunic.

I glanced down at the trembling woman.

She looked up. "Sister?" she said, pleading.

My gloved hand shot out to rest, firmly, on Hosea's. "Kha, please, let me."

He glanced at me, then down at his patient's worried brow. His hands fell to his sides.

"Shh," I said. I brushed the woman's brow. "Be easy. Shhh."

Slowly, she lay back.

I unlaced her tunic. I pulled back the pleats to expose the tops of her breasts.

When I finished, she held out her hand. "Sister," she said.

I pulled her hand to my cheek.

"This won't hurt my baby, will it? Do you promise?"

I glanced at Hosea, who nodded. "I promise," I said. I kissed her palm. "Now rest."

She closed her eyes.

My eyes met Hosea's over the mound of her belly. His were no longer hot with rage. Slowly, he nodded his approval.

I dropped my chin. My chest felt thick and good.

He returned to his work. "She's in an early stage of the fever. She's not coughing regularly, and she's young. This is the medicine we're using for now." He displayed the tin tub for my inspection.

"The medicine we're using for now?" I said, curiously.

"I'm still experimenting with the best remedy."

"What's in that?"

"Eucalyptus, white camphor, ginger root, and other herbs. It sooths the cough and loosens mucus in the chest." He dipped his finger in the congealed substance then handed me the tub. "They'll need a good amount applied every hour. Also apply around the nose, like so." He smeared the gel around the woman's nose.

She winced in her sleep.

"It's painful," I accused. "You said it wouldn't hurt."

He shrugged. "It hurts some on the open wounds. It can't be helped. Put it on, no matter how they protest. It's essential to their healing."

It was on the tip of my tongue to ask him how he knew that. How he knew to mix eucalyptus, white camphor and ginger root together to make medicine. I held back, sensing I already knew the answer. Those books in his room: *Basic Botany*, *Botanical Gardens*, *The Secret World of Trees*. They weren't for gardening, as I'd suspected. He was interested in plants for medicinal purposes. Hosea was a healer.

"What's the draft?" I asked, pushing my luck. By showing me how to tend to the workers' physical needs, he'd already conceded a great deal.

He hesitated. "The draft is another medicine."

"Why are you withholding it from the young man over there? The one coughing so badly."

Hosea led me away from the concentration of patients.

"I'm withholding it because the draft will put him to sleep."

"He's exhausted. Isn't sleep good?"

"Not always. The fever has several stages. During some, they need to cough to clear their lungs. If they don't, they die. I administer the draft when it's clear they won't make it."

"What do you mean—when it's clear? What else does the draft do?"

"It allows them to sleep peacefully."

My brows dropped. "Murder," I translated.

"If I don't give them the draft, they will die anyway. Trust me, I've watched many go violently." He gestured to the far half of the room, where I'd studiously avoided looking.

"I don't want to give up on anyone but, sometimes, peace

is all you can offer." Catching himself, he paused for a long moment. "It seems you were right, Cobane." He looked down at my schoolbag, then back up. "I judged you earlier, and I shouldn't have."

I nodded, accepting his apology.

"But I meant what I said. I don't want to see that quill out again. No more unnecessary lies. We do it only if it will save a life."

A part of me wanted to argue—*what made their physical health more important than peace of mind?* But I held my tongue. "I was only trying to help," I said.

He placed a container of ointment in my hand. "Okay, then help. If we can get a handle on this early, we might save Cobane from a worse fate."

"I'll stay as long as I can." I bit my lip, thinking of Jones. I wanted to know what he meant by *a worse fate*, but something told me to let it be.

He gestured to the ointment. "If you'll bring that to Robin, I'll take care of Sky and Kiwi."

Just then, the young man's cough began again, blitzing the room.

"Hosea, come!" Robin shouted.

I jumped. She was bent over the young man's bed.

"You go," Hosea said. "Do whatever Robin tells you."

As I got to Robin's side, the young man fell quiet. His body lay limp on the bed. "Is he conscious?" I asked.

"Barely. Hold his head up, like this," Robin said. "Make sure it doesn't fall back."

She transferred the man's heavy head into my palms. It was slippery with sweat. I almost dropped it when he began to vomit. The covering over his mouth loosened and, within seconds, the front of my cloak was splashed with bile and blood. I held on tight. If I let go, all would be lost. He would collapse back and suffocate on his own vomit.

Shifting my hands, I moved to his back to prop him up. He shook between bouts. He lifted his hand to wipe his mouth, but he was weak. It withered back to his side. Without thinking, I folded the sleeve of my *pallium* and pressed the thick cloak to his mouth.

He opened his eyes. The whites were red with crooked vessels. "Thank you, sister," he said.

I swallowed my pity and smiled into his gaze. I longed to offer him courageous words, but none came to mind. A second later, he was unconscious again. I eased him down to rest. His breath clattered in his chest. His brow burned with fever. Below the tourniquet, the bandage on his arm was spotted with blood.

Wintry thoughts assailed me. *Thank you, sister.* Had those been his last words? Would they cover him soon? Reduce him to an odorous mound of death? I dashed my hand across my beaded brow. *I will not panic.*

"Did Kha give you the medicine?"

I jumped, turned. "I'm sorry. Wha—?"

"The medicine," Robin repeated. "Did Kha give it to you?"

I fumbled in the pocket of my *pallium* for the jar. I held it up.

"Good. You tend this part of the room. I have to go."

"Wait! Where are you going? You can't leave me here! This man needs a doctor!" I pointed to the young black cannon. "I'm not a doctor!"

"Nor am I," Robin said.

"But you have experience!"

"Only a few more hours than you."

"Robin!"

She lowered her eyes. "Yes, Ma'am."

I stiffened. Her tone, her face, her hopeless resignation struck me. An echo of my own voice filled my ears—*I am your Mistress, Robin, not Arika!*

Misunderstanding my distress, Robin hurried to explain. "Now that the sun is up, I have to remove the oldest bodies. They can't stay here. But I will be back; I promise." She gave my hand a friendly squeeze, taking care to hide the gesture from sight just as I'd trained her.

I hung my head, barely listening, as my guilt ripened beneath her kindness. Kindness, I realized, I didn't deserve. When she was sick, I had not rushed to the kitchen. And I didn't believe her when she told me of the fever. More, I had lied to her about her baby.

I forced myself to look up. Robin's face was carefully blank, but I felt her gauging me. Watching for my reaction, just as I watched Jones. My inner eye burned with shame as I saw our relationship, clearly, for the first time.

"Don't worry, Ma'am. You are not alone; Crane is with you," she said.

I didn't answer. I could not speak past the ache in my chest.

William put his stalwart hand on my shoulder. I looked at it a long time. My gaze traveled up his arm to his eyes. "I stay here," he said.

I watched Robin walk away until she was out of sight.

•

Finally, I turned back to the young man, still unconscious on his makeshift bed. I opened the jar of medicine Hosea had given me. The smell made my eyes water. "It's strong," I said.

"Fever is strong," William countered.

I dipped my fingers and spread the ointment on the young man's chest, as I'd seen Hosea do. "That should do it," I said, glancing at William.

He nodded down at me.

I pulled the cover over the young man's chest and turned to find our next patient. William's hand on my arm stopped me.

"Arika, you take," he said.

He opened my schoolbag and handed me the pad I'd used to take Sky's and Kiwi's stories.

"No." I pushed it away. "Hosea—I mean, Kha told me not to do that anymore."

"Kha not right. You take." He forced the pad into my hands.

I looked over my shoulder at Hosea. He was out of earshot. "If he sees me with that, he'll throw me out."

William shook his head. One hand moving to his club. "You stay here."

I bit my lip. I'd promised Hosea I would not lie to the dying patients, but maybe I could still take their stories. Not with quill and paper, that would raise Hosea's suspicion, but—. "I have an idea," I said. "Put this away."

Reluctantly, he took the pad I handed back to him.

"I don't need it," I said. "I'll memorize their stories, and write them out later. It won't be perfect, but it might work."

"You do that?" William asked.

"I haven't done it before, but—" I shrugged. "It's all I can offer."

He nodded. "Okay, we go."

THE BOY, FOUNT

I am not a healer. And, technically, I was not authorized to take records as I was not yet a Record Keeper. Nevertheless, for the next several hours I doled out medicine and massaged each chest to hasten the ointment's work. Moreover, when asked to, I took informal stories from the people, glancing frequently in Hosea's direction. He never seemed to suspect.

The patients were in various stages of death. However, when word spread that I could read and write, the worst of the lot, the very old and sick, would refuse pain medication, preferring to suffer with clear heads for the chance to be heard.

We had none of the niceties usually associated with recording. We were not in a listening room, but a noxious warehouse. The storytellers did not have the luxury of days to explain, only a few pressured minutes. I held hands with seconds of life in them, and listened to dying confessions. We spoke together, not as First and Second Brothers, but in dialog—although I attempted to limit my part. With rare exception, most grievous to me, I am unable to recall their names. What I did record in every instance is their visage. Their faces and smiles, their essence and eyes; I carry them with me still.

Toward the end of my time there, I encountered a worker younger than the rest. His diction was better than Robin's and far better than William's, indicating he had yet to undergo a Rebirth. I imagine he was just out of the Academy.

"You are the Record Keeper physician that the people are whispering about?" he asked.

I was checking his pulse, and waited to finish before responding. "I am a Record Keeper in training only, and not a healer."

"Do you live in the big house with the white ghosts?" he asked, bluntly.

I smiled. "I suppose I do."

"Why?"

"Because that is where I go to school."

"Why?"

"Because when I was a baby, the white ghosts, as you call them, chose me to be a student of Record Keeping."

He nodded. "I go to school. I learn to sing and dance. Do you learn these at your school?"

"No, but I have my own room, and lots of books to read."

"*O-bi*! You mean, you sleep alone?" he said.

"Yes. I see my classmates during the day. But at night I sleep in a bed, quite alone."

"*All* night?"

"Yes."

"Do you get afraid?"

I laid a hand across his mouth. "Hush now, I have to take your pulse."

He cocked his head and waited until I'd finished. "That is the second time you have taken my pulse."

"And I must take it once more before we're done."

"Why?"

"Because Kha has instructed me to take it three times, and I don't argue with Kha."

"I think you are very wise. Is Kha your friend in the big house?"

"No. Kha and I just met." I checked his nose for a telltale matrix of scabs. To my relief, it was merely blistered. He had not been sick for long. "Now, I have a question for you," I said.

He perked up.

"Why do you call him Kha?"

"Because that is the name he answers to!" The boy smiled, as if I'd asked the silliest question. "Do you know that my special gift is to sing?" he went on, seamlessly. "Father Potoo told me this."

"Is that so?"

"Yes. He said, 'Fount, you sing better than all the rest of the flock, but not better than me.'"

I examined his thin chest. I estimated he was in the first stage of the disease. He had yet to start the crippling cough which, I thought grimly, would silence his singing voice for days.

"I will be like Father Potoo when I am older," he said.

"You want to be a medicine man?"

He shook his head. "I want to be the Master of Music."

"I think you mean the music teacher, at the Academy."

He shook his head. "No, Auntie, I don't."

Auntie. I paused, fighting the urge to gather the little boy into my arms and run as fast as I could. I swallowed and the feeling settled in my chest. Fount was still waiting for an answer. "If you want to be like Father Potoo, you want to be a music teacher," I explained. "That is the position that Father Potoo holds, medicine man and music teacher."

"Yes, but Father Potoo is in charge of music in Cobane," Fount replied. "I will be in charge of music all over the Kongo. The Master of Music." He spread his hands in the air.

I smiled, gently. "I don't believe such a master exists."

"Not yet." He settled back. "I will be the first."

My smile died. After being erased he might not remember this ambition, let alone achieve it. "What about the Rebirth," I said, tentatively. "It's coming in just a few weeks. Soon you will be old enough to participate."

"Yes," he said, simply.

I waited for him to add more, to show some sign of dread. But he was too young, I realized. He had not learned enough about pain to dread the future. I began to rub ointment on his chest, feeling sadder with every slight beat of his heart against my hand.

"Tell me your name again," I said.

"Fountain. They call me Fount."

"What a special name."

"Father Potoo says, on the day I was born, a crow came down from a great oak to croak on the window ledge of the birthing hut."

"Now, why would a crow do that?"

"Father Potoo says a conjure man sent the crow to curse me."

I stopped rubbing. "That's terrible."

"Father Potoo says the curse means that I will grow only so high, and no more. So I should not think of becoming the music teacher instead of him, for the music teacher must be seven feet tall."

"I haven't heard of this rule. Why seven?"

"So that, when he stands before the people to lead them in song, he can be seen."

I rolled my eyes. In my estimation, Father Potoo seemed most concerned with protecting his own position. "Father Potoo told you that, did he? Do you believe that you've been cursed?"

"Of course! Father Potoo is very wise." He leaned forward and whispered, "But see, Father Potoo doesn't know that I do not wish to be the music teacher."

"Oh yes, I remember. The Master of Music." I spread my hands in the air, imitating him, and we laughed together. He began to cough. I patted his back as the fit subsided.

"I once led all of Cobane in song," he said, weakly. The coughing had exhausted him.

"Did you?"

"Yes. Father Potoo was away. I stood on a chair on top of a table, and I led them all."

His breath came slower, and his words slurred on the brink of sleep.

"What song?" I asked.

His eyes closed. "Auntie? Are you there?"

I squeezed his hand. "I'm here, Fount. I asked you a question. What song did you lead?"

He spoke, around a yawn. "My favorite song."

"And what's that? What is your favorite song?" Knowing this one thing was suddenly vitally important to me. I shook him. "What is your favorite song, Fount? You must sing it to me before I go."

He paused for so long, I thought he had not heard. I was about to shake him again, when the ghost of a smile tilted his mouth. His eyes remained closed, but he took a deep breath, filling his thin chest—and sang. "Will I go away someday; will I fly? Someday, someday, someday."

He held the last note then his face went blank in repose.

My throat contracted. "He didn't finish," I said.

"He did," William assured me.

I tore my eyes from his face and looked up. "So short?"

"Not short for us. We sing over and over, for many hours." He arranged the blanket around Fount's small frame. Finished, he turned to me. "We get water. Arika must drink."

"I know where the tap is now. I can get it myself." I picked up the water bucket, knowing what William would say even before he shook his head, obstinately.

"We go together," he assured me.

Seeing the stubborn set of his jaw, I knew it was pointless to protest. I passed him the water bucket. "Fine, we go together," I agreed.

I pulled off my mask and gloves as we stepped onto the porch. The night was warm and the wind wailed mournfully. Gray clouds covered the moon in a transparent veil. Below, a thick, sticky fog had settled in the village. Its wetness collected on my cheeks. As we walked, a fat drop shimmered down my chin. I stopped, suddenly, seized by a powerful need to say... *something* about Fount, the sick room, what I'd witnessed. "William," I said.

He stopped alongside me. "Yes, Arika."

I opened my mouth. Nothing came out. I closed it, wiping at my damp face.

As we started again, William's hand, the size of a supper plate, rested gently on my back.

THE MESSENGER

We were near our destination when a sizable crowd of Kongos came into view. They were gathered in front of the waterspout at the end of the street. A man stood on a crate addressing the crowd. He had a red bandana angled over one eye.

"Who's that?" I asked.

"Trouble," William answered, eyeing the man. He pulled me into an alley. We were far enough away that no one had noticed our approach, but we could still hear the man in the bandana from atop his ad hoc podium.

"I have told you what the brother said. I will not tell you again," he shouted.

"And what assurance have we that this brother does not lie?" someone in the crowd asked.

"Or that you, yourself, do not speak false?" said another.

I stepped out of the alley to get a better look. William yanked me back.

"Hey!" I protested.

He covered my mouth. His eyes were wide with trepidation. "He must not see Arika," William warned.

I nodded, and he removed his hand. "Why not?"

He put a finger to his closed lips, then his ear, advising me to be quiet and listen.

The man on the crate was still speaking. "What reason do I have to lie?"

"To drive up prices," a voice suggested. "We all know you trade goods in secret. We ought to turn him in. Let him swing on the gallows."

"Maybe I trade on the black market—maybe not. This much is true: the price of my goods remains the same, no matter what happens there."

"What proof is there that anything happened at all?"

"I told you, the messenger! He reported that someone set fire to the Point Landing village, and it was no accident."

"Why would anyone set fire to a village? It doesn't make sense. Why burn a plantation?"

"A fine question. One the messenger could not answer," the man with the bandana said.

"Well, then, *you* answer. Why would a Point Lander burn his own village down?"

"I do not think it was a Point Lander who set the fire," the man retorted. "I think it was someone else."

"So, you are a Rebel!"

The crowd murmured, disturbed by the idea. The man on the crate waited before responding.

"I am not a Rebel," he said clearly. "I am an honest merchant and I have no wish to fight."

"A good Kongo works the field, according to the Compromise. You say you are a merchant. Well, then, honest or not, you might as well be a Rebel!" someone challenged.

"And look! He wears an electric bracelet!" someone else cried.

"It's not an electric bracelet; it's a watch from the old world.

It's used to keep time," the man defended.

"*Wreckage* ware," someone said, appalled. "Only Rebels wear *wreckage*,"

"I'm not afraid of old-world technology. And yes, I fix broken relics from time to time. That doesn't mean I aspire to the Assembly like the Rebels."

A belligerent voice arose from the crowd. "Answer this! If you are not a Rebel, why do you accuse our First Brother of burning down Point Landing? From the time of the Last War, the First Brothers have watched over us as their own. We know this! It is written in the Sun Tower of Hasting. Our father, the Great Obi Solomon, giver of the Omen of the One, signed the Compromise for the good of our First Fathers, and their lineage. We are that lineage! To break the Compromise is to break with Obi, to forsake the coming of the One who will save the Kongo. I, myself, will never doubt. I'll never forsake the way. God keep Obi and soon come the One. *Soon come the One!*"

"Soon come the One!"

The Loyalist crowd took up this cry so loudly, the man on the crate had to shout to be heard. "I don't doubt the Omen! And I did not say it was a Record Keeper who burned down the village. I merely said it was not a Point Lander."

"Then who do you say it was?" the belligerent voice demanded.

"That's what I want to find out!" the man on the crate cried.

"How do we do that?" someone asked.

"Yes, how?" said another.

"We establish a delegate of men," the man said.

"And women," a female voice interrupted.

"And women," he repeated. "The delegates will travel to

Point Landing and observe for themselves what happened. If the delegates find foul play, we will present that evidence to the Assembly and seek justice, through lawful means."

"And what about our work?" said a new voice.

"Yes, what about the quota?" another said.

The belligerent voice championed this argument. "We all have work to do under the Compromise. We're working extra now, to make up for the sick among us. If three more leave for this so-called delegation, the Seed won't be planted and the quota will be forfeit. What would the Overseer say?"

The man on the crate threw up his hands. "If someone is burning down Kongo houses, I think we need to discover the criminal more than we need to plant crops to keep the Keepers fat."

Several people gasped. A lone voice whispered, "Rebel!"

"Get the noose," a voice shouted. "Call the Guard!"

"Raise the gallows!" another voice agreed. "We'll drag him out!"

The man on the crate squeaked out a defense, but his voice was lost in their resistance.

William drew my attention. "You stay here," he said. He strode from the alley.

I nodded, certain a lynching was about to take place.

The crowd yanked the slender man from the crate. They had him, hoisted above their heads, when William arrived.

"Who's there?" someone asked.

"It's Crane," another answered.

Their white-hot fervor dimmed considerably.

Silent, William walked to the middle of the crowd, a head taller than the tallest man.

"Crane, you have no business here." I saw now, the belligerent voice belonged to a stout youth with medium-brown skin.

William pointed at the crowd's slender captive. "Put down."

"Move aside, Crane," the stout youth demanded.

Instead of answering, William crossed his arms.

I saw the crowd. All but the stout leader wanted to comply. They exchanged looks. Then, as one, they returned the slender man to his feet and dispersed.

When the crowd had gone, the man adjusted his bandana. "Thank you, Crane. I don't know what I would have done if you had not intervened."

Beside the giant, I saw the man was older than I'd first guessed upon hearing him speak. His language was unusually clear for someone who should have undergone several Rebirths. The Loyalist workers in the crowd had been much younger, which explained their language, but what of him? He looked to be thirty, at least. Not a single misfire in all those years?

"Point Landing—tell me," William demanded.

I strained closer, not wanting to miss a word of the man's story.

"I don't know much, just what a Point Landing brother relayed to me earlier," he began. "I don't know his name. He was injured when he got here. He asked to speak with Kha. So, I took him to the big house, where Kha was rumored to be."

"And?"

"And he refused to go. He was burning with fever and injured. I could tell he wasn't going to last long and I didn't want to take him to Potoo, that old fool. So, I forced him to tell me his news."

"What news?"

"That the Point Landing village is nearly gone. Burned to the ground in a fire. Many of the workers died. He didn't know how the fire started, but he said it was not a normal fire. He wouldn't say anything more. He just demanded to speak to Kha."

I stepped from the alley. "What do you mean, it wasn't a normal fire?"

Shocked by my appearance, the young man looked from me to William.

"What do you mean?" I repeated.

He took a step back. "Are you one of them?" he asked. "A Record Keeper?"

"I am."

My answer scared him. He backed away, glaring at William.

"Wait, don't go," I said. But he was gone.

William turned to me.

"Don't look at me like that!"

"I told you stay," he said.

I lifted my chin. "Well, you weren't asking the proper questions. If there's been a fire at Point Landing, it's likely the work of Voltaire's Army. Point Landing is mere miles from Cobane. We have to inform the authorities. I'm a favorite of Jones. I can alert her. I can help!"

"Jones?"

"The Headmistress at the Schoolhouse," I explained.

William looked appalled. "Not tell Jones."

"We've got to get that man, the one with the bandana, back here."

"No," William said firmly. "He not talk more. We get water."

"I want to know about the fire," I protested.

William took the bucket from my hand and refilled it from the spout. "We get water," he said again. "Arika must drink."

"I'm not drinking until you tell me what you know. Who was that man with the bandana?"

William looked at me a long time. He sighed. "The man is Martin," he said, emphasizing the first syllable. "He is Kongo Rebel."

"But, he said he wasn't a Rebel," I breathed.

"He lies." William's eyes held mine, inviting me to see the truth of his conviction.

"Tell me more," I demanded. "Where is Martin's messenger? Does Martin know Voltaire? Does Voltaire know of the New Seed?"

Behind us, another voice shouted, "Do not answer that!"

I gasped and jumped around. "Hosea!"

"Did I tell you to leave the sick room?"

"You told me to stay with William."

"Yes, in the sick room, by the sick beds. Not out here, where you can do actual harm."

"We were just getting water."

"That's not what it sounded like."

"William, tell him!"

"Leave William out of this." Hosea lunged forward.

William stepped in his path. "Kha not touch Arika."

From behind the wall of William's body, I watched Hosea stop as if shackled.

For all his size and strength, William's power lay in his tremendous will. Once his mind was made up, he became immovable. Earlier in the evening, Hosea and I had tended patients one bed apart and William, as was his habit, was humming softly to himself—the same short tune. The song had been unfamiliar to me at first, but he sung it so persistently that I was humming along with him when Hosea, just a few feet away, paused in his ministration to ask sardonically whether our song had words. William's face had turned to stone. He eyed Hosea and said, firmly, "*We sing song.*" Motioning to me to continue with him, he had begun at the top of the verse, no louder than before, but no quieter either.

Hosea puffed air through his nostrils. "I'm not going to hurt her."

"Kha not touch Arika," William repeated.

At his back, I smothered a smile with my fist. In just a few hours, William had changed from my guard, to my shield.

Hosea glared at me. "Look, will you call him off. I just want to talk."

I stayed behind William and called out, "I want to know about the fire at Point Landing. How did it start?"

"I don't know."

"Tell me about Martin's messenger."

Hosea sighed. "There's nothing to tell. He's dead."

"When? How?"

"A few minutes ago. He bled to death. There was nothing anyone could do."

Stunned, I said nothing.

"Remember the built young man we tended tonight?"

"The cannon!" I recalled. "He was the messenger? Did he say anything before he died?"

"There wasn't time," Hosea said.

I deflated as the trail of information came to an abrupt end.

If I wanted to know more, I would have to find and question Martin, the Rebel.

I stepped into the open. "It's okay, William. I want to talk to Kha alone."

William didn't move.

"Why don't you go back to the sick room?" I suggested, placing a hand on his arm. "I'm sure Robin could use your help."

After a moment, William sent Hosea a dark look and strode away.

THE FACTIONS

When William was out of sight, Hosea stalked toward me. When we were toe to toe, he pulled a pink, fragrant square from his back pocket.

"What is that?" I asked.

"An invitation. According to this, I'm the only student in residence from the Vine, which means I'm on the Joust Planning Committee by default. So, we have to go."

I stared, nonplussed. The preliminary meeting had taken place already, and the first official Committee meeting wasn't until Saturday night. Could it be that I'd spent the whole of Saturday in the village? "What day is it?"

"It's Saturday, Cobane. We have thirty minutes. Now, let's go."

Suddenly, I thought of the empty black book. It felt like a millstone in my pocket. A whole day and night of absence would not go unnoticed by Jones. She might, even now, be awaiting my return. I needed information about the Director, and I needed it now!

I glanced at Hosea from the corner of my eye. "You know, if you miss the meeting, the worst Jones will do is expel you."

He frowned, suspicious.

I smiled to cover my nerves. I was fishing, hoping he'd let a clue slip as to his intentions at the Schoolhouse.

"Perhaps I want to graduate and become a Senator," he said.

"Do you?"

"Doesn't everyone?"

I huffed. He was toying with me, and I didn't have time! I gave up all pretense. "Be straight with me, Hosea. I want to know why you're here. If not to graduate, then why? It's important."

He scoffed. "You school brats are all the same. Whatever you happen to want becomes important, just because you want it."

"Don't forget, this school brat was right beside you in the sick room tonight! There's blood on my hands too."

I lifted a hand to show him and realized, to my horror, I was a mess, covered all over in blood and filth. I touched my hair where soft curls sprang haphazardly. "*Obi Solomon!* I have to change," I said.

"There's no time. We have to go."

I balked, imagining Jones' reaction to the dirt. "Late or not, I can't go back like this."

He looked me over. Resignedly, he took my arm and led me to an abandoned hut. He took a turn around the single room, ensuring it was safe, and left me alone with a shout. "You have five minutes."

I didn't waste any time. I stripped and took a square pile of garments from my bag. I plucked up the first square, an underskirt, and stepped into it. Then I pulled a soft blouse over my head. I shook out the last square, my *aura*, and began to wrap myself in the broad strip of cloth.

I started with a long drape around my hips, tucking it in at the waist of my underskirt. I made several pleats and tucked those in too, creating a fan pattern across the top of my thighs. I pulled the next part of the cloth tight around my knees, hobbling them together. I secured the remaining length around my back and over my shoulder. With the small steps required by the close nip of my skirt, I retrieved the thick studded belt I'd discarded earlier and cinched it around my waist.

Finished, I surveyed myself. The pleats were unfashionably wide and I'd tucked the skirt poorly, so the hem hung unevenly. I'd managed a tight hobble, which was most important to Jones. It would do. A knock sounded at the door.

"Are you done in there?"

"In a minute." I gathered up the length of my torn *aura* and folded it with my *pallium*. I was shoving both into my bag when the door opened.

Hosea had cleaned himself and changed clothes. He held up a bucket. "I thought you could use some water," he explained.

I blinked. "I—yes—thank you."

He set his offering on a window ledge.

I brushed past him to wash. As I rinsed my hands, I was keenly aware of his gaze.

He relaxed back against the ledge. "How's your thumb?"

"Excuse—?" My voice squeaked. I cleared my throat and tried again. "Excuse me?"

"Your thumb, you gouged it in class."

"Oh, that." I stared determinedly at the water, scrubbing extra hard. "It's fine."

"That's good. Don't forget your face," he added, "you've got dirt on your chin."

I splashed cold water on my warm cheeks.

"You're missing it—it's right here." He leaned forward and lifted his hand.

I jerked back just in time. "I'm—fine," I whispered.

He crossed his forearms over his broad chest and gave me an odd look.

I scurried to my bag and wiped myself dry, keeping my back to him until he left the hut to empty the dirty water into an alley.

Side by side, we left the village behind, weaving our way through the tangle of streets. We crossed the perimeter and started through the meadow between the village and the Schoolhouse.

"I was thinking about what you said earlier," he said, breaking the silence. "You were right, again."

"Right about what?"

He made a sweeping motion with his arm, clearing a path for me through the high grass. "You *were* in the sick room tonight, covered in blood, just as I was."

"Oh, that." I picked my way around a clump of dirt. "I had no idea what I was doing."

"But you did it anyway," he said. "Which is more than most people would do. I was wrong to imply otherwise." Abruptly, he stopped walking and looked at me.

I stopped beside him. A hot breeze trickled through the grass, tickling my ankles. "You're staring," I said.

"Am I?"

I nodded. "You do it a lot."

He was quiet for a long time. "I've traveled all over the Kongo. I meet new people every day," he said.

"So?"

He stuffed his hands in his rear pockets and hunched his shoulders. "So—they rarely surprise me."

My breath caught in my chest. My stomach quivered. My

face felt hot and my hands were too big. I turned away and hid them in the folds of my skirt. The long finger of my right hand grazed the edge of the black book and I flinched, curling my hand into a fist.

"If you still want to know why I'm here, I'll tell you," he said.

I looked back at him. I sensed he was testing me again. On what, I couldn't guess. And it didn't matter. Jones wanted answers. If I wanted to be a Senator, I needed to ingratiate myself—just one more time. "Tell me," I said.

"Okay, but let's hurry. I don't want to be late."

He took the lead and gestured for me to walk behind him.

•

"The rumors started a month before I came to Cobane," he began. "Talk of a fever sweeping through the Kongo. The symptoms were similar to a fever that plagued the Vine last quarter. I wanted more information. So, I went to Point Landing."

"Was it the same sickness?" I asked.

"It was—only worse. At the Vine, the medicine man refers people to me. At Point Landing, he was still in charge, dosing with salt and liquor. He'd even turned the nursery into a hash tent, so the smoke could *heal* the children. By the time I got there, over a hundred people had fallen ill."

I inhaled. "That many?"

He nodded. "Production shut down once the northern diplomats became aware of the problem. The house fell into disarray. They failed even to designate a hospital. So, the sick and healthy were still sleeping and eating together."

"Why didn't the Overseer notify the Assembly?"

"Fear. When it comes to the Kongo, the Assembly cares

about one thing—the quota. The North is overcrowded. Food storage hasn't kept pace with population growth. They have enough to sustain them for six months to a year, tops. After that, if the Kongo doesn't send food, thousands will starve. A wise Overseer never admits that the quota is in danger. If he did, the Assembly would give his post to another diplomat, eager to take his place. The Overseers have it good here in the Kongo. Our territory is bigger than the two northern territories put together. So here, they have space."

"Well, considering the death toll, doing nothing about the fever makes even less sense than informing the Assembly," I said.

"I agree. I think his hope was that the fever would die out quickly. Like I said, the same fever plagued the Vine last quarter. It ran its course in a month. The Overseer there was able to get back on schedule before anyone noticed a problem. We lost nearly fifty workers, but he worked the remainder hard in the aftermath and made up for lost time."

I grimaced. "Did any of the Overseer's men fall ill?"

"No, not at the Vine. When I arrived at Point Landing, the Overseer and his men were barricaded in the big house—with their Kongo house staff, of course."

I hid my distaste for their cowardice. "How does the fever spread?" I asked.

"Good question," Hosea said. "That's the most confounding part. I haven't had time to research the origin and spread. All I know is it has something to do with smoking hash."

I thought of Jetson and the others, who smoked hash regularly. "Hash! But that's impossible. So many more would be sick."

Hosea nodded, his brow wrinkled in thought. "I've considered that. My guess is that only a few shipments of hash were contaminated. Or, perhaps the hash merely makes workers vulnerable to catching the fever, but doesn't cause the fever directly."

"Well, have you petitioned the Assembly? They could set aside funds to conduct research."

Hosea snorted. "Cobane, the Assembly doesn't *care*. Remember, for the English and Clayskin Senators, the purpose of the Kongo is to fulfill the food quota."

"Well, then, the Record Keepers, or the Kongo Senators can—"

Hosea cut me off. "The Kongo Senators are just as worried about saving themselves as the Overseers. They're not going to admit there's a problem, and risk getting ousted, unless they absolutely have to. Besides, the current political fighting over the New Seed is overshadowing every other concern in the Assembly. No one cares about a few hundred Kongo individuals. What matters under the Niagara Compromise is the quota. We all only exist—"

"For the greater good," I finished. He was right. The Compromise valued efficiency and abhorred waste. If the remaining Vine workers were able to meet the quota, then, according to the Compromise, the felled workers had been superfluous to begin with, useless mouths to feed. "Population control is essential to the perpetuity of the human remnant on Earth," I quoted, thinking of the birthing control laws. "The old world was woefully overgrown. The Earth couldn't keep up."

"Exactly," Hosea agreed. "Some even theorize that the hacker who planted the catastrophic computer virus was an environmentalist who worked for the old World Health Organization."

I nodded. "I read something about that during my Silver Award research. So, what happened next, at Point Landing?" I asked.

"Well, we were achieving good results treating the young and otherwise healthy, but the older, more feeble patients invariably died. Eventually, news of the fever spread south."

I shivered. "Don't tell me. The news reached Voltaire's Army?" I guessed.

He nodded. "As soon as they heard of the fever at Point Landing, they came to recruit. I guess they thought the fever would breed discontent with the current class system."

Suddenly, I was angry. "Voltaire is despicable. Capitalizing on death? Using illness to further selfish aims? I wish the Kongo Guard could find the Army's headquarters and blow it up, all at once. Then we could be done with it."

"I'm sure they would," Hosea said, "if Voltaire's Army had a headquarters."

My mouth gaped. "They don't?"

"*Obi*, they keep you school brats sheltered. Listen closely. Voltaire's movement started out as a ragtag group of kids in Hannibal. Voltaire, the leader of the gang, stopped taking the Rebirth and coached the other members into refusing the Rebirth too. It might have stopped there, if Voltaire hadn't been so extraordinarily blessed."

"Blessed? With what?"

"The gift of the written word. Two years ago, Voltaire started publishing pamphlets theorizing that the Rebirth is morally wrong and demanding that the Record Keepers disavow it.

The pamphlets spread like wildfire. Hundreds joined the Rebel gang."

"How extraordinary. A Second Brother mentally capable of constructing theories."

"And arguing them convincingly," Hosea added.

"So, what happened?" I said.

"Well, nothing at first. The Record Keepers didn't care about Voltaire's cause. For them, it was business as usual. Nothing changed until Voltaire orchestrated a silent protest. The gang published a pamphlet that persuaded hundreds of workers to sit down in the middle of the field and refuse to work or eat for three days."

I gasped. "But what about the harvest?"

"Exactly," Hosea said. "When the Overseers grew concerned about the quota, they blamed the Record Keepers, for not keeping the Second Brothers in line. Of course, the Record Keepers blamed the Overseers. It was a mess. In the end, the Rebels got attention, which is exactly what Voltaire wanted."

"But the laws didn't change. The Rebirth is still staunchly observed."

"Actually, Cobane, the laws *did* change. The fugitive yesterday is a prime example."

I frowned. "The fugitive? He was convicted of distributing illegal paraphernalia."

"Illegal paraphernalia, otherwise known as Voltaire's pamphlets."

"Oh! So they outlawed the pamphlets?"

"Yes, along with any writing that discourages or disparages the Rebirth."

"Oh…" I frowned. Somehow, that didn't seem right.

"Of course, Voltaire continued to write and, eventually, got caught."

"So, Voltaire is dead?"

Hosea looked surprised. "Not at all—far from it. The punishment for distributing illegal paraphernalia is not execution, but intermittent Rebirth. Since Voltaire was convicted of publishing ten different pamphlets, ten Rebirth pills were administered as punishment."

I gasped. "Ten on the same day! The possibility of misfire would be astronomical."

He nodded. "Everyone thought the rebellion was over—"

"But?"

"But Voltaire survived the dosing, escaped in January of this year and went into hiding. After Voltaire's exile, the gang changed. They turned militant. What's more, they went undercover. They used to boast of their Rebel state. They grew their hair long and wore these bronzed extension cords looped with bits of old-world *wreckage*—ink cartridges, computer chips, coils. But now they've stopped all that. They blend in, so they're indistinguishable from Loyalists."

"If Voltaire is in exile, who's leading the Army?"

Hosea pressed his lips together. "Some think Voltaire is still conducting it, using a secret network of spies and allies to distribute information about when and where to strike. The Army members surface a handful at a time and conduct their suicide missions, knowing they'll be caught and executed for it."

I shivered. "But there must be some way of recognizing them before they strike."

Hosea shrugged. "For now, there isn't. After the Joust this

year, when the workers partake of the Rebirth, Hasting will have a better idea of who to suspect."

I frowned. "I just don't understand. Why does Voltaire's Army want to turn the workers against us Record Keepers? We're all on the same side."

"Maybe, but they want the Second Brother to represent himself before the Assembly. You saw the condition of the village. They want more for the people."

"They need medicine and better shelter, but why aspire to influence the Assembly? They have us, the First Brothers, to care for their needs."

He shook his head. "They don't believe the Record Keepers are taking care of the Kongo workers' interests."

I tried to speak, but he held up a hand.

"And, according to them, it's too late for the Keepers to change their ways. Food and shelter isn't enough. They want education and direct participation in government."

"That's nutty! A Second Brother making law? Their psyches would collapse with the effort."

He frowned down at me. "Careful, Cobane. In the wrong crowd, those words will get you killed."

I didn't know what to say.

Hosea went on. "The Rebels in Voltaire's Army are smart. Smarter than Jones would have you believe. They're tired of being patronized by Hasting. They want the Record Keepers gone, not just from the Kongo, but from the face of the Earth."

My heart pounded. "How many workers have joined Voltaire's Army?"

"I don't know, but it's growing fast. It's difficult to gauge with all the fighting."

I nodded. "And where do you stand in all this?" I asked. "I assume you're a New Seeder." I bit my lip. This was a question Jones would undoubtedly want answered, but I asked it casually, keeping my eyes down to hide my deceitful intention.

He hesitated. "I'm a medic, a scientist. I want no part of Kongo politics or war."

"And what about all those things you said during class, and the weapons book I found in your room? Your father doesn't condone that kind of thing—does he?"

When he didn't answer, I looked up, willing him to disclose something, anything. We were nearing the Schoolhouse and my future depended on his candor.

He shrugged. "I was playing devil's advocate. Murder, for any cause, turns my stomach. I've seen more than enough for a lifetime. At Point Landing alone, the death toll tripled when Voltaire's Army surfaced. It wasn't safe to walk out at night. I can fight disease, but no one can save the Kongo from itself, and I won't waste my time."

His cynicism left me deflated. The people in the village looked up to him, but he spoke as if he didn't care. "So, that's why you left Point Landing," I said. "But why did you come here?"

"I told you, I'm a medic. I heard a rumor that someone was sick. So, my father arranged for me to come here and take the Final Exam."

His father arranged it! That was important. I wet my mouth, determined to remember every word he said—*nothing lost in translation.*

"He didn't do it for me," he said, grimacing at the thought of his father. "I now owe him a favor, and I'm sure he'll collect in due time. But I couldn't resist the opportunity to study the fever again." He looked at the sky and cursed. "*Damn*, Cobane. We have to hurry. We're already late."

"Wait, if you don't care about school, why are you so set on getting to this meeting? Shouldn't you stay in the village?"

"You're forgetting what happened at Point Landing. So long as we keep what's happening in the village quiet, I have a chance of finally understanding this fever. If Voltaire's Army learns that the sickness has spread here, they'll begin recruiting. Some workers will join them, but others will push back—just as you saw tonight. There will be fighting, stoning and lynching. The Overseer or Jones will double the Guard stationed here, and chaos will ensue. If Jones finds out that the pair of us weren't at the meeting—"

"She's sure to investigate why," I finished.

"Exactly. She'll draw attention here, and Voltaire's Army will follow. The minute I think Jones is catching on, I'm gone."

My lip curled; I couldn't help it. "You would leave all these sick people, just to avoid a fight?"

He lifted one eyebrow. "Are you advocating war, Cobane?"

"No, but—"

"Then we agree. Anything done in pursuit of peace is necessarily justified by it."

I bit my lip, hearing my own words thrown back at me.

"Look, I'm not saying I won't leave medicine. I will. I just won't be here to supervise. My father has tried to involve me in politics since I was a kid. The one thing I learned is that fighting leads nowhere. I'm a man of peace."

We had reached the gate. He produced a key and walked in ahead of me, gesturing for me to stay behind.

I leaned in the open doorway and called after him, "So, if

you aren't willing to stand with the Record Keepers, and you won't fight for the Rebels, what do you want?"

He appeared before me. "I just want to be left alone with my work. It's all clear. You can come." He stopped, one hand on my arm, just before we went inside. "Remember, not a word of what's happening in the village to anyone. I'm here for the meeting only."

THE COMMITTEE MEETING

Covington called the Committee to order just as we entered the room. She narrowed her eyes on us.

East Keep tossed her long braid. "You're late."

"Our apologies," Hosea said to Covington. He ignored East Keep.

Covington remained silent.

"Sorry doesn't explain why she's late—again," East Keep said scathingly.

"Or where she was yesterday."

I stared at the twin who had taken East Keep's side. Her shield was up as she waited for my retort. I signed, tiredly. My toil in the sickroom made our Schoolhouse rivalry seem petty in comparison. All I could see was the stack of bone bracelets around her wrist. Just one would buy a week of food for Fount. Before I could speak, Covington cut in.

"Cool it, West Keep!" she said. "Arika, relax and take a seat."

I squinted, thrown by her capitulation, but grateful. I had more important matters to see to. By some miracle, Jones had not been waiting on the porch to expel me. With luck, she would never discover my sojourn to the village. Once I returned the black book to her, I'd be free to hunker in the library for the rest of the week.

As I sat beside Jetson, he jabbed me with his quill, reminding me that I'd promised him information. I snubbed him studiously. He would just have to understand that I couldn't keep that promise. Things had changed. The political data I'd discovered was for Jones. It was my currency, my ticket to the Assembly. And the other information—about the fever—well, that had to be kept secret too. If it got out, Hosea would leave Cobane and abandon all those sick people.

I gnawed on a knuckle. Jetson poked me again, but I ignored him. He hadn't seen the sickroom, he didn't understand. Clean air was a luxury. He was well-fed. Medicine, if he fell ill, was a call away. Hosea Khan was all the village had. For their sake, I had to keep his secret.

"Arika," Jetson whispered.

"Leave me alone." I scooted away, but I felt his anger rolling toward me in hot swells.

"Fine," he said. "You'll get what's coming."

"Fine," I hissed. I didn't meet his eyes as I fumbled in my bag for a quill.

Covington continued with the meeting. "So, where did we leave off?"

"You were about to take roll," Jetson offered. His voice was chilly. "I have the latest list for you, right here."

It wasn't until he'd produced a neatly pinned sheet of paper that my preoccupied mind registered his words. My head snapped up and I snatched for the paper—too late. East Keep plucked it from Jetson's hand and passed it to Covington.

The room went quiet.

According to protocol, Teacher Jones would have had the most current list of attendees delivered to the Secretary's room—my room—the night before the first meeting.

One twin touched her pointed chin. "But, I thought Arika was the Secretary."

The other twin tilted her head and tapped an identical spot on her own chin. "Yeah, I thought so too."

Jetson looked grim. "You're right, the pair of you. Arika is the Secretary."

It took them a second to process. "So, why doesn't she have the roll?" one twin said. Her eyes darted to her sister.

"And why do you have it, instead?"

The answer was obvious. If Jetson had the roll, then he had been to my empty room to get it. He would know I'd lied to him, and he would guess that I'd spent the night in the village.

Slowly, I looked to my right, meeting his cool green eyes. "Jetson, don't."

His mouth tightened. "I won't cover for you. There's too much at stake."

"Just trust me, please," I whispered.

"I *did* trust you."

My mouth gaped, but what could I say? He was right. For years, he had been my only ally in a school of sharks. Now those sharks were swimming around me, scenting blood.

"Do tell, Jetson," East Keep said, her sharp nails snapping along the arm of her chair. "How *did* you get that roll?"

The twins leaned in, their small ears perked as they waited for Jetson's answer.

"It must have been from her room."

"That's where Jones would have sent it," they said.

"I was at her dorm," Jetson confirmed. "I went last night. The roll was by her door."

A sickness twisted my gut. Once they knew I was in the

village overnight, they would fight over the opportunity to report me to Jones. Covington would win that battle. She'd been after me for years. The black book would offer some protection, but how good was the information I had? Would Jones assume I was conspiring with Hosea? Would I be able to convince her of my loyalty? Probably not—not now that I'd stayed in the village all day and night.

"Go on, Jetson, tell us the story," East Keep said. Her nails clicked.

"I found the roll and knocked," he went on. "I wanted to hand it to her personally, because she'd been sick."

I clenched my quill.

"No one answered, so I went away. I thought she was asleep, but I came back an hour later. I knocked again, harder. I came back every hour—for the whole night."

I glared at him. "And did I answer?"

He looked away. "No, you didn't."

East Keep smiled. "So, little miss perfect wasn't in her room last night."

West Keep leaned forward. "You're not allowed to leave your room after lights out, you know."

I wanted to point out that Jetson had been out of his room after lights out, but I bit my tongue, knowing it was no good.

Hannibal looked concerned. "If she wasn't in her room, perhaps she has an excuse. Arika?"

I scoured my mind. I could say I was in Hosea's room, but that wouldn't put me on the right side of the rules—or Jones. I could say I was in the nurse's office, but she wouldn't lie for me. My best bet was to say I was sleeping. I'd hit my head and didn't hear Jetson's knock. It would be his word against mine.

I had just opened my mouth to lie when Covington spoke.

"She was with me."

We all turned to gawk at Covington.

Catching myself, I closed my mouth.

"Wait, who was with you?" one twin said.

Covington rolled her eyes. "Arika, you nut."

"With *you*? But you hate Arika," said the other.

Rather than deny her dislike, Covington shrugged flippantly. "I changed my mind."

East Keep looked between us, her full cheeks flat with jealousy. The title of second most popular girl had been hers for years. "I don't believe it," she said, zeroing in on me. "What were you doing together?"

I lifted my chin. "We were talking."

She snorted. "About what? Nothing we discuss could *possibly* be of interest to you," she mocked, making the twins titter.

"What we talked about is none of your business," Covington interrupted.

They stopped laughing.

"But, if you must know, we were discussing my nomination for Committee Vice Chair."

East Keep's wide mouth paled. "The Vice Chair? But—that's already been decided."

I looked between them. By law, the valedictorian of the class was named President of the Committee. The President, in turn, nominated a Vice Chair to keep order in her absence. When I gave up the Presidency to focus on my studies, I had assumed Covington would pick East Keep. The two were inseparable.

"Who—who will you nominate?" East Keep asked.

"As President, I nominate Arika Cobane for Vice Chair."

East Keep slammed a hand on the table. "No! Arika doesn't even want the Vice Chair. And I've wanted it forever!"

True. The President and Vice Chair got to pose for pictures in the Main Hall. We'd learned that fact early on in our secondary years, and East Keep had been angling for the honor since.

"Arika won't accept!" she shouted.

Covington rolled her eyes. "Of course she will."

I said nothing.

"Well, you can't just appoint her; she has to be confirmed by the Committee!" East Keep challenged.

Covington didn't blink. "Fine. All in favor, say 'aye.'" There was a moment of silence, then Covington snapped her fingers at the twins.

They jumped and spoke together. "Aye."

In the end, the count was ten to one, with one abstaining, in favor of my appointment.

Covington's rings clinked as she folded her hands. "Arika is Vice Chair."

East Keep shrieked, "Noo!"

"It's done, we're moving on."

"But she voted against herself!"

"Actually, she abstained," Hannibal said.

"Hush up, Hannibal!"

"Hey, don't shout at her," Jetson said. "You lost fair and square."

East Keep's pug nose quivered on the verge of tears.

My stomach rolled guiltily. If there had been any other explanation for my whereabouts, I would have declined the job, just to remove that wounded look from her eyes.

She stood up and backed toward the exit, looking around the room as if we were strangers. With the exception of Covington and myself, the Committee avoided her gaze. It was terrible to see her pain. But, I figured, I owed her that much.

At the door, she turned to deride Covington.

"You all follow her like she's something special, but she's not and she knows it. She's only President of the Committee because Arika declined the post."

Her eyes raked me. "And you—you're too nutty to care what happens at the Joust. You don't care about any of us. All you've ever cared about was your marks, and your reputation with the Teachers. And that's all you care about now."

She tossed her head toward Covington. "Do you know she wanted the Silver Award? She works just as hard as you, only she does it in secret in case she doesn't win. She doesn't want to come in second, again, to *you*."

I dropped my gaze to the table.

She sneered at Covington. "I'll get you back for this."

Before anyone could reply, she left.

•

I couldn't lift my eyes from the blank parchment in front of me. Why had Covington lied for me?

Covington broke the silence. "As President of the Committee, I move to remove East Keep as Treasurer. I move to elect Hannibal as Treasurer in her place."

"Technically," Hannibal said, "we can't elect new officers without every member present. If East Keep doesn't return, we can't even hold a meeting."

Covington rolled her eyes. "Don't be ridiculous, of course we're holding the meeting."

A secondary student spoke, his voice small. "Hannibal's right. According to the rules, nothing we do is official without every member present. That's why attendance is mandatory."

Covington sighed. "Fine. I'll talk to East Keep and we'll meet back here in an hour."

No one moved.

"What are you waiting for? Go!"

The secondary students scurried away. Hannibal and the West Keep twins followed close behind. I stayed in my seat, flanked on either side by Jetson and Hosea. At the far end of the table, Covington sank dramatically into her chair.

"Are you going to tell us what that was about?" Jetson asked.

She looked up, her chin in her hands. "Your guess is as good as mine."

He turned on me. "You and I both know you were *not* with Covington last night. You were in the village—with him." He jabbed a finger at Hosea.

"You can't prove that, Jetson," I said. "And if you consider me a friend, you won't try to prove it."

"I can't ignore the fact that you're working with a Rebel enemy of Hasting. Don't you know they hate our kind?"

"No!" I pleaded. "I'm not working with anyone! I swear it. All I want is a fair shot at the Senate seat."

"Then why were you in the village last night?"

I glanced at Hosea, feeling torn. "I can't tell you."

Jetson jumped to his feet, grabbing Hosea by the shirtfront. "What have you done to her?"

"Jetson, no!" I jumped up.

"Relax, Cobane," Hosea said. "Jetson isn't going to hurt anyone, least of all me."

Jetson bared his teeth.

Hosea went on, calmly. "You were right. He can't prove anything. All he has are allegations."

I looked between the two as they towered over me, evenly matched. What Jetson lacked in size he made up in zeal. He looked ready to murder Hosea who, for all his height and bulk, hadn't lifted a finger to defend himself.

They stood there, breathing heavily, their eyes locked. Remembering Hosea's mysterious weapon, my gaze dropped to his waist. Close up, I saw it was etched with what looked to be ladders. Two pairs of vertical lines, each pair intercrossed with shorter horizontal lines. The ladders wove back and forth together, forming an intricate braid.

The sight of the metal tube sent a chill down my spine. "Jetson," I tried again. "For your sake, just let this go."

Jetson focused so intently on Hosea, I wondered if he'd heard me. After several long moments, he shoved his captive away. "You're not worth it," he said. He stomped from the room.

Hosea straightened his clothes, glanced at me, and followed after Jetson.

THE ULTIMATUM

As the door closed after them, I sighed. I had managed yet another narrow escape. After one more assignment life would return to normal. It was time to fill out the black book. I pushed back from the table and stood.

Covington stopped me. "Sit down, Arika."

I looped my pack around my neck. "Not now, Covington, I'm behind as it is. I mean, thanks for covering for me, but—"

Her eyes flashed. "I said, sit down."

"Why?"

She touched her chin. "Well, let's see—because if you don't, I'll tell Jones exactly what happened last night."

"After lying to save me? Why would you do that?"

She ticked off the reasons on her jeweled fingers. "Because I don't like you. Because you're a traitor and a rat. Because I can? Mostly, I'll turn you in, Arika, because East Keep was right. All you care about is yourself. *Your* reputation, *your* marks, *your* schedule. That's all you've cared about for seventeen years, but you're going to change. You're going to change *tonight*."

"Was she right about you?" I shot back. "Bidding for the Silver Award? Studying in secret? Not wanting to come in second?"

Covington laughed. "I don't regret *my* choices. Do you?"

I lifted my chin. "Get to the point. What is it you want?"

Her tone went flat. "I want answers. I assume you spent the night in the village, nursing the workers?"

"How do you know about that?"

"I'll tell you once I know whether I can trust you. Now sit."

Curious, I sat, thinking. She must have overheard my conversation with Jetson. She'd seen me sneak out and guessed where I was going. "I was in the sick room," I admitted.

"How bad is it?"

Her concern surprised me. "Bad when I got there. Better now," I said.

She nodded.

"And you exposed yourself to risk—just to help? Not for any other reason?"

"No other reason," I lied, smoothly, then reiterated the truth. "I wanted to help."

She sat back. The gold hoops in her ears swayed. "So it would appear. But I can hardly credit *you* with such... generosity."

I shot to my feet, chin angled. "If I'm so awful, why did you stick up for me?"

Her eyes lit with conviction. "Because, if there's even a chance that you're with us, I couldn't ignore it. Voltaire's Army grows every day. The Kongo is cracking at the seams. If we don't stick together, there won't be enough good Record Keepers left alive to save Hasting."

I sat back down. I could no longer claim ignorance. I knew about Voltaire's Rebel Army. From all accounts they would, indeed, murder us in our beds. If it weren't for the greater issues at play—the divide in Kongo leadership, the black book, even now waiting to be filled—it would make sense to join with Covington and the other students. As it was, securing my place in the Assembly was more important. Once there, I could focus on helping others.

"I won't deceive you, Covington," I said. "I've worked my whole life to be a Senator. Once I have my seat in the Assembly, I'll do what I can to quell the Rebels and neutralize Voltaire's Army. I want peace for all the Kongo Houses—but I can't think of that now. For now, I have to keep on Jones' good side and graduate. So excuse me, I have a Final Exam."

Covington looked at me a long time.

I slid my chair back.

I had just reached the door when her voice stopped me again.

"I can still go to Jones whenever I want. You'll be ruined."

I walked back to the table. "You wouldn't dare."

She stood. "Don't presume to know *what* I would dare, Arika Cobane. You've always thought you were too good for the rest of us, even in primary school. Did you ever think about us while you fought Jones? She punished all of us, not just you. Then, when you decided class was alright, you stepped on everyone in your race to the top."

"I did not!"

"You skipped every gathering to sit in the library and memorize books that weren't even required! You made sure you were the first to raise your hand, so that no one could get a word in edgewise. And when we did, you were always there to correct us. If the date was off a year or the name mispronounced—there came Arika!"

My shoulder stiffened. "That's not fair. There's only one top spot. You can't blame me for competing for it."

She looked down her long, thin nose at me. "Okay, I've tried reasoning. I give up. Here's what's going to happen. You're going to wait here for twenty minutes. Then you'll go to the Rec Room."

"Why?"

She went on with her instructions. "By that time, I will have patched things over with East Keep."

"There's no way! East Keep was vexed!"

"I'll patch it over," she repeated. "And you'll have fun for four hours while you're at our party."

"Have fun?" I said, bewildered. "At a nail party? What can you possibly hope to accomplish?"

"It's not a nail party, Arika. It's a braiding party. And you'll be there."

I grimaced—I couldn't help myself.

"We're having another tomorrow night. If you don't have fun tonight, you don't have to come tomorrow. You go your way and I'll go mine. But you have to give it a chance. No snide remarks and no talking about books, exams, the Assembly or Hasting. You're there to make friends, deal?"

Seeing she was in earnest, I bit my lip. "Can I answer later?"

"No."

"Can I—"

"No, you can't! Like it or not, we've got to stick together if we're going to defeat the Rebels. Which means you, Arika Cobane, have got to realize that you're not too good to associate with the rest of us."

"It's not like that! I'm not too good. I'm just... busy."

Covington crossed her arms. "If you're not in the Recreation Room in twenty minutes, you'll be meeting with Jones in thirty, once I tell her you snuck off with Hosea."

"But that's blackmail!"

"Yes, it is." She stood. "And, Arika, if you're not there, on time, having fun, I fully intend to follow through. Keeper or not." She turned on her heel and left.

THE PARTY

For fifteen minutes I sat alone in the meeting room, reliving the past hour. I felt Jetson's disappointment. I heard Covington call me selfish. I saw East Keep's face, a mask of contempt, insisting I'd never cared. All of it bothered me because most of it was true.

I'd grown accustomed to the great divide that separated me from my classmates. Reconciliation was impossible, I'd assumed. And for all these years, I'd figured they agreed. Sure, they invited me to parties, but that was formality. They did not truly want me there, any more than I had wanted to be there—which was not at all.

Liar.

I grimaced, searching myself for the truth. If I didn't care, why had Covington's proposal of alliance struck such a nerve? I glanced at the clock. Why was I waiting on pins and needles for twenty minutes to pass? Why was I hoping she would patch things over with East Keep? If I didn't care, why was I trembling at the possibility of a truce?

At nine forty-five, I jumped to my feet and hurried out of the meeting room. I walked through the Main Hall on shaky legs. Perhaps this sentimentality was residue from the village. For a few hours there, I'd been a daughter, a sister, an auntie—part of a family. Perhaps being back at the Schoolhouse felt lonely in comparison. Was Covington right? Could we reunite once we left the Schoolhouse? Could we face the Rebels together and mend the Kongo? I could hardly believe it. But then again, anything seemed possible at Hasting. And, as Senator, I would have security. I could make friends and afford to remain loyal to them. I wouldn't be subject to Jones.

I approached the Recreation Room and slowed. I saw my reflection in the clear glass of the Rec Room window and, through it, I saw my peers. They sat in a close-knit circle. No doubt, I would have to fight for a place among them. It would not be easy. On the other hand, if Covington was right, if there was even a sliver of a chance—I wanted to try. Shifting my school pack to the opposite shoulder, I pushed open the door and stepped inside.

•

East Keep was the first to notice my approach. The half-smile on her lips died. She nudged Covington and nodded in my direction. The urge to turn on my heel doubled. If not for Covington's gaze, warning me of ruination, I would have fled at that moment.

As it was, I pressed on, keeping my pace steady and my expression neutral. The West Keep twins wore stern expressions, but both were fidgeting. Hannibal's arms were folded, like the others', but her hands were open, not fisted. I knew, instinctively, her heart was not in the fight against me.

The one to placate was East Keep. On that first day of school, she'd been doodling so intently I had already mounted the nearest desk by the time she looked up from her parchment. She looked at me and, finding nothing of interest, turned back to her page. I caught a glimpse of it as I fell. It was dotted with nonsense—droopy-eyed puppies and loops of garland. She hadn't looked up again, even when my flailing foot dislodged the container of ink on her desk. Her eyes had followed it down instead of me.

I forced a smile as I stopped. "Hi, East Keep."

She tossed her braid.

I glanced at Covington who nodded, urging me to continue.

I tried for humility. "Look, East Keep, I'm sorry about what happened in the meeting."

Her lips twisted petulantly.

"You were right, I didn't want the position." I glanced at Covington. "You were also right about other things. I've always focused on my studies and maybe… perhaps I could have been more sociable."

After a long while, she gave a small shrug. "Since you're here, I assume you received my invitation."

"Yes, I did. I thought it was… pretty." *Lie.* In truth, one drawer of my desk was permanently scented, stuffed with a decade of perfumed and bedazzled invitations I hadn't bothered to read.

Her mouth softened. "I tried something new with that last batch. The twins gave me a stationery kit for my birth month. It came with twenty-four colors of ink."

"They must have gone to a lot of trouble."

One twin interrupted. "Not really. Covington's boyfriend is a merchant from Point Landing. He gets us whatever we want from the—ouch!" She broke off as her sister jabbed her in the side.

I looked between them. "I won't tell anyone about

Covington's boyfriend, if that's what you're worried about."

East Keep scooted close to Covington who seemed, suddenly, sad.

"What is it?" I asked.

Covington dabbed at the corner of her eyes, her gold rings flashing in the crystalights above. "You might as well tell her, West Keep. You're in a talkative mood."

The twin who had spoken out of turn rubbed her side sheepishly. "Covington's boyfriend had to leave Cobane today. He broke up with her before he left. We just heard the news. I—forgot."

"You're an idiot," East Keep said.

"Am not! I said I was sorry!"

"No, actually, you didn't," East Keep said.

"Ladies, can we just get along, please?" Hannibal said, gently. "We've been through enough today already." She glanced around, seeking confirmation from each of us.

I nodded my assent along with the twins.

"I guess we *are* here for fun, not fighting," East Keep said.

"And to do our hair, don't forget!" one twin said. "You promised."

East Keep smiled reluctantly. "I remember."

Except for Covington, they each took out bags of grooming supplies and began arranging the jars and bundles on a large coffee table. Covington remained seated, her arms crossed over her body. West Keep had let it slip that Covington's boyfriend was from Point Landing, just like the messenger. *Had they known each other?* I moved to sit beside Covington, but kept my questions to myself.

"No, no. You can't sit there!"

I looked up to see one twin shooing me away from my seat. "Why not?"

She rolled her eyes. "If you sit there, you'll be at the head of the braiding line, and Covington's always at the head of the braiding line."

I stood up. "What's a braiding line?"

"Oh, dear."

Before West Keep could recover, Hannibal took my arm and led me away. The twins rearranged six chairs, so they were front to back around the coffee table. Hannibal settled me down in the last one.

"A braiding line is how we keep ourselves looking so stylish. Not that it matters," she added more quietly. She sat down in front of me. "Haven't you ever noticed how difficult it is to twist your own hair?"

"My arms tire, I guess."

"Exactly! Twisting and shaping four dozen braids takes hours," the twins said. They sat in the two chairs in front of Hannibal and took turns explaining.

"Then you have to pin it up."

"Or do a beehive."

"Victory rolls are so glamourous; don't you think?"

Before I answered, East Keep sat down behind Covington, completing the line. "We do a braiding line every week. We all have to braid someone's hair, and we each get our own hair styled. This way, it's easier on all of us. Plus, before each session, we catch up on all the latest gossip." She clapped her hands. "That's the best part."

"Not everyone likes that part, East Keep," Hannibal said. "Some of us would do quite fine without it."

"Well, *we* relish news—right, girls?" East Keep grinned at the twins.

They nodded agreeably.

Covington smiled, though I saw her mind was elsewhere.

"Arika, you'll learn quickly which of us is fun and exciting, and which of us is a lame nut," East Keep said. She laughed along with the twins, then hurried over to kiss Hannibal's cheek. "Oh, you know I'm just teasing, don't you, Hanni?"

Hannibal grinned. "I suppose."

"Good!" She clapped her hands. "Now, who has something to share?"

The twins began talking over each other in their effort to tell the same story.

I listened with only half an ear. I'd wondered how Covington would get East Keep to forgive me, but, after only a few minutes, the answer was clear. East Keep was as changeable as the twins were affable. From anger to teasing to laughter and back again—all in the same minute.

"Now, has anyone heard anything more about the rebellion at Point Landing?" East Keep said, turning the talk to more serious matters.

My ears perked up.

"Well, we know it's the third this year," Hannibal said. "One at Hannibal House, one at Bankhead, and now one at Point Landing. And we know that Record Keepers were murdered, which brings the total to seven. I also heard rumors about a fire," Hannibal added, her face tense with apprehension.

"I heard the same rumors," Covington said. She sat forward, blowing her nose in a handkerchief. "Do you know if the fire damaged the crops? Will it affect the quota?"

"I don't know," Hannibal said, apologetically.

Moved by their anxiety, I spoke up. "I know something about Point Landing."

They both turned to me, eyes wide.

"I can't tell how I know, but the fire was in the village. The outfield crops weren't damaged."

Covington sighed. "That's good, at least. If it had reached the outfield, I'm afraid the Assembly would have to be informed—which would be really bad news."

I bit my lip. "Not necessarily. I'm not saying the Assembly should get involved. But the Senators do have power and there may be some truth to the Rebels' complaints, at least when it comes to the poor condition of the village."

"No, really!?" East Keep sounded more scandalized than disappointed.

The twins gasped.

My eyes met Covington's. Instinctively, I knew she would see my revelation for what it was: a disturbing twist in the current political happenings.

"Have *you* heard there are poor conditions in the village? We know they don't live in luxury, but it's not so bad, is it?" Covington asked, directing her question to Hannibal.

"Well, if I remember correctly, I read something about how the Record Keepers murdered at Bankhead were on a mission to take inventory of this mysterious fever when they were killed. It wouldn't hurt if the Assembly earmarked more funds for upkeep and medicine."

I nodded my agreement. Then a thought occurred to me. My brow furrowed. "So, Hannibal, how do you know all this?" I asked.

Hannibal's mouth quirked. "I subscribe to the *Northern Light* under Professor Saxon's name. She gets two papers delivered, and I slip one into my pocket when I get her coffee in the morning. She's so scattered, she doesn't even notice."

It was a terrible violation of the Schoolhouse rules, but it was bold and clever.

"It's not perfect in the way of information gathering," she went on. "I only subscribe to the Sunday edition, since serving her coffee every day like a servant would raise suspicion. I miss a lot of what goes on during the week. But most of the big news is recapped in the Sunday paper."

I nodded. "Ingenious. I would never have thought of that."

"Who are you kidding, Arika?" East Keep said. "Even if you had thought of it, you're too much of a toady to follow through." She glanced at the twins for confirmation and they giggled together.

I ignored them. "What I want to know is how the Record Keepers plan on addressing the legitimate concerns of the Rebels. The New Seed will help, but more is needed. They must demand funds from the Assembly."

Covington answered me. "It won't be easy to get all the Record Keepers to agree on anything. Corruption is rampant at Hasting and, unfortunately, some of the Kongo Senators are so terrified of being ousted, they'll flatly refuse to petition the Assembly for more money, or more fair Overseers. I suppose, once we get to Hasting, we can combat the bad Keepers."

"We'll have even more power if one of us manages to become Senator," Hannibal said. "Of course, that will depend on whether Hosea and Jones are politically aligned."

I lowered my eyes, and said nothing.

Covington nodded, agreeing with Hannibal. "*Obi Solomon* save us if Jones selects the Vine Keeper to be Senator, and he goes against the New Seed. If the New Seed doesn't pass, we're in danger—grave danger."

I shivered. "The failure of such a worker-friendly bill will give the Rebels all the ammunition they need to defeat us Record Keepers."

"Right," Hannibal said. "We've got to find some way of convincing all of the Second Brothers that there are enough good Keepers left to spare our lives. In the end, we all want the same things."

"Not all the same things," East Keep amended. "They want to take our seats, and we don't want any dirty ferals in the Assembly."

Hannibal looked pained but didn't disagree. She met my eyes and explained, "East Keep's right, actually. We want to keep the lines that separate the First and Second Brothers. More, the Rebels want to repeal the Rebirth and, generally, we're in favor of the pill."

"Not in its current state," Covington added. "We want more oversight and more research into why the Rebirth misfires."

"Botched erasure," I said, thinking of the workers I'd met in the village. "It's unconscionable and must stop."

Covington lowered her voice and leaned in. "I know I shouldn't say this, but when I consider the ills of the Rebirth, this mysterious fever and the work they do in the field—well, sometimes I'm not sure I blame the workers for rebelling."

My eyes locked with Covington's, and I felt myself nod ever so slightly. However, I remained silent. I'd already said as much as I dared. After several tense minutes, I took a deep breath. "So, why is Covington always at the head of the line?" I asked, changing the subject.

The twins exchanged an amused glance, and East Keep smothered a laugh.

Covington sighed. "They put me at the front because the person at the front of the line doesn't actually do any work."

I nodded, seeing that what she said was true. Because the ends of the line weren't connected. The person at the front, Covington, wouldn't have a head to style. And the person at the back, myself, wouldn't be treated. "Do you not like to braid?" I said, treading carefully. The tension between us was just dissipating and, despite my misgivings, I was having fun.

"Well, none of us *likes* to braid," Covington replied.

I pressed on. "So why don't you rotate positions, or shift the chairs closer?"

She crossed her arms defensively, mumbling something I couldn't hear.

All the girls burst into laughter. The twins were holding each other and wiping tears of mirth from their eyes.

"I don't get it," I said, but I was smiling in my curiosity.

East Keep recovered. "We don't rotate, because Covington's not allowed to touch anyone's hair—not anymore." She dissolved into laughter again.

"What is it?" I asked, laughingly.

Hannibal turned to me. "Remember that terrible bang West Keep had last year?"

I had no clue, but I nodded anyway.

"Well, she didn't exactly cut it on purpose. After Covington did her braids, her hair was so knotted that West Keep had no choice but to cut it."

One West Keep twin sobered, touching the front of her hairline. "It's really not all that funny. I had to take off nearly a foot of hair."

"Oh please, it wasn't that much," Covington scoffed.

"Who cares about what came off," the other twin said, wiping her eyes. "Do you remember what was left? It wouldn't curl back! It just hung there, straight as a sting, no matter what we did."

"She had to wear that scarf for three months," East Keep added. "Like an old-world movie star. What color was it?"

"Yellow. It was yellow," West Keep said, still fingering her injured scalp.

Her sister leaned over and gave her a hug. "But remember how Covington almost got caught by Jones when she tried to get you another color?" she said.

They smiled at each other. "Yes. She brought back every color of the rainbow, two of each shade."

"So we could both wear them," they said together. They'd told this story before.

I glanced at Covington. Her eyes, still red-rimmed, glowed as she surveyed the twins. "Eventually they forgave me," she said. "But now, no one trusts me anywhere in the line, except at the front."

Everyone laughed and the air in the room shifted, gently—to welcome me. Because it pleased her to boss me, I let East Keep choose my style for the next week.

"You'll see. A chignon will be perfect," she said.

My brow lifted. "How can you tell?"

"Well, first, it's simple and classic, like you."

I smiled.

"And also," she said, making a face, "it's low maintenance. Let's face it, after today, you probably won't even look at your hair until it needs twisting a month from now."

"Is it that obvious?"

Covington rolled her eyes. "Arika, you've literally had the same hairstyle since the first day of school. Neat braids pulled back into a giant, angry bun."

"So?"

"So," she went on, "that was ten years ago. None of us are as in vogue as East Keep, but you're off-the-charts nutty."

Everyone laughed.

I smiled good-naturedly. She had a point. "If it's that easy to do," I said, "then you should be able to fix it."

Covington paused, surprised. "I can do your hair?"

To prove I meant it, I scooted my chair so it was positioned in front of her.

The other girls sat frozen, looking between us. By my trusting their leader, we were all on the verge of a tentative truce.

I took a page from Covington's book. "What are you waiting for?" I said. "Shift!"

They jumped and adjusted themselves around in a circle.

"What if your hair knots?" one twin said.

"You'll have to cut it off!" said the other.

I shrugged one shoulder. "Bangs aren't so bad."

"But, what if you have to cut it *all* off? You'll look like a field hand."

I turned to East Keep, who had issued this challenge in patent disbelief. She was right. The long braids and twists we wore weren't only by preference. An old Schoolhouse rule, intended to separate us from the workers, required they shave their heads every year. Conversely, we were to keep at least two years of length.

I looked at Covington. "You know I'm a stickler for rules," I said.

She rolled her eyes. "I might have picked up on that."

"Then you'd better not muck this up."

She smiled, slowly. "I wouldn't dare."

THE BLACK BOOK

The drums played that night, for an unprecedented second time in one week. We paused the party, letting half-complete twists unravel, while we crowded around the window to squint into the night. Within minutes, the fugitive was surrounded by a group of workers. This time, they didn't let him go free.

I forced myself to watch as two dozen workers formed three beams of wood into a triangle. They hoisted the triangle up and supported each point on three more beams. A rope was slung over the structure and a noose coiled at the rope's end. Ten minutes later, the fugitive swung.

As I walked back to my room for the night, my scalp tight beneath the braids, I thought back to Martin's speech, so clear and articulate. With his red bandana and rousing message, everything about him had been sharp and intelligent—unimpaired. Was he now hanging beneath the moon, slain by his own Kongo brothers? And what had been his crime? Daring to suggest that individual Kongo lives were more important than the quota?

At my desk, I listened to the rumbling of my stomach as I made notes in Jones' black book. I listed all the facts I'd learned about Hosea and the Director. There weren't as many as I wanted, so I took the next hour to add my conjectures to the list. As I wrote, I saw Hosea's strange brown eyes on the page. My pen dropped twice from my shaking hand before the task was complete.

Even so, I refused to acknowledge the shame that nagged me. I told myself I had no choice but to report to Jones—my assignment was clear. More, to *really* change the Kongo for good, I had to make it to the Assembly. Which meant, I had to appease Jones.

Finished, I placed the book in a locked compartment of my desk alongside a small bag of dried orange wedges—a rare fruit in the Kongo. I took the bag out and held it to my nose. I'd gotten the treat as a reward from Teacher Rowan last fall. Instead of ripping into it that day, I'd decided to save it, to eat on my journey to Hasting. I closed and locked the compartment then took out a clean notebook. I had a promise to keep.

The details of my time in the village were already blurring around the edges but, starting at the top of the page, I recorded everything I could remember about the people I'd met there. I'd spoken to so many that their stories ran together. *Three and four grown men to a bed. Pregnant with one whilst nursing two. Can't remember my real name, but they call me Scamper. I don't eat much, weren't much to eat. Got erased twice that year, once more the next, for missing work. Had a good woman once, I believe, two Rebirths ago.*

Tears coursed down my cheeks as I wrote their tragic stories and remembered their faces. As desperate as they'd been, sick and dying, they had found reasons to laugh with each other, tossing out their precious recollections like dice. They had rolled out the village fool for a laugh. He was so stupid, they said, he thought every day was Sunday. He would sleep in until seven, waiting for worship, then hop up and race to the field. At twenty he'd been erased so often, as punishment for being late, that he was no longer good for anything but shoveling manure. The Guard wouldn't even have him. On and on—they'd laughed and hooted between coughs. Only I knew that such forgetfulness was a medical condition, most likely the result of a misfire.

I worked late into the night, hammering out a dozen stories. It wasn't easy. After a lifetime of Rebirths, the workers recalled their lives in bits and pieces. So, the act of recording was patchwork. We collected segments, here and there, and we made sense of them. No one understood why some memories were scattered, some were repressed and others lost entirely, but the English were constantly searching for an answer. They issued new and improved formulas every few years, but the wipe was never clean.

The workers nurtured their own set of beliefs concerning this. To them, the pieces that remained at the end of a lifetime were sacred and indestructible—morsels of their soul. Consequently, a letter from Hasting was, to them, an invitation to heaven. A pass to eternity, made even more precious by the fragmented life they'd lived.

I closed the notebook and got into bed, the teeth of the matter still sunk in my throat. I fell into an exhausted sleep filled with dreams—pale hands, dark faces, and memories of my old nursery.

THE SECOND TRIP TO THE VILLAGE

"Arika, come now," a voice said.

I jerked awake. A hand covered my mouth.

"It is I, William," he said. "Arika, come now."

I couldn't distinguish his face in the night, but his tone was unmistakable. Something was wrong.

I didn't stop to ask how he'd gotten into my room. I pushed his hand aside and whispered, "Get my shoes."

I donned my sandals and cloak and he scooped me up, one hand beneath my knees and one under my back. Instead of moving to my door, he went to my window—which was open! He must have scaled the Schoolhouse wall to get to me. I sat on the sill as he tied a rope around his waist and pulled me onto his back. I clung there as he climbed to the ground. He set me on my feet, then swept me up, high on his chest, and sprinted toward the village.

"Is it Fount?" I said, shouting as he ran. "Is Fount sick?"

As I said it, I realized that it was my worst fear.

"Many sick people," William said. "Arika need pray."

"Obi save us," I whispered.

He pressed my head against his neck.

After a few moments, a troublesome odor penetrated my panic—a scent I couldn't identify. "What's that smell?" I shouted.

At my words, his step faltered, and his tone, when he

answered, was grim. "Arika need pray," he said.

In the Schoolhouse we preferred logic to mystique. In personal study, I enjoyed the fables surrounding the ancient deities—Zeus, Jesus, and Pope in particular. They were amusing, if not particularly awe-inspiring. After all, none of them had had the power to stop humanity from nearly destroying itself in war.

The workers, in their ignorance, still believed in the divine. And their devil, Petro, was anything not derived from living matter. In essence, they worshipped creation, which, I supposed, was as noble an idol as any. It was out of respect for William, rather than religion, that I bowed my head that night. I hung my head and, for the first time in seventeen years, the first of many times to come, I prayed.

William's hair and brows were dusted with white powder as he set me on my feet in front of the sick house. The same substance floated in the air and collected in drifts on the ground. I held my palm out to catch a speckling of flakes.

"William," I said. "What is this?"

Slowly, he shook his head.

The flakes weren't cold and they smeared between my fingers. I looked up, shielding my eyes as the wind whipped a light blizzard above us. "It's not snow," I said. "What is it?"

Again, he shook his head, refusing to answer.

"William, please!" Fear tickled my dry throat.

He spoke reluctantly. "Many sick people."

I turned to the warehouse. It was quiet. The shutters were pulled tight. I remembered how, in my naiveté, I'd thought the sickness had smelled like fresh clean fish. Only later did I recognize the stench of blood. Speckled spots of mucus, coughed into the air by a roomful of dying people. The lucky ones were placed on tables, covered in blankets; the luckless had stiffened at our feet. Robin had borne the task of dragging the dead to the pyre.

Suddenly, it hit me. I'd seen the pyre's fire from afar as William had carried me across the meadow, but I'd failed to put the pieces together. I didn't look back to William for confirmation. I didn't have to—I knew. The persistent stench of a hundred burning brothers was inescapable. I covered my mouth but it seeped in, clogging my pores, scorching my eyes. I could taste it. I gagged, but my stomach was empty.

"Tell me about Fount," I gasped. I was down on my knees between bouts of nausea. "Is Fount—?"

Slowly, William shook his head.

"Oh no! *Obi, Obi!*" I jumped to my feet to run, but there was nowhere to go. I dug my nails into the flesh of my palm and slammed a fist against my mouth, splitting my lip. "My God, my God!"

"Arika. You hurt hand."

He grabbed my wrist but I jerked away. *Fount!*

"Arika, stop!" He pried my fist open and wrestled me to the porch steps.

Finally, I slumped, burying my face in my lap. He patted my back and hummed softly. It was the same short tune he'd sung as we'd nursed the sick in the village.

"Don't be mad at William," Robin said from behind us. "*I* sent him to find you."

I looked over my shoulder. She was standing in the open door of the warehouse. Behind her, the sick room was silent and dark.

I swiped at my tears. "What happened, Robin? How can this be?"

She looked as adrift as I felt.

"Are they all dead? All of them?"

Slowly, she nodded. "The first round of patients are gone, except Kiwi. He wants to speak to you first."

"Kiwi?" I said, rising. Hope bloomed inside me. Perhaps I could change his fate.

"Yes. He's inside, but you must hurry."

THE TRUTH ABOUT THE FEVER

Kiwi lay amidst the dead that littered the warehouse floor. His whole body labored to breathe and a viscous mix of blood and mucus covered his nose. After securing a black scarf around Kiwi's face, Robin tied my white mask.

I took Kiwi's hand. "Kiwi? It's me, Arika."

He took a shuddering breath.

"Robin!" I called over my shoulder. "He needs the ventilator!" I had used it several times before with great success. It would temporarily clear Kiwi's air passage.

She shook her head. "It's no good, Arika. I meant only for you to comfort him. Here, he'll take it from you." She held out a bottle of the sleeping draft.

I knocked it out of her hand. "Don't talk like that! He's going to live," I vowed. "We need a ventilator."

She and William exchanged a look. "I'll find one," she said and left.

I examined Kiwi. "I think it's his hair. The medicine can't get to his lungs." I called to William over my shoulder. "Find me a razor!"

He left without a word.

"Arika," Kiwi rasped.

I sat, and untied my *pallium*. "Hush now. We'll talk when you're better." I draped my cloak over his body, and he relaxed in my embrace.

My arm fell asleep where it held him. My breath caught between each of his.

After several minutes, he opened one eye. "Arika?"

"I'm here, Kiwi. We're waiting for the ventilator."

"No time," he said. "I got to speak. Sit me up, girl."

"Not now. Now, you rest," I urged.

"Up!" he insisted. "If I lay back, the memory will leak from my ears."

"Leak from your—?" I gave a choked laugh and wiped away a tear. "Oh, Kiwi." Hugging him close, I shifted my legs and maneuvered his frame until his upper body was propped on my crossed legs. He rested there a moment.

"I came as soon as possible, Kiwi."

He nodded. "I say to myself, I must tell Arika. I must not leave it untold."

"You mean your story from earlier is unfinished?" I said, finally understanding why I'd been called instead of Hosea. "You have more to say." Seeing he was determined to speak, I propped him higher on my knees, so the words would come easier. "Is that better?"

He nodded, forced a deep breath, then spoke. "I remember when I was a boy; I was not yet in the field. Too small, no use for the quota, see? My brothers—we ran naked, like chickens. We got some clothes, if we were lucky. But we were not much lucky. I had no pants," he confessed. "Just a shirt I wore like a dress and my brothers—they poke at me. *Kiwi is a woman!* I had no shoes, but they said nothing about this. Only about the dress—*Kiwi is a woman!*"

My heart clenched, hearing the shame in his voice.

Kiwi went on. "So one night, we sneak out and look for

clothes. We did this many nights, but each night, I came back with only my dress. Then, one day, we saw a pair of britches hanging from a clothespin. *Boy-o!* I had them britches on like *that*." He wheezed out a chuckle. "They fit too big. I tied them up with rope. But, I had pants."

He wheezed for a while then cleared his throat. "Night came, and my brothers—they go to look for more. They call me to come, but I said, 'No thanks.' I was happy with my pants, see? Too happy, I think."

"How can you be too happy?" I asked.

A fat tear rolled from one eye to the fold of his black mask. "When you forget you have no shoes," he said. "That is when you are too happy."

I nodded slowly, sensing a flicker of truth in his words, but failing to digest it.

"My brothers did not ask me to come again. And so, for years, until I took to the field, I had no shoes. My feet bruised up and I stubbed my toe until the blood ran." He nodded to the mangled mess of his feet, one foot with four toes.

I winced.

"Arika, please, when you write my story, write this first: in my next life, we must remember to be miserable. We must make a terrible fuss. Fuss until we got all three. Shirt, pants—" He choked and held up three fingers.

"I understand. Shirt, pants, and shoes. I got it, Kiwi. I've got it written down."

He began to cough, making a soft pecking noise that, I knew, signified death.

William came with a straight-edge razor.

"It's no good," I said, holding back tears. "He's moving too

247

much. We need a ventilator! Where is Robin!?"

William sat down and hummed softly as I supported Kiwi's upper half. Suddenly, I had an idea. "There's a technique I read about," I said. "Hurry, William! Help me lay him down."

"What you do?"

Grunting, I lifted Kiwi's head from my lap. In my hurry, my neat chignon loosened and my hair fell to my waist. "I'm going to breathe for him," I said.

William looked skeptical.

"Please, just help me." I took off my white mask and removed Kiwi's black scarf.

"*Arika*," William said, his voice low.

Ignoring his warning, I ordered him again to help me. William obeyed. He held Kiwi's weight while I positioned the old man flat on the ground. After, William held my hair as I bent over to squeeze Kiwi's nose shut. When he stopped coughing, I blew into his mouth. Nothing happened. I tried again, and his chest rose. He twitched, and gave a harsh cough. Something cold landed on my chin, and I wiped it away, ignoring the smell. "Look, he coughed. It's working!"

William nodded, grimly.

I managed to prolong Kiwi's life by an hour as my knees grew cold, then painful. My legs went numb, and the difference between Kiwi's breath and mine shrank to nothing. At some point, my back seized. William pushed me aside and took over. I retook my position as soon as I could—breathing and blowing, barely using the air before giving it over. I did this until two strong hands took my shoulders and pulled me away.

It was Hosea. "Arika. He's gone."

"No!"

"He is, look! You're prolonging his suffering." He forced my chin up.

Kiwi's skin had a ghastly hue. The truth was plain. Every breath he took, slight and irregular, was numbered. Without my help, it was already a thin whistle. Seconds later, his ghostly bellows haunted the room. Robin, who stood over us, blocked the noise with her palms and left. At my nod, William went to comfort her.

Kiwi lived for twenty-five minutes, panting like a dog, so I thought his chest would cave in. And then, with a gasp, he died.

•

"Where are the tables?" I said. I draped a sheet of blood-speckled cloth over Kiwi's furred torso.

Hosea took a breath. "Why do you need a table?"

"I want to lay Kiwi out and wash his body on a table. I can get water, but someone moved the tables." I sounded lost, even to my own ears.

Hosea stood. "I don't have time to move a table back in here. Besides, they're all in use."

"Fine, I'll check the abandoned huts." I stood, determined. "I'll move it myself, or William will help."

"William is busy, Arika, and so is Robin. We're all needed in the other sick rooms."

I bristled at his tone. He hadn't called me *brat*, but he might as well have. Suddenly, his words registered. "What do you mean, *other sick rooms*?"

"You might as well know. In the last few hours, the fever has spread. There is no single sick room. We're urging the sick to avoid the streets." He swiped a hand across the lower half of his face. "They bring the dead here to await the pyre."

"How many are sick?" I demanded.

He resisted.

"Hosea!"

"A fifth of the village at last count, but the number is rising."

I covered my mouth. "I thought you said it was under control."

"I never said that—you assumed. There's no way to contain a fever without knowing how it spreads."

"How did you stop it in the Vine?"

"I didn't. It died out."

"And at Point Landing?"

"Before I left, I'd lost count. And then the fire…" His voice trailed off.

"*Obi,* Hosea. What do we do?"

To my horror, he began to count the likely survivors on one hand. "Well, you and I will live. The fever spreads like fire. If we haven't gotten it now, we likely won't succumb. Robin and William seem to be immune too. Everyone else…"

I reeled away before he could say more. I hurried to the door, tripping over the dead. "There has to be something we can do."

Outside, the streets were piles of ash; the air was suffocating. I flung an arm across my face, shielding my nose. I stumbled to the nearest hut. I leapt the steps, threw open the door and gasped, falling backwards.

There were four of them. An old mother and a nest of three, curled together in the last stage of the fever. The door cracked against the adjacent wall and their heads turned. Caught in their stare—I froze, and I watched. And I listened. Their eyes spoke volumes.

Hosea was there. "Arika, you're not well."

I tuned him out, straining to hear their tales. The themes were pain, and confusion. Short stories with tragic endings. A *crack* sounded in my head and a deluge of other images poured forth. In the kitchen—malnourished children with bloated bellies, heads too big for their bodies. Blank eyes—*not content at all*—but dull with misery. Dark skin marred with ropes of scars. I'd averted my eyes—diligently. But, somehow, I had seen. Evidence had been mounting for years.

"Arika? Let me take you home."

I shook him off. "I've *got* to do something," I realized.

"There's nothing we can do," he said.

"There is!" I insisted. "I can breathe for them, like with Kiwi!"

"Not all of them, Arika."

"Then one!" I was in a frenzy. "Please, Hosea, we have to try."

"Arika."

I took handfuls of his shirt and shook as hard as I could. "*We have to try!*"

•

He let me have my way, however misguided. We moved from house to house. He tended with medicine and, when he couldn't treat them, I knelt and breathed for them, mouth to mouth. They would puff out broken pieces of story that made little sense to me—but I persisted. Kneeling, breathing, blowing. Blowing, breathing, kneeling, until it felt like all I ever breathed for was to breathe for another. I recalled how confident I'd been when I'd first come to the village. I'd entered the sick room with the giant at my side. I'd felt certain, with my quill and pad, that I could make it better.

It's good that I didn't know then how it would end. If I had seen the truth, I might have guessed the worst part. Not my aching knees, or the smell of blood—spilling and soaking. Not the shallow catch of a family gasping for air, like fish out of water. Not even the taste of their dead mouths—like cold salt cod.

No, the worst part for me was not being able to fix it! At that time, I imagined knowledge was force. My faith said I could manage my world through wit. I was valedictorian, all-powerful. And yet that night, I could not fix the fever. No matter how I breathed for them, they died terribly one by one, gasping. Realizing that I could not save my people—that was the worst part. It upset my faith and made me fear, in my gut, that I could not save myself.

"I need more medicine," he said in my ear, between Houses. "I'm running low."

I turned to him. He was spotted all over with blood. "Can you get more?"

"I can make more, but there's not time. And besides, it's not enough. They need something stronger, decongestants and antibiotics."

My eyes went wide. "Medicine from the North."

He nodded, grimly.

We both knew that was impossible. It wasn't that English doctors weren't compassionate toward Kongo people, but a sick Kongo man was of absolutely no use to America. Which was to say, he was of no use at all—just another mouth to feed. An English doctor would be obligated to put the sick worker down, for the greater good.

Suddenly, I stopped walking.

Hosea traveled on a few steps then looked back at me. "What's wrong?" he asked.

I bit my lip, testing the train of my thoughts. "I just had an idea."

He came back. "What is it?"

"A few sick workers are in danger of being put down. But, at this stage, the fever is an epidemic. It's already killed hundreds, and it's spreading." My eyes searched his. "Do you see what that means? If we don't save them, who'll finish the planting? Who'll bring in the harvest? At this point, medicine *is* the greater good."

He caught on quickly. "I see what you're getting at, but no one would—"

"I can talk to Jones!" I said, not letting him dissuade me. "She'll intercede in the Assembly! Explain the logic! I can *make* her understand!"

He scoffed. "Jones doesn't care about logic or the greater good. She cares about herself. I doubt she'll even listen, unless there's something in it for her."

I thought of the black book in my desk—my ticket, my currency. "I have something she wants," I said.

"What is it?"

I couldn't meet his eyes. "Information. She trusts me to spy for her."

He looked appalled. "You would work with Jones again? Spy for her, even now? Arika, listen to yourself."

"I *am* listening!"

His mouth curled in disgust. "If you go to her, I'll leave today, at first light. With the pyres going all night, she's sure to know about the fever. But, as you can see, she's done nothing to help. If you go to her now, you'll be no better than her—worse! You'll be a—" He broke off.

Workers gathered on their porches to watch our argument.

"Go ahead, say the word!" I shouted. I pushed at his chest. "Say it!"

"Say what?"

"Say I'm a traitor! That's what you're thinking, isn't it? That's what you all think. But you're wrong, my information is going to buy medicine—and save the people!"

"Don't do it, Arika. There are other ways."

"Wrong!" I roared. I pulled at the sleeve of my blouse. It ripped and slid down, revealing the four crescent scars on my upper arm.

"I don't understand, what are those supposed to mean?"

My eyes were bright and open too wide. "Don't you see, Hosea? They mean we have to play by her *rules*. It's the only way to get any power. And power is the *only* way to *stay safe*!"

He looked confused, but I couldn't explain—there wasn't time. I turned on my heel, picked up my skirt and, for the first time in ten years, I ran.

THE SENATOR

After I survived the Pit and that first beating, I limped away from the cracked window and followed Headmistress Jones. She flexed her hand as she walked with satisfied strides, back down the wood-paneled hall. Holding my aching ribs, I kept my gaze on my feet. We went down a wide staircase and through an airy room. We walked another long hall and rounded a corner before starting down the same wide set of stairs. Realizing we'd walked in a circle, I raised my head. The airy room we passed through not five minutes before was below—a dining room. Every student in the Schoolhouse was present for supper.

Seeing them, I faltered, but Jones kept walking, intending to parade me through the gawking crowd—*again.*

Students turned to stare as we marched down the center aisle. Their pity poked at my mortified features. We passed several Teachers, including one with raspberry-red hair who frowned sympathetically.

Finally, we left the audience behind and marched on. My relief was short-lived. After a series of turns, I saw that we were, once again, heading to the wide staircase for a third showing.

Just then, a woman appeared at the top of the steps. Seeing

Jones, she started our way. The seams of her purple and gold robes were stitched with emerald-green thread. Heavy animal claws hung at her neck and ears and a single bone studded with tiny lavender gemstones pierced her nose. As she neared, I saw she was not an unusually tall student, as I first suspected from her coloring. She was too old. I picked apart her features. Large eyes, but not like the Clayskin maids. Too dark to be English. So, by default, she was Kongo. Only, she was *not* a worker. She moved upright with uncompromising strides.

She stopped before us.

"Senator Osprey," Jones said.

The dark-skinned woman nodded stiffly. "Teacher Jones." Her tone was authoritative.

Jones smiled tightly, tugged at the shirt of her uniform. "As you know, Senator, I was promoted this year. I'm now Headmistress of the Schoolhouse. *Headmistress* Jones."

"Director Kumar informed us of the change."

Hidden behind Jones' bulk, I gulped. She was, clearly, displeased by the *change*.

"What brings you to House Cobane?" Jones said. Her words strained through clenched teeth.

The dark woman gestured to her right and, suddenly, I saw the raspberry-haired English Teacher was with her. The Teacher's curls frizzled about her head like magenta feathers. "I'm meeting with Teacher Saxon about her technology course proposal," the dark woman said.

Teacher Saxon smiled weakly, twisting her fingers together in an anxious knot.

Headmistress Jones glared openly, her eyes hard with hatred. The dark-skinned woman didn't flinch. "Teacher Saxon!"

Saxon jumped. "Yes, Senator."

"Take this student to the infirmary."

My mouth fell open. I looked around, confirming what I knew. *I* was the only student present. I gazed back at the woman as Teacher Saxon hurried me away. Her bedecked neck, dark and strong, went on. Inch after inch. She was tall enough to look down on all of us.

When we were out of earshot, I whispered. "Who *was* that?"

"That was Senator Osprey," Teacher Saxon said.

"A Record Keeper?"

"More—she is a Kongo Senator."

So, she was Kongo—like me! "How—how did she—?"

Teacher Saxon bent so our eyes were level. "After Director Kumar," she said, "Senators are the most powerful people in the Kongo."

My breath caught. *Power*, immune to reclassification—*safe forever.* "Could I?"

She shrugged. "If you excel in your studies, then yes, one day you can aspire to a seat in the Senate. But—"

"I can do it," I said, bullishly.

She shook her head, making her bright spirals shimmy. "You're behind, Arika. And Teacher Jones—"

"I can do it," I repeated. "I'll be the *best* student ever."

Saxon's hand lingered on my cheek as she straightened. We never spoke of Senator Osprey again.

THE GAMBLE

Ignoring Hosea's shout, I ran from the village, ripping the hobbled skirt of my *aura* as I crossed the meadow. I stopped at the Schoolhouse gate just as the sun peeked over the horizon on Sunday morning. Heaving for breath, I crawled under the loose fence post and circled the porch. I was sweaty and dirty, and I took the stairs two at a time. At my desk, I withdrew the black book and sat down to write.

Minutes later, I cleaned myself and dressed properly. Book in hand, I left my room and wound my way around the Schoolhouse to Teacher Jones' office. It opened just as I stopped, before I could knock! Terrified, I froze. All the light in the world seemed to flicker on and off. *She'd known I was coming.*

•

"Come in, girl."

Seeing that I wasn't followed, she shut the door. "You were to contact me tomorrow," she hissed.

I forced myself to meet her stare. "I came to give you this, Teacher." I held up the black book.

"You fool. I told you Monday. Monday, not Sunday."

"Yes, Teacher, but the matter is imperative."

Her eyes bored into mine.

I didn't dare blink.

"Hand it here."

I placed the book in her outstretched hand and let out a breath. It was finished. There, in her grip, she had it all. My life, the lives of my peers, Hosea and the village. If information was currency, I was now bankrupt.

If someone had told me yesterday that, today, I would give up everything in exchange for medicine for the village, I would have laughed.

Now, as I watched her read, I knew something inside me had changed. For Sky and Fount, I would give everything ten times over. I bit my lip, tasting blood. *Would it be enough?* I had added more to the book about Hosea and the Director. They were of special interest to her.

Then, for extra credit, I'd added information she hadn't asked for. Details about Saxon and Rowan. I often overheard them discussing Jones. Old Teacher Purnell gossiped when she crafted late at night. With only me for company, she let many treasonous morsels slip. I'd tattled every disloyal word. Covington's boyfriend, Jetson's political leanings, Hannibal's newspaper scheme. It was all there for Jones' consumption.

Faces spiraled around me accusingly. *Traitor*, they whispered. My throat clenched. It was true. I was a rat. But I held my shoulders stiff beneath their disdain. I forced my head high. All that mattered was gaining her trust and using it to save my family. I pictured them in the field, even now, bringing in the quota. Their brightly colored scarves every color of the Kongo: burgundy, spice, indigo, teal, coconut, grape—and brown.

Finally, Jones set the book on her desk. "You mentioned time-sensitive information, Arika."

"Yes." I cleared my throat. This was my opportunity. "It's

come to my attention that the fever I wrote about is spreading out of control. It's killed hundreds of workers, and many more are sick. If we don't intervene and tell the Assembly, the fever will decimate the workforce. The Seed planted now will die, and all of America will suffer."

"Your point, girl?" Her voice was colder than I expected.

"I—I want to make a bargain, I'll give you my service and allegiance. With my marks, I'm an excellent candidate for the open Senator seat in the Assembly. I'll have the power to cast any vote you like. I can even gather votes—get more information. I'll do anything you want."

She turned her back to me, facing the small window in her office. Through it, the morning sun grew hotter every minute. "And what do you want in return in this—bargain?" she asked.

I plowed forth. "I need you to petition the Assembly. I need medicine from the North. Decongestants and antibiotics."

There it was. I had done my part. Gotten her information. Kept her secrets. I was her perfect pet. I had *assimilated*, groveled, drooled on command. I'd horded her goodwill knowing, one day, I would need it. Today, with the taste of blood still on my lips, was that day.

She was silent for a long time, her gaze shifting back and forth—from the new dawn to the tower of polished plaques on the adjacent wall. When she spoke, her tone was pleasant. "I, too, was valedictorian; did you know?"

Uncertain, I remained quiet. The sun was cresting over the high peaks to the east, awakening the room inch by inch.

Jones went on. "I was at the top of my class in a better university than this school could ever dream of being." Her mouth puckered around the word *school*. "I was valedictorian, but the *boy* under me was chosen for the Assembly. And the three imbecile *boys* after him were chosen too. But not me, no, I was told to complete a teaching certificate. Do you know why?"

I stayed quiet.

"Do you?" she hissed.

"No, Teacher."

"Of course you don't." She crossed her arms. "English women aren't allowed to speak in the Assembly, Ms. Cobane. If we want power, we must take it. *We're* forced take it, but you—you Kongo *bitch!*" The word burst forth like the punchline of a joke, then she ducked her head and laughed. "I bested them all and yet, here I am, entertaining bargains—with dogs."

Her head came up. A muscle ticked in her jaw. Heavy cords bulged in her neck. Worse, her eyes—so glassy I saw my reflection. Not the teacher's pet, I realized, too late—no, never that. Nothing so cherished. I was not a pet, but a pawn.

She picked up her steel-lined ruler. "Do you remember your assignment, Arika?"

The horror of my error crashed over me. I stepped back.

"You were to earn the Vine boy's trust and report back to me everything he said." The ruler *snapped* against the palm of her hand.

I stepped back. A spout of fear gushed up, pooling behind my knees.

"Instead, I hear the pair of you were playing nursemaid."

I stepped back. "I—I helped because the fever posed a danger to our cause—*our* cause. You must see the logic. I thought—"

Snap. "Your job, Ms. Cobane, is to execute my thoughts, not question them."

"But the harvest—"

"Is secure!" She finished. "We saw to it weeks ago. Your task was to infiltrate Director Kumar's inner circle via the boy— the boy! That was your job." She strode forward.

I scrambled back until my shoulder blades touched the far wall. Then I slipped into the darkness.

She'll beat you like nothing for this. More 'cause you've made her wait. Never forget, she likes to see the marks.

"Look at me!"

I tried! I tried to see her, to dodge what I knew was coming— no good. Her first blow drove me to the ground.

She kicks like a donkey.

I curled up and covered my head, protecting my vitals as she vented her rage.

She knelt down, peeled my hands from my skull and hit me in the ear. I heard something *pop*. I covered my temple. She seized my hand, pushing the little finger sideways. *Snap!*

"I said, look at me!"

My overwrought senses obeyed. I saw her in vibrant color: her red face, her blue eyes, her crystal-clear excitement.

"The Assembly is three weeks away from passing the most significant piece of legislation the new world has ever seen," she spat in my face. "The only thing capable of defeating us is Dana Kumar. My job is to find out what insurrection he's planning. Yours, you stupid beast, was to find out whose side he's on!"

She punched me viciously then threw my hand down. I whimpered. She dragged me to my feet, kicked a chair forward and pushed me into it.

"Now, listen to me, girl. The New Seed is already in the

ground." She slapped me. I felt my lip split. "Are you listening?" I nodded vigorously but my finger throbbed and spots dotted my vision. She snatched my hand up and squeezed, forcing my loose knuckle into place. I screamed, fully alert.

"The New Seed is already in the ground," she repeated.

Her words penetrated. *The New Seed is in the ground?* "I don't understand," I said.

She shoved her face close to mine. "The first batch of New Seed was ready at the first of the year. The workers have been planting it for days now. It's done, and there's nothing anyone can do to reverse it."

I shook my head. She lied. Surely she lied.

"Now you're listening," she growled. "The harvest will flourish with or without the workers. Your fever merely saves us the trouble of extinguishing that which is now of no use to America."

I closed my eyes, resisting the import of her words. The New Seed! How had I not seen its inevitable consequence before? Without a harvest to tend, the workers were of little use to America. Their role would be diminished and the strict efficiency of the Compromise would demand that the population of workers be controlled to avoid waste.

"But the bill hasn't passed," I said, logically, trying to think past the pain in my hand. "It's illegal to plant the Seed without Assembly approval."

"Which is why the bill must pass, to ratify the progress we've already made. We'll keep fifty percent of the workers to harvest. The rest will be useless mouths to feed. Once the Kongo undergoes population control, America will have the space we need to expand our research facilities into the south. The Assembly will have no choice but to utilize their top

English talent, male *or* female, to ensure success." She clasped her hands. "The future is here!"

I recalled the greedy gleam of Rowan's tone as she'd professed a similar sentiment. "You and Rowan are on the same side," I guessed.

"She doesn't know it, as I've remained loyal to Dana in public. But yes, we are both in support of the New Seed."

I thought of the twins and East Keep. "What will happen to the Keepers?"

"Your class will live."

"And the new students transferred from the nursery?"

"Less to train, less to feed. Resources are scarce, girl." She sniffed. "You're not suggesting we keep them?"

I gripped my hand.

"Arika!"

"No," I whispered. "They must die." At that moment, Fount's face materialized before me. I bit my lip as something inside me collapsed.

Jones paced. "You've made a mess of things, but there's a chance to redeem yourself." She turned on her heel. "The Vine boy has knowledge that we need. I'd bet on it. You'll stay with him. Go wherever he goes. Get to the Director and learn what his plans are for the New Seed vote."

"That's impossible. Hosea hates me. He'll never trust me again."

"You'd better hope that's not the case. If you're of no use to me, you'll be the first to perish."

My chin sank to my chest.

"The vote takes place in three weeks, just after the Final Exam. When I have what I need, you may take the test and

I'll ensure you become a Senator." She sat behind her desk and removed a clear jar from a drawer. It contained a silver hairpin.

"If you have to leave Cobane, so be it, but you must come back in three weeks. If you're not back, I'll have you arrested. If you're caught before then, don't let them take you alive. Do you understand?"

I nodded. I knew too much to be questioned by anyone not under her influence.

"If they come for you, jab the point of that pin into your flesh." She pushed the vial toward me. "Be sure to break the skin. It will be over in seconds. Is that clear?"

I stared, barely breathing. There was only one thing to say. "Yes, Teacher. It's clear."

THE FALLOUT

Jetson found me in my room. "I've been looking for you," he said. He stepped inside and closed the door. "Why are you packing?"

"You didn't knock," I said, keeping my face down. "You're not allowed in here without written permission from a Teacher. Produce a pass, or leave."

"I'm not leaving. We had a fight, but I'm still your friend."

My chest constricted. "I didn't ask for your friendship, Jetson."

"You didn't have to, Arika. Are you going somewhere?"

His eyes were boring into the back of my skull.

"You told me before that you needed one night," Jetson said. "Then you would answer all of my questions."

I went to my desk and began riffling around blindly, opening and closing drawers. I had to get through the next hour. Just this one hour, then I would face the next.

Jetson went on. "If you think you can't trust me, you're wrong. I'm just about the only one you *can* trust."

I took out ink, several quills, and a new notebook. I placed them in my bag and pulled the straps shut, cinching them tightly. A piece of *bambi* broke off in my bandaged palm and the throb in my little finger intensified.

"Is this what you really want—to be alone? If so, tell me and I'll leave."

Tears dropped from my eyes. "Oh, Jetson, do you really believe any of us can get what we *want*?"

"Not here, with Jones watching our every move, but at Hasting." He came up behind me, trying to pull me around. "A change is coming. The New Seed will usher in a new age for the Kongo. We'll make a bid for more power in the Assembly. We might even—well, Covington was talking about reinstituting marriage."

My heart cramped. "Oh, Jetson!" I turned, revealing my damaged face.

He shrank back. There was only one person capable of such violence. "What did you do to her?"

"Nothing," I said. "Don't you see? You were right. It's not logical. It doesn't make sense. We have no control, and we never will. This is what we get when we *bid for power.*"

"Did she find out you were in the village? Did that scum from the Vine tell her?"

I turned away, seeing he would never understand. He still believed Hosea was the problem. He still believed there was a solution. "It's not Hosea's fault," I said. "Jones already knew I was there. She knew everything."

"It's *his* fault you were there in the first place. You shouldn't have gone."

I thought about that. If I hadn't gone to the village, I would never have met Kiwi, Sky, Fount, or the others. I would not have tried to save them. I would be at my desk now, studying. The black book, in my secret compartment, would be ready to give to Jones in the morning. I would still have a perfect record and the illusion of safety that it brought me.

"What are you thinking?" Jetson asked. "And where are you

going? Please, just tell me." His eyes pleaded. They were the sunny color of fresh-cut grass. Soon, news of how I'd betrayed him and the others would spread, and he would never look at me this way again. I don't know why I did what I did next. Maybe I was grateful.

I set my bag down and stepped into his arms. I put my hands on his chest and stretched up. I placed my mouth on his.

•

After a while, a knock sounded on the door.

"I pulled my mouth away. "Someone's at the door."

His mouth curved in a soft, silly smile.

"The door," I said, tugging at his arm. "Someone's at the door. You have to get in the closet."

He snapped to attention. "Who is it?"

"I don't know. Just get in there—and stay." I pushed him toward the closet. "Promise you won't come out."

"Fine." He stepped into the closet.

"Promise," I insisted.

"I promise."

I shut the door and hurried across the room. If Jones was knocking, she wouldn't wait long. I wanted her attention as far from Jetson as possible. The knock sounded again.

"I can hear you breathing, Cobane. Open the door."

Hosea! He was here! He'd said he would leave at first light. I had been prepared to chase him across the Kongo. I opened the door. Dressed in black *bambi*, he was ready for travel. His eyes were rimmed with sleeplessness. "You're still here," I said.

He stepped in, forcing me backward. "Not for long. What in hell happened to you?"

"It's nothing. How is the village?"

"No better. But, no worse—no thanks to you," he added. He was murderously mad, but he withdrew ointment from his bag. "Sit down. I'll see to your wounds."

I moved to my desk and sat as he ministered.

"I assume Jones didn't like what you had to offer."

Acutely aware of Jetson's presence in the closet, I chose my words carefully. "I tried to help. You may not have liked my methods, but I tried."

He didn't answer. He wore a strange expression. Half pity, half something else I couldn't identify. Was it guilt, or was that my own heart projecting onto him? He moved with stiff, impersonal motions. He hated me. How would I convince him to bring me back into the fold, even closer than I'd been before? How would I convince him to take me with him from Cobane? I was caught in indecision when he wrapped a hand around my wrist.

"Cobane, you're coming with me."

My jaw dropped.

"I'm taking you to Director Kumar."

I couldn't believe my ears. Had he read my mind? "Wha— you're taking me to the Director? Why would you do that?"

"He's ordered it, and I owe him a favor. He'll determine what's to be done with you."

I balked. "I don't understand. What does he want with a student? How does he know my name?"

"I don't know."

"Hosea Khan, you're lying!" I accused. The lie was written all over his face. "Tell me what he wants," I demanded.

"Let it go, Cobane. It makes no difference. He wants you.

You can come with me peacefully, so that others won't be hurt. Or, you can fight."

I gritted my teeth. He was offering me exactly what I wanted, access to Director Kumar. And, with his grip tightening on my wrist, I needn't even feel guilty. He was begging me to spy! I could get Jones' information and return in time for the Final Exam. I could leave for Hasting and maybe, as a Senator, I could find a way to fix the Kongo. It was perfect, but the urge to flee overwhelmed me. I didn't want to work for Jones. And I didn't want to betray him, or anyone, ever again. I jumped from the chair.

I made it halfway to the door.

He caught me by the arm. "I was hoping you wouldn't do that, Cobane." He pulled me back and tied my wrists with a strip of *bambi*.

Suddenly, I remembered Jetson. He would no doubt try to rescue me. I had to apologize to Hosea, tell him that no one had to be hurt. I opened my mouth, just as Hosea stuffed a balled bandage between my teeth. *Obi—no!*

He pushed the cloth back, close to my throat. "Don't try to talk, or dislodge it. You'll only hurt yourself." He tied a strip of cloth over my mouth to hold the gag in place. He bent to lift me over his shoulder. The closet door slammed open.

No! The full force of Jetson's body slammed us to the floor.

Jetson bounded to his feet. He grabbed my arm, pushed me onto the bed, and moved to face Hosea. Jetson's entire body was tensed for battle. "You'll never take her from here."

No! He would be hurt, and it was my fault. I kicked, trying to get his attention.

If Hosea was surprised by Jetson's ambush, he didn't show

it. He stood straight, his hands spread at his sides. "I want no quarrel with you, Jetson."

"Then don't try to take Arika from Cobane."

Hosea nodded to my packed bag. "As you can see, she was on her way out."

"Not with you, she wasn't."

"Are you sure about that?"

"Arika would never risk expulsion. If she was leaving, you were making her."

Hosea moved, suddenly, faster than my eyes could register. When he was still again, his weapon was in his palm.

No! I kicked, but they ignored me.

"Go ahead—ask me what it is," Hosea said, displaying the small tube on the flat of his palm.

Jetson's jaw jutted. Tension radiated from his back.

"It's a weapon," Hosea supplied.

"It's not going to stop me from protecting Arika."

"Be assured, brother, it *is* going to stop you," Hosea said. "The only question is how much suffering you'll have to endure."

"I'm not your brother."

"You're not my enemy."

"Yet you come at me with that." He nodded toward the device.

"Only to show you how futile resistance will be." Hosea moved and the tube rolled over to rest on the back of his hand. He made a quick fist, bumping it into the air. Like magic, the flat circles at either end of the tube lengthened into snub points. The points peeled back, and pushed outward again and again, sharpening with each revelation. When the device was four times its original size and glinting, it rested. The whole process had taken less than a second. "Do you need to see more?" Hosea asked.

Jetson raised his fists and hunkered down. "You're not leaving with her," he insisted.

I groaned deep in my throat.

"So be it." Hosea tightened his fist, and the spear lengthened, sharpening further. The points at either end were razor sharp. "This position is for hand-to-hand combat. Or, if I don't want to get too close, I can do this." He flipped the daggered spear into the air. It curved into a longbow. A glowing blue string shot from either end of the bow and connected in the middle, sending off sparks. He caught the bow just above his head. With his arm straight out and the longbow extended on either side of his hand, he hooked the blue string with two fingers. As he drew back, a blue arrow formed in the half-moon arc of the bow. The further he pulled, the larger the arrow grew, until, finally, its blue feathers quivered in the air by his ear.

"This arrow is pure energy," he said. "If it pierces your skin, its force will rip you apart at your most basic level. Your cells will combust." He let the arrow fly toward the closet door. Blue veins laced out from the point of impact and the door burst, scattering in a million directions.

A fine mist of wood dust settled over my face. I'd seen enough. I rolled onto my stomach and struggled to my feet. Jetson blocked my path, but I dodged him to stand behind Hosea.

"He's not taking you!" Jetson cried. His eyes skated, searching for his next move.

Just then, someone tapped at the door. I turned—*Covington!* She stepped inside, dressed in an intricately embroidered *aura* and blouse. The brassy length of her hair was piled atop her head. As always, the steep slope of her nose was offset by her tendency to point it toward the ceiling.

"You don't want to be here, Covington," Jetson said, glancing between her and Hosea's bow.

"To the contrary, Jetson, I do. Now hush!" She smiled, looking like a fox. She closed the door and sauntered toward us. "I couldn't help but overhear your dilemma."

"He's the one with a dilemma," Jetson said.

Covington smirked. "Oh, Jetson. Don't be a cliché as well as a fool. Arika isn't worth it."

Jetson's eyes narrowed. "Whose side are you on?"

"Your side," she said.

"Well, I'm on Arika's side."

She tilted her head. "And have you asked her whose side she's on?"

Jetson didn't respond.

"I thought not." She flicked a disrespectful finger toward Hosea's weapon. "That *thing* won't be necessary."

Hosea hesitated a moment, then dropped his arms. By the time they rested at his side, the bow was, once again, a metallic tube.

Covington licked her lips. "Now, move away from her."

He didn't budge.

"*Obi Solomon*, not you too! I'm not going to hurt her. I just want Jetson to see her face, so he knows I'm not lying."

Hosea looked over his shoulder at me.

I dropped my gaze and nodded. I knew what was coming and I knew I deserved it. I couldn't stop myself from trembling as he took my arm and guided me forward.

"That's better," Covington said, icily. She never liked me, but at least she had respected me. Now, I'd lost even that small affection. I'd wheedled my way into their circle only to betray them—again.

"What's this about?" Jetson said, looking between us.

Covington thrust her face close to my cheek, almost kissing me. "This is about Hannibal in the Pit," she answered.

Her words struck me like a blow, and I bent at the waist. *No!* Jetson jerked. "Hannibal is in the Pit? Why?"

"Why exactly." Her voice shook. "Why is Hannibal in the Pit, Arika? Hannibal is the best of us. She never has a bad word for anyone, even when they deserve it."

I rolled my shoulders forward, trying to stave off the guilt.

"Explain yourself—now!" Jetson shouted.

She met his gaze. "There's nothing to explain. She's in the Pit and your precious Arika put her there. She told Jones that Hannibal stole newspapers, and Jones had her room searched. There was twenty months of evidence. So, she'll have twenty days, without food, in the Pit."

My head flew up. I found Covington's eyes and accused her silently. *You lie!* Most people didn't last twenty hours in the Pit. With ten days, I held the record. I emerged a shell, but I'd emerged. Twenty days was a death sentence.

"The hell you say?" Jetson took Covington by the arms and shook her.

Her face crumpled and tears welled in her eyes. "It's true, every word."

Jetson let her go and ran both hands across his face. "Arika? Tell me she's lying."

Instead of answering, I cowered inside my own body. If

Covington spoke the truth, Hannibal was gone forever—and I had killed her.

He didn't ask again.

From the fog that seemed to engulf me, I heard him speak to Hosea. "You can take her. She's yours."

PART THREE

THE KONGO

I am not the One, but
One is coming—mightier than I.
OBI SOLOMON

THE DESERT

Determined to deliver me to Director Kumar, Hosea carried my unconscious body across the Cobane perimeter and into the wild Kongo desert. The minute I awoke, every moment of the past two days washed over me. Accusations blared and Covington's last words made me wish I was dead. *Why is Hannibal in the Pit, Arika? Pit, Arika? Pit, Arika?*

Despite my wish, I remained begrudgingly alive. Blindfolded and gagged, I was crippled with pain. My wrists chafed beneath a leather strap. The little finger Jones abused throbbed and my temples ached mercilessly. My right ear, which had taken a direct blow, felt thick. My stomach dropped as falling sensations consumed me, disoriented.

The physical agony paled compared to the silence. Hosea was there, just beyond the blindfold. We traveled by horse. His chest to my back, his breath on my cheek. And, through my gag, I railed at him: *Speak to me; this silence is worse than the Pit.* But he did not listen. And so, for a day, I suffered as revelations mounted an attack on my psyche. Years of suppressed knowledge marched forth, loosed by Jones' hypocrisy.

The law is supreme, she said. And yet, she ignored the law as she pleased, planting the New Seed without consent. She claimed efficiency justified her actions, but I was not a fool. Imposing a law before the Assembly enacted it was not efficiency—it was tyranny.

But then, the Kongo had suffered many tyrants, beginning with the Great Obi Solomon. I'd known for some time that something about Obi was wrong. My latent suspicion began one evening, years ago. I was reading in the library when a picture captured my attention: *Obi Solomon poses, triumphant.* In the photo, the Great Obi sat on a carved rock.

The photograph was staged. Sternly upright, legs splayed, hands on his knees. His hands were always fists since, years before the end of the War, he lost the little finger on his left hand, and didn't like to display it. He often exchanged his Kongo attire for English frocks when he traveled north, so his English clothing was not why I stared. Something about the picture was *wrong*. At the time, I hadn't been willing to name it.

Suddenly, the horse jolted beneath me, yanking me from the past. My binds tightened and strained my *little finger*! Just like that, the nature of the wrongness came clear. The picture formed inside my blindfold and I took in every little detail. Obi, dressed in English fashion with a tall white collar framing his dark jaw and chin. Under his boots, a patch of snow. On his knees, his hands—*unmangled* and splayed. Two perfect Kongo stars on his English trousers.

His hands dated the picture to years *before* the end of the War, which begged a dangerous question. Why had the Great Obi Solomon been dressed like an Englishman before the Niagara Compromise was signed? The answer could upend the peace that anchored America. Terrified, I forced the matter from my mind as waves of heart-palpitating guilt attacked me.

My sins—selfishness, arrogance, betrayal—mocked me.

Would Hannibal die in the Pit, or had Covington rallied the others to split her punishment between them? If Hannibal died, I would die—unforgiven. *She's yours*, Jetson had said. Jetson, my only friend, was lost to me.

Hosea tried to feed me water and food he'd packed for the journey. Overwhelmed by guilt, I refused nourishment. I spat out the nuts and seeds. I turned my head so the water dripped down my chin.

"You school brats are all the same," he said, breaking the silence. "You'll drink when you're thirsty."

Only I didn't. Eventually, he gave up trying and I dehydrated in the heat of the desert. My tongue dried, my fingers shriveled and my eyes ached. Perversely, beads of anxiety dribbled down my back, itching mercilessly.

At night, Hosea dismounted and lifted me down. He left me alone as he spoke to someone in the distance. I couldn't guess who. As the sun set, he came back, and ordered me to sleep. The night grew cold as I lay on my side beside him. When his arm, draped with a blanket, came around my waist, I kicked him off and wormed away in the sand. Cursing, he gave up and slept.

My blindfold had shifted in the tussle and it clogged one nostril. The other was nearly filled with sand. As my breath grew thin, I tottered on the edge of demise—and I welcomed it. There are no thoughts on the brink of death, only wild imaginings. A hot continent of fauna and sugar cane, a high canopy of trees, a rippling undergrowth. Feathered wings unfurled and flew me to a place called *home*, where I ate a watermelon, seedless and waist high. I chewed and swallowed. Then, finally, I slept.

THE GUST

The next morning, Hosea shook me. "Wake up, Cobane."

I leapt into consciousness.

"Are you awake?" He ripped the blindfold away.

I squeezed my eyes shut, pressing my face against my shoulder as he hunkered down to untie my wrists. Blood rushed painfully to my hands and I cried out.

"Hold on, don't move yet," he said. He lifted my arms around to rest in my lap and massaged them, one by one. When he was done, even the pain in my little finger had dulled considerably. His shadow fell across me as he inspected my dirty bandages. The leather tie had abraded my wrists. Grimly, he removed my gag. Bits of it had been eaten away in the night.

"If you were hungry, you might have said something," he growled, tossing the chewed remains away. "Will you drink now?" He put the waterskin to my mouth.

Still guilt-ridden, I turned my head so the fluid spilled down the side of my neck.

"You're wasting water, Cobane. Don't be a fool. We're in the middle of the desert."

When I turned away again he grabbed my jaw, and forced my mouth open. It stung and I cried out, gulping a mouthful of water.

"What the hell?" He leaned in, holding my mouth open for

his inspection. "*Obi*, what have you done?"

He didn't have to tell me what he saw. Along with water, I'd swallowed a metallic mouthful of stale blood. My inner cheek was shredded with teeth marks. I tested the damage with my tongue and studied my bare feet apathetically.

He bared his teeth. "Ignore me, but if you don't drink, you'll die faster than you think."

With a shrug, I rested back against the ground.

"Oh, no you don't."

A second later, water flooded my face. It came quickly and I swallowed a good portion. Against my will, it tasted good. He got another skin of water and forced me to drink again. Stubbornly, I took a deep breath, filling my lungs with liquid. I gagged and some of what I drank came back up.

"Damn you!" he shouted, but he stopped pouring. A second later, the blade of his knife was at my chin. "Is this what you want, Cobane?" he said. The knife moved to my jugular. "Do you want to die?"

Confronted with immediate death, adrenaline shot through my veins. Rubies encrusted his knife. It was razor sharp and I strained away. The answer was *no,* I realized. The revelation surprised me. *I don't want to live,* I thought, *but I do not want to die.*

I kept my eyes on the glint of his blade. The past two days had soured the idea of a return to the Schoolhouse. Even for a seat in the American Assembly, I would never be able to face my classmates. So, what *did* I want? In a flash, I saw the fugitive crossing the Cobane perimeter. My heart pounded— *escape.* I had nowhere to go. But, if I was lucky—

The point of Hosea's knife broke my skin.

"If you want to die, I can kill you here and now," he said.

I blinked, giving him my attention. His mouth was a cruel slash, but his eyes told the real story. They were red from sleepless nights spent tending to the sick. Even after I betrayed him, Dr. Hosea Khan had dressed my wounds.

He reiterated his threat. "I'll kill you, just say the word."

"*Kha*," I croaked, calling his bluff.

His eyes registered surprise. Then, resignedly, he lowered his knife. "Well, you might get your wish, Cobane, whether I like it or not." He pointed off into the distance.

I sat up and looked west. The hills were spotted with familiar vegetation—palm, agave, jojoba, fishhook, beavertail, and prickly pear. In the distance, however, the plant life disappeared beneath a cloud formation. It hung dark against the Earth, covering everything in its path. Before I could ask what it was, a new voice explained.

"Big gust coming, Arika."

I jumped and turned. "William!"

"I am here," William declared, smiling warmly.

I smiled back as more life flowed into my limbs.

Hosea grunted. "If you don't know, Cobane, a gust is a sandstorm." He pulled me to my feet. "William has been tracking us since Cobane. He made contact to warn us of the storm."

"I bring horse for Arika," William said. He smiled. "See here—Mary."

He retrieved the reins of two horses, a dark-brown stallion and a jet-black mare. Sensing the mare was mine, I stepped toward her on unsteady legs.

"Mary," I said. I rested my cheek against her nose.

William patted my back and hummed softly.

"Do you know how to ride?" Hosea asked.

"No," I whispered.

He looked grim. "Cumin can't get to full speed with both our weights," he said, patting his horse. "I'll have to guide you."

William nodded. "Big gust coming," he repeated. "Arika must ride."

I looked at the clouds brewing in the distance. I was not ready to die. Not with the hope of escape sprouting in my mind.

As Hosea packed the camp, I ate a handful of nuts and drank as much as my stomach would hold. When I finished, he lifted me into Mary's saddle. He produced a rope and handed me the end. "Wrap this around you twice."

Wetting my dry lips, I did as I was told. I gave back the slack. Hosea knotted it around Mary and pulled to secure it. "That's too tight," I said, my face pressed firmly to Mary's neck. "I can't move."

"That's the point, Cobane. I don't want you falling." He patted my exposed cheek.

William checked the knot Hosea made. Satisfied, he nodded. "Tie is good, strong." He mounted the brown stallion.

"Our aim is that precipice," Hosea said.

I looked to where he pointed. To me, it looked no different than any other rock formations surrounding us.

"There's a wood in a valley just over the hill," he continued. "We need to get there before the storm."

Hosea held my reins as we started at a fast trot. Within the hour, the wind picked up, speeding the storm's approach. It closed in from the south and west, spanning the sky and blotting out the horizon. At this pace, the gust would catch us before we reached shelter.

Hosea signaled to William as he reined in. "We have to move faster."

William nodded.

Hosea dismounted and untied the rope from my waist. The wind whipped harder, looping one of my braids around his neck. He deposited Mary's reins into my left hand as he detangled himself. "You'll have to learn quickly," he said. "These give you control. Give slack for speed and tighten if you want to slow down." He glanced over his shoulder at the sky. "For now, you'll want to give her her head. Whatever you do, do not let go of the reins—understand?"

I stalled, my heart in my throat, but I nodded.

"Good. Pull left to go left and right to go right," he said.

I wiped my hands and made a fist around the *bambi* reins.

"If she gets away from you, don't panic. Just hold tight. She'll lead you someplace safe."

The wind spun wildly in cyclones. Up close, I saw the fog was not a cloud formation, but a solid wall of sand. The horses stamped nervously. Hosea remounted Cumin and turned to me, his mouth tight. "Stay close, Cobane. If we get separated, head in that direction." He pointed again at our target.

The howl of the wind made speech impossible. Hosea nodded and, tremulously, I nodded back. He turned forward, slapped Cumin's rear and bounded off. William did the same. I swallowed hard, and loosened the reins.

•

Mary reared up and I slid to the left. I screamed and gripped the saddle, certain I was going to die. As we gained speed, so did the wind. It weaponized the sand, a thousand tiny canines biting my skin. I doubled my hands on the horn, but my palms, slick with sweat, refused to hold. I threw my head back and bellowed for help. The pounding hooves drowned me out. I was entirely alone. My fingers slipped. I glanced back. Instantly, I wished I hadn't.

To my terrified mind, the thing behind us was not a storm, but a demon. A smoke-wall of dust, arching back and bulging forth, consuming everything. Its pull was irresistible, advancing like a pack of wolves. One beast surged forward and I saw its eyes—like black steel. Another lunged over me, snuffing every joule of light. With a shout, I curled into the saddle, covered my head and dropped the reins.

Later, Hosea said our time behind the wall of the storm lasted a minute or two. I called him a liar, but William's corroborating nod confirmed his story. For me, it lasted an eternity as terrifying images whirled around me. Jones, breathing red flames. William, cradling a baby. Sky, palms up, pleading. Kiwi and Covington, pointing bloody fingers. An empty-eyed Hannibal, a pyre. The images turned on a reel, around and around, screaming like banshees. Jones, Fount, Hannibal—Hannibal, Kiwi, Covington. Their bodies warped in the middle, bending back and bulging forth. Careening and spinning around until, suddenly, on the most disturbing image—William's face—it stopped.

THE COMPROMISE

I opened my eyes and looked around—*where was I? Not the desert.* I lay on the ground, surrounded by sparse forest. Branches of dark foliage loomed overhead. Beneath me, yellow flowers bloomed in patches of dirt, instead of sand. The air was moist with pungent spring vegetation. My jaw dropped. Only one place in the Kongo was rumored to be this lush. Somehow, I'd woken up in an oasis.

"Arika?" William came forward and bent over me, blocking out the beautiful scene. His face filled my view, just as it had in my nightmare during the gust.

I gasped, forgetting the paradise, as my eyes narrowed on the mole on his cheek. It seemed to swell as I stared, not believing my eyes. I touched my own cheek and reared back from him. "Get away from me!"

He leaned closer. "Arika, hush. You safe now."

I rolled away and emptied my stomach, losing precious ounces of water.

"Arika?" He reached out to help.

I fended him off with a fist, my eyes on his face as if seeing it for the first time. "*You*—don't touch me!" I shouted.

He sat back, confused.

I jumped to my feet and glared down at him. "Don't ever touch me again."

Before he could speak, I turned and ran into the nearest clump of trees. Hosea shouted behind me, but I ignored him. Trunks lined my path, their branches reaching out like dark hands. I blinked. *Dark hands, pale faces.* I forced my eyes open and sped up; the memories persisted. I saw myself as a baby, leaving the nursery, arriving at the Schoolhouse. I'd seen two faces that night. The pale face of Teacher Jones—and the serious black of William's. It was *his* dark hands that had delivered me to the Schoolhouse.

Suddenly, Hosea tackled me.

I gasped as we clamored to the ground.

Recovering quickly, I shimmied away.

His arm clamped over my ribcage.

"Let me go!"

"You're not going anywhere." He breathed hard.

"You can't stop me."

"I *will* stop you. You had a choice in the village, Cobane. You chose to spy for Jones, and you'll pay for it!"

I bit his hand and scrambled a few yards. He caught my foot. "What's got into you?!" He wrestled me to the ground. I wormed and scratched. He wrapped his arms around my trunk, trapping my arms at my sides.

"Where is he?" I cried. I strained to look around.

"Who? You look as if you've seen a ghost!"

Seeing that William was nowhere in sight, I collapsed.

Hosea landed on top of me.

Not a ghost, I thought—*an enemy from my past.* My chest heaved as I struggled to inhale beneath Hosea's weight. His silver necklace dangled above me, slapping my face. "Hosea, I can't breathe!" I shouted.

He rolled off me but fixed a hand around my wrist. We both gasped for air. No wonder William was kind to me in the village. He recognized me. I'd seen his guilt then, but had not understood its origin. *Well, William, I remember you now,* I thought bitterly, remembering all the secret smiles we'd shared. Hosea shifted and I glanced over at him. He held me with one hand and, with his other, he removed a length of rope and a gag from his bag.

Suddenly, I recalled my plan to escape. Thanks to William, I had squandered a prime opportunity. I'd been unbound and on horseback. But, instead of biding my time, I'd exposed my intention to run away. I snarled as my anger toward William increased. He was just one more reason I had to get away.

I cleared my throat. "Please, Hosea, leave the ties off. I'm sorry I ran." I had to placate him, get him to let his guard down.

"No way. I told my father I'd deliver you, and I will," he said. "Besides, it's dangerous to run off by yourself."

"That's just it," I insisted. "I'm telling you, I won't run away anymore."

He snorted.

I shifted my angle. "What good will I be to the Director if I'm sick?" I reasoned. "I'll eat and drink if you leave off the binds. And I won't run away," I said again.

"Good. Taking off in the *wadi* would be suicide."

I nodded agreeably. "I don't want to die," I said, honestly. "I won't run into the desert." *But I will,* I thought, glancing around, *take my chances in this oasis.* "Besides, the ties hurt." I cradled my bandaged hand against my stomach.

He studied me a long time. When he sighed, I knew I'd won. "Stay close to me, unless I tell you to go with William."

"I'll stay close."

He put the ropes back in his bag and helped me to my feet. "If you run again, I'll tie you to your horse."

●

To earn his trust, I became Hosea's shadow. When he drank, I matched him gulp for gulp, and I ate every bite of food he offered. I helped him wipe down the horses and sat obediently as he changed my bandages. Later, we tethered Mary and Cumin to a tree as they grazed in a patch of sweet clover. All the while, I plotted my escape.

I stared into the distance. Deep in the maze of that wood was a hot spring capable of supporting my life. Mary was intelligent and gentle. I would lead her away that night, find the spring, and hide until Hosea gave up trailing us.

Just after noon meal, Hosea stood and stretched. "Are you ready?"

I groaned inwardly. I was exhausted, and I needed rest for my flight later. "Ready for what?"

"We need to collect firewood."

I looked up. The sky, visible through the forest trees, was clear. The afternoon was hot. *So why did we need a fire?* Shrugging, I forced myself to my feet. When our arms were filled with kindling, he guided us back to the clearing and bent to arrange the wood.

My thighs screamed as I squatted beside him.

His chuckle broke the silence. "It keeps the animals at bay, Cobane."

"Huh?" I swiped sweat from my brow.

"The fire," he explained. "You're wondering why we're

making a fire when it's warm and light outside. It's for our protection. Fire will keep animals away while we sleep."

I squinted at him. "We're sleeping here?"

"We've been making camp all day." He made a face. "What did you think we were doing?"

I answered honestly. "Waiting for William to return."

"And when we set the perimeter?"

"You mean, when we moved those stones into a circle?"

"Yes." He smiled and tossed more wood on the pile.

I shrugged, feeling foolish. "At the Schoolhouse, it went better for us if we didn't ask too many questions. I do what I'm told."

"Well, you're not at the Schoolhouse anymore, Cobane. Remember that." He sounded smug.

I lifted my chin. "If you want questions, Vine Keeper, I have plenty. What does the Director want with me? How does he know my name?"

He stopped smiling. "I'll tell you when you need to know."

"Once I'm under his control, is he going to execute me?"

He didn't answer.

"If he tries—to kill me, I mean—are you going to let him?"

He looked wary. "I think you've made your point."

With a satisfied smile, I layered the logs on top of each other in a small circle. As I finished, a sliver of wood pierced my palm. My breath hissed. *Dammit.* It was bleeding. I was about to call out to Hosea for help when, suddenly, I froze. I set the log down and surveyed the trees lining our camp. Their dark limbs were menacing. My smug satisfaction vanished. I might have made a point earlier, but so had he—though he hadn't intended to.

There was a gaping hole in my plan to escape. If not for Hosea's curtly issued orders, I would have had no idea what to do with the firewood. I didn't know how to set a perimeter, or ward off animals. I couldn't cook, find water or make clothes. I picked at the splinter in my hand as Hosea moved to the other side of camp with a sample of plants he'd collected earlier.

I watched covertly as he settled down, emptied the pouch and made several rows of leaves and roots on the ground before him. Working with great care, he selected a small heart-shaped leaf and compared it to an illustration in a book he took from his pack. His brow creased in concentration.

The sliver of wood came free and I tossed it aside. There was no help for it, I realized. I could not escape tonight. I would stay a few days, watch Hosea, and learn what I needed to survive. I raised my voice and called across the clearing, "Where did you learn about medicine?"

He made a notation in his book and called back, "Books, practice—apprenticeship."

I scratched my chin. "Books, I assume, you got from your father."

He nodded.

"And your first patients were Vine workers. You told me that much before."

Again, he nodded.

"But who did you study under?"

He inspected another leaf and continued writing. "I studied medicine under my birth mother."

"And where did she learn?"

"From my grandmother, who learned from her grandmother just after the War."

I recalled Saxon saying Hosea's mother had been young during her affair with the Director. "Your mother must have been talented." Hosea didn't correct my use of the past tense.

"Why do you say that?" he asked.

"Well, because you're quite gifted."

He looked up at me. "I do more than numb the pain, which is all the medicine men do. But, barely more."

I didn't argue with him. "How did you know I was wondering about the fire earlier?"

I'd caught him off guard, and he responded without pretense. "Your eyes. Everything you feel is written there. Most of what you think, too." He hesitated. "You should guard yourself more closely, Cobane."

I leaned in, meeting his gaze in the afternoon sun. There was something in his voice that worried me. *Did he know I intended to escape?* His eyes flashed and I felt, again, he was trying to warn me of something. Before I could guess what, the light shifted and the feeling faded. I sat back, chafing my hands along the crescent-moon scars on my arms. Hosea returned to his work. By late afternoon, William had yet to appear.

THE SCORPION

Hours later, Hosea served my supper on a crude plate. He ordered me to sit then walked beyond the scope of the firelight. I heard him talking to someone in the distance, but I stayed put. I figured he was testing me, watching from the trees to see if I could be trusted.

"Don't worry. I'll be right here—for now," I whispered. I'd jittered with impatience all day, but I'd made great strides toward my escape. I'd followed him as he foraged for edible leaves. Then, at my insistence, he let me wash them. I memorized their particulars so I could find them again when I was on my own. When he'd ordered me away as he chopped the leaves and mixed them with oil to make a green paste, I watched from afar so I could repeat the process.

Imagining his eyes on me, I stuffed my mouth full of noodles slathered in the green paste. I picked up my pack and moved to my bedroll, to analyze my situation as I ate.

During the journey from Cobane I'd been blindfolded, but I faintly recalled the direction of the sun on my face each day. If my memory could be trusted, we were far north, east of Cobane, close to the Kongo border.

I took a bite and chewed slowly. From my studies, I knew the only destination northeast of Cobane was the Obi Forest, the verboten land. By my calculation, Hosea had been headed there before the gust. I frowned. The Obi Forest had a murky history.

After the Last War, tens of thousands died of famine as the remains of the Earth could not produce food without innovative help. To develop a solution, the Compromise delegates commissioned a team of scientists to bolster advancement in the area of agriculture.

Months later, a solution emerged. Using hydroplane irrigation technology and a cocktail of synthetic minerals, the super-team set forth a plan to nourish the land. They tested multiple versions of the synthetic mineral mixture on a strip of the Kongo, dubbed the Obi Forest. The land ran the length of the northern Kongo border, providing a barrier between the Kongo and Clayskin territory.

After the Compromise was signed, the Obi Forest was deemed uninhabitable, having been treated with unstable radicals. According to law, it was hazardous to carbon-based biology. Nevertheless, tales of illicit voyages made their way back to Cobane. According to rumors, the experimental land was wild, home to mutant trees and animals. Everything from killer mosquitos to talking snakes. In legitimately published literature, I read about an English-made antitrespassing device that made the Obi Forest difficult to find and impossible to pass through.

If that was true, then why was Hosea headed in that direction? A piece of information scratched at the back of my mind, something Rowan had said while arguing with Teacher Saxon.

And the missing planes? Rowan asked. Explain that!

How many did your contact say are missing? Saxon said.

Four, at least, according to her last letter. The Kongo Technology Center doesn't keep an inventory of planes that are out of commission.

Then how can she know four are missing? Saxon asked.

At least four! And she knows because she's a staff engineer at the KTC, she knows what's missing. Besides the planes, remember, she warned us of a private, secret project Kumar is developing using government funds. The question is not how many planes, but what possible purpose the Director could have for misdirecting them?

My heart throbbed. The clues pointed to a dangerous conclusion. Hosea was going to the Obi Forest because it was no longer abandoned. Director Kumar, using hydroplanes hijacked from the Kongo Technology Center, had nourished the land for his own purpose—I couldn't guess what. However, if I didn't escape soon, I would know it all. With a few hours of hard riding, we'd be at the Obi Forest and wise to the Director's secret project.

Using one finger, I scooped up the last of the paste and popped it into my mouth. I wiped my hands, set my plate aside and retrieved ink and paper. I sketched a scale map of the Kongo from memory. The northern perimeter of America was seven hundred miles across at its widest point. From there, it narrowed through the Clayskin lands.

I drew a jagged horizontal line to represent the Obi Forest. From either end of the forest I angled two more lines, bringing them to meet at a point, the southernmost tip of the Kongo. I sketched a star there and wrote *Hannibal House*. I made eleven other stars, including one labeled *Cobane*. Starting there, I traced our progress north, trying to pinpoint exactly where we were. If I couldn't escape Hosea before we left the oasis, I would need a map to guide me back.

Something crept across the edge of my vision.

I glanced up, thinking to see Hosea. Instead, a large scorpion scurried across the way. I jumped to my feet. Hosea was nowhere in sight. I hunkered down, eyeing the creature's arched red tail. There were nonpoisonous varieties of scorpions, but I was no expert. It was inches from the open mouth of my pack when I moved, bringing my notebook up to smash it. Before I could, Hosea appeared. He took the book and knocked me off balance. His arm stretched across my chest to right me. In a flash, he deposited me by the fire, my notebook in my lap. My chest, where he'd touched me, tingled with warmth. He hadn't even spilled my ink. Shocked, I watched him return to move my bag from the scorpion's path.

"Will it come back?" I said, watching it go.

Hosea shook his head. "The fire will keep it away." He knelt beside me. "Are you okay?" He took my shoulders and ran his hands over my arms and back, leaving trails of sensation. I stared up at him. He'd moved like a blur. Faster than possible—but how?

"There was no need to kill it," Hosea explained, seeing the question in my expression. His arms were lifted behind his head and I saw he was retying the leather string that held his silver medallion. It must have come loose in our tussle. "We probably disturbed its home when we made camp," he went on.

I nodded. My eyes found the weapon at his hip. He was armed and so very strong, and yet he refused to hurt even the most insignificant of creatures. "It's getting late, I'm tired," I said. I put my ink and notebook away. I arranged my bag beneath my head. Hosea moved his blanket close to mine before he lay down.

·

Later, I rolled onto my back. I let out a small sigh and shifted to my side, toward the fire.

"What's the problem, Cobane?"

Not bothering to feign sleep, I propped myself up on one elbow. "In my room, before we left, your spear appeared in your hand like magic. And just now, to save that scorpion, you came from nowhere."

"What's your point?"

"You move so fast. I want to know how," I said, bluntly.

"I shouldn't tell you anything. You'll inform Jones the first chance you get."

I said nothing, unable to promise him loyalty, as I fully intended to escape.

He sighed. "What do you know about Clayskin history?"

"Not much. Why?"

He sat up. "Knowledge of Clayskin history would make it easier to explain. What do you know about the Last War?"

"Everything," I said confidently. I sat up.

"Then I'll start there," he said. "In the final years, there were five factions left fighting the War. The Kongo and English had the largest armies, followed by the Indu. Then there were two smaller forces that had formed an alliance early on."

"The Mandarin and Pacific-Asian forces," I said. "I remember. They suffered a plague that decimated their female population. Both armies nearly perished."

Hosea nodded. "Yes, before the plague they had impressive

numbers. But, in the final days, they were forced to ally with each other against their foes. The key to their survival was their expertise in hand-to-hand combat.

"Well, in the last days of the War, the armies looked to the future. Habitable land was scarce and they questioned their methods of war. What good was victory if the winning army had no place to settle? The big three—the English, Indu, and Kongo—agreed to stop using heavy bombs altogether. And so, hand-to-hand combat became essential to victory."

"Which is why the Indu fell behind," I said. "They had been losing ground for years, because the English controlled all the raw materials needed to produce danomite swords."

"Right, the Indu fought with steel and titanium, no match against the danomite fire sword. Additionally, the Indu lacked the brute strength of the Kongo. When it was obvious to the Indu that they would lose without better training, their general offered to ally his force with one of the two smaller armies—either the Mandarin or the Pacific-Asian armies."

I frowned. "I don't remember this. I don't believe it was in our books."

"Schoolhouse literature is censored," Hosea said. "The English write the curriculum to reflect what they want you to know."

I frowned. I knew our readers were censored, but I'd shied away from considering why until that moment. "Which of the armies did the Indu align with?" I asked tentatively, wanting to know more, but afraid of where the answers would lead.

"That's just it, the Indu general didn't choose a force," Hosea said. "Instead, he pitted the two groups against each other, forcing them to break their alliance. Since both groups knew they didn't have a chance without the Indu's help, they fought it out in a tournament, using their specialized hand-to-hand combat styles."

"They had specialized fighting styles?" I said. "I've never heard of them."

"Few have. The styles are carefully guarded. No one knows them all, but I've mastered a few techniques. Sword and grappling, strike and stick—*Kyudo*."

"Kyudo," I said, practicing the word on my tongue."

"The art of archery," he explained. "Every style was fair game in the tournament, and every fight was a death match with the Indu as spectators. I believe the Indu leader was trying to flesh out the most successful techniques. Several styles perished during the tournament, when the last master fell."

"So, who won the tournament?" I asked.

"Neither side won, which is exactly what the Indu general wanted. After a month, when both forces had dwindled so as not to pose a threat to the Indu combined, the general called an end to the tournament, and offered the remaining people sanctuary if they swore allegiance to him. More importantly, they had to agree to teach the Indu their combat styles."

"That's awful," I said.

"Yes," Hosea agreed. "The smaller armies had been fighting for alliance, not allegiance. The general's plan was to give the Mandarin and Pacific-Asian people working-class status in the Indu nation. The nation he believed would rule the world." Hosea laughed.

"What's funny about that?" I asked.

"Well, it's ironic, isn't it, how it all played out? On the other side of the War, the English didn't care what the Indu general intended. To them, the Indu, Mandarin and Pacific-Asian armies were essentially the same: *not* white. They called the new force the *Clayskin* army, and the name stuck."

I suddenly understood. "So the general brought about the end of the Mandarin and Pacific-Asian armies, but his final efforts to turn the tide of the War precipitated the fall of his own people too," I said.

"Exactly, and even more ironic is the fact that the Clayskin became the middle-class people of America under the Niagara Compromise. The general got a taste of what he'd planned for his enemies."

"No more than he deserved," I said.

"The point is, masters of any style are extremely rare. It's against the Clayskin law to teach the styles to the other two races. And it's even fallen out of practice among the Clayskin. In the old world, they called it an art and its primary use was discipline and self-defense. It was during the chaos of the Last War that the old-world *Art of Mars* was manipulated for aggression. After the War ended, it wasn't necessary for survival. So they got lax with it, stopped teaching it as religiously as they had before. My father is half Clayskin, half English. He has Clayskin blood from the both the Pacific-Asian and the Indu line. He's one of the few masters left alive."

I nodded, recognizing his Clayskin blood in the almond shape of his eyes. By breaking the law, the Director had produced a quintessential American citizen in Hosea Khan. He had Kongo, Clayskin, and English blood. The mix was mesmerizing. I looked away. "This combat style," I said, feeling out of breath. "It's why you can move so fast?"

Hosea nodded. "It's part of the training. The art of fighting without weapons. Victory rests on the warrior's speed and wisdom, the strength of his resilience."

"Or hers," I whispered. I sent a long look toward his weapon. A thought occurred to me. "You call it fighting without weapons, but you have a weapon," I said.

He removed the etched cylinder and twirled it between his long fingers. "I have it, but you won't see me use it to fight. Only to make my opponent yield."

"What are the markings on the side?" I asked.

He shook his head. "It's getting late, Cobane."

"One last question and I'll leave you alone."

On his back, he squinted over at me.

"Do you ever think what would have happened if Obi Solomon had plotted against the Mandarin and Pacific-Asian armies? In that case, the Kongo would hold the secrets of combat art."

His eyes gleamed. "Arika Cobane, are you *questioning* the wisdom of the Great Obi Solomon?"

The way he said it brought his whispered words to my mind, *If I don't see you again, Cobane, know this... you must question everything.* "No," I said, "I'm not questioning his wisdom. But—"

"But what?" Hosea propped himself up again.

I bit my lip, unable to stop the spiral of my own curiosity. In the last days of the War, the Kongo outnumbered its enemy two to one. Kongo women as well as men were trained warriors, berserkers in battle, superior in size and strength to any other people on Earth. It's said that one male and one female, fighting back to back, could take out a platoon of combatants. If the Last War had continued to the bitter end, the Kongo would have prevailed.

"I've studied it for years," I said, finally. "For years, and I still don't understand. Why did Obi Solomon sign an agreement that allotted our people so little? When the tasks were divided, why did he lead his people to choose the most difficult portion of all? Why did he—?"

I pressed my lips together. Underscoring my doubt was the picture I had tried so desperately to forget. The one of Obi with his perfect hand on his fancy English clothing. He had fraternized with the enemy before the Compromise, *which means that*—I shoved a fist against my mouth.

"Cobane?"

My eyes flew open. Hosea waited for me to finish. I cleared my throat and said all I dared. "It seems to me," I whispered, my tongue as dry as sand, "it seems all of America was ours for the taking and he—he just gave it away."

"Is that right?" Hosea asked, his eyes bright.

My heart beat hard as our eyes locked. "I don't know. Yes!" The word flew out before I could stop it. "The workers toil endlessly, while people in the North spend their days learning and experimenting. We achieved peace, but the best life went to the English."

Hosea didn't answer me except to lay back down. "Go to sleep, Cobane."

I lay back, trying to sleep. Instead, disillusionment plagued me. My misgiving regarding Obi could not be forestalled. It overshadowed my guilt and edged out my fear. By morning, a relentless suspicion lodged in my gut, slithering around like a serpent.

THE ARMISTICE

William returned that night, surprising me as we broke camp. He didn't explain his absence, but, it seemed, he had come to stay. He took the lead, singing a short tune as we started out into the wood. I recognized the song as the one we sang together in Cobane. Annoyingly, it reminded me of his gentleness that night in the sick room. Ignoring the sound, I strode behind him. Hosea kept up the rear.

In my hobbled skirt and *bambi* blouse, I was uncomfortable—except for my feet. Along with Mary, William brought a perfectly fitting pair of thick-soled shoes from Cobane. He'd presented them while we ate breakfast. My instinct had been to reject the gift. Before I could, however, Hosea accepted on my behalf.

"We'll be hiking for miles, Cobane," he explained. "You'll need shoes."

I frowned, but said nothing as I finished my meal, reminding myself that I wouldn't be in their company long. Hosea had prepared more leaves that morning. He'd added oil to make the paste then spread it on crackers he'd brought with him from Cobane. I'd watched like a hawk and made mental notes. More importantly, I'd heard him discuss our water supply with William.

"We'll need to track down water before the end of the day," he'd said.

In response, William had nodded toward his horse. "He find water."

Hosea had glanced at William's mount with surprise. "So, your horse has been trained to seek out water in the desert. I've heard of such training. Will Arika's Mary find water too?"

As if he sensed my bated breath, William had looked directly at me as he answered. "Yes, Mary find water for Arika."

I digested the information. Before long, I would have all the knowledge I needed to escape.

Late that afternoon, Hosea called for a halt. Exhausted, I collapsed onto a patch of dirt. Instead of resting, Hosea catered to the horses. Mary moved to nuzzle a bush, Cumin joined her, and William scouted the path ahead.

After sitting a while, I went farther into the densely packed trees to relieve myself. The moist ground gave beneath me as I walked, creating an unfamiliar sucking sensation along my soles. This oasis was more vast and lush than anything described in books. Even in rumor, the oasis islands, surrounded by dry desert, were only a few miles wide—one or two at most. However, the forest around me was thirty times that. When I'd asked Hosea about the discrepancy, he'd laughed and told me not to believe everything I read.

I finished quickly and wandered out to a large rock. A trio of colorful lizards scattered as I sat to empty my boots of soil and pebbles. This particular oasis had to be an anomaly. Something about its location, nestled between two mountainous rock ranges, made it more verdant than the oases described in library books. It supported one main species of tree, foreign to me. Their trunks were tall and thin. In lieu of leaves, round crowds of needles vied near their tops, bunched at the end of spindly limbs that tangled together high above us. Through them, I saw the sun. We were headed north, still, toward the Obi Forest.

Hosea's voice startled me. "I told you not to go far, Cobane."

I studied him. His mouth was pulled in at the edges.

I rubbed my aching forehead. "I was thinking. I didn't realize how far I'd gone."

Concerned, he stepped forward, but I held him off. "I'm fine, Doctor."

"You worry too much," he retorted.

I flexed my foot and shook my boot. "If I'm worrying, blame yourself," I said. "If what you told me last night is true, then we live in dangerous times—worry is inevitable."

"You're going to make yourself sick," he said. "Nothing is worth your life."

"Nothing?" I challenged. "Not even the Kongo?" I pressed my fingers into my temple and stood, feeling like an old woman. My doubt had not dissipated overnight as I'd hoped. Instead, it grew stronger every hour. The damning picture of Obi Solomon haunted my thoughts. I told myself that his disloyalty was all the more reason to focus on escaping. However, instead of plotting my own freedom, my mind continued to ponder the unsolvable mystery of the man. If the father of our nation was a traitor, then nothing could be trusted. Not the Teachers, or the Assembly, or the Compromise. How would the Kongo survive? I looked at Hosea. "Don't you care about the Kongo?"

Instead of answering, Hosea sighed, placed a hand on my back, and shuffled me back toward the horses. "What you need is water. This way, Senator," he teased.

I smiled reluctantly. With William scouting most of the

time, the canopy of trees created an illusion of privacy. Under it, Hosea and I enjoyed a tentative armistice. We were not friends, exactly. But, as the miles had passed, neither were we Cobane and captor. The ease had revealed a pleasing playfulness in Hosea's nature. I found he could make me laugh, however grudgingly.

Back at our temporary camp, I accepted a skin of water, drank thirstily and set the skin aside. A while later, I gnawed on my bottom lip as I thought. According to the Teachers, the boiling seas to the west of America were uninhabitable and impassable. But, I knew now, the Teachers couldn't be trusted.

I took my notebook from my bag, and checked to ensure that Hosea was nowhere in sight before I flipped several pages to my hand-drawn map of America. Quickly, I retrieved a quill and spat on the ink dried on its tip. I had just enough lubrication to write the word *land* among the squiggles to the west of the America border. Beside the word, I drew a question mark.

I picked up the waterskin and took a big gulp just as William drifted into my line of vision. He nodded once but kept his distance, pointing to his right. "Water east," he said. He patted his dark horse and set out in that direction.

I forced the mouthful of the water down my tense throat, closed my notebook and shoved it in my bag, grateful William hadn't seemed to see my drawing. So far he had left me alone, but the matter between us remained unsettled. Eventually, he would approach me and I would have to shun him directly. I did not relish the prospect.

I jumped to my feet as Hosea placed a hand on my shoulder from behind.

He laughed. "Relax, Cobane. I'm just going to check your wraps while we're stopped."

Taking a breath, I sat down again and held out my right arm. He made quick work of exposing the abrasions on my inner wrist. They were scarred with light-brown ropes of skin. He unwrapped my other wrist and compared the two. "These are healing nicely. You can remove the wraps in another day."

I nodded, barely hearing him as he tied the new bandages. He placed a hand on the back of my neck and I relaxed my head into his palm without his direction. "Left," he said.

I turned my head.

"Now right."

I looked the other way.

"Any pain here?" He squeezed my nape.

"No."

"What about your cheek?" He tilted my chin up and to the side to check the marks on my face.

"There's no pain," I said.

His routine changed. He pressed his fingers into my jaw, massaging the muscles there.

"Any pain in this area?"

"Ouch!" I pulled back. *How had he known?*

"You were grinding your teeth last night," he explained.

I touched my jaw.

"You were grinding them again just now, before we stopped walking." His mouth quirked. "I hope you weren't thinking of me."

"Not you," I said.

Hosea went to his pack and removed a small tub. He handed it to me. "A balm for lacerations."

I opened the lid to see a white paste. "Coconut oil," I said, inhaling the familiar scent. "I use it on my hair."

"Well, it also prevents scarring. You have a nasty cut on your ear that hasn't healed yet."

I touched my ear and immediately thought of Jones' hypocrisy. She hadn't bothered to remove her ring when she hit me, as was her *right*, under the dubious Compromise. I glowered. If the Compromise was a fraud, then what right did she have to discipline the students at all? The answer was clear—she had *no* right. My belly clenched and rumbled.

Hosea let out a breath. "There you go again, grinding."

I looked up.

He was standing over me, his hands on his hips. "As your doctor, I order you to stop worrying." He bent down and clasped the knot of my jaw, making me wince. "You're giving yourself tendonitis, Cobane," he whispered.

My mind went blank as his fingers worked expertly over my jaw.

"Better?" he asked.

His eyes were light brown now, and his jaw was dark with his growing beard. It obscured the cleft in his chin. My heart skipped and I jumped to my feet. "We should get going," I said.

"William's so far ahead, I can barely hear his song." I was talking too quickly.

Hosea didn't seem to notice. His hands dropped to his sides. "Okay, just let me check the horses."

I drank more water as Hosea checked the knots securing our gear. When he was done he started again, rechecking each tie. He went through the same steps, meticulous and measured, at every stop, no matter how short. In fact, he was measured in everything he did, which made memorizing his actions easier. I turned my back to him and looked around the wood. As the miles passed, I grew more comfortable. I would leave in just a few days. "Do you hear those birds?" I said, after a while.

He cocked his head. "Yes, whippoorwills."

"I thought so, too." I frowned.

"You're grinding, Cobane. I can hear it." He glanced over his shoulder. "What's the problem?"

"They've been following us, calling incessantly for an hour," I said.

"And?"

"And their calls sound close. Only, I haven't seen any whippoorwills."

He grinned crookedly, showing a dent in his right cheek. "Perhaps they're hiding."

Rolling my eyes, I stepped further into the wood. "I'll only be a moment," I called back.

"Don't go far," he said. He turned back to the horses.

I walked deep into the forest and stepped behind a dense patch of trees as the whippoorwills called, sounding closer than ever. I spoke loudly to Hosea over my shoulder. "Listen to that. They never stop!" I said, adjusting my *aura*. "It's the most confounding thing. I've seen other birds, parakeets, a hawk." I brushed at the sand in my blouse. "I've seen two blue jays but—"

Hosea cut me off with a shout. "Hush!"

I froze. His tone was tense. "What is it?" I called.

"Do you hear that?"

I listened. "Hear what? I don't hear anything," I said. Then it hit me. The hair on the back of my neck rose. "The whippoorwills. They've stopped singing."

Something was wrong. Hosea's uncharacteristically heavy footsteps rushed toward me. I hastily retied my *aura*, eager to get to his side. I stepped from behind the trees and ran. I took one step—two. A group of men materialized around me, their spears gleaming. I came to a sliding stop and opened my mouth to warn Hosea, but a hand snaked around my throat.

"Move and you die, English."

Something sharp pressed the side of my neck. I froze.

THE BANDITS

A minute later, Hosea appeared in the clearing—captured. He looked me over, then his eyes found the bandit behind me. He tensed and his lips parted expectantly. I sensed their eyes meeting over my head; then the bandit tightened his grip on my neck, and the expectant look faded from Hosea's gaze.

I frowned, wondering if Hosea recognized our captors. A second later, the suspicion passed as three men with spears guided William into our midst. Two more came with our horses. Including the man at my back, I counted six men in all.

There were terrible stories of the outlaws that lurked in verboten lands. Scavengers and cannibals. I rolled my eyes to catch a look at the one that had me.

He sneered, revealing red-stained teeth. He wore a patch over one eye. His other winked cruelly as he moved his spear along my cheek.

"Do you smell that, English?" he said, his eye catching mine.

I stifled a whimper. His weapon smelled like dung.

"That," he said, poking my jugular, "is the smell of rattler venom. If the bleeding doesn't get you, the poison will. Make no mistake. Move and die." Baring his red gums, he glanced at my pack. "I'll have your sack, English."

He was so close his saliva was wet on my cheek. I shivered.

To produce my pack, I'd have to bend my neck, which strained to avoid his spear.

Hosea called out, "Here, take mine." I looked at him. His hands were spread in surrender, low at his side, close to his weapon, which they hadn't seized, likely not realizing it posed a threat. His eyes flashed to mine, revealing his plan. He couldn't go for his weapon with the bandit's spear so close to my neck. But, if the bandit moved the spear from my throat in an effort to get his pack, we were saved.

The lead bandit, holding me, showed his bloody grin around the clearing. "Don't mind if I do," he said, and the other bandits leered back.

"Fly Man, move!" the leader shouted.

A boy, no more than ten, bounded from behind a tree and scampered to Hosea. The top of his head barely reached Hosea's holster, but he showed no fear. He grabbed the pack and tugged.

"You got to bend over, English," the boy said, scratching one round ear.

Hosea bent down, his mouth tucked in. My hope of rescue perished. The satchel transferred to the leader without incident.

"The sack is heavy," the leader confirmed, nodding his approval.

"We're peaceful travelers," Hosea said. "We lost our way in the storm. Take what you want, only leave us one horse and water."

The leader emptied Hosea's pack onto the ground, revealing bandages and medicine. He nodded for another of his men to guard me, then he riffled through the items. He opened one tin tub and sniffed, disappointed. He walked over to Hosea, his one eye unblinking.

"What do you say, men? Shall we leave them water?"

Inexplicably, the little boy, called Fly Man, covered his mouth and giggled.

"Here is your water, English," the leader declared. All at once, the circle of jackals spat onto the ground. Wet flecks touched my cheek. A glob of red stained Hosea's moccasin.

Hosea looked from the mess, to the leader. "I'm not English," he said.

The leader growled, spat again—and missed.

At the last second, Hosea stepped out of range.

With a growl, the leader knocked Hosea's chest with the side of his spear. He reared back for a second blow, aiming with the point.

"No!" I cried.

The leader jerked to a halt. In a flash, he crossed the circle to shove his face close to mine. His eye snapped to Hosea, then back to me.

"What was that? Say it again—English."

Every eye turned in my direction. The point of his weapon slid across my jaw and prodded my throat. Fear flooded me. Seeing Hosea in danger, I spoke without thinking, recalling, too late, his weapon. *And what do you have to defend yourself, you fool!* My heart skipped violently as the leader slid his spear over my shoulder. He tapped twice on my bag.

"I'll have your sack," he said. "And, English, it had better be heavy."

"I—I have nothing of value."

"Give it to me!"

I obeyed, shaking. He riffled through it with one hand as dark lines of fear blurred my vision.

Finally, he cried triumphantly. Turning in a circle, he extended his arm so everyone could see. I squinted at his bounty. In his hand was a simple scroll of parchment. On it was a worker's story. He stepped forward and hit me across the face with the scroll.

I cried out in surprise. It hadn't hurt.

Across the way, William grunted.

"You call this nothing, English?" the leader shouted, so his chin glistened with spittle.

I didn't know what to say.

He untied the scroll. "These words," he spoke slowly, watching for my reaction, "are plans of attack, laid out in English letters. The details of a plot *against* me!"

The bandits buzzed, shaking their heads, hands tight on their weapons.

"No!" I said. "You can't be serious."

"Did you write these letters, English?" the leader said, his eye narrowed.

"Yes, but it's not a battle plan. It's only a story. I'm a student, a Record Keeper."

The leader's face stiffened with dislike. His eye strained left and right as a new hum sounded among the bandits. "A student." He spat red. "If you are a student, then you should know who I am." He reached into his frock and removed a tattered piece of paper. He held it out for my inspection, nearly touching my nose.

It was the title page of a book. I calmed my trembling enough to read out loud. "*Candide*, or, *The Optimist*, by—" My heart shriveled as I read the last word. "—by *Voltaire*," I whispered.

The leader dropped his arm. His eyes brimmed with contempt.

I didn't see what happened next. A flash of light exploded in my head. Something hit me from behind, knocking me to the ground. A war cry from William, a clattering skirmish. I tried to roll over to see what was happening but something, a foot or knee, pressed against my back. I shook my head, throwing the heavy drape of my hair from my eyes. Just then, William escaped his captors. The boy, Fly Man, was beneath his arm.

Voltaire screamed, "Haaaalt!"

Everyone stopped.

The Rebel leader was behind me, his foot was on my back, his spear pointed across the clearing—at William. His sneer was gone but, with his red teeth bared, he looked more dangerous than ever. "Put him down," he hissed. His eye bulged from its socket to fix on the boy, clutched to William's chest. Suddenly, he remembered my presence. He repositioned his weapon against my neck. "You have three seconds before she dies."

"No hurt Arika!" William shouted.

"One!"

"Arika!"

"Two. Now!" Voltaire shouted.

I squeezed my eyes shut, not wanting the Rebel's face to be my last vision. His spear was so close, the slightest movement would end me.

"William, let the boy go," Hosea commanded.

I opened my eyes. William's stony gaze was on me. Everyone else stared at Hosea.

"Let him go," Hosea repeated.

Reluctantly, William set the boy on his feet. The child

scampered into the woods. William raised his arms in surrender.

I let out my breath.

"You are wise, English," Voltaire sneered. "A second longer and your warrior would have your woman dead."

"I am not English," Hosea repeated, calmly. "He is not my warrior and it is you, Voltaire, who must consider your options before you and your men are dead."

The bandit leaned on my back. The poisoned spear slipped down my sweaty neck.

"My options? Explain yourself, English."

"You're Voltaire, right, the notorious Rebel leader?"

Above me, Voltaire must have nodded, because Hosea went on. "I've heard you're looking to add weapons to your artillery. I can see why. Poison-tipped spears are nothing compared to the weapons of Hasting."

"We do well enough," Voltaire said.

"Perhaps," Hosea agreed. "But we both know you can't fight the Kongo Guard with spears. I can help you."

Voltaire thought this over, easing the spear on my neck. With the spare inch of space, I turned to look up at him. He wore an odd mix of clothing. A dingy brown English frock over loose, worker-style britches. Polished boots, and a very fine red scarf around his waist. His foot was heavy, but his frame was slight. Except for the boy, Fly Man, he was the smallest bandit by far. No taller than me.

His eyes narrowed on Hosea. "You, help me? English, what do you know of war? My handful of men immobilized yours in seconds." He propped one small fist on his waist.

"I'm at your mercy, but only because you grabbed her first," Hosea said, nodding at me. "If you hadn't, you would all be dead. By that turn, if you let her go, I will help you."

"You still haven't said how, English, and you're running out of time," Voltaire said.

"Weapons," Hosea replied. "I have English biotech weaponry at my disposal."

Voltaire stiffened above me.

I strained to see Hosea's face—*did he lie?* I thought not. He was the Director's son, after all, and Kumar had uninhibited access to the Kongo Technology Center, the perfect place to hide cutting-edge weaponry. Had Hosea stolen the technology from the KTC? Had the Director given it willingly? The inscription in his illicit weaponry book formed in my mind— *May you also find the gift in death.*

"I'm going to show you the weapon," Hosea said. He shifted, revealing the tube at his waist. He lifted it in his palm and stepped forward.

"Don't come any closer," Voltaire said.

Hosea stopped and held out his hand. The weapon winked in the sun. "Do you recognize these markings on the side— here, and here?"

Voltaire puffed up his chest. "I am not ignorant, English. I have read many books and seen many such symbols."

Before seeing the ladders etched into Hosea's weapon, *I* had never seen the marks. I doubted Voltaire had either. But I kept my mouth shut.

Hosea nodded, accepting Voltaire's answer. "May I still explain what it is, for their benefit?" He gestured toward the other members of the band.

Voltaire agreed. He lifted his chin, but his eyes fixed curiously on the ladders whipping to and fro, hypnotically.

"The symbol you see here is a double helix," Hosea explained. He ran a finger along the etchings as he spoke. "If you don't know, a double helix is what we call the shape of life."

He twirled the tube, making the ladders dance. They didn't resemble any lifeform I'd seen before. Still, I was mesmerized, tracing their movement back and forth.

"Inside each of us are trillions of these strands, encoded with genetic information. They're the building blocks of everything alive. Man, beast and bird."

Voltaire scoffed. "Do you mean for us to believe that silver bat is alive?"

"Believe what you want," Hosea said. "But no, it's not alive. It *is* encrypted with life. My DNA, to be exact."

"Your what?" He had completely given up his pretense of prior knowledge. More, his patch was lifted up, revealing a perfectly good eye beneath.

"Deoxyribonucleic acid: DNA," Hosea repeated. "I could explain, but it's easier to show you."

He closed his fist around the weapon, causing it to awaken. In a flash, the blunt tube became a needle-sharp spear. The bandits backed away. Voltaire, however, moved closer, pressing me beneath his foot. Hosea twirled the spear skillfully, dipping it on either side of his body, before demonstrating its ability as a bow. Birds scattered as a tree on the edge of the clearing exploded into dust.

Voltaire cursed. He grabbed my blouse and pulled me up, my back to his chest. As I'd guessed, we were the same height. I made a complete shield between him and Hosea.

"Kick your weapon over here, English, or I'll kill her where she stands."

"No," Hosea said.

"I won't ask again, your weapon for her life." His words hissed in my ear.

"My weapon won't do you any good," Hosea replied, calmly. "That's what I've been telling you. It's mine. My double helix, my DNA, my life, my weapon. It only responds to my touch."

"Then what good is it to me? I'll kill her, then you along with her."

"I can get you more," Hosea said. "One for yourself and five others. We'll encode them with whomever of your men you choose." He glanced around the circle. The bandits shifted, excited by the possibility.

"Our own weapons, just like yours?" Voltaire asked.

"Not exactly the same," Hosea explained, patiently. "Everyone's DNA is unique, and their weapons will be too."

"Will they be as powerful?"

"Every Helix is exactly as powerful as its wielder."

"As powerful or not, English! Yes, or no?"

Hosea hesitated. "If you let me train you—yes."

"Not a chance," Voltaire scoffed.

"Then no. You'll have your weapons, and the biotechnology will match mine. But, they'll be no more than swords and spears in your hands." He spoke to the other men now, making an argument. "It took me years of study to wield the Helix. Self-exploration, self-control, discipline, fortitude. When you master these, and not before, you will master your Helix. I can teach you what I know."

My breath caught. He spoke of combat art, but why share the secrets with Voltaire? Such knowledge, in the Rebel's hand, would destroy the First Brother regime and the Kongo as we knew it. Is that what he wanted? I gasped inwardly. *Is that what the Director wanted?*

"Where will you get these weapons?" Voltaire asked. "I've looked, they're not in your sack."

"I'll have them brought here. If you let my friend go, I'll call for them and you will have them tomorrow."

"How will you call?"

"I have a comm-unit," Hosea said.

"Impossible," Voltaire whispered, speaking for us all. The original comm-units were the size of a room. Even the compact-design models were too big to transport easily.

"I assure you, English innovation has made much possible. They hoard technology in the Northridge, more than the average Kongo could ever dream of. I *do* have a comm-unit. And with it, the weapons are at our fingertips, a call away."

"This comm-unit, show me," Voltaire demanded.

"Not until you agree to my terms," Hosea said.

"You agree to stay here and train my men. You will provide us with weapons. And, in return, you want her," he said, thoughtfully. "You'd do *all* that for *one* girl. Why?"

The same question nagged at me. Hosea despised war, and yet, he would teach these bloodthirsty men to kill in exchange for my life?

"Not for one girl," Hosea said, slowly. He released his fist and watched the Helix disarm. When it was a harmless-looking tube again, he holstered it. "War is coming. The White-Face soldiers will kill until the First Brothers have no choice but to retaliate—or face the Assembly. The lines are drawn and no dark man will be spared. I've been to villages all over the Kongo, and I've been to Hasting. More,

I've been to the Schoolhouse and observed the Record Keepers of the future."

I cringed. Between my betrayal and East Keep's materialism, he had seen the worst we had to offer.

"War is coming," he said, again. "I find all sides objectionable, but yours the least so. If I have to choose, I'll join with you and the Rebels."

"I don't believe you," Voltaire said.

Hosea shrugged. "Believe what you want. Only take my help. If not for yourself, do it for your men. You've led them this far. Now, give them a fighting chance to survive."

Voltaire didn't respond.

"What choice do you have?" Hosea prodded. "War is coming, and you're not prepared."

Voltaire lifted his chin. He looked over Hosea, and weighed his next words. "That may be true," he said, solemnly.

Hosea nodded. "Then let me help."

Voltaire looked around at his men, then into the woods, where Fly Man had disappeared. "Contrary to what you've heard," he said, finally, "I am not the leader of the group known as Voltaire's Army. After my exile, the leaders of the so-called Voltaire's Army stole my name, and my cause. So, the current violence is not at my command. In fact, I doubt the leaders of the so-called Voltaire's Army know that I, the true Voltaire, am still alive."

This revelation shocked me, but Hosea seemed to take Voltaire's words in stride.

"My followers, my true followers," Voltaire confessed, "are numbered. Just what you see here and a few more. Will you still help us?"

Hosea didn't hesitate. "With the right weapons, it will be enough. I will get you the weapons I promised, and I will train your men. Then, we will part ways. Agreed?"

Voltaire lowered his poisoned spear from my throat.

THE SILVER PIN

Over my sigh of relief, an amicable conversation began around me.

"How long have you made your camp in these woods?" Hosea asked.

"About two months," Voltaire answered.

"Is there room for three more?"

"You'll have to clear your own resting place if you want privacy, but there's always room by the fire."

"Sure, sleep by the fire, if you can stand old Walker's chattering," someone said.

Several bandits laughed.

Shaking, I hurried to my horse. I accepted my pack from Hosea, slung it across my body and put my foot in the stirrup. I tried to mount Mary, but slipped and fell instead. William came to my rescue.

"Arika—"

"No—leave me alone!" My voice stuck out poorly in the cooperative atmosphere.

"Arika, are you okay?" Hosea asked.

"I just want to walk," I lied. My body trembled so, I didn't have a choice.

"If she prefers to walk, it's not a great distance," Voltaire said, helpfully.

"Okay then, we walk," Hosea agreed.

Hurt by my rebuff, William retreated to his own horse as our caravan moved forward. Hosea and Voltaire walked side by side, discussing the future of the Kongo. Behind them, shame burned my eyes.

One prick, I thought, as the dream of escape died inside me. One prick of Voltaire's spear and I'd have been back in the Pit—with *her*. The girl who'd limped down the hall after Jones, dripping blood and snot. Our eyes too swollen to see the others. But we felt their whispers like hot pokers. Fumbling in my pack, I found Jones' glass vial. Pulling it out, I gazed at the poisoned pin. *Do you need more?* Quickly, I stuffed it back in the bag. Tears blurred my vision.

I'd been a fool to dream of freedom. Even if I outwitted Hosea Khan and learned to survive, Jones would never let me go. I knew too much. When I failed to return, she'd set a reward for my capture—and one prick of a bounty hunter's knife was all it would take to destroy me. I swallowed. I didn't want to spy, but there was no escape. The only way forward, for me, was back to the Schoolhouse, and to spying for Jones.

Reluctantly, I lifted my gaze to Hosea, in the midst of debate with Voltaire. My ears perked as the phrase "New Seed" drifted back to me. I bit my lip, knowing what I had to do—but hating to do it. With a few quick steps, I was close enough to overhear their conversation.

THE BANDITS' CAMP

The ten of us arrived at a grassy clearing. At its center, another bandit tended an iron pot hung over a fire. The smell of stewing meat made my mouth water.

Following the others, I handed Mary's reins to Fly Man. With an easy smile, he guided the horses to the edge of the clearing, which was lined with pup tents and bedrolls.

I stuck close to Hosea, who kept up his conversation with Voltaire. So far, nothing pertinent had been said, but I was on high alert. The smallest tidbit could prove valuable to Jones.

The eighth bandit was older than the others. An apron strained over his hefty gut. His bald head gleamed in the firelight as he leaned over to stir the pot. "You boys are late," he said flatly. "I added more water to the stew. Now you got to wait for it to boil down."

Voltaire sat down on one of the logs surrounding the fire and addressed Hosea. "You say they're powered by English technology, but they are here in the Kongo. How is that possible?"

"The technology was paid for by an Assembly grant to an English research center," Hosea said. "So it has English origins. The swords arrived in the Kongo when the scientist that managed the bioweapon project relocated to the KTC over two decades ago."

"Your father," I whispered to myself. Hosea heard and turned to me.

"Dana Kumar relocated to the Kongo twenty-four years ago to assume the Directorship," I said.

Hosea nodded. "When he came, he brought the technology with him. It wasn't viable when he left the North, but he continued to develop it for our use."

I frowned—*our use?* The KTC was the hub of Kongo Technology. However, it did not produce technology for *our* use. Technology was known to engender discontent.

I'd completed my Silver Award research under Teacher Saxon, a scholar of old- and new-world technology, so I had some expertise on the subject. In her office, she had ferreted away relics of the old world. She had a computer, a cellular phone, a VCR and more. I'd heard her advocate for the broader use of technology in the Schoolhouse, but even she would have drawn the line at a KTC development center. To begin with, the KTC was serviced by the Vine House. The risk of knowledge leaking into the village would have been untenable.

"What do you mean, he developed bioweapons for *our use*?" I said. "It almost sounds like the Director is interested in distributing arms."

Hosea stared at me. "The Director is an advocate of an independent Kongo nation. Surely you've put that together by now. He developed the Helix for years, and it just recently—in the past year—became viable."

"In the past year," I repeated, my heart thudding. "Just as Voltaire's Army turned violent."

Voltaire glared at me. "The so-called 'Voltaire's Army'!" he said. "Get it right—*English*—or keep my name from your mouth. Those white-faced villains have nothing to do with the real Voltaire!"

I ignored Voltaire's interruption. Hosea was about to hand over the exact information Jones had requested. "Does the Director have a plan to use the weapons to stop the New Seed from passing muster in the Assembly?"

"I don't know," Hosea said. "Perhaps he'll answer that himself."

"Then we're still going to meet him at—" I bit my tongue before I said *the Obi Forest*. I would not expose that I knew our original destination. "—at the end of our journey?" I finished.

"No, we're not traveling to meet him anymore."

"Well then, he must be traveling here to the oasis," I said, trying to appear casual.

"I believe so," Hosea said. "He protects the Helix technology. The development of each sword is an expensive endeavor. He'll want to know the warriors I entrust them to."

I bit my lip and turned away, wanting to write down all I'd heard—*nothing lost in translation.*

Voltaire stood and shouted triumphantly. "We will have our swords, tomorrow! Do you hear that, men? Tomorrow!"

•

We all sat awaiting supper, when the bandit who'd guarded William returned to the fire. He had a beak nose that hooked sharply at the end. He carried a jug of alcohol.

"Booster, not too much drink," Voltaire cautioned.

The burly man took a swig from the jug. "I'm man enough to hold my spirits, Voltaire."

Before Voltaire could respond, Hosea spoke. "Anyone who drinks tonight cannot train in the morning. To master the Helix quickly, you'll need a clear head."

The burly man, the largest of the bandits, flexed his onyx chest so it rippled in the firelight. He eyed Hosea, drank defiantly from the jug and wiped his chin with a fist of knuckles. Holding Hosea's gaze, he passed the jug to his right. A slender bandit with ears that stuck straight out from his head immediately passed it back.

The burly man roared. "Come now, Pidge. You would let him take the hair from your chest?" He pounded his black sternum.

"I've got plenty of hair, Booster. I don't need drink to grow it."

The burly man laughed derisively and handed the bottle to the next man, shorter and even more slender than the first. "Finch, brother. Tell me you're more a man than your skinny shadow here."

Finch had a friendly face with a wide mouth and a set of small ivory teeth that he showed often. He looked thoughtfully at the jug. He sniffed the open lip and wiggled his eyebrows appreciatively. He shifted woozily, pretending to swoon from his stool. Just before he hit the ground, he popped back up with a gummy grin. He set the bottle at his feet.

"Come now, Finch," the burly man roared. "I don't believe it, not you too." He bent at the waist and shoved his face close, forcing Finch to lean back. "Why not?" he growled.

Finch pretended to grab something at his waist. He held up his empty fist and flicked his wrist left, just as Hosea had in the clearing. He watched, wide-eyed, as his imaginary Helix lengthened into a spear.

"Won't he speak?" I whispered.

"Not a word," Voltaire answered. "Pidge usually translates."

I turned back in time to watch Finch mime-shooting

an arrow into the distance. With both hands he mimed an explosion. Struck by the blast, he leapt from his seat into the air. He flipped backwards, catching himself on both hands. With his slim body straight up, balanced on his palms, he picked his way to the inside of the circle and flipped delicately back into his seat.

I marveled as he grinned, showing all his teeth.

Pidge cleared his throat. "I think Finch says he would rather train tomorrow with the English than drink tonight with you, Booster."

Booster glared. "I heard him." He snatched up the bottle and handed it to Voltaire. "You will drink, Voltaire."

Voltaire shook his head and handed it to Hosea, who passed it to me. Following course, I turned to my right. The man beside me was stout with a bulbous nose.

"Would you like some?" I said. "I don't know your name."

"That's alright. I'm Hurley." His voice was nasal, as if he was sick and couldn't breathe properly. He held out a hand.

I shifted the jug to one knee and took it. "Arika," I said.

On the cusp of replying, his face scrunched up. Booster and the others leapt backwards. A second later, I understood why. Hurley sneezed violently *one, two, three* times in a row. The blast was gigantic, spraying wetness so wide, the fire sizzled.

Voltaire moaned. "*Obi*, Hurley! Where is your handkerchief?"

I wiped my moist face discreetly.

"Lost it in the scuffle, boss." He held a hand over his mouth.

The man in the apron handed Hurley a towel.

Hurley blew his nose for several seconds and slung the towel across his shoulder. He looked gratefully at the man in the apron. "Thanks, Walker." He still sounded stuffy.

"No problem, boy." Walker pushed aside his apron and squatted so he was eye level with me. "I'm Walker. I do the cooking around here and I like company. Come by anytime."

I nodded.

"Are you thirsty?" he asked. "Sure you are," he answered. He went to the fire. "The main waterhole is through those trees there, but I've always got a bucket by the hearth." He filled a rough wooden cup with water and returned to take the jug of spirits from me.

"Thank you," I said, taking the water. I was so thirsty, I drank in large gulps.

When I'd finished he filled it again, then got water for William and Hosea. He picked up a large hat, styled in a manner I vaguely remembered seeing in a Reel Room movie about the old-world American cowboy. His kind had lived it in the western lands and eaten a dry grassy leaf that the old Americans had called *hay*.

"I'm Walker," he said again, settling the hat on his head. "You know Hurley here, with the nose. That's Voltaire and over there's Fly Man with the horses. Those two bean-poles are Finch and Pidge. And the mean one's Booster."

The burly man, Booster, grunted and sat down, his arms crossed over his chest.

•

Later, as the fire died, the bandits wandered off with full bellies. The stew had been heavy with meat and seasoned with herbs and spices. Finch had eaten with gusto, slurping his drink and patting his stomach appreciatively. What he couldn't get across in funny gestures, Pidge translated.

"Finch likes the stew," Pidge had surmised.

"Finch always likes the stew," Fly Man said, giggling.

Booster grunted. "I wish he'd shut up about it. For a mute, he's noisy."

Finch had laughed quietly and smacked his lips.

After supper, Voltaire had called for entertainment. They took turns each night, and tonight had been Finch's turn. He bounded from his seat and onto the campfire stage. With larger-than-life gestures and the occasional dry translation from Pidge, he explained that he would perform a dangerous feat over the fire. He ordered Fly Man to add more logs and cautioned us all to remain silent until the end. His calisthenics amazed me. Cartwheels and twisting backflips, forward hand-springs and aerial somersaults. After, he bowed gallantly at the waist.

"Finch wants to teach me how to tumble," I said to Hosea. We were rolling our bed mats out side by side in a secluded corner of the clearing.

"Good, do it," Hosea replied. "It will only enhance your training."

I paused and looked over my shoulder at him. "My training?"

He was busy with his pack and didn't look up. "Yes, your training. I'm going to train you along with the others."

Slowly, I sat back, my mouth agape. I knew I'd heard correctly, but I couldn't wrap my mind around it. Remaining calm, I tested his intentions. "I suppose you'll want to keep an eye on me before you turn me over to the Director. That would be impossible unless I'm in the training field with the others. But, I won't actually have a sword." My eyes fixed on his back.

Hosea turned. "On the contrary, you will. I spoke to the Director after supper."

I stood. "Hosea, are you saying you're going to give me a Double Helix? And you're going to train me to use it?"

"Yes and yes," he said, simply.

Biting my lip, I attacked the idea. "You don't have a communit; Voltaire checked your bag!"

"I assure you, I have a unit, Cobane. And I did speak to my father."

"But, the Director *knows* I've spied for Jones. Why would he give me a sword?"

"Does it matter?"

Suddenly, my knees felt weak. I sat back down. "No, I suppose not." Still, I was reluctant to get my hopes up. I smoothed my bedroll as my mind roved over the facts. "It doesn't make sense," I said finally. "You said Director Kumar wants the Kongo to be independent of the North."

Hosea nodded. "I did."

I tilted my head. "Well then, how does arming me further that aim? It's as if he thinks I might help him. Why would he think that I—a Record Keeper—would help him break the law?"

Hosea inched closer to me and lowered his voice, as if we were not the only ones listening. "You said yourself, it doesn't matter why you get a sword, so long as you get one. So let it go, Cobane. Civil war is upon us. There's no way to avoid it. Believe me, I've tried. The White-Face Army will strike at the Joust just over two weeks from today. I'd bet my right hand that Hasting will deploy the Guard in force. It will be their last chance to stop the rebellion before the Assembly gets involved. The other Keepers will be sitting targets. At least, with a weapon, you can take care of yourself. Accept the gift and stop asking questions."

I leaned in. "But *you* told me to question everything."

"Not this," he said. "Trust me, you don't want to know. So stay out of it."

My breath caught and my skin rippled with gooseflesh. I could see in his eyes that he was trying to protect me because, somehow, he cared for me. I fumbled for words. "Hosea—I. Thank you."

He shook his head. "Don't thank me. I'm only following the Director's orders."

"But you spoke to him on my behalf. You convinced him to spare me." I lifted my chin, daring him to deny my words.

He shrugged. "Believe what you want, but take a look at your wrists, Cobane. I bound and gagged you. You're right, these are dangerous times. You've got to learn to watch out for yourself."

For the second time his eyes flashed a warning. I shifted and looked down at my wrists. I could smell the coconut cream he'd given me along the lacerations. I looked back at him. "You bound me, but then you let me go," I said.

"So?"

"So—you may not be my friend, but you're not my enemy."

Instead of answering, he turned away, busying himself with his bedroll. He climbed inside and turned his back on me. "Be ready to train in the morning, Cobane."

THE OPTIMIST

That night, I lay awake unable to contain the confidence brought on by Hosea's news. I saw myself by the Schoolhouse window. Jones towered over me. She lifted her leg and I heard the familiar whisper of fear—*she kicks like a donkey*. But, instead of cowering, I stood tall, Helix in hand.

I rolled onto my stomach, biting my nails. Once I escaped, my home would be the oasis. My walls, a solid rank of trunks. My roof, an awning of leaves. The Guard would come for me. But, with the sword, I would protect myself. Even if Jones came in the flesh; *I* could master *her*. My eyes darted, searching for a hole in my plan. I couldn't find one.

Somewhere in the distance, Hurley sneezed three times. Booster commanded him to use his towel, and Voltaire shouted at them both. Walker's slow drawl hushed them all. And their animosity quieted into snores. I smiled. They were dangerous outlaws, but they were family. I rolled onto my back, wove my fingers together and placed them behind my head, imagining a family of my own.

A moment later, my gut kicked as a dark reality occurred to me. Even after I escaped, a family was out of the question. Whether from fever, war, or regimented extermination, the bandits—and most of the Kongo—would be dead within the year. And under that *hoax* of a Compromise, I was still powerless to save them. Trying would merely forfeit my own safety. I gasped suddenly, as something hard hit my temple. I sat up, rubbed my head and looked around. In the wood beyond the clearing was a dark figure—Voltaire! He held a finger to his mouth, warning me to be quiet. He waved me closer.

I hesitated. During supper, a mouthful of water had rinsed the red from his gums, and he'd removed his eye patch entirely. When I asked about the source of his bloodstained teeth, Hurley had wheezed with laughter. "*Berries*," he'd said, his nose honking. "*Them were just berries*." Finally, curiosity won out. I stood and followed Voltaire.

He stopped at his bedroll, laid out beside Fly Man. He was dressed for sleep in a nightgown. But, true to form, he wore an elaborately decorated band on his head, noisily proclaiming his leadership. I sighed. "What am I doing here, Voltaire?"

"You are a Record Keeper," he said.

My hackles rose. I knew he despised my classification. However, taking in his bare feet and headdress, I couldn't muster the energy to care. I deflated. "And if I am?" I said.

"Then I require your service." He pulled a book from his gown. "I taught Fly Man as much as possible, but we ran out of time. He can't read the big words." He handed me the book.

I glanced at the boy. In sleep, Fly Man reminded me of Fount.

"He sleeps like a rock," Voltaire said, following my gaze. "If that's what you're worried about, we won't wake him."

I studied the coverless book in my hands, wondering what he meant about running out of time. I didn't ask. Instead, I guessed the book's title. "*Candide, or, The Optimist*, by Voltaire," I said. "Is that where your name comes from? This old-world book?"

Voltaire looked grim. "I'm not sure. I found it sewed into the lining of my trousers when I woke up here—after my trial."

I remembered Voltaire's men had rescued him, but not before ten Rebirth pills were administered as punishment.

Voltaire went on. "I want to read it, to find clues about my life before, but Fly Man can't read the big words," he repeated.

"So, you want me to read it to you?"

He nodded. "I think I've read it in the past. But I don't remember."

The pills had robbed him of his ability to read and write. He had come to me in the night to protect his image before the other bandits, who believed his intellect was intact.

I frowned, swallowing my pity. He'd terrified me with his poisoned spear and berry-stained teeth. "Why should I help you?" I said. "Your army has been killing my kind for months."

"I told you," Voltaire protested. "I'm not in charge of the so-called Voltaire's Army. They're using my name."

"Your name *and* your message," I said. "You want the Record Keepers gone just like they do. You want an end to the Rebirth. You want to make laws and vote in the Senate."

Voltaire shrugged. "Yes, that's my message, or so I've been told," he said. His headdress slipped to the side.

I bit my lip. "You really don't remember, do you?"

"Do you think I'd have come to *you*, to ask for anything, if I did?"

I opened my mouth to answer.

Voltaire cut me off. "Believe me, English," he whispered harshly. "If there were any other way, I'd take it. I don't remember everything, but I do know the workers deserve freedom from their misery. Not forgetfulness, not ignorance;

freedom—and I'm going to help them get it."

His eyes were hot with passion. He didn't know it, but we were not in opposition. He wanted freedom, and so did I. After seventeen years, I realized that the students in the big house were no more free than the workers in the field. Voltaire would realize it too, in time. "I'll do it," I said, finally. "But I want something in return."

"Name it."

"I'm to train with you and your men tomorrow and—well—I need a pair of britches," I said. "You're about my size."

"Done," Voltaire said.

We shook hands.

I took the book and sat down beside him to read. "Okay. Where should I start?"

He squinted scornfully. His chin thrust out again and the sneer was back in his tone. "Where should you start? At the beginning, English—where else would you start?"

An hour later, a dark figure hovered behind me as I picked my way back across the camp. I couldn't see his face, but I knew it was William. He'd been there the moment I left my bed, and had stayed beside me since. I pulled the covers up to my chin and rested back, wide awake. Finally, I closed my eyes. A moment later, a twig snapped in the distance as he found his bed for the night.

THE FIRST TEST

I woke, instantly alert. I checked my surroundings. Hosea was not in his bedroll. Slipping out of bed, I found his pack and the ruby knife he stored there. I lodged the knife in the waistband of my skirt, grabbed my own pack and hurried away.

In a dense clump of trees, I tried on Voltaire's britches. They were made of soft, breathable cloth that gave easily. The fit was good, but it could be better. I ripped my *aura* into strips and used it to seal the britches to my body at my calves and knees. I cut some of the length for a blouse, and tied it as I'd seen the worker women do. I wrapped it around my neck, crossed it over my chest and again at my back. I tied it tightly around my waist. The tail end dangled between my legs. So, I knotted it at the small of my back, tucked it into my britches, and fashioned a belt to secure it.

I flexed my arms and back, relishing the freedom that came without a hobbled skirt to maneuver around. With my shoulders bare and my legs defined in the britches, I felt compact and aerodynamic.

"Walker called for breakfast," Hosea said.

I jumped around. He was propped casually against a tree. My eyes scurried to his knife on the ground between us. "How did you find me?"

"I see you borrowed my knife," he said.

"I would have asked, but you weren't there when I woke," I hurried to explain.

He stepped across the remains of my *aura* to pick up the knife. The red jewels glimmered as he slid the blade into its leather sheath. "I got an early comm-unit call," he said. With the sheathed knife, he gestured toward the leather string around his neck. He lifted the string so that his ugly silver medallion dangled in the air.

My jaw went slack. "You're serious? *That* is a comm-unit?"

"It is."

I stared at the charm, hiding in plain sight, deceptively insignificant. "You can find anyone in the world with a unit, hone in on their exact location and speak to them, with that?"

He nodded. "I can. I detached the honing component on this particular unit, so I can't be tracked. But, I can still make contact and communicate."

"It's so small," I said.

"The device is small, but the three-dimensional holograph it produces is life-sized. I hold it in my hand and the image projects up from the center of the coin. It's like talking face to face."

"They told us there was only one comm-unit in the Kongo," I said, bitterly.

Hosea smiled, sympathetically. "They lie." He took a worn strip of *bambi* from his back pocket and came forward. He held it out, along with the ruby knife. "Keep it," he said.

I took the knife. It was warm from his hand. And I felt warm as he knelt to show me how to tie the strap into a holster for the blade.

"If you wear it around your calf, like this, you'll never have to take it off," he said, his hand still wrapped around my ankle.

Bending at the waist, I admired it, invisible beneath the leg of my britches "When will my sword come?" I asked, adjusting the laces of my moccasins.

"It came hours ago." He smiled and held up a hand when he saw my excitement. "No—no more questions for now. We'll start training later this morning. Now, we eat breakfast."

Breakfast was bread slathered in nut paste, an oily mixture of finely ground forest nuts and seeds. It had the consistency of drying glue, but it was high in fat which, Hosea assured us, was good for training. With that in mind, I scraped the paste from the roof of my mouth and requested more. My ability to wield the sword was my key to freedom. With a smile, Walker filled my plate again.

Hosea led us to a training field half a mile away. It smelled like freshly cut firewood. Instead of grass, a thick blanket of felled needles covered the ground.

In the middle of the clearing, Hosea stopped and pointed to a row of narrow tree stumps. "Each of you line up behind a pole," he said.

I moved obediently. The surface of the stump was smooth, ten inches in diameter. I guessed Hosea had leveled it with his Helix. His weapon hung from his waist but, as I surveyed the field, ours were nowhere to be found.

"Step onto the post," Hosea ordered.

I looked around. There were five of us training. William had explained, again, that he no longer lived by the club which, for him, meant he would only fight in defense of a loved one. He had no need for such a powerful weapon. Along with him, Walker and Hurley admitted to being too tired and old to train. All three had remained by the morning fire as Hosea rounded us up.

"Where is my sword?" Voltaire asked. He crossed his arms over his thin chest.

"The swords are close by," Hosea said.

"I want mine now," Booster said. He too remained stubbornly on the ground.

"You'll have it when you're ready, and not before," Hosea said.

"And when will that be, English?" Voltaire said.

I looked between Voltaire, Booster and Hosea. He was unmoved by their defiance.

"Not before you get on the post," he said. "Now let's go, each of you."

Finch shrugged and he and Pidge climbed up. I followed, along with Booster and Voltaire. My feet barely fit on the flat surface. I looked around, to see how the others fared. Booster struggled, with both heels hanging from the back of his post. Next to him, Voltaire stood squarely, his booted feet jutting just over the edge. Pidge looked uncomfortable up on his toes, but Finch relaxed on one foot. His long toes curled around the post like fingers. His hands rested casually against his hips.

Hosea paced in front of us as we settled on the posts. He squinted up at the sky. "It's just after seven. Your training begins now."

"Without swords?" Booster shouted. His tenuous hold on the post faltered and he fell.

Hosea turned on his heel. "Booster, you'll do one hundred push-ups and circle the field ten times. When you're done, get back on your post. Your training will begin at fifteen after. If you fall, you're done for the day. You'll start training tomorrow. The same goes for everyone. Stay on your post."

"What for?" Pidge asked.

Finch gestured wildly.

"For how long? Can we sit down? Can we switch feet?" Pidge translated.

"We'll break for noon meal," Hosea said. "You can do anything, except talk or set foot on the ground. As for why we're doing this, be patient. The answer will become clear." He paused. "I'll tell you this, which is more than I was told. The wise among you will heed it. When the pain attacks, look inside yourself and meditate on what you observe. Do this and you'll master your Double Helix. Booster, get going."

Booster began his punishment with a grunt of annoyance.

"Any more questions?" Hosea asked.

We looked at each other, full of apprehension. No one spoke.

"Good—silence begins now." Moving, once again, more quickly than my eye could register, Hosea jumped onto a post a few feet in front of our post arrangements. *Surprise.* He, the teacher, was going to stand with us. More, his post was further from the ground and smaller in diameter than ours. He stood on one foot, switching back and forth, with great athleticism. Then, his eyes on a point just before him, he settled in.

•

An hour before noon, my thigh muscles began twitching in protest. At the same time, the arches in my feet twisted violently. The tightness in my calves seized into cramps, shooting excruciating pain in every direction. Stiffness worked its way into my back, making me long to stretch. Each time I tried, I lost balance. If I fell, I knew, my training would be delayed—an unacceptable fate. The Helix was my key to freedom. I conjured up a picture of Jones' hateful face, clenched my jaw, and forced myself to be still.

I heard the others struggling as well. Booster's breath howled and Pidge gave a guttural grunt. Voltaire was bent in an uncomfortable seated position that he didn't seem able to get out of. Finch alone had yet to break down. Like Hosea, he had remained on one leg, switching periodically. I'd even seen him stretch, tilting forward at the waist, one leg lifted behind and both arms extended from his sides.

I peeked at Hosea. Straight ahead of us, he stood on the ball of one foot. The other dangled over the edge of the pole. His arms relaxed at his sides and his eyes anchored on a single spot of earth. He might have been standing on solid ground. *How was he doing it?*

Booster cried out and tumbled from his pole. Walker and Hurley, watching from the sidelines, hurried forward with water. The sight of cool liquid trickling down Booster's black chin shook me. I tilted sideways. Flinging my arms out, I sank into a deep squat, regaining my balance just in time. The fire in my thighs exploded. Pidge shouted loudly and collapsed back, joining Booster on the ground.

"Water, water," Pidge said. Hurley hurried to splashed water on Pidge's legs, which shook dangerously. He was in no condition to go on. He and Booster would begin again tomorrow.

Time passed as I panted. Sweat dripped rhythmically from my earlobe to my shoulder. Desperate, I reminded myself of why I had to stay strong. *Free-dom, free-dom, free-dom.* I clenched my jaw. *How much longer?*

My back muscles clamped at my spine, pinching my nerves. My shoulders solidified. My neck convulsed. I heard someone moaning, and realized it was my own voice deepened by pain. I screwed my eyes shut. Voltaire began praying, and Finch breathed in rasps. *Free-dom, free-dom. Oh God, Obi— freedooom!* I imagined myself roaming the oasis as another minute ticked by.

In the end, my legs crumpled involuntarily. Unable to stand, I toppled to the ground, just as Hosea called time. Terrified I had failed, I pushed myself aright and looked around. Voltaire lay on the ground, as did Finch. We had all fallen at the same moment Hosea had released us. Tears came to my eyes and I collapsed back to the floor. I had passed. I had passed the first morning of training.

•

On our way to camp, Walker and Hurley gushed congratulations. Even Booster and Pidge shook our hands, goodnaturedly. I accepted their praise, along with Voltaire and Finch. However, I was too worried to revel in my triumph. It was easy to see why Voltaire and I had withstood the trial. It was not skill, but luck. Our feet had fit flatly within the diameter. Pidge's and Booster's task, standing on half of one foot, had been measurably harder. Finch had his acrobatic skills to rely on. If not for that, he too would have fallen.

I worried my lip as I sat by the fire. If mere luck propelled me through this first trial—what would happen when my luck ran out? I hated for the Helix, my means of escape, to rest on such tenuous terms. As I accepted a plate of food, my gaze—unbidden—sought William's. He smiled and shook his head. *Arika not worry.* I understood him as if he'd whispered directly into my heart. His familiar hum drifted across the fire to me. The same short tune. My shoulders relaxed. He lifted his cup and nodded his approval.

•

That night, I read to Voltaire. He lounged on his back, his hands crossed over his middle. "You're skipping, English," he said.

Short-tempered, I rolled my shoulders. I'd asked Hosea about the training schedule after dinner, hoping to receive an extra tip. He had laughed in my face. *This isn't the Schoolhouse, Cobane. You'll learn with everyone else.*

Seeing Hosea's smug expression, I glared at Voltaire. "I'm not skipping," I snapped.

He ignored me. "Go back—three pages."

"One," I countered.

He opened one eye. "Three."

I sighed and began again, through clenched teeth.

"You're going too fast—English!"

I snapped the book shut. "I am *not* English!"

Fly Man stirred restlessly. Voltaire sat up to adjust the boy's covers. "Of course, Record Keepers aren't English," he muttered. "You speak like the English and you live in the white house with the white ghost. In the Assembly, you vote like the English, to the harm of your own people. But, I see now. Oh, mighty First Brother, *you* are right—you are not English."

"I was forced to live in the white house," I hissed. "The white ghosts—the *Teachers*—forced me to speak as I do. I had no choice."

"Yet you benefit greatly from all the choices you did not have."

"I had food and clothes, yes, but nothing else. I'm no more free than you!"

Voltaire scoffed. "For all your letters, you—*English*—are quite dull. You'll never understand what you have until it's taken from you."

I threw the book on the ground. "Fine. If you're so smart, you read it!" I jumped up and stomped away, muttering to myself.

Insufferable, ill-tempered, insane! When he wasn't plaguing Hosea with questions or quizzing me on the logic of the English way, he strutted around, sneering at everyone else's intelligence, and bragged about his own! It was all a show. Put on to intimidate others, just like his red-stained teeth.

I fumed all the way to my bedroll, snatched off my moccasins and lay down fully clothed—in Voltaire's britches. I bit my lip and rolled over, determined to rest. However, after several minutes, I sighed.

Voltaire and Fly Man were bent together when I returned, the book between them.

"But I'm still sleepy," Fly Man protested.

"Don't be a weakling," Voltaire said. His voice was gentle. "Finish this verse."

The little boy clawed at his eyes and yawned. "Okay, okay." He held the book close to his nose, as if proximity would help him decipher. "'Do you believe,' said Can—Can—"

"Candide," Voltaire said. "That's his name."

"Oh," Fly Man yawned and continued. "'Do you believe, Candide, that men have always mass—massacred each other as they do today, that they have always been liars, cheats, traitors, ingrates, bri—brigands, idiots, thieves.'" He yawned loudly. "I'm sleepy. Can't we read tomorrow?"

"No! You always say that and you never read. At that rate, you'll never improve."

I stepped away from the trees. "Let the boy go to sleep."

Voltaire glared. "You. What do you want?"

"We had a bargain." I held out my hand for the book. "It's only fair."

I saw his battle. He wanted to throw my fairness in my First-Brother face. Fly Man, however, was already sound asleep.

Without another word, I resumed my position.

"'Do you believe,' said Candide, 'that men have always massacred each other as they do today, that they have always been liars, cheats, traitors, ingrates, brigands, idiots, thieves, scoundrels, gluttons, drunkards, misers, envious, ambitious, bloody-minded, calumniators, debauchees, fanatics, hypocrites, and fools?'

"'Do you believe,' said Martin, 'that hawks have always eaten pigeons when they have found them?'

"'Yes, without doubt,' said Candide.

"'Well, then,' said Martin, 'if hawks have always had the same character why should you imagine that men may have changed theirs?'

"'Oh!' said Candide, 'there is a vast deal of difference, for free will—'"

THE BREATH

Finch and I planned my calisthenics training for the next morning, while Booster and Pidge completed the pole challenge. Eager to start, I woke and hurried to find Finch by the fire. Voltaire and Fly Man were with him. William stood by the hearth, whittling and humming the same old tune. Walker peeled and chopped vegetables. Beside him, Hurley dozed. The three of them were similar in age and often huddled together like so, apart from the rest of us.

Voltaire's scowl darkened at my approach and Finch jumped to his feet, gesturing frantically. I couldn't make out what he said. I sat on the log I usually shared with Hosea and asked him to repeat himself. He turned to Fly Man and gestured, huffing loudly.

"He says," Fly Man translated. "That you woke too late. So you'll have to go with him to tickle up some fish for Walker before you start."

"Start what?" Voltaire asked.

"Finch is teaching me acrobatics," I said. "Yes, Finch, I'll help. But, what is tickling fish?"

Fly Man giggled, covering his mouth.

"Tickling fish is what we call fishing around here," Walker explained.

"Uh-uh," Fly Man said, shaking his head. "I use a pole and

Voltaire uses a spear. Only Finch tickles them, Walker," he corrected. He turned to me and whispered, showing several holes in his teeth. "Only ferals tickle fish."

Finch gestured again and Walker laughed. "Finch says he ought not have to fish at all today. He says, if Fly Man was any good with a pole, there would be plenty of fish left over from yesterday." As he translated, Walker handed me a bowl of food. "He sure has that right, little man. Now, hush and eat."

Chuckling, I looked down at the selection of nuts and wild grain in my lap. It was mixed with dried fruit, and I took my time picking out the combinations I liked best.

After several minutes Finch let out a breath and came to stand over me. I squinted up.

"He says he doesn't have time for you to eat so slowly," Fly Man said with a shrug.

"Arika must eat," William declared, setting his whittling aside.

I looked between him and Finch, both with their arms crossed.

"I'll take it with me," I said. "I'll eat while you fish."

I ate in handfuls as Finch led me down to the stream. In addition to the food, William had given me a carved wooden canister of water. I uncorked the top and took a long drink, eyeing his handiwork. I'd overheard him say he learned to whittle when he was young, and, miraculously, had never forgotten the skill, despite his many Rebirths.

It was strange to see such a large man wielding a sharp blade so gently. His hands moved quickly, making tiny cuts and angles in the soft wood. His work was unplanned. So, it was impossible to guess what he was making until the moment he finished. Along with my water container, he'd completed a wooden warrior for Fly Man, and a small etching of the five trainees on stumps.

"I wonder how Pidge and Booster are faring," I said, swallowing the last of my food.

With no one around to translate, I watched Finch closely for his answer.

We can walk by the field if you want, he said. *That way, you can have a look for yourself.*

"Okay, let's do that."

He grinned, happy to have made himself clear.

According to Finch, Pidge and Booster were both in their third hour on the pole. To my surprise, Hosea was, again, completing the challenge with them. If I didn't know exactly how much pain he was in, after three additional hours, I would have dismissed his efforts. As it was, my respect for him grew more robust. It settled, like a warm flush, in my chest.

"How does he do it?" I said, urgently. His endurance on the post was the key to his superior skill with the Helix. If I could muster half his ability, I would never be afraid of Jones again. "How does he stand the pain?"

Finch answered quickly, as if he had considered the question before. He lifted his hand and inhaled, slowly, bringing his hand down, running it along his throat and chest, all the way to his stomach. He held his breath a few seconds, then exhaled.

"Breath?" I guessed. "You think Hosea bears the pain with his breath?"

Finch nodded, smiling.

"I don't understand."

He explained more, turning me so that we faced each other

squarely. He took another breath, then he pointed at me.

"You want me to breathe?"

He nodded.

Obediently, I inhaled.

He clapped his hands harshly and shook his head. *You're doing it wrong.* Taking my hand, he placed it on his stomach. It ballooned out as he inhaled and it filled with air. It flattened when he exhaled.

When he pointed at me, I tried again. My chest and shoulders rose, but my stomach remained flat. "I'm doing it wrong!" I said, convinced.

Finch demonstrated the technique once more. His stomach ballooned up, his chest stayed flat.

I turned to watch Pidge and Booster and, suddenly, Hosea's advice came back to me.

When the pain attacks your balance, look inside and meditate on what you observe. Do this, and you'll master your Double Helix.

From a distance, I saw that Hosea, like Finch, was breathing from his stomach. It worked rhythmically, in and out, as the rest of him remained immobile. I closed my eyes and focused. Once again, I tried to fill my abdomen with air. Instead, my chest rose and fell. My stomach remained deflated. Frustrated by my repeated failure, I opened my eyes.

"We should go," I said to Finch. "Walker will be expecting fish."

Finch looked about to protest, but shrugged. He led me the rest of the way to the stream.

THE CHAMPION

That night we celebrated all the trainees passing the first test. At the feast, Pidge and Booster soaked their feet in water as Pidge recounted the tale of Booster's initial fall from the post. As they laughed, I surveyed them. Each man did their part to support the camp.

Voltaire was ornery, but brilliant. Pidge, possessed of a steely will, was an expert trapper. Booster was arrogant, but mighty. He could kill a desert antelope with a single blow. Walker cooked and gathered food. Hurley, when he wasn't dozing, maintained a potted garden of vegetables that he painstakingly shuttled from camp to camp when they moved. Even Fly Man did his part by keeping the horses. Unlike the students at the Schoolhouse, they needed no prodding to work together. They had to survive.

I ate my fish slowly, ignoring the twinges in my body, which ached from my lesson with Finch. I'd picked myself up from the ground again and again, telling myself the training was less painful than returning to the Schoolhouse and playing the traitor for Jones.

My gaze moved on to Hosea Khan, who ate in silence. Earlier, I'd seen him talking to William in private. They had been too far away to hear, but William's cross-armed stance had relaxed as they spoke. The giant had rested one affectionate hand on

Hosea's shoulder and squeezed before walking away. When he was out of sight, Hosea had turned to catch my eye. I shifted out of sight, just as he gave a mock salute. He'd known I was there all along. Just as I knew, somehow, that *I* was the subject of their exchange.

I took another bite of fish and let my eyes narrow on his flat abdomen as he inhaled. A flush of admiration settling in my chest. Finch switched to shallow chest breathing often, especially when frustrated at my slowness. Hosea, in contrast, breathed deeply, as if it were second nature to him. For hours now, I had tried to catch him unawares without success. *How did he do it?*

Just then, Booster stood and raised his cup. "I propose a toast," he said, "to me."

I tore my eyes from Hosea and laughed with the others.

"And why are we toasting you this time, Booster?" Pidge asked.

Booster adjusted his feet in the water bucket, so he stood taller. "We toast me because I will be our Champion at the upcoming Joust."

Pidge stopped smiling. Confused, I set my cup aside. The Joust consisted of a Champion from each of the twelve Kongo Houses. No other group could participate. More, the bandits' pictures had been circulating the Kongo for months on *Wanted* posters. They would be arrested on sight if they entered Cobane. I looked at Voltaire, certain he would refute Booster's claim.

Voltaire remained silent.

"You speak too soon, Booster," Pidge said. "The Joust is weeks away and we all agreed that Voltaire will pick our Champion."

"Voltaire and I spoke today. I will be Champion," Booster argued.

All eyes turned to Voltaire. He stood to explain. "As you all know, I plan to return to the Kongo people on the night of the Joust," he said.

My mouth dropped. The others, however, including Hosea, weren't surprised.

Voltaire continued. "With the help of the Hannibal Champion, who agreed to let one of us take his place, we will infiltrate the Joust, win the tournament, and prove, that the *real* Voltaire is the true leader of the Second Brothers' Rebellion."

I nodded. It was a good plan. If Voltaire's Champion won, he would have the people's favor.

Voltaire continued. "This morning I spoke with the Cobane Champion, William, formerly known as Crane the Conqueror. William told me that the so-called Voltaire's Army will *also* fight in the Joust. Because of this, William says that Booster is our only hope of winning."

Stationed between Hurley and Walker, William whittled a long block of wood. He did not confirm his conversation with Voltaire.

"And so," Voltaire concluded, "Booster will be our Champion."

Pidge threw his cup. "You base our strategy on the word of a man you've just met. Where do his loyalties lie? Where did he get his information?" Pidge asked.

Voltaire's chest rose and fell rapidly. "William Whittle is not only the former Cobane Champion," he said. "Before he gave up the club, he led the so-called Voltaire's Army."

My mouth dropped again. Finally, William finally set aside his whittling. The image he presented, his hands in his lap, didn't mesh with the pictures I'd seen of the White-Face men. William, however, didn't deny Voltaire's claim.

"You were our leader?" Booster asked.

Eyeing Booster, William performed a series of identifying hand motions.

"You were our leader." Booster confirmed.

"Booster! You were a White-Face soldier?" I asked.

Booster glanced at me. "Yes. I was entranced by Voltaire's writings. I did anything for the cause, even kill. Before I learned that the true Voltaire was against the Army, I wore the white-face. Hurley and Walker saved me from a mob of Loyalists set on hanging me. Pidge, there, was always a Rebel."

"And Finch?" I asked.

Finch stood and held up a hand to Booster. *Quiet Booster, I will tell my story myself.* Respectfully, Booster withdrew. Walker removed his hat, holding it to his chest as Finch cleared his throat. I sensed Finch's tale would not end well.

•

"I was a household servant at House Bankhead," Finch began. "I served with my brother. We were born from the same egg on the same day. He was shorter than me by a quarter inch, so we called him Little Finch. Each night we entertained the English diplomats at the big house, and the English treated us well in return. We ate the fat, and slept by the kitchen fire. And, because they feared we would forget our act, they shielded us from the Rebirth.

"Life was good until Little Finch found a Rebel pamphlet. I could not read as Little Finch could. And so, the English letters did not plague me like they plagued him. For him, they were like a fever. They put ideas into his head. And after, he would not perform. Instead, he hunted for more pamphlets and stole paper to copy the old ones. So, the English sent us both to the field.

"Work in the field was hard. Sunup to sundown, without enough to eat. And still, Little Finch longed for the pamphlets. They had become like hash to him. I begged, but he would not give them up.

"Then, one day, we were sent to the outfield for work. It took all morning to get there and, when we arrived, we were punished for being late, though it was not our fault. The next day, we took a shorter route, through the bush. It was a dangerous route, but we ignored the danger. We were afraid to be punished.

"My brother was ahead and that is how I saw the snake—twice the length of my arm, and as thick as my wrist. It did not make a sound, I swear, not a sound. It slid up. I cried out and I crushed its head, too late. The snake killed my brother. One minute, Little Finch was alive. The next, he was dead. The last thing he said was this:

"'*Finch, find the one who writes the pamphlets. Pledge your allegiance, forever, to the end of the age.*'

"I did not care about the pamphlets. I hated them, as they had possessed my brother. Even so, I could work no more at Bankhead, the House of the snake that murdered my Little Finch. I got one of his cursed pamphlets and followed the name on it, Voltaire, across the Kongo—to Hannibal. When I found Voltaire, I pledged my allegiance and, together, we fight all the snakes. First, we were Rebels. Now we are bandits. Next, I do not know."

He lunged over the fire to Voltaire's side. He placed the other over his heart and gestured for several seconds, tears in his eyes. Pidge did not translate. There was no need.

"Where you go, Voltaire, I will go. If the Conqueror Crane is your friend, he is also mine. If Booster will fight for you in the Joust, he will also fight for me. To the end of the age."

Finished, Finch retired to his log.

Pidge broke the silence. "I do not disagree with you, Voltaire. I too have a story of allegiance, though I will not tell it. I do not *disagree* with you. But I will not follow anyone blindly, as I did the English." As he said this, he sent me a nasty look.

He considered me as English as Jones. After Finch's story, could I blame him? I bowed my head. I was a First Brother, part of the group charged with protecting the workers. Part of the group that betrayed them for our own gain.

"I want an explanation," Pidge went on. "What is this White-Face leader doing among us? And why do you seek his council?"

William returned to his knife and wood, leaving Voltaire to answer.

"I seek his council because the White-Face strategy for the tournament was formed before he resigned his leadership." Voltaire said. "Last night, William told me of their plan."

The bandits murmured.

Voltaire went on. "Two men now lead the so-called Voltaire's Army. The first man, Martin, speaks for the Army. The second, Condor, is their military head. It is Condor that wears the white-face."

Pidge began to pace. "How do you know Crane isn't here as a spy? Did you consider that possibility?"

Voltaire nodded. "There are two reasons I believe him. As we all know, the identity of the White-Face soldiers is a well-guarded secret. I did not suspect William was one of their number, until he came to me of his own free will."

I nodded, seeing his reasoning. Why would William expose himself, if not to help?

"Second," Voltaire continued, "we found his group in the woods, driven here by a storm, not the other way around. That proves he was not seeking us for any ill purpose."

Pidge crossed his arms. "If he was ever the leader of the so-called Voltaire's Army, he can't be trusted. He is responsible for many deaths."

At this, William stood and walked away from the fire, back to his bedroll.

Anger surged in me. "What's past is passed," I said, glaring at Pidge. "William no longer lives by the club."

"On the day we met, he nearly killed Fly Man." Pidge insisted.

"He would never have harmed a hair on that child's head," I said, standing. "He only wanted Voltaire to release me."

Pidge pursed his lips.

"If William says Booster is the right choice, you should trust him," I said. I sat down, feeling awkward. Of all people, William should have been the last person I stood up for.

"I agree with Arika," Hosea said, lending his support.

Pidge sighed and kicked the ground.

"Now, hold on," Hurley said. He blew his nose and stood. "No one is asking *why* Booster the best choice."

"Damn right," Walker added. "Did William explain himself?" He pushed his hat back and looked to Voltaire.

"He did," Voltaire answered. "He said that the White-Face Champion to fight in the Joust will be one of the leaders of the so-called Voltaire's Army."

"Condor," Pidge exploded. "I relish the chance to fight this man, face to face. He equates the name Voltaire with violence."

Voltaire held up a hand. "I appreciate your loyalty, but the White-Face leader is a trained Kongo Guard and a large man."

"I am not afraid of the Guard or a large man!" Pidge protested.

"Not just large," Voltaire insisted. "Condor is colossal. William himself cannot stare him in the eye."

Pidge fell silent.

My heart shook with fear. "What's your plan?" I asked Voltaire.

"My plan is to send Booster, my strongest Champion, to fight and win the Joust," Voltaire said.

I blinked. "That's it? Booster isn't even as large as William!"

Voltaire turned stony. "I know that, *English*."

"He'll be slaughtered!"

"But he'll fight anyway," Voltaire snapped. "He *wants* the honor of dying for the cause of the Second Brothers' Rebellion."

Booster stood tall, his arms crossed over his chest.

Pidge moved to stand in front of him. "I too want the honor of dying for the Second Brothers' Rebellion. We get our swords tomorrow, Booster. If I can best you in a match two weeks from today, you'll give up your spot in the Joust and I will Champion us—agreed?" He held out his hand.

Booster hesitated only a moment, then took it. "If you can beat me, brother, you're the Champion."

They both turned to Voltaire, who nodded his consent.

THE INVINCIBLE

Later, I lay in bed breathing in and out. I had yet to take a single proper breath, though I'd practiced for hours, just as Finch had instructed me. A cold rock of apprehension sat in my stomach. I couldn't stop picturing my life of freedom. Slaying Jones and bellowing my triumph, alone, in an empty wood. My stomach grumbled. I would be free, but *what good was my freedom, if I spent it alone?*

I thought of the bandits, their nobility and their passion. Finch in tears over his blood brother. Pidge and Booster vying to serve Voltaire. Hurley and Walker had remained silent but they had stories too. They were each in the oasis for the good of the Kongo and only *I* knew the futility of their effort.

Even *if* they won Joust and subdued the White-Face Army— they still had to contend with the future of America. The New Seed would diminish the Second Brothers' role under the Compromise. Like unproductive vines, thousands of Kongo people would be cut off and thrown into the fire, for the greater good. Northerners would flood south, hungry for land. With luck, the Second Brother might overcome the First, but how would either overcome the Compromise?

Suddenly, Hosea growled my name.

In a flash, he leapt from his bedroll. He landed beside me. "Here and here," he said. He placed two warm hands against my abdomen. "These are the muscles you use to breathe," he said. "As you take air in, drop your diaphragm."

He cupped a soft place beneath my sternum. "This is your diaphragm, here. Let your lungs fill from the bottom to the top. Compress your stomach to make room. To release the breath, push up from here." He pressed my lower belly. "Squeeze from the bottom up. And, *damn,* Cobane, breathe through your nose. You sound like a congested power fan."

He was so close, I forgot to take offense. Instead, I smiled a little. I'd never seen him so bothered. His face screwed up, uncharacteristically. Bent over me, his wide shoulders blotted out the sky. A succulent curiosity wet my palms and I gave into it, pressing a shy hand to his torso.

I was about to speak when he swallowed audibly. "No—no questions. Close your mouth."

I did, withdrawing my hand.

"Now, breathe and concentrate on what I said."

I wet my lips. Inhaling through my nose, I dropped my diaphragm and filled my lungs from the bottom, just as he said. I pictured making room for the air in my body and, slowly, my gut inflated. I held the breath, then squeezed my lower belly until it deflated. "I did it!" I said.

Hosea dropped his hands to his sides; his mouth tilted at one corner. "Very good." He rocked back on his heels. He'd turned to go to bed when I stopped him.

"Is that how you managed to stay on the post?" I asked.

He was still for so long, I thought he wouldn't answer. He turned back. "Breath is life, Cobane. It's how I completed the challenge. It's how I do anything." He took my hand and placed it back on his abdomen. "Close your eyes."

In the dark, I felt him breathe for several seconds.

"In and out, in and out," he said. "It's a circle. A perfect exchange." He let go of my hand and I opened my eyes.

"You push out weakness." He pushed his arms forward, palms flat. "And you take in power." He separated his hands, then raised them over his head. In a smooth motion, he closed his palms like a praying mantis and pulled them down in front of his chest. Without stopping, he pressed them out again, palms up, completing the cycle. "It's a circle," he repeated. "A perfect exchange."

I followed along as he continued the pattern, breathing in and out with each movement. "I can feel it," I said. "You call it power, but it calms me to my core."

"Good," he said. "In combat, we use the breath to fight. But, its power is peaceful and immeasurable."

I frowned. "Immeasurable, because we can't see it?" I asked.

"No, Cobane—immeasurable because it's limitless, infinite. It's everything unseen in the world and beyond. In the stars and beyond that. Like a breath, we can hold it only a few minutes. But, if you're very quiet, you can meditate on the power and learn to move with it."

"In and out, in and out," I said.

He nodded. "The more you meditate, the more you will learn." He tapped his temple with a finger.

"Learn what?" I asked.

He lifted one shoulder. "Everything. How to move. When to move and where. You'll learn to read others and predict their movements."

I remembered noting Voltaire's anger—not by his voice, which had remained calm, but by his breath.

"The goal," he went on, "is to move in perfect alignment with your breath. To meditate in motion."

"I think I understand," I said. "I need to align with this power, so I can master the Helix."

Hosea shook his head. "It's not about swords, Cobane. It never is. When you achieve perfect alignment, you will have long since stopped relying on swords."

"Because, when I get there..." I stopped. The end of the sentence escaped me.

"When you get there," Hosea said. He touched my cheek, tucked a braid behind my ear. "When you get there, Arika, you'll be invincible."

Our eyes locked and I inhaled, suddenly understanding everything.

His mouth hovered over mine. He breathed out and I breathed in.

When he dropped his hand, I jerked. "Hosea?" I whispered.

"No," he said, but his voice cracked.

"No, what?"

He shook his head, resisting me—or himself. I couldn't tell. A second later, he slipped into his bedroll.

THE DOUBLE HELIX

The next morning, I arrived late to breakfast. Pidge and Booster were arguing with Voltaire over Joust strategies. I hurried by them, skipping the seat I usually shared with Hosea, which was empty. I settled next to Walker and William, who generally kept out of the others' discussions.

Walker tilted his hat back. "See, William, she has arisen."

William glanced up from his whittling and nodded. He resumed his soft hum.

"William demanded I make a take-away breakfast for you," Walker continued. "He had no faith you would wake in time."

"Arika no sleep," William explained.

Walker flashed his big smile. "So you said, old man." He reached down to pick up my water bottle and a pouch of food.

I took it and tucked in. William was right. I had not slept well. I'd lain awake, struggling with discontent as well as my growing affection for the Vine Keeper.

I took a sip of water and glanced over my shoulder at Voltaire and Pidge. They were listening intently to Booster. I looked away. I'd considered the matter from every angle and there was no help for it, the bandits were doomed. I had to keep them at a distance. I was in the oasis to master the Helix sword and gain my freedom! *However, if I failed*—I bit my lip and grazed one hand over the crescent moon scars on my arm.

If I did not master the Helix, I would have to return to Jones. I would take the Final Exam and become a Record Keeper. Jones would torture me for information before I left for Hasting, and I was not strong enough to withstand her. The thought made my stomach toss. With such a cross-purpose in mind, one thing was clear: I could not make friends with the bandits. The less I knew of their plans, the better.

I looked up as Hosea arrived with a trunk. He held the container with ease, letting the widest part rest against his stomach, exactly where my hand had rested last night. My mouth went dry and I coughed, drawing his attention. Our eyes met over the fire. There was nothing out of the ordinary in his. Surely none of the hot feathers I felt in my own stomach. I forced my eyes back to my plate and finished eating.

When it was time to train, there was an acute air of excitement among us as we followed Hosea, with the mysterious trunk in tow, to the training field. He led us to the posts and set the trunk down. We all gathered around him. Instead of opening the trunk, however, he straightened.

"Line up," he said, folding his arms. "And strip down. I want your chest and feet bare. Arika and Voltaire, keep your shirts, but step forward. Arika, you first."

I obeyed automatically. He knelt on a knee before me and took a knife from his pocket. He grasped the hem of my blouse and cut an L shape up and to the side. Resting the knife between his teeth, he gripped my blouse in both hands and ripped six inches from the bottom.

Cool air touched my middle.

"Voltaire," he said, dismissing me.

I resumed my place with the other men, who were now bare-chested. I felt exposed, but I understood why he'd stripped us. He'd explained it last night—a man's breath mirrors his soul. With our midsections bare, nothing could be hidden. Every catch of fear, every hiccup of anger was on display for observation and discipline.

Another rip split the air and Voltaire stepped back in line, sneering. I looked curiously at Voltaire's midriff. It was barer than my own, as Hosea had taken ten inches of shirt. My eyes narrowed. Lean and muscular, Voltaire's midsection tapered at the waist before flaring out again into round, unmistakably feminine hips. My breath caught.

I stared, open-mouthed, as my mind flew over the conversations I'd had with and about Voltaire. Surely someone had told me the notorious Rebel Voltaire was a man? Instead, I realized, I'd been told no such thing. Now revealed, the truth was obvious. My eyes flew over her. The thinness of her wrists and ankles. The soft curve of her firm jaw. Even the swagger with which she carried herself, chin tilted pugnaciously, was distinctly feminine.

I glanced around and saw that none of the other trainees were surprised. No one stared at her; or me. Hosea had demanded their attention. I struggled to focus on his words.

"The task you endured yesterday was not strictly a training exercise," he said. "It was a test. I, myself, endured it before you at the hands of my own teacher—Director Kumar. The purpose of the test was to aid me in choosing which weapon will best complement your strengths while guarding against your individual weaknesses."

Finally, I tore my eyes from Voltaire. Had we passed or failed? None of us knew.

Finch waved angrily at Hosea. *You promised us swords, not tests!*

"Finch is right," Pidge said. "You said our swords would be like yours."

Hosea placed a hand on Finch's shoulder. "Trust me, brother, your weapon will be extremely powerful. The technology used to make it is identical to my own. But, as I've explained, the nature of the Double Helix is such that no two are exactly alike. Each one takes a unique form." He removed his weapon and twirled it to life. "My sword takes the basic form of a bow. The daggers and spear are both secondary forms that I call up at will." He switched forms back and forth with practiced ease.

"How many forms can it take?" Pidge asked.

"The range is limited only by the will of the wielder."

"So, it can do everything we command it to," Booster said, his eyes wide with greed.

Hosea shook his head. "Not everything you command it to," he clarified. "Everything you *will* it to."

Booster snorted, dismissively.

"You snort, but I think you'll find that honing your will is no easy task. The Helix takes years of practice to master. It's an extension of you and will bear with you your failings."

Finch waved his hand. *How does it work?* he asked.

"It's complicated. More so than I have time to explain. Think of your Helix as you would a third arm that reads and reacts to your energy. See here." He twirled his weapon, in spear form, along his fingers. "Though it's quite heavy, I can maneuver my spear in a large circle with only the slightest effort. Ordinarily, such a weight would take great strength to wield."

"Then how are you moving it?" Pidge asked.

"With my energy," Hosea said. "The Helix responds to the muscles in my fingers. But also to the potential energy stored elsewhere in my body."

"Your potential energy. Where is that?" Pidge asked. His eyes roamed Hosea's form, looking for a muscle group.

"It's everywhere," Hosea answered. "My muscle, and tendon, of course. But also, my bones and joints. And deeper, my marrow and cells. The atoms that make up the elements in my cells and the bonds that hold them together. These store a tremendous amount of energy."

Finch waved. *So, Booster has an advantage over us. He's bigger and has more muscles and, therefore, more energy.*

"Not necessarily," Hosea said. "Booster has greater body mass but, remember, the Helix reads energy, not mass. A thought, for example, is energy and the Helix can measure it. Moreover, passion is energy in its purest form. With superior emotional control and mental prowess, someone Voltaire's size can strike harder, faster and with more skill than a giant like Booster."

Or Jones! My heart raced. This is what I'd hoped for. The ability to best Jones, or anyone, in battle would assure my freedom.

Hosea continued. "The easiest form to achieve is the Helix's basic form, as it's hardwired into your weapon and requires the least amount of energy to shape. Your sword will take this form as soon as you hold it. As for secondary forms, the more complex their shape and the farther that shape is from your weapon's basic form, the harder it will be to achieve. Any questions?"

When no one spoke, Hosea went to the trunk and lifted the

lid. Inside, the cylinders were individually wrapped in *bambi*. "When I call your name, come forward. Unwrap your Helix and hold it lightly, in the palm of your hand."

Booster was first. He took the sword and moved several feet away. His massive shoulders heaved with his quaking breath. Finally, he grasped the bare tube tight in his fist.

The Helix came to life, leaping from his grip into the air. A line of blue fire erupted from the top, forcing its base back toward the ground. Shouting, Booster caught it and fell to his knees.

I sprang forward, concerned, but Hosea held me back. I twisted away, then froze as Booster lifted his head. His face was lit, as bright as a star. But he was not in pain. He was lit with power. It coursed through him. His eyes bulged, his arms trembled, his fist vibrated around the weapon, which took the form of a whip. He got to his feet and struggled to raise the blue whip over his head and bring it down in a proper arc.

His fist gripped the stock, the tail trailed at his feet. Inch by quivering inch, he forced it up with sheer brute strength as if it weighed hundreds of pounds. It was at his ear, above his head, as high as he could reach. Suddenly, the whip sprang into motion. The blue tail flew up past Booster's body, past the length of his arm and into the air. It sparked against the sky like lightning. Booster bore down and the cracker snapped back, striking the ground. Earth flew, smoke billowed. I turned my face, coughing and choking. When I looked back, the whip lay in a crater of its own creation.

Booster collapsed. We all rushed forward. Hosea rolled him over. "You fool. I told you to hold it in the palm of your hand. Not grasp it. This display proves you're not ready yet."

Booster shook his head, unable to speak.

Hosea took his pulse. "Perhaps next time you'll listen before you act rashly," he said. "Your physical prowess leads you to imagine you're invulnerable. You must manage your strength so it works for you, instead of against others."

Booster's mouth hung slack. His eyes brimmed with fear.

"You won't be able to talk for a while, but you'll be fine," Hosea continued. "You'll rest the remainder of the day." Over Booster's weak protests, he wrapped the whip in *bambi* cloth and tied it to Booster's hip. William and Hurley carted Booster away.

Hosea turned to the rest of us. "Booster's weapon—"

"What *was* that?" Pidge interrupted, as shocked as the rest of us.

"It was a flail," Hosea said. "A spiked ball attached to a chain. It's the simplest Helix, but it takes great strength to wield, which is why I chose it for Booster."

"Simple?" Pidge said, incredulous.

"Yes, archaic. The flail essentially batters its victims. It takes no great skill to maneuver. The spiked ball is large enough that your aim can be imprecise and still be very effective."

Finch waved his arms. *You say the flail has a spiked ball, but there was no ball at the end of Booster's whip.*

"When the Helix is fully formed, the ball will gather at the end and produce spikes. Booster dropped the weapon before it had fully activated."

My jaw dropped.

"You mean that wasn't a display of its full power?" Pidge asked, voicing all our fears.

Hosea shook his head. "Not even close. As I said before, the basic form requires the least energy."

Finch grabbed his forehead. *But it left Booster drained like the dead. And he was the strongest of us.*

Again, Hosea shook his head. "Booster got the least sophisticated weapon because he is the weakest in many ways. He relies too much on his physical strength. He's neglected other, more potent, avenues of power."

Suspicion surged in me. My eyes narrowed. "You knew that would happen," I guessed.

Hosea's face was set like stone.

"You knew, from your test, that Booster would not heed you. That he would grip the weapon in his fist and cause it to overpower him. You knew, and you let him do it anyway."

Hosea shrugged, not denying my accusation.

"You did it to teach us a lesson," I said, angrily. "Do you care that he was terrified?"

"*I* don't care," Voltaire announced, not waiting for Hosea's reply. "And if he was hurt it serves him right." She lifted her chin.

"I agree," Pidge said. "Booster's too arrogant for his own good. If humbling him teaches us a valuable lesson, so be it."

Seeing I was outnumbered, I said nothing. Still, it was not right. Booster had his flaws, but he was a Kongo brother. I did not like seeing him ill-treated.

Hosea picked up the next weapon from the trunk. "Pidge," he said.

Pidge stepped forward, his ears prominent. His upper back worked rhythmically, revealing his inner demons. He followed Hosea's instructions to perfection, holding the tube in the palm of his hand as a thin sword formed. It didn't look particularly menacing but, at Hosea's bidding, Pidge sliced the sword along one of the balancing posts. Without any apparent effort from him, a transparent peel of wood curled up from the stump.

"Sharper than a razor. It will never rust or dull," Hosea said. "It's called a rapier."

Finch's Helix formed a lance, which he took to immediately. He used it like a human slingshot, propelling himself through the air. When his demonstration was done, Finch secured his lance against his hip and grinned.

Hosea turned to Voltaire and me. I had avoided looking directly at her. But now I glanced her way, taking in her masculine dress. Worker women covered their short hair with colorful scarves. Voltaire's head was intentionally uncovered, to fool others into overlooking her true sex. It was easy to guess why she hid herself. She was a woman maintaining dominance amidst men, any one of which could best her in a physical altercation. No doubt she, like myself, hoped the Helix would even the playing field.

Hosea was locked in indecision. He stared, trying to discern which of us—two women with something to prove—would receive the more powerful weapon. His eyes bored into mine. *Would I have the power to wield it, the potential?* My stomach flinched. I needed the Helix to attain freedom. But, in a way, I cared less about the sword than Hosea Khan's conclusion. My heart turned over as his gaze roved over my body.

He dropped his eyes, his decision made. "Voltaire," he said. "You're next."

THE APEX

That night, I didn't wait for Voltaire's summons. I went to her camp, deciding on the way not to tell her I'd been fooled by her disguise. Fly Man was awake and Voltaire was mending a pair of britches. "You're early—English."

"I know. Can we just start now?"

She made a face. "No, we cannot start now—English. If you don't know, the world spins on an axis and *you* are not its center."

"Fine, I'll wait."

Fly Man giggled and waved me over to sit next to him.

I smiled sadly. He reminded me so much of Fount, but I had to stay away. Reeling my heart in, I declined his offer and sat cross-legged, a few feet away from their beds.

Voltaire snorted. "If you can't sit *with* us—English—kindly wait by your own tree."

I looked guiltily over my shoulder. I'd hurt Fly Man's feelings. For that alone, Voltaire would take pleasure in torturing me the rest of the night. I stood and stalked away.

I had nowhere to go. Most everyone else was by the dinner fire, but I had no right to be with them—not until I mastered the Helix and put spying for Jones behind me forever. My own bedroll was off limits as Hosea was there, mixing his medical potions.

Out of options, I walked by myself. In the silence, there was nothing to distract me from recalling the climax of the day's training. Hosea had snubbed me, again.

Soon after he handed Voltaire her weapon, it assumed its basic form. Two lethal blue bars, connected by a chain. After a demonstration, she had wielded her nunchucks, as Hosea had called them, in a few basic patterns, swinging them around her body in a blue fan. At full speed, he said, the fans made a complete shield. He had chosen her for the nunchucks, he said, because the spin patterns were complicated, requiring keen intelligence.

Voltaire stepped back in line and Hosea called me forward. I minded my breath, giving away as little as possible as I accepted my weapon. Hosea avoided my gaze. I had no idea whether I had won the contest between Voltaire and me.

The Helix was heavy as I pushed back the *bambi* wrap. Up close, the ladders were even beautiful. I felt strangely connected to them and my eyes relaxed, searching the tube from end to end. A thrill of power quivered down my spine as I caressed it.

I took the weapon in my bare hand. It grew warm, then so hot I almost dropped it. Then the heat felt good. It settled into my skin, and the urge to close my fist around it became unbearable. I resisted, closing my eyes. It pulsed as it lengthened on my palm, creating all sorts of sensations. Vibrations quivered my nerves. Heat popped along my bones and sizzled in my marrow. My cells, and the bonds that held my elements together, hummed like a tuning fork.

Finally, I opened my eyes and looked down in my palm to see—a curved *stick*. I blinked, shook my head, but there it was—a stick. Disappointment gripped my chest. I stared stupidly at it, then up at Hosea. *Had it malfunctioned?* His opaque gaze was solemn. I knew, then, he had given me the weaker sword. He had chosen Voltaire.

"What is it?" I asked. The betrayal I felt was evident in the shallow breaths I couldn't control.

He cleared his throat. "It's an Apex, or some call it a boomerang."

"Boo-merang." It sounded silly, like a toy. "What does it do?"

"You throw it and hit your opponent from a distance."

Curious, I looked down at the cold arch in my palm—*could it best Jones?* I threw it. It landed harmlessly on the ground a few feet away. Embarrassed, I retrieved it quickly.

After an hour, using all my strength, I'd heaved it far enough so that it curved back toward me. It fell short of returning to my hand, as Hosea said it was meant to do. There were no spikes, no blades. No blue fire whips. My hope had careened down. I felt the others snickering at me. I felt my old classmates and the rest of the Schoolhouse laughing, too.

Even now, as I left Voltaire's encampment behind and hurried toward the spring, I was still cringing with shame. I blamed Hosea Khan. Why give me the weakest weapon? Did he find me pathetic? And what was wrong with me? Why couldn't I wield the sword?

By the time I reached the spring, I was running. I leapt to the far side of the bubbling eddies. I was miles away from camp when I stopped. I threw myself into the black water and swam back the other way. With the last of my energy I pulled myself out and fell into an exhausted sleep.

•

Voltaire woke me with a kick.

"Hey!" I cried.

"Good, you're awake," she said.

I rolled over. "What do you want?"

"They sent me to make sure you didn't harm yourself. Well, William sent me. No one else cares."

Jerkily, I sat up.

"I refused to come. But he's persistent. He sent you this." She dropped a bundle in my lap. A thermos, and something else I couldn't make out. Curious, I held it up to the moonlight. I inhaled softly. It was a beautiful wooden replica of my Apex. It fit nicely in my hand and was lightweight. So, unlike the Helix, it would be easy to throw. Etched along its smooth side was a girl. Her long braids flagged behind her as she ran. With this model Apex, I could practice aiming my weapon without exposing the humiliating limits of my strength.

Voltaire waited for my reaction. I blinked rapidly, unable to find words.

"You could say thank you," she supplied, her tone more caustic than usual.

Taken aback, I looked at her. She was grim-faced and accusing. She sensed the strain in my relationship with William, how he hovered over me like an old watchdog. She'd seen him be gentle and harmless, and she had judged my halfhearted response to his care.

"I don't want his gifts," I said, finally. "Take them back."

"I won't. Crane laid down his club, but he's proud and I won't humiliate him."

She didn't say that I *had* humiliated him, but she didn't have to. I had rejected him repeatedly.

I ignored the thermos and went to the spring. Water ran down my chin as I drank.

Voltaire snorted. "Well, if you're not going to listen to reason, at least be fair. You're supposed to be reading to me and instead, I'm here coddling you."

I didn't answer.

"And, if you want to know the truth, you could use help with your Helix. We all saw how pitiful you are. You're weak!"

"I don't want his help!"

She threw her hands up. "Why not? Because he's a worker and you're an *illustrious* Record Keeper? You can't stomach the idea of help from a feral?"

"That has nothing to do with it."

"Suit yourself—English." She turned to walk away.

I don't know what compelled me to stop her. Maybe, despite our differences, I felt kinship with Voltaire as a woman. Perhaps she was just so unlikeable that I didn't fear my heart becoming entangled with hers, as I did the other bandits. Or perhaps, I just had to get it off my chest. "I don't want his help because William is my birth father," I said.

She whipped around.

"My birth father," I repeated. Relief swept through me as I released the truth. "He knows who I am," I went on, "but he doesn't know that I recognize him. I didn't at first, but now I'm certain. There's no doubt."

She stomped back toward me, mouth open.

"They blindfold the mother, not the child," I explained, before she could snap at me. "On the day I was born, I saw William. I don't know how he managed it, but he was there when they took me to the nursery."

Voltaire was shocked. "And you remember—how? No one remembers being born."

"I don't know how, but I remember almost everything about that day."

"Don't be a fool."

I shrugged. "I remembered my birth father, didn't I?"

She hesitated, then came to sit down, still absorbing the revelation. After a while, she rankled. "That doesn't explain why you hate him. Most of us would kill to know our birth father."

"If you were a Record Keeper, you wouldn't." I swallowed. "At the Schoolhouse, knowing your birth father means you know exactly who gave you away."

"Don't be stupid," Voltaire said. "It's not his fault you were chosen."

My throat burned with anger. "You've got to stop seeing it as a privilege; it's not! William took me to the Schoolhouse himself. I remember his face as he handed me over."

"He had no choice."

"*I* had no choice! He took my choice away. Don't you see? I went quietly because of him. I trusted him. In their hateful crib, I thought he was there watching me from the shadows. I cried for a week! I nearly died trying to reach him because I *believed* in him. I thought, if he just heard me, he would come."

Voltaire said nothing.

I stared at the ground, thinking back to the gust. In that nightmare, the years had fallen away. I'd seen William, his birthmark prominent, looking down on my swaddled form, tucked in the crook of his arm. A moment later, the scene had changed to Covington pointing at my own birthmark, the Devil's mark, as she called it. It was closer to my mouth than William's, but the same size. When I woke, I put the two pictures together.

Voltaire touched my shoulder. Her voice, for once, was kind. "Arika?"

I remained quiet for a long time, then I shrugged her off. I jumped to my feet.

Voltaire rocked back. "Where are you going?"

"To the training field."

"But why?"

I oriented myself and jogged into the darkness. I called back over my shoulder, "To train!"

If she argued, I was too far away to hear. At the training field, I hopped onto a post. Clearing my mind, I focused on my dream of freedom. Hours later, wracked with pain, I turned my mind toward my hatred for Jones—which refueled me. I had to master the Helix. I could not go back to the Schoolhouse. Finally, when the pain became a roaring dragon breathing along my spine, I remembered Hosea's advice and turned my focus inward on the movement of my breath. *In and out, in and out.*

As I staggered, finally, from my perch, William came forward from beyond the line of trees. I swayed, my legs seizing. He took my hand, squeezed it, and turned it over. He placed the wooden boomerang in my palm.

"Arika *must* practice," he said.

He waited a moment.

My heart filled my throat. It was on the tip of my tongue to ask him why he'd done it. Instead, I tucked the boomerang into my belt and turned my back on him.

THE TRAINEE

In the following weeks, I trained as if my life depended on it. I threw the boomerang three hundred times each morning. When my fingers were raw, I pictured myself, back in Jones' grasp. I saw myself betraying my friends. I felt the hot poker of pity. And I picked up my Apex and threw it again and again.

I also engaged the bandits to learn their expertise. From Walker, I learned to salt meat for storage. I removed innards and cleaned them for eating, covered in thick gravy. With a mortar and pestle, I learned to grind nuts into flour, and to make bread from it. I added oil to the nuts and created butter for the bread.

I took over watering and weeding Hurley's garden, and I learned which part of the plants were edible and which would make me sick. We made soap from animal fat, and mended clothes with needles and hand-spun thread.

I coaxed Booster into taking me hunting. We waited high in the trees and rappelled down with only a thin rope to break our fall. I lugged a desert antelope back to camp and, later, I helped skin the beast. I scraped the hide and presented it to Hurley for tanning.

I followed Pidge as he checked his traps for small game. All the while I peppered him with questions. How many traps? How do you set them? How do you choose bait?

With Fly Man, I flipped rocks to find edible insects and gathered dry kindling from bushes. He showed me how to dig worms for fishing, and collect bird eggs without disturbing the nest. He demonstrated his skill as a groom, showing me to cool and brush Mary after riding.

Hosea, I had to admit, was an excellent teacher. We learned dozens of maneuvers. Strikes, kicks, punches and blocks, as well as defensive moves to counter each attack.

"Every body part is a weapon," Hosea said, again and again. "The hands stab, quick and strong, like daggers. Your elbows strike like the mace. Your knees chop, left and right. They are battle-axes. Use your legs like a staff. Pummel your enemy and vault away. Keep your shins and forearms ready. They protect you, like a suit of armor. You have eight limbs now; use them!"

We sparred with each other. I paired often with Voltaire, but also tested my strength with Pidge and Finch. Once, I sparred with Booster for over an hour. Three full matches.

I lost the first match in minutes and did not fare well in the second match. In the third, however, Hosea had coached me from the sidelines, reminding me of the techniques he'd drilled into us from the beginning.

"When you can't strike, what do you do?" he asked. It had been our second day of training and no one knew what to expect. "Say your opponent has a sword and you are disarmed. How do you defend yourself? Say your opponent is twice your size. Or say, you've been injured. You've got one good arm to fight with. What do you do?"

No one answered.

Hosea pointed at Finch. "Finch, tie my right arm behind my back," he ordered.

Finch moved to comply.

"Booster, come here."

Booster strutted forward, beak up, a few inches taller than Hosea.

"Now, attack me. If you forfeit, tap the ground. Got it?"

Booster had grinned cockily. He lowered his stance and the two had circled before Booster, seeing an opening, attacked aggressively. A second later, Hosea had pinned him on the ground. Booster tapped submission, grunting in pain, no longer smiling. Hosea released him and they went at it again—and again. Each time, Hosea won. When Booster struggled to rise, Hosea called a halt to the demonstration. Finch untied his hand.

"Booster is bigger in size than I am, yet I bested him."

"How?" Voltaire asked, hungrily. "Teach us how."

"I have already begun to teach you," Hosea had said. "The key lies in the art of yielding, the technique of softness. The old world called it *jujitsu*. When striking is ineffective, neutralize the threat. Throw, lock, pin. Don't oppose your enemy's aggression. Take his energy and turn it in your favor."

I remembered those very words as Booster came charging in the third match. I ducked and scooted between his legs. I had avoided him thus far, but I had to find a way to attack.

Booster heaved with fatigue, annoyed by my escape tactics, which made him look the fool. When he turned to face me again, there was malice in his eyes. All at once, he ran, full force, in a final attack. I set my jaw, cautioning myself to wait. When he was inches away, I stepped to the side. He blew past. I raised an elbow and pummeled his back. He stumbled and fell to his knees, dazed, but not submitting. Hosea's words came to me again.

"Don't be afraid to use your weapons," he said. "Trap, hold, gouge, bite. Your hands are swords."

Booster was still on the ground in front of me. Quickly, before he could recover, I chopped at his throat. He fell forward, cursing. While he sputtered, I put a knee in his back. I couldn't hold him long. I lifted one of his massive arms and grabbed his thumb. I twisted it just as Hosea had showed us. Booster's shout of pain was like music to me. A second later, he tapped submission. I had won. It was the first and only match I would win against the other trainees.

Our Helix training consisted of long hours on the poles, balancing as Hosea Khan paced before us, explaining the elements of battle.

"Your enemy is not your opponent. Your battle is not against flesh and blood. There are three conflicts to conquer. Confusion," he tapped his temple. "Fatigue," he tapped his chest. "And fear," he rested a hand on his core. "To master the Helix, you must master these. Discipline your mind, determine your strength, and breathe."

For hours, we stood on the poles. The others complained restlessly and, eventually, Hosea relented, dismissing us to practice with our weapons. Improvement in this area came daily. Booster no longer set trees ablaze with his whip and, sometimes, he formed the ball of his flail.

Hosea constantly cautioned him, shouting across the field. "Moderation!"

Pidge accosted falling leaves. With the tip of his rapier, he carved them into stars before they drifted to the ground, smoking and singed.

Finch, an expert with his staff, was the only one who

managed a second form. When he flipped his lance upright and pulled back at the elbow, an axe formed over his shoulder. He held the form for a few elated minutes, as he ran about chopping wood for Fly Man. After, he dropped to his knees, exhausted. Hosea had come forward to rip the weapon from his hand. "Moderation!"

Voltaire learned to alternate her swing so that her nunchucks protected either side of her body. She could also trap a weapon in the chain between her shafts. Both Pidge and Finch had fallen prey to this maneuver while Hosea looked on, nodding approval.

I became good at tossing William's boomerang. With a split second of calculation, I could hit a bird midflight and knock it from the air. Pidge didn't set traps for fowl, and Booster didn't bother with small bounties. So I, alone, provided the camp with poultry. Often, on my way back from a morning run, I would nab a bird for Walker to fry up for our noon meal. Accordingly, the bandits' respect for me increased.

Despite this, I was the only trainee who had yet to wield the Helix. My Apex remained a cold weight, too heavy to throw more than a few yards. I forced myself to eat, but I rarely slept. Instead, I trained.

I also avoided the others. They discussed Joust strategies around the campfire, so I ate alone by my bedroll, reminding myself that affection was contrary to my survival—and theirs. Even so, affection crept upon me like a spider, spinning debts of loyalty I couldn't afford.

I would cower in my bed as their voices, buoyed with hope, drifted across the clearing. I was just so cowered on the night William entertained the group with the story of how he became Champion. Each detail, spoken in his broken English, sent shocks of longing through my body.

He had a wife when he was young—*my mother*. And they'd had a baby—*me*. Despite the birthing laws, they found a way to know the child and were careful to keep their knowledge a secret. One day, when their baby girl was an infant, his wife snuck from the field to the village nursery. The Overseer caught her and kicked her. As fate would have it, she—*my mother!*—had fallen and cut her neck on a rock, bleeding to death in minutes. Enraged, William seized the Overseer's weapon and killed him with it.

"The Overseers longed to kill me for taking that life," he said. "Murder shined in their eyes. But, I was a strong worker. I brought in three times my quota. To kill me was to lose the crop. Their greed could not stand it."

"So, what happened?" Voltaire asked.

"They did not kill me. No, they said, '*William, you will be in the Guard*.' I got a new quota—to beat the workers each day. I became the sword of the Overseer. I became a beast. And I hated that beast like the Devil. All of Cobane hated that beast. In my first Joust as Champion, they wanted me to die. My death would end their misery."

"They don't hate you now," Voltaire said. "You're revered."

"What you speak is true. At last, their hatred became love. Near and far, people knew the name Crane the Conqueror. They cheered me and my love for them was strong. I could not beat them. I lost my stomach for it."

"What about the Overseer and his men?" Voltaire asked.

"The Overseers fear the people together. They would not do me harm. The people together are the strongest sword of all."

He went on to describe how he spent the next years of his life as a bounty hunter. With workers—not just in Cobane, but everywhere—on his side, he became virtually autonomous. He traveled between Houses, hunting outlaws, and delivering them at his discretion. He was welcomed everywhere. He used his fame to build a secret network of men that he trained as soldiers, teaching them all he learned in the Guard.

"A White-Face murdered my sister," Pidge said, his voice petulant. "They kill without caution."

"I did not teach them that way," William replied, his voice grave. "I teach them to honor and protect. To strike fear in the First Brother's heart, to ease the way of the worker."

"So, what happened?" Voltaire asked.

"I trained a man, Condor, to second my command. But, at last, his heart became dark. He ordered attacks. He joined another worker, Martin. And so came Voltaire's Army. Martin is the brain. Condor is the muscle. The Rebels who wear the white-face have anger in the heart. They said to me, '*Crane, we do not want you to lead. We chose the way of Condor.*' On that day, I laid down my club."

In my bedroll, tears trickled from the corners of my eyes. I clasped my hands behind my head and considered the leader, Condor. He had rallied the White-Face soldiers. I, too, had rallied my people. *Comrades, to me!* What might have been, if my peers had picked up their quills, like daggers, and followed me from the Schoolhouse into rebellion.

THE TRUTH ABOUT VOLTAIRE

Later, I went to Voltaire. Since learning my secret, she'd softened toward me. She was not kind, but she was no longer derisive. And, sometimes, she called me by my given name. I stepped into the light of her campfire.

"It's about time—English."

I ignored her bad mood. We had finished *Candide* and were reading through it again. In return, she gave me another precious pair of leggings. They stretched over my legs as I sat down beside her.

Hoping to catch her off guard, I spoke quickly. "Is Fly Man your birth brother?"

"He is," Voltaire said.

"How do you know?"

She hesitated, then pushed aside her blouse. She turned, showing me a mark on her back.

"Does he have the same birthmark?" I said, thinking of the mole I shared with William.

"It's not a birthmark, it's a scar." She traced her finger along it. "It's a bird in flight."

I squinted. The mark was raised like an old burn. A sprawling M shape, the bird was pale against the brown sky of her shoulder blade.

"We think our birth mother gave it to us to mark us as hers,"

Voltaire said. She covered her shoulder.

"Did you claim Fly Man as soon as you knew he shared your blood?" I asked.

"Yes. When my auntie, a nursery attendant, told me our scars were the same I went that night to the nursery and compared our tattoos."

"Were you found out?"

"Yes. They sentenced me to an intermittent Rebirth, but I ran away. I planned to leave for good. But, after a few weeks, I went back. I couldn't stay away from Fly Man."

I compared her loyalty to William's abandonment and bitterness filled me. "Were you erased when you returned?"

She shook her head. "I changed my appearance so they wouldn't know it was me."

"You mean, you began dressing like a male."

She lifted her chin. "And what if I did?"

"I don't judge you," I said. "What happened next?"

"I hid out with my sister, and saw Fly Man when I could," she said. "When I got older, I took up with a group of smart kids."

"Rebels," I guessed.

"They were just kids at the time," she corrected. "We refused to be subject to our equals, especially those who don't care if we live or die."

I barely heard her, unable to shake the image of William handing me over. "It was good of you to risk death for your blood family, Voltaire," I said, finally. "I wish all Second Brothers were as decent as you."

She eyed me with contempt. "No one here feels sorry for you, Arika, least of all me."

"If you knew my life, I think you'd change your mind."

"The fact that you can make up your *own* mind means you're privileged. Only, you're too privileged to see it."

I scoffed. "You think feeling betrayed is preferable to the bliss of erasure? It's not!"

"It is! Do you know why I'm here in the oasis?"

I shook my head. She was on her feet, shouting at me. "Well, neither do I," she said.

I was confused.

"I don't know, because the Record Keepers had me erased! Ten pills!"

Her pain was palpable.

"I don't even remember the plans I had for the Rebels. Walker says that I told him to head this way before I went under. We were to continue heading north, but I don't know where or why."

"You didn't leave yourself notes?" I asked.

She shook her head. "I was afraid to. Spies haunted my every step in those days. I told Fly Man and Walker there would be an oasis, and to wait here, but not much else. I hoped that some spark of memory would light when we got here. Something that explains why we headed north to begin with. But I'm as lost today as I was when I awakened."

I frowned, remembering how I decided Hosea was leading our group to the Obi Forest. Had Voltaire been going to the forbidden lands too?

"I never thought my own people, my First Brothers, would use the worst English weapon against me in such an underhanded manner," she said.

"The Rebirth was never supposed to be a weapon," I defended, automatically. In my guilt, I wanted her to see my side. "It was supposed to be a peacekeeping measure."

"Sure," she sneered. "It keeps the workers in line so that the Record Keepers can take advantage of our ignorance."

I couldn't deny that. "Not all Record Keepers are self-serving," I said. "Plenty of us want to restore strength to the village."

"You can't restore strength by creating weakness—Arika."

"The Rebirth doesn't create weakness," I said. "That's what they told us."

"And *you* believed them!" she accused.

Her words scattered on my skin like hot coals. I shook them off. "There were studies that proved it. That's what they told us! An *animus rasa*, a clean slate!"

"Well, I didn't want a clean slate! I used to write for hours every day. Now, I'm bartering supplies with someone I *hate*, just to read a single volume of literature."

I lowered my head. She was right, and there was no use arguing. "I'm getting up in a few hours to train. If you want to read tonight, we have to start now."

The corner of her mouth curled bitterly. She handed me the book.

THE OMEN

The next day I woke with a feeling of dread. Time was running out. The New Seed vote was nigh. In seven days, Jones expected me back at the Schoolhouse with information about the Director, and I still could not wield the Helix. Afraid, I jumped up and began training.

I redoubled my efforts to remain aloof from the bandits. I ran longer in the morning, ate alone, and filled every spare minute with strength training. To compensate for my inability to wield the Helix, Hosea obliged me with extra combat lessons. Early in the morning the two of us would meet at the clearing and, while I stood on the post, he lectured.

In time, I excelled theoretically. I perfected the physics of aiming my Apex, accurately predicting the arcs and angles, even in heavy wind. I improved greatly, but it was not enough. Without use of the Helix, I was bested in every competition. Even when Pidge twisted his ankle, he challenged me and won the match in seconds.

On the day before Jones expected me back at Cobane, I gave up hope. I admitted to myself that I would never live free in the oasis. Instead of despair, icy numbness settled over me.

I woke early that morning and watched Hosea as he prepared to rise. By now, I knew his morning routine. He would go about bathing before the morning birds awoke. After, he meditated in the forest near the spring. I had adjusted my own schedule to fit his, rising with him and running until we met in the training field.

Bitterness burned my throat. Had he known all along that I would fail? Had he intentionally tempted me with the Helix, knowing I would never master it? Had he done it to distract me from spying for Jones? To be fair, he had warned me that he wasn't my friend.

"Hosea," I said, into the darkness.

He turned, his eyes curious. And there, in the tightening of his mouth, was the opaque wall he'd erected between us. I'd surmounted it on the night he'd explained the breath to me. But, the next morning, he'd fortified his shield. He pushed me away and he kept me at arm's length—and I knew why. There were questions he didn't want me to ask.

"What is it, Cobane?" he said.

I went for the jugular. "The Helix—did you know all along that I was too weak to wield it?"

He shook his head.

"Then tell me, why did the Director give me a sword? You said before that I don't want to know, but I do."

He didn't flinch from my blunt query. Hosea Khan never shied from a fight. He avoided violence, to be sure. But against his will, he cared too much to shut me out completely.

I played on his affection. "If you care about me, even a little, you'll not keep me in the dark. I want to know why I have a sword, and I want to know *right now*."

He took a breath. "I do care for you, and more than a little."

I swallowed. "Then tell me."

"You're better off in the dark, Arika."

"Tell me!"

He grimaced, searching for the right words. "The Director gave you a sword, because he thinks that *someone* can save the Kongo. He believes that the *One* is among us today."

My eyes went wide. It was the last thing I had expected him to say. "The *One?*" I croaked. "You can't possibly mean—"

"The Omen," he said.

I felt the hairs on my neck rise up. The Omen had been spoken by the Great Obi Solomon himself, right before he signed the Compromise.

Before I could respond, Hosea spoke the sacred words out loud. "'I am not the *One*, but *One* is coming—mightier than I.'"

I stared at him. His words hung in the air between us.

I shook my head, trying to think logically. "You told me that the Director wants the Kongo to secede from the North, but the Omen isn't about seceding," I said. "It's about the future of all America." I knew the legend by heart and quoted from an old reader. "One day, the Northridge will invent a piece of technology so powerful, the whole world will be healed by it. The Earth will return to its former glory and no one—not Kongo, Clayskin, or English—will labor again. At that time, the *One* Director of the Kongo will usher in a new age of peace."

Hosea made a face. "That's what you learned in school—that the *One*, the savior of the Kongo people, would be an *English* Diplomat from the Northridge?"

I bit my lip, feeling small. "That's what they taught us."

"And after all you've seen, you still believe it?"

I shook my head. "I don't know what to believe."

"Well, figure it out, Cobane! You're the *one* that wanted to know."

My heart drummed against my ribs. "If you're implying that I have something to do with the Omen, you're mad. I can't wield the Helix to save *myself*, let alone save the Kongo." Tears burned the back of my eyes. "Hosea," I whispered, "what's wrong with me?"

He didn't ask my meaning—he knew. "Something inside you is stopping the flow of your breath. You'll have to remove it in order to see improvement."

"Yes, a block, you said that before in lecture," I said. "How can I remove it?"

He shrugged.

My frustration boiled over and I confronted him physically, butting him with my chest. "Don't shrug, Hosea! Don't shrug. Time is running out. Help me!"

Our eyes locked. We stood, with my chest to his middle. He took my shoulders. "Believe me, Arika, I would help you if I could. No one can help you do this. Whatever it is, is between you and your own demons—your own God, if you claim one."

"Then tell me more. What is a block? Explain it."

"The explanation depends on the problem. If it's here," he touched his chest, "it's an emotional block. Or, it could be in your head. Breath is like water, it needs to flow. And right now, something is stifling you, sapping you of the strength you need to wield the sword. It's like you're trying to swim with a boulder around your waist. You can't get far."

"Whatever this block is, how do I find it?"

"You have to ask yourself, Cobane." He turned and went to the stream to wash.

I waited a few moments and followed. I walked straight to the water, letting the moon, high in the sky, fall over me. "I need to see the Director," I said.

Chest-deep in the stream, he cupped his hands and lifted water, scrubbing vigorously before answering. "What for?"

"I have information for him, regarding Jones." The lie came easily. Once I accepted escape was impossible, I had tested several methods of deceiving him. In the end, I'd decided keep it simple. Once I was face to face with the Director, I would find some way of manipulating him into revealing his plans for the New Seed vote. I would take that information to Jones in exchange for her protection.

I waited impatiently as Hosea continued to wash. He was as meticulous about cleanliness as he was about everything, and he took his time. Finally, he moved to the waterside.

He had a tattoo high on the left side of his chest. The intricate design swelled as he flattened his palms on the ground and propelled himself out of the water. Sheets of liquid cascaded down his torso. I turned away.

When my breath slowed, I called over my shoulder. "Will you arrange a meeting?"

"I don't see why not." His voice was muffled as he pulled his shirt over his head.

I shoved a fist against my mouth. *Would it really be this easy?* "How soon can it happen?" I said. I heard the slip and rustle of more clothing falling into place. I turned to face him. "It needs to be in the next two days."

He knelt to lace up his moccasins. "The day after tomorrow is when the Assembly votes on the New Seed," he said.

"Yes. Before that."

His eyes met mine and I stared back, trying to appear innocent.

"I'll contact him and let him know you have information,"

he said, finally. "Whether or not he answers will be up to him."

I nodded and turned away, hating myself—and him. Didn't he know that I was weak? I *needed* him to block my path to betrayal. Instead, he had given me exactly what I didn't want— his trust.

Just before I left the clearing, I looked back at Hosea Khan. His eyes were on the ground, fists clenched at his waist. His shoulders, ordinarily squared, were bent. I squinted, trying to name the emotion vibrating from his frame. My stomach clenched when it hit me. He hadn't been deceived. As always, he knew exactly what I was about, and he hadn't tried to stop me. He wasn't even angry. No, he was disappointed.

•

I turned and ran from the spring. Back at my bedroll, I didn't slow as I grabbed my pack and continued to run. I raced past the outskirts of camp—into no-man's-land. When I was completely alone, I slowed to a jog. I riffled through my satchel with one hand until my fingers closed around the glass vial Jones had given me. I pulled it out, knowing what I had to do. If I stayed in the oasis, Jones would find me. She would drag me back to the Schoolhouse and, eventually, I would betray Hosea Khan. Tears obscured my vision. I was out of choices.

Just then, my foot caught on a thick root and I stumbled. I hit the ground hard, sprawling on my stomach. I didn't bother to get back up. Clutching the vial, I rolled onto my back and fumbled to open it. Darkness, blacker than the Pit, descended upon me.

Hosea had said no one could help me, that I had to ask myself what demon haunted me. It was no secret. She whispered to me every night. *Fall down with the first blow, okay? She kicks like a donkey.* She was in my head and in my heart. My constant companion—myself. *Don't plead, but grovel and play dumb. Can you hear me?*

My hand shook as I withdrew the silver pin. It glowed like a crystalight. Taking a breath, I pressed the tip to the large vein at the side of my neck. I began to sob. I closed my eyes and pressed harder. The first pang of pain registered in my mind. *Dear God, it hurts. If only I had the strength to wield the Helix!* Biting my lip, I forced myself to press harder. The skin of my neck was nearly broken when Hosea Khan's voice pierced the darkness.

It's not about swords, Cobane. It never is. When you achieve perfect alignment, you will have long since stopped relying on swords.

I hesitated, opened my eyes and saw it. There, high in the sky above me, the sun shined and wind blew through the trees— like a breath. My fingers, slick with sweat, dropped the pin.

I don't know how long he stood there, watching me in the dirt. He didn't make a sound, however, as he crept toward me. My only warning of his presence, a twig snapping beneath his foot, came too late. I had just enough time to turn and see his face, black but painted white, as he threw a sack over my head. I managed a single shout before he hit me. I opened my mouth and let loose the first thing that came to my mind. A cry for rescue. Not *please*, or *help*, but, "William!"

THE JOURNEY BACK

I awoke, suffocating. The blindfold, meant for my eyes, now covered my nose, and my mouth was sealed shut. I remembered running from Hosea right before he, the White-Face soldier, came upon me. From the feel of it, I was folded into the sack he used to cover my head. Inside, without air, I was already faint. If I lost consciousness once more, I doubted I would wake again.

I tested the ties around my wrists. He'd tied my feet as well, and he'd knotted the two ties together, taking no chances. Suddenly, the ground moved and I tipped from my sitting position. I was being dragged on my side, like a sack of vegetables. I rocked and grunted, trying to get my captor's attention. He'd taken me alive, so surely he didn't want me to suffocate—not yet.

I cried out, but he didn't stop. Instead, a weakness in my binding revealed itself. My mouth piece had slipped during my struggle. Latching onto this, I worked my jaw until, finally, I wiggled free. I gasped, filling my burning lungs. I was abducted, but I could breathe.

Gripping my neck and thigh through the sack, he heaved me onto a horse that whinnied with my weight. I tottered precariously, and another pair of hands steadied me. There were two of them! Who had sent them? Was it Condor and

Martin, the leaders of the White-Face Army? In that case, I had to warn the bandits that their enemies were close. Just then, one of my captors spoke. His words filtered through the lining of the sack.

"This her?" one asked.

"Yes, this her," the other confirmed.

I heard the rustle of paper unfolding.

A limb brushed my head as my captor passed the paper to his mate, who took it, then untied my sack. Air rushed in, and I sensed him comparing me to the likeness he held.

He grunted his approval and retied the sack.

Inside, my mind raced. They'd made no mistake. It *was* me they were looking for—but why?

Minutes later we rode, hard and fast. I jostled continually, but managed to stay on the horse. I barely noticed my pain and thirst as I focused on collecting tidbits of information that would help me navigate once I escaped. The sound of the horse hooves on the ground, the feel of the little light that filtered through to me, the smell of the air and tilt of my body as I swayed left and right. Over time I worked my hands free. I untied my blindfold and tugged at the knot around my ankles. Finally, around midday, I was loose.

I stayed put in the sack, however, afraid to alarm my captors and lose the element of surprise. Before I made a move, I needed a plan. The sack had a tight lattice weave, but it was not impermeable. I found a small hole and widened it, with my little finger, into a peephole. Through it, I saw one of my captors. He was huge. He sat bareback, his thick legs gripping his beast like a vise. He held the mane in one hand and a giant battle-axe in the other. His skin was the color of soot, which made the white paint on his face more fearsome. The horse I occupied was tied by a rope to his waist.

I kept blood flowing to my limbs by shifting periodically as the day wore on. They didn't offer me food or eat themselves. The one I watched took his eye off the horizon only twice, to drink a few sips of water and to check a compass. He signaled to his companion before he adjusted our direction from south, to west. As we turned that way, a sick feeling settled in my stomach. I checked the light again as we continued to ride hard, into the sunset. There was no doubt about it: we were headed straight for Cobane.

We continued to ride late into the afternoon, slowing down only when the horses showed signs of fatigue. The desert sand reflected the light of a full moon and illuminated everything in our path. Through the sack, I saw the terrain changing, becoming more familiar. We were mere hours away from Cobane. What business could two White-Face soldiers have there? Jones would have them arrested on sight. I feared what she would do with me, back before the deadline with only bits and pieces of the information she'd requested. I knew the Director was up to something, but I didn't know what or how it would affect the New Seed vote. Would I be able to protect Hosea and the bandits? My thoughts chased each other in circles as I tried to formulate a plan.

•

We halted unexpectedly. We were still several miles from Cobane and I thought my captors would ride through to the Schoolhouse. I wasn't prepared to stop. My body shifted forward and I cried out—a loud cry, clearly unimpeded by a gag. Through my peephole, I saw my captor's head turn sharply. His eyes narrowed as he studied me through the bag. I froze. If he found me unbound, all would be lost. He was still eyeing me when his companion called out.

"We have luck. Our prey follows in the open."

The first captor's attention shifted away from me. The second captor dismounted, rounded my horse, and handed something to his mate.

"Look here," he said.

The first man held the proffered telescope to his eye and aimed it east, the direction from which we'd come. He looked for a moment, then smiled, revealing broken, yellow teeth. "We have luck," he repeated. There was greed in his voice. "We have the girl. And now, we will have the man. The prize for him is great."

The second man unfolded a *Wanted* poster from his pocket. "A bag of coin," he said.

"And Condor will be pleased," the first man said. "We will stop here."

"But, he is almost upon us. He will make war."

"He will not catch us," the first man said.

The second man frowned. "You make no sense."

The first man dismounted from his horse and explained. "We stop here and wash our faces. When he is close, we make her scream." He gestured to me. "Then we ride to Cobane. For her, he will follow us into Cobane, but we will get there first. We will alert the Guard."

"I see," the second man said, smiling again. He held up the poster. "He is now a wanted man, and the Kongo Guard is in Cobane in great number for the Joust."

"Yes!" agreed the first man. "Two, he will overpower, even ten. But no man can best a Guard ten thousand strong—not even Crane the Conqueror."

THE TEACHER'S PET

Hearing William's name made my heart stop. They were not just White-Face soldiers; they were hunters after William for bounty. Without my help, they would catch him unawares and his life would be forfeit. Grasping this, I took action. I didn't think or plan. I hooked two fingers in my peephole and ripped open my hiding place. I shouted, "Ahhh!"

My captors fumbled for their weapons.

Acting on instinct, I jumped from the horse and slapped its rear as I shouted, "Hiyah!"

The horse spooked, just as I hoped. It reared with a scream and galloped into the *wadi*. My first captor flipped into the air and came flying toward me, pulled by the tie on his waist. I hopped over his skidding body with keen agility, landing on the balls of my feet. I heard him cry out. I felt the spray of sand against my back, but I didn't stop.

I ran forward, aiming for the next man. He was ready. He squatted in a wide stance to catch me, a sneer on his white face. I put my head down and ran directly toward his trap. At the last moment, I veered left and walloped the horse at his side. It screamed and took off running. Distracted, the second captor called the horse back as I pivoted, in search of the last steed. It was yards away. I started toward it.

Realizing my plan, the man stopped chasing the runaway

horse. He turned toward me. I had a head start, but he gained ground quickly. I heard him at my back. I was yards from the mount when he lunged at my feet—too late.

I leapt onto the horse, landing on my stomach. He was bigger than Mary, but Finch had taught me well. I lifted a leg over the horse's haunch and pulled myself up by the mane. I slapped its hindquarters. "Hiyah!" And I was off.

•

The flanks of my horse heaved beneath me as I reached the gates of Cobane. Patting my mount, I bent low against his neck. "Come on, boy. Just a bit farther."

With a burst of speed, he carried us through the village, across the meadow and up to the Schoolhouse fence. I forced open the entryway with a kick then slowed to dismount. I lifted my leg over and slid down one heavily lathered flank. I landed lightly on the Schoolhouse porch. I turned on my heel and opened the front door. I came face to face with a kitchen maid. She screeched.

"You," I said. "There's a horse outside. Take him to the stables and have him fed and watered." I didn't slow or wait for her reply.

I took the stairs by threes, passing bewildered students. Thankfully, I saw no one from my class. I avoided the corridors where Teachers tended to congregate. They would try to stop me running, and I couldn't be stopped. I had slowed the bounty hunters down, but they were greedy. They would, eventually, regroup, find William and trade him in for coin. He would be easy to track. If not for my stubborn anger, I would have known the truth. It was achingly clear to me now.

As sure as the sun, William was on his way to me. William would not leave me to the hunters any more than he had abandoned me at the Schoolhouse those many years ago. If I had ever been alone, it was because he had no choice in the matter. From the moment of my birth to this very day, he had watched over me.

Arms akimbo like a perched eagle, observing that we were not sick. He'd covered us like an ebony shade, the worst of the heat on his back. Say papa, say papa. Come now, say papa.

My eyes stung. The hunters had only to follow me, and they would have him. I could have ridden east and warned him of their plot but something, the niggling beginnings of a plan, had told me to ride to Cobane.

I would save William and win the Senator seat. It wasn't the freedom I'd hoped for, but I would survive and, perhaps, be well positioned to protect the Kongo from the worst of the New Seed proposal. I sped up as I rounded the corner to Jones' office.

I came to a skidding stop. My chest heaved, though not from my exertions. I told myself to calm down. For once, I thought, *I* had the advantage. She was not expecting me. I took a deep breath and lifted one hand. To my horror, Jones opened the door just before I made contact. Heat flooded my face as my bravado flickered and died. Instantly, I was seven years old again, at her mercy. I lowered my head. "Teacher."

•

She waited for me to sit, then towered over me. Instinctively, my hand crept to the holster at my back, where I had strapped my Helix that morning. It was empty. My Apex was with the bounty hunters or back in the oasis. Not that it mattered. It was useless in my hand, anyway.

My teeth chattered but I forced myself to focus on my plan. There was only one way to spar with Jones, I realized. I would have to let her win. Play her game. Embrace exactly what she wanted me to be—a feral spy. I would be her pawn just like before. Only now, I lacked even the illusion of power. She would win, but, this time, she would suffer along with me.

I swallowed past the bitter taste of my tongue and began—exactly as I'd practiced. "You were right," I said. "Director Kumar does not honor the law. He breaks it." I looked up. "Only, not in the way you suggested."

"What do you mean, girl? How does he break the law?"

"He's been reassigning hydroplanes north, to an oasis near the Clayskin border," I said.

"Are you sure?" she asked, surprised.

To be exact, I believed the hydroplanes were nourishing land *inside* the Obi Forest—but I held that part back from Jones. "Yes, Teacher," I said.

Jones stepped toward me, greedy for more. "What else?" she said.

I hesitated. The next piece was even more speculative than the first. I pretended to gather my thoughts as I reconsidered the facts. At first blush, it appeared we had stumbled upon the bandits by accident. A second look, however, made me certain the encounter was planned.

Hosea himself admitted he intended to support Voltaire. *War is coming to the Kongo*, he'd said. *Lines have been drawn.* I didn't think it a coincidence that the two had met, both on their way to the forbidden land.

The piece that edged me toward confidence, however, was the Helix. Hosea had said the Director guarded the biotechnology. So much so, he wanted to meet exactly who it was given to. Only, the Director had never appeared, not even by comm-unit. It all led me to believe the Director had *planned* to recruit Voltaire to lead the rebellion. He'd known exactly where she was because, although she couldn't remember, she'd been sent there to await Hosea's training.

"The Director is building an arsenal," I confessed to Jones. "He's gathering an army in preparation for war."

"How can you know that?" she hissed.

I chose my words carefully, unwilling to betray the bandits. "I know he plots war, because he told me about the weapons."

"Weapons." Jones got to her feet. "You heard this in person, from the Director?"

"Not in person. We spoke via Master Vine's comm-unit."

"What did he say? Could you see his location? Where was he when you spoke?"

I fabricated. "He said that the weapons are being built at the Kongo Technology Center, in a secret lab. I don't know where he was when we spoke. From what I could see, it was someplace dark." I understood comm-unit mechanics in theory. I hoped my answer made sense.

"Perhaps he was somewhere in the secret lab. Perhaps it's underground," Jones hypothesized.

"Yes, maybe," I said.

"What kind of weapons did he say he was building?"

"Some kind of sword, I think."

"Think, girl! Was it a sword, or wasn't it?"

My heart skipped. "I'm sorry, Teacher, but weapons aren't

permitted in the Schoolhouse. Learning that was not part of my training." I ducked my head, expecting a blow. But I would not reveal what I knew of the Helix, the bandits' only weapon in the coming war. My eyes found a bump on the small knuckle of my right, the one she'd dislocated. If I tried, I could still hear it—*snapping*.

"Look at me!"

My eyes flew to her face.

"Did you see the Director's army?"

"Ye—yes, Teacher. I saw but not clearly. I couldn't see their faces. I don't think I could identify anyone." I stopped and took a breath. If I talked too fast, I'd give myself away.

"Was it a large force?"

"Not exactly."

"Was it small?"

I let my lip hang and shrugged, appearing the ignorant feral. "It was medium," I said, dumbly.

"Medium?"

"Not too big, not too small."

"I know what medium means, you idiot. I need numbers. Does he have enough to hijack the Assembly? Can he stop the vote? Is that his plan?"

I had no idea of the Director's intention. I doubted he would try to stop Jones. He had bigger goals in mind. "I don't think his goal is to stop the vote," I said.

"How do you know?"

"The vote takes place tomorrow, but the army I saw was just beginning to train," I said, logically.

"Are you sure? Answer carefully, girl. Your life depends on it."

I wasn't sure, but that was the beauty of this hoax. By the

time either of us knew the Director's intentions, her threats wouldn't matter. The vote would take place *after* the exam. I hoped Jones' treason was exposed. Either way, I would be safe.

I nodded confidently. "I'm sure, Teacher."

She walked back to her seat, sliding her thick fingers along her desk. She opened a drawer and removed a book of Supply Room passes. She tore off three sheets and placed two in the middle of her desk. "Get clothing and shoes. You look like a feral."

Shame burned my cheeks. I recalled how she called me a dog not three weeks ago. I forced myself to move slowly, so as not to, in my annoyance, snatch up the passes.

"I'll send your maid up for a late bath. You need one. Also, check under your door tomorrow for your copy of the final essay. Hand it in, and you'll maintain your class rank."

I blinked. She believed me. She'd swallowed every word. After the Final Exam I'd be a Senator in the Assembly. I waited for happiness to overtake me. It never came. Instead, my whole body seethed.

She sniffed pointedly. I jumped. "Thank you, Teacher, I appreciate your generosity," I said. I heard myself as if from a distance. But I didn't feel the words. My palms were wet with sweat as my body worked to cool the heat in my belly.

She fingered the last pink slip and set it down. "Take this too. Get anything you want. Consider it a personal gift to you, from America."

I glanced at the slip then gazed at her desk. As usual, it was spotless. Nothing to mar the gleam of fresh polish, or hide her reflection in it. She was smiling at me, conspiratorially—as if we were allies in this cruel world.

Thousands were dead from the mysterious fever, and thousands more would perish. The Kongo Guard would murder the White-Face soldiers and Rebels would slaughter the Loyalists. In the end, they would all die. Population control was for *the greater good*. My head steamed. The greater good meant only the good of the English—not the Kongo. Never the Kongo.

Jones interrupted my thoughts. "Go on, girl. Take the passes, they're yours."

Obediently, I leaned forward to take them.

She went on. "A good dog deserves a treat."

My limbs turned to stone.

She smiled, showing square gray teeth. Suddenly, her smile went stale and she crossed her legs, bobbing one snakeskin boot.

Whatever you do, stay far back from her feet. She kicks like a donkey.

I picked up the pass, moving like a marionette. I stood and I walked to the door. I had come to Jones for two things: to ensure my safety, and William's. I took a cool breath. It was time to implement the heart of my plan.

With one hand on the knob, I turned. "Oh, Teacher. I forgot to tell you," I said.

She frowned. "Yes?"

"On my way back to the Schoolhouse, about a mile east, I saw two feral men. They seemed to be headed this way."

"Travelers, from the other Houses," she surmised. "They come in droves for the Joust."

"I know, I saw them walking."

"If you know, then why are you asking?" she snapped.

"These men were different." I paused, as if the act of recalling overwhelmed my feral mind. Then, slowly, deliberately, I laid the bait. "They had white paint on their faces. They might have washed it off now, but it was odd. I wonder if they had the proper passes to travel between Houses. I thought I'd tell you—just in case."

Jones was on her feet again, just as I'd hoped.

"Were they riding or walking?"

"They were walking, but they had horses." I gave her a detailed description of the bounty hunters as well as their two remaining mounts, knowing she would pass it on to the Kongo Guard. Within the hour, the two men would be arrested. My heart warmed incrementally. I could not save everyone, but William, at least, would live.

THE GUARD AND THE NOTEBOOK

I went directly to the supply closet, eager to rid myself of the passes. Three passes in payment for services rendered, and each of them made me sick. I reminded myself of the logic—the Seed was the future. I was powerless, but logic didn't settle my stomach.

The deserted hall seemed smaller than I remembered. The main stairs, the porch, the schoolyard and its picket fence had all seemed small too. Three weeks ago, when I'd gone to the village, I had worried about opening the gate. Today, one swift kick had reduced it to splinters. I hadn't even paused. As if, once breached, the fence was no longer a barrier to me. Out of nowhere, I recalled a line from Sky's story.

"We been here so long, it's like a fence and we can't get out," I said to myself.

I walked more slowly, recalling her passion as she'd tried to tell me—*what was it?*

"Listen to me, daughter. Write this down. You don't belong to that skin," I said. My voice echoed in the hall. If a Teacher had been lurking in an empty room, they would have heard. I didn't care. I closed my eyes and pictured myself taking stories in the sick room. At the time I spoke to Sky, her words had been babble, the ramblings of a fevered old woman. Now, however, I puzzled over them, sensing their significance. They blew by me, brushing my cheek like an exhaled breath. *You got to look up*, she'd said. *You got to look up.*

"Pass!"

I snapped to attention. The Supply Room Guard, the Chalk-Hand Guard, was glaring at me. I had stepped into his hall without showing my pass. Quickly, I handed him Jones' pink slip. His eyes roamed over it, then over my un-Keeper-like britches.

"It's a real pass," I said, making no excuse for my clothing. Contrary to Jones' assessment, they weren't filthy. Hurley had seen to that. A lump congealed in my throat as I remembered how Hosea had added decongesting herbs to the hot wash water. Hurley had snored and sneezed no less.

The guard handed my pass back and, for the first time in all my training years, I stopped to look at him. I noticed the fingernails on his left hand were crusted with a dried pasty substance. He looked tired.

"Do you stay here throughout the night?" I said.

The guard looked around before responding. The hall was dark and empty. "Yes, Mistress."

I noticed other things about him. He was tall, even for a Kongo, very black and well muscled. He was younger than William but old enough to have sired me. His hands were extremely dry, as was his face, causing his skin to have that ashy white sheen I associated with him. "Don't—I mean, you don't have to call me Mistress," I said.

He dipped his head, clearly worried we were being watched. To ease his mind, I took a step back. If old Barrett was watching from the Supply Room, we wouldn't appear to be talking.

"Are you hungry?" I asked.

"No, Mistress!" I'd shocked him.

"What's your name?" I asked.

He looked pained, but whispered, barely moving his lips. "They call me Jay."

"I'm Arika," I said, noticing how his eyes ferreted away as he spoke his name.

He didn't respond. He was so uncomfortable, I knew I had to move on. This was not the oasis, where workers and Keepers toiled alike. There was no Voltaire ordering me about, reminding everyone that the pecking order started with her.

I started down the hall. Then, on impulse, I turned back. "Do you need anything, Jay?"

He glanced at me. "Ma'am?"

"Do you need supplies? A blanket, shoes, anything at all. You just say it, and I'll get it for you. I have more passes than I need."

His chalky chin came down a fraction of an inch as he took in the passes crumpled in my hand. I saw his eyes were a rich mahogany. "No, Ma'am," he said, softly. When I would have insisted, he added, "Ma'am, move on, now, before you get us killed."

My heart sank. He was right. At the Schoolhouse, there were ferals and madams—nothing in between. I stuffed the passes into the pocket of my britches and backed away, mumbling an apology.

From the Supply Room I selected the simplest *aura* and blouse in stock. I set the items down before Barrett and produced my passes.

"Just these, dear?"

I stalled. *Dear?*

Her thin lips wrinkled into a smile. "Why not a leather

journal too?" she offered. "I restocked them today."

She pulled a stack of notebooks from the fabled compartment under her desk. I took one without thinking. It was bound in embossed red leather. I touched my finger to the spiked ivy etched into the cover. The foliage ran up from the bottom of the spine. At the top, I traced sideways, down and back again. From there, the leaves bloomed up and out. They tangled together, weaving a nest in the center of the diary. In the middle of the nest a dark splotch of imperfectly dyed leather made a black oval egg, about the size of my thumb. I pressed my finger to it and felt it grow warm. Surprised, I yanked my hand back.

"Is one not enough?" she said, seeing my hesitation. "Here, take two. And quills and ink." She rushed to collect these, stuffing it all into a take-away bag.

"I only have three passes," I protested.

She waved a benevolent hand. "Consider it a token, a welcome-back gift—*from the Party.*"

I winced. Another gift was the last thing I wanted, and especially not one from the New Seed Party. I took the bag from her and removed several items. "I have quills and ink," I said. "I'll take the journal, but only one."

I had an idea for what to write in it. One journal was enough to accomplish my goal. Without meeting her ingratiating gaze, I bade her goodbye and left.

THE HEARTBREAK

Back in my room, I found everything exactly as I left it. My toiletries in ranks and lines. My curtains tied back in neat knots, no bows. My readers, crisp on the corner of my desk, each edge lined up in perfect right angles. I knelt on the floor by my desk and rummaged through my drawers. Finally, all the way in the back, I found a stack of East Keep's invitations. Pressed down and tied together, they were still three inches thick. I unbound them and spread them in a fan across my desk. The smell of stale perfume and stationery ink wafted up from the envelopes. Not a single one had been opened.

I was fumbling for a letter opener when a quiet knock sounded at my door. *My maid, my dear Robin!* I set the invitations aside. Until that moment, I hadn't realized how much I'd missed our friendship. Besides that, she was my link to the village news. She had nursed alongside Hosea and me. She would know who had made it and exactly how many were lost.

I flung open the door and froze. My smile died.

"Hello, Ma'am."

Instead of Robin, a little brown maid stood there, skinny and barefoot. I recognized her thin sack dress and solemn eyes. This was the girl that slept in the kitchen by the fire. The one who had brought me bad tidings about Robin before.

A terrible premonition tickled my throat. "What is it?" I asked.

"I'm here to draw your bath, Ma'am."

"Where is Robin?" I forced the words from my contracted chest.

She blinked, and looked down at her toes.

"Robin, my maid," I said, nearly shouting. Black spots obscured my vision. I wanted to take her thin shoulders and shake out a reassurance.

She shook her head.

No! I thought the word but couldn't say it.

The little maid's eyes were glued to the wood-paneled floor. "I'm sorry, Ma'am," she said, "Robin is—"

"Oh, no!" I reeled back.

She fell silent. Her thin lips sealed around the bad news.

I covered my head and sank to my knees. Robin was gone. Grief swooped down with a sharp beak. It bit my eyes and tore open my throat. Finally, too late, I said her name. "Wren." It pulsed out, like blood from a vein. "*Wren, Wren Wren, Wren Wren.*"

THE RECORD KEEPER

Once I'd spoken Wren's name, I couldn't stop. I repeated it, again and again, as the little maid stepped over me and into my room. She drew my bath as instructed. When that was done, she pulled me to my feet, as I mumbled incoherently. She walked me to the warm water. Finally, I grew quiet. Still in shock, I stared blindly into the dark distance. With the little maid's prodding, I undressed and stepped into the tub where I sat, like a limp doll. She talked to me as she helped me wash.

Robin died just after the Kongo Guard arrived en masse at Cobane. They'd not come only for the Joust, as the bounty hunters had presumed. They came weeks ago, to protect the English Teachers from fever, as Hosea had warned. The rule was, no one left the Schoolhouse gate and no one entered. The Guard enforced quarantine with threats of arrest.

Without the sick to tend, Robin faded more each day. Then, one morning, a worker found her hanging from the kitchen rafters, a length of brown *bambi* at her throat. She had finally found the strength to join her little Wren. Without Robin's care, many more in the village had died. The little maid didn't know how many, but they built another pyre to accommodate the bodies. She said many other things, but I didn't hear.

I was preoccupied, following a crooked line of logic. If I hadn't gone to Jones about the fever, Hosea might have stayed at Cobane. He might have found a cure, or at least kept the death toll down. Jones might not have called the Guard. If the Guard hadn't come, Robin would not have died. Her death was on my head—*guilty.*

"Mistress?" the girl shook my shoulder as she spoke into my ear.

I started. "Yes?" I managed.

"Do I wash your hair?" she repeated, talking loudly.

I looked around, confused, hearing her as if through a fog. I took in her sweet even features. Dark, intelligent eyes, too big for her face. The kind of eyes that appreciated minute details, imagined grand scenarios, recorded every slight. Her small lower lip was bitten raw with worry. I shook my head, to clear it. I noticed more. She was soaked with water and shivering. *How long had she been here?* Long enough for the bath water to have grown cold. "No, my hair is fine," I said, finally. She was freezing; I had to get her dry. I stood and stepped out of the tub.

I found two nightgowns made of thick warm cloth. Donning one, I wrapped the other around her shoulders. I heard her teeth chattering and felt ashamed. She spoke of disease, death and suicide. She was too young for such things. Robin had been *her* friend as well. And yet, here she was, taking care of me. The unfairness of her situation struck me anew.

"It's dangerous out there," I said. "Why don't you stay here tonight?"

She seemed surprised but, unlike Jay, she boldly accepted my offer. I heated more water for washing and tied a colorful scarf around her head to hide its nakedness. Finally, I settled her in my bed with a portion of nuts. I found the dried orange wedges in the locked compartment of my desk and gave them to her.

"You look to be about seven years old," I said. "You remind me of someone I used to know."

She smiled mischievously, but said nothing, sipping her tea.

My heart flipped. I remembered Robin at seven—*fluffing a pillow and setting it back in its place. She smiled. "If you are seven and I am seven, maybe we were born the same year!"*

I pressed my lips together. I could not save anyone, not even myself. But, I *would* keep pain away from this one girl, for this one night, if I could.

She loosened up quickly, chattering like the child she was, as I watched her eat. I heated more water and brought her tea which she slurped, greedily. At one point, another knock sounded at my door, but I ignored it and whoever it was went away.

It was late when the little maid fell asleep, mid-sentence. Her eyes drifted shut and her hand clasped reflexively around mine. I held it for a long while.

Later, I sat at my desk with the fine leather journal, thinking of the future. William would likely come to me after the Joust. The Kongo Guard would march from Cobane and I would finally be a Senator—with power of my own. I would use it to help my people. I would join the Assembly, but I would be different. I would be a true First Brother.

Strife loomed over the Kongo. War, fever, and the New Seed. Many would die. I sighed. Many had already died. I thought of the slain and allowed myself a single tear. It traveled down my chin to my desk, where I wiped it away.

I reined in my emotions. Robin was gone, and I hadn't said goodbye. Never again would I wait to make amends, as

I had with her. When I saw William next, I would apologize, first thing. He would welcome me and, with a single word—*Papa*—I would bind every wound between us. Then, in my first act as Senator, I would issue him a formal invitation to Hasting. For my second act, I would arrange for myself to record his story.

I opened the leather journal, and wrote *For William* on the front cover. I stared at it a long while then added, *the Whittler.* It seemed right somehow that this journal, my *gift from the Party*, should be given to him. More, it was right that I, his daughter, should be the one to record his story in it. I hugged the book to my chest. What wisdom he gained in his life with my mother was my birthright, and I would claim it tomorrow.

BACK TO THE PIT

I slept deeply that night, more than I had in years. When I woke, I found the kitchen maid had disappeared. Two packages had been delivered. The first, I knew instinctually, was from William. Somehow, he'd snuck into my room and left my pack from the oasis. Inside were the parchment rolls of stories I'd collected, as well as my spare pair of leggings, my Helix and the wooden boomerang he'd made me. I picked up the Helix. It warmed immediately and composed itself into its basic form. I tossed it up into the air, testing its weight in my hand. It was as cumbersome as ever. I replaced its sheath and returned it to my bag.

As promised, the second package was from Jones. I opened the folder, slipped beneath my door in the night, to find an essay written in stylized calligraphy. We'd been trained to produce the uniform script since primary school. So the handwriting in this essay would be indistinguishable from any other student's. Without reading it, I put the essay in a small sack along with quills and ink.

Instead of a skirt and blouse, I slipped on my leggings and vest. I draped my *aura* over them both. I folded the *bambi* in pleats and wrapped it around my hips and shoulders, before securing it with a broad belt around my waist. I looked in the mirror with some satisfaction. The tight binding still hobbled my knees but, beneath all the material, my britches were undetectable. And, beneath my britches, my ruby knife warmed my leg.

It had remained undetected in its harness during my capture from the oasis. It was so much a part of my body that I'd forgotten its presence until last night, when I found it in the pile of clothes I discarded before my bath. In her ignorance, the kitchen maid must have removed it. *Never again will it leave my body*, I thought. If I couldn't wield the Helix, the ruby knife was my only weapon against the violence that was about to swallow the Kongo.

I laced my sandals on feet spotted with tiny cuts that would disappear now that I wasn't training. Some of the deeper abrasions would scar. I didn't mind. At Hasting, they would be a cherished reminder of my days in the oasis. After giving my face a good scrub and pulling my hair back in a mound at the crown of my head, I left my room to take the Final Exam.

The hall was ripe with anticipation. Students and Teachers alike would leave the Schoolhouse within the hour to observe the festivities. I stopped at the nearest window and looked out. The Clayskin contractors had erected a temporary arena in the meadow just outside of the Schoolhouse gate. Clayskin medics and armed Kongo Guards surrounded every entrance. They scanned the crowd waiting to enter. Anyone with fever would be turned away, or worse. I watched as a Kongo Guard led a contingent of workers, some obviously ailing, away from the arena. They walked toward a waiting line of gated wagons. Instinct told me those wagons were not headed back toward the village.

In the Main Hall, I stuck close to a group of chattering

secondary students as they took their place in the breakfast queue. I grabbed food quickly, intending to slip out of the hall and eat alone in the library. I couldn't stand to face my class—not yet. I was almost back through the exit when I hesitated, wondering. *Would Hannibal be with the others at the breakfast table? Would she be crippled—maimed? Had Jetson tried to rescue her and been injured himself?*

Biting my lip, I glanced over my shoulder at the senior table. To my surprise, it was unoccupied. I turned back into the crowd and made my way around the Hall, dodging maids and heavily laden tables. I made two laps and concluded that none of my classmates were present. I stopped at the senior table, where a battalion of secondary students discussed where to sit.

"We can't sit at the senior table until after Break, when we're officially seniors."

"But the primaries have taken over *our* seats."

"Then we'll just have to tell them to move!"

"Where? The Clayskin administrators have commandeered the primary table for registration."

"Maybe we should ask a Teacher."

Three curious pairs of eyes turned to me. I started, realizing they waited for me to weigh in on their discussion. I was a senior, valedictorian of my class, nearly as good as a Teacher in their minds. I looked at each of them, then told the truth. "It doesn't matter where you sit," I said.

They exchanged curious looks, but said nothing.

I lowered my voice. "What matters is that you sit together. A wise man, a worker named William, told me that. There is no stronger sword than the people together," I said.

I'd stunned two of them into silence. The third student nodded as if she understood.

I turned to her. "Have you seen the senior students this morning?"

"No, Keeper Cobane."

"Arika is just fine. I'm not a Keeper yet. Do you know where they are?" I asked.

"Yes. They're in the test room suite. The kitchen staff set a breakfast for their exclusive enjoyment."

I nodded. Jones mentioned the special breakfast on the last day of class. "Thank you," I said, resting a hand on her shoulder. "And don't forget what I said."

She stood straight and nodded again.

As I discarded my tray, I considered what the next year would be like for her class. In light of the New Seed, many of them would be unnecessary—fewer workers required fewer Keepers to keep them in line. The Teachers would likely divide the students into two groups. One would go on to Hasting and the other would be deemed *nonessential*. They'd be exterminated and their lifeless bodies thrown into the pyre. I ascended the stairs, deep in thought. The old worker song played in my mind.

Swinging the sickle, cutting the wheat, tossing the wheat, swinging the sickle.

How would the chaff be separated from the wheat, I wondered. As students of Record Keeping, we were trained to believe that our noses, hair, and lips signified our superiority. So, what now would justify the slaughter of half the elite? Would it be by height or weight? Maybe the relative lightness of their skin? So a student with Jetson's fair complexion would be safe, but one with my medium skin tone, or darker, would be killed?

Whatever the Assembly decided, the new barometer would be no less arbitrary than the measures currently in place to separate the First Brothers from the Second. The illogic of the law could no longer be denied. I knew, firsthand, the Second Brothers' capacity. Voltaire, for example, was a genius. More intelligent than the sweet but nonsensical twins who were classified as First Brothers. I had nursed the village workers, and eaten with bandits in the oasis. I spoke with the young and old alike. I had friends or family in every political faction and I, myself, was a Keeper. This much was clear: what separated my class from the ferals was not intellect or design, but the Rebirth. They were subject to it, and we were not. Who knew what the workers could achieve intellectually, if they could only recall who they were before the Compromise?

As I mounted the top level, my doubts circled around the dark figure who set the Rebirth in place—Obi Solomon. All revered the name, but the man himself was obscure, draped in shadows and legends. I had, at least, some evidence that the Great Obi Solomon was not a loyal Kongo. The ancient tales needed, once and for all, to be untangled. The Omen regarding the mighty *One* needed research and verification. Was there a Kongo savior? Was he—or she—coming? I would search for the truth at Hasting.

I stopped walking, abruptly, at the door of the testing suite. I stood there a long while, catching my breath. After speaking to the younger students, I knew I needed to face my peers. We would need each other in the upcoming days. Somehow, I had to bridge the rift between us.

I entered the room. Relief washed over me as I counted their heads. *One, two, three, four, and the twins!* Five females, one male, and all intact—for the most part. Jetson had a patch on his chin, Hannibal had a wrist brace, and all appeared more haggard than I remembered. But, they were alive!

To my credit, I didn't shrink from their scrutiny. I met their eyes in turn. Jetson's were cold, Hannibal's blank, the twins glared daggers along with Covington.

East Keep's squinting expression was inscrutable. She stood, hands clutching her sides. "What are you doing here? We thought you were dead!" East Keep said.

I stepped further into the room. "As you can see, I'm very much alive."

"Well, you shouldn't be," she said, harshly. "We wish you weren't. Hannibal's wrist is broken. She'll walk with a limp for the rest of her life because of you."

I bowed my head. "I'm sorry. So sorry."

"It's not enough!" East Keep declared. She stormed out of the room.

With the sound of the slammed door still echoing, I faced the remainder of the class. Shame churned in my stomach, but I faced them squarely. They had every right to strike back at me for the strife I'd caused. Let them do their worst! I would stand it.

"I know a doctor," I told Hannibal, quietly. "He'll look at your limp. If there's anything that can be done, he'll see to it."

Hannibal acknowledged me with the barest nod.

Several minutes of silence. My chin trembled, but I waited—resolved to stay.

Finally, Jetson spoke. "Why did you do it?"

"*Obi*, Jetson! I don't care why she did it," Covington snapped. "It's done, that's all that matters."

"We don't care either," the twins added.

"Well, explain it to me then," Jetson said. "*If* you can."

"I can, and I want to," I said, searching his eyes. The secrets I carried longed to be exposed. More than that, my peers needed to know the truth, for their own safety. I positioned myself in view of the door. Jones would be administering the test and I didn't want her to sneak up in the middle of my story.

"It started the day Hosea Khan came to class," I began. "I went to the kitchen that night to find Robin, and, on my way back to my room, Jones caught me out after dark."

I went on to explain everything. The secret assignment I'd been given, the fever, nursing in the village and why, even after I promised to reveal myself, I kept all I knew a secret.

Jetson uncrossed his arms. "So, it's as I thought! That Vine feral blackmailed you!"

"No," I said quickly. "Hosea would never do that. He wants peace above everything. He saw what happened at Point Landing and he didn't want it to happen at Cobane. I was in the wrong, not him. Hosea is—kind and good." My voice trailed off as Jetson's eyes narrowed on my face.

"So why did you go to Jones?" Covington asked. She didn't look at me but her head was cocked attentively, waiting for my answer.

Seizing upon this encouragement, I explained. Telling them how my plan to bargain for medicine had backfired. I told them I had not escaped unscathed. Jetson spoke up for me then, confirming that Jones had, indeed, beaten me severely on the day of my departure.

East Keep came back just as I revealed the truth about the New Seed. She came to crowd around me with the others who were stunned to realize, too late, that they'd been on the wrong side of the political battle.

"So, the New Seed is actually bad for the workers," Hannibal said.

"And for the Keepers," Covington added. "I don't know how I didn't put that together before. As soon as the Seed is harvested, some northern Senator is sure to petition for population control."

"I agree," I said. "We do outnumber the other two races, and we consume a lot of food. Population control is vital to the greater good." My voice trailed off. There was nothing more to say. With the New Seed in place, the fate of the Kongo was sealed.

Covington's mouth trembled. Her fists clenched. She looked how I felt—helpless. I glanced around to see everyone was upset. They were elitists, certain that their birthright was to rule the workers. However, it was plain to see, now, that they were not without compassion.

"We're all safe, at least," I said, knowing this was little consolation. Like me, they wanted everyone, all of the Kongo, to be safe. "If the Rebels don't cut our throats tonight, we'll go to Hasting as planned. It'll be our job to convince the Assembly that the Second Brothers are worth saving."

"That will never happen," Hannibal said.

I tore my eyes from Covington. Tears dripped from Hannibal's chin. "No," I agreed, finding I needed to be honest. "It won't."

"What happens to the Keepers that stay behind at the Schoolhouse?" East Keep asked.

I looked at her curiously. There was a strange note in her voice and her face was ashen.

"They're going to die," I answered, unable to soften the horror of it. "Not all of them, but most will be deemed nonessential. Jones said about half is all we'll need in the future."

Her face grew even more severe.

"East Keep, are you okay?" I asked.

Before she could answer, a bevy of trumpets resounded, announcing the beginning of the Festival. As one, we adjourned to the window; except for East Keep, who took her seat. She heard only the tail end of my explanation and so, I assumed, she was still angry. I turned back to speak to her privately when something strange about the arena caught my eye.

"What's that at the far end there?" I asked.

Jetson answered. "It's a gallows. You've missed quite a bit in your absence."

"Tell me," I said.

"Do you remember that fugitive who escaped custody a few weeks back?"

"The one that broke through the line," I said, nodding.

"Well, Jones has been on a witch hunt to discover how he was able to get through. She's taken a dozen political prisoners since then. There've been rumors of torture in the Pit. A few days ago, she caught up with Martin."

"The Rebel!" I said. "I heard him speak in the village before I left."

"He's not just a Rebel," Covington said. "She believes he's a key figure in Voltaire's Army, and he's been causing all sorts of trouble."

"I'll bet." I recalled how the man in the red bandana agitated the workers, stirring them into a lynch mob with his words. And later, the repulsion and fear he showed toward me once he discovered I was a Record Keeper. He was the Martin that co-led the White-Face Army. The one William had called *the brain*. "It all makes sense," I said.

Hannibal's haunted eyes fixed on the gallows. "Some of the worst criminals, Martin included, are being held in the Pit now. They're to be executed today," she said.

One by one, we drifted back to our seats. Jetson moved gently at Hannibal's side, helping her adjust her leg so that it stuck straight out into the aisle.

My mouth tightened with pity. Her mangled leg had been perfect just a few weeks ago.

Jetson noticed my gaze and hurried to explain. "When she bends her leg too long, it cramps."

Before I could respond, something powerful jerked low in my belly. I bent over as the cramp tightened. An angry voice I didn't recognize echoed from deep inside me. *Wrong! So very wrong!*

Jetson watched me. "Arika?"

My head snapped up; my lips twisted in a vicious snarl.

He stepped back, shocked.

I looked away, forcing myself to relax. I straightened my shoulders and stood upright. "I'm sorry, Jetson. I don't know what came over me," I said.

His eyes narrowed on my face.

"I'm fine now." I smiled, for his sake. I turned and found my seat.

I rested a sweat-dampened palm just over my belly button, which quivered and jerked. I wasn't fine, I realized. I was trembling all over. My stomach ached and that strange voice coiled inside me like a cobra, repeating a name that refused to be denied. "Dr. Adam Dagnyyyy," I hissed, letting it out.

Quickly, I covered my mouth. I hadn't thought of Dr. Dagny in some time, and I wasn't sure why his name plagued me now. He was a Finnish defense specialist that died toward the end of the old world. He'd plummeted from the side of Mount Fiji in a tethering rope accident. Miraculously, the doctor had landed in snow so soft, he could have walked away uninjured—if only he'd walked away. Instead, according to his fellow climbers, he'd lain there, raging at the rock he'd fallen from.

He'd come up during my Silver Award research because, in the year before his untimely death, by avalanche, Dr. Dagny had invented the blueprint for the first heavy bomb, the most lethal weapon ever created. Just one could demolish several hundred miles, laying flat everything in its path. Its force was so great it left cracks in the Earth's surface, causing the man-made phenomenon known as lava geysers. After it was first tested, it was banned by international agreement. It was simply too dangerous to exist. Russia, China, India—all claimed to disarm. None did.

•

Jones entered the room, a treacherous frown on her stern face. She was looking for a fight. "Take out your essays and pass them forward," she said briskly.

She wasn't allowed in the room once we had the test in hand but, as moderator, she would collect our essays, distribute the Final and watch us from a small side room attached to the testing suite.

I took out my essay and, as I awaited further instructions, I read the prompt for the first time. *"Discuss the biological modules of the Niagara Compromise."* I pressed a fist into my rumbling stomach. It was a fair question. One we had discussed often over the years. In crafting the Compromise, the Founders had relied on a careful study of past civilizations, human nature and biology. In their study, they found that each race had its own inherent strengths and weaknesses. According to the Compromise, the key to living in harmony was to rely on the strength of our differences while bearing each other's faults.

I glanced down at the content of the essay Jones had delivered to me. I wasn't surprised to see it was, essentially, an exhaustive list of the Kongo's weaknesses, complete with dozens of examples from the new and old world. When discussing the biologics of the Compromise, the dialog always turned to the shortcomings of dark men. We were never asked to debate the weakness of the English.

The old world had been ruled by the English, and not by accident. The English had dominated by force. For hundreds of years, they had operated under the belief that ruling the Earth, to the exclusion of other races, was their birthright.

The Founders had rejected that paradigm outright. The Compromise did not favor one race to the exclusion of others. Instead, it divided the races. Separate but equal spheres of influence. The sum tasks required to sustain life on Earth were divvied up so that each race had an indispensable role. We enjoyed a symbiotic relationship. They couldn't eat without us and we couldn't advance without them.

It was perfectly logical but, even as I brooded on the facts, something inside of me rejected the conclusion they led to. The Founders had improved on the old-world order of English domination. But, somehow, I knew that they had stopped short of the truth.

A stifled cry jarred me from my ruminations. I turned to look at Covington in the seat behind me. She was shaking with sobs.

"Covington?" I whispered.

Outside, trumpets sounded and a loud voice announced the name of the first criminal to be executed. *Hawk*—I couldn't hear his House name. It was drowned out by the sound of East Keep's chair, screeching as she scooted into the aisle toward Covington.

She leaned in. "I'm so sorry, Covington. I didn't know. I swear, I didn't know."

I looked between them, confused. Covington cried as if she'd received a death sentence and East Keep appeared even more bereft. Before I could ask again what was happening, I noticed Covington's desktop. I glanced around. Everyone else—in their hands or on their desk—had a handwritten essay. In contrast, Covington's hands clutched her face and her desk was empty.

The crowd outside roared as the criminal—Hawk—was executed.

"Covington, where is your essay?" I said.

She didn't answer.

I looked again at East Keep and I knew. She'd vowed revenge, and she'd taken it. With me presumed dead, she had used Covington as my proxy. Covington, who had vouched for me. Covington, who had chosen me as Vice Chair. Covington, who had betrayed her once too often.

"I took it from your bag this morning," she confessed, her voice barely a whisper. "I tried to get it back when Arika came, but someone must have taken it out in the garbage," East Keep said. "I'm so sorry. I—"

I didn't hear what East Keep said next, whether she explained her malice, stood by it, or offered amends. All I saw was Covington—my sister—weeping. All I felt was my own heart, moving me to act. I took my own essay in hand, and set it on Covington's desk.

·

"What are you doing," Jones snapped.

I froze. She stood over me.

"Covington dropped her essay," I said.

I swallowed hard. I had acted on impulse. But now, I had to explain my own empty desk to Jones. My mind worked on overdrive. I had two points in my favor. Jones could not openly admit to giving me the essay. And two, I was her spy! If I stayed another year, I could hope to be deemed essential—but Covington would surely die. My eyes flickered to Covington, warning her to keep quiet. I turned forward in my seat, my head bowed, meekly.

"I'm sorry, Teacher. I don't have a final essay. I don't—"

I broke off as the trumpets boomed again. The same loud voice announced the next criminal to be executed. "Crane the Conqueror!"

My breath caught. Surely I had heard wrong.

"You don't what, girl?" Jones barked. She was dangerously annoyed.

"Champion of House Cobane," the announcer said.

I stood. There had to be some mistake.

"Sit down!" Jones snapped. She tried to block my way to the window. I knocked right into her, caught her off balance, and pushed her aside.

"Cobane! You filthy, filthy—"

Her shouts faded into the background. I reached the window, frantically searching the arena. Surely I had heard wrong. Oh, God! William was easy to spot in the open space. He was the tallest man—a giant. There were three Guards escorting him to the gallows.

"No! No! No!" I pounded on the window. I had to break it.

Behind me, Jones' fist caught my head and I whiplashed forward, headlong into the window overlooking the arena. A gash split my forehead.

I didn't even feel it. I continued to flail. "No! There's been a mistake!"

She hit me again, opening another cut. It spewed blood.

Red washed over my eyes, blocking my vision. I blinked as fast as I could, but not fast enough. I couldn't see a thing.

Jones took me by the neck. She dragged me down to the ground. I pushed away violently. I was on my feet in a flash. Back at the window, I smashed blindly with both fists. "We have to break it!" I cried, incoherent with panic.

No one answered.

Vaguely, I heard Jones at my back, rummaging through her desk.

Tears were washing the blood from my eyes, and soon I could see again. Out to the arena. Right near the gallows. William and three Guards. William, stepping onto the wood stairs, mounting them. *Up, up,* without even a struggle. A rope around his neck. A sack on his head.

"No! Fight!" I screamed. My throat was raw. "Fight!" If he tried he could throw them off, but he wasn't trying. He wasn't fighting. He had laid down his club. They tightened the noose. There was a lever by his leg. The third Guard, the smallest, pulled it. A resounding *thunk*, as the platform dropped from beneath him—my *father*.

"Papa, Papa, Papa! I'm sorry. Papa, I'm sorry, forgive me. No!" I threw myself at the window, opening more wounds, again and again. It was too late. I was too late. He was hanged. I started to wail. "No!"

Suddenly, Jones was back. She was shouting, incoherently. Her fist came down. The lights flashed and the wailing stopped.

•

I woke disoriented. I was on my side in the Pit—the dream Pit. I sat up and looked around. I frowned. Something was different. I was on the ground as always, having landed here from the hallway above. To my left, down the way, I saw the mewling girl, rocking and mouthing as always. But there, just above me. *That* was different! There was a small square of light up there as if someone, whoever made dreams, had forgotten to close the Schoolhouse hole I'd fallen through. Voices echoed through it.

"Is she dead?"

That sounded like Hannibal.

"She'll live. Boy, get water, and hurry."

I grimaced. That was Jones. Just hearing her voice made my gut clench. Everyone got quiet as *the boy*, Jetson, fetched water. Presumably, Jones would use it to wake up my unconscious body still lying above on the classroom floor. I hadn't seen the weapon she had pulled from her desk, but she'd hit me hard. Hard enough to send me here, to the brink of hell.

"Here's the water, Teacher."

Jetson was back! They all got quiet again as, I assume, Jones tried to revive me. With one hand, I felt my forehead and temple. I wasn't in pain, though I should have been, given what had happened up there before I'd fallen. I remembered everything. Giving Covington my essay, defying Jones, running to the window, cracking my forehead. I remembered it all, but none of it mattered down here—except what I'd seen on the gallows.

The Guards must have arrested William last night, when he'd snuck into my room. Jones had had them patrolling the streets of the village, looking for men wanted in connection with the fugitive. There was no way someone as large and famous as William could have passed undetected. So, why had he come? Why hadn't he waited until after the Joust, when the risk of discovery was low? Oh, William!

Following the announcement of his name in the arena, a stunned silence had fallen over the crowd. When he'd been halfway to the gallows, someone had started to hum his tune. As he'd mounted the steps, the masses had not been cheering, as they had with the other criminal. They had all taken up the tune and sung him to his death. I cocked my head. I could hear them humming still. Their voices drifted up from the arena, across the testing suite and down to me.

My papa had been well loved. His people had honored him

as a king, and he had watched over them—silent and strong. My heart ached and I curled over, longing to be with him.

After a long while, my sobs subsided. I pushed myself upright and dried my face. Of all the people my father had loved, he had loved me best. Love was why he came to me last night, despite the danger. He risked his life to bring me my Apex. In the oasis, he encouraged me to practice, so that I would be strong.

He had laid down his own club, but he would not want me to languish here in the Pit. He would not want me to abandon my body above and go further into the darkness. No, my papa wanted me to fight. I stood, knowing what I had to do. I walked down the hallway to confront *her*.

I watched her for a while. Her sharp nails dug their crescent moons. "Do you know that you are my block?" I said.

She didn't answer.

"You make me weak," I accused.

She rocked and mewled silently.

"You stop me from fighting—from wielding my sword."

The grate opened above us. "Do you need more?" dream Jones asked.

She didn't answer and neither did I. Shame filled me.

Dream Jones shut the grate with a loud *click*. I jumped and hunched my shoulders. The sound had been loud and it lingered. Resounding around the hall—*click, click, click*. It bounced up and down and boomed inside my chest— *CLICK*.

Silence fell.

My heartbeat tripled and my breath pumped *in and out, in and out*.

Slowly, I lowered my shoulders and raised my head. I looked up at the dark bars of the grate. I looked down at the girl. Up and down again. I saw her, as if seeing for the first time. *She was just a child.*

"I was just a little girl," I said. Something hot filled my throat and deepened my voice. I swallowed but it washed back up. "Just a little girl," I said, again.

Suddenly, I began to shake. My legs trembled. My bowels quivered. I jerked and weaved. My knees bent and I fell to the ground as something inside of me was unleashed. A black, hot rage such as I'd never known. Lithe and fanged, it whipped through my body. I clamped my head, trying to control it, but it was no use. My mind looped around a single thought. *A little girl is nothing to be ashamed of. The evil, the true monster, is watching from the grate above.* My neck snapped back and I glared up into the darkness.

"Jones!" My gut cramped. "Jones!" Wrath fired my belly and boiled my tongue. "Jones! Jones, Jones!" *She* was the vile one. *She*, the monster—not me. *If I'd a dozen heavy bombs, I would launch them all at her—the Earth be damned.* The thought shifted across my mind like a shadow.

I crouched on the cold stone ground, breathing heavily, my arm wrapped around my middle. I glanced back at the little girl. We had been divided too long. Now, finally, I understood—she was my ally. Fiercely protective, I scooted over and settled myself beside her. I sat for a moment then said what was on my mind. "You know, we have a sword now. We have power. We don't have to be afraid."

I jumped when she moved. She lifted her head, as if she'd heard me.

"Can you hear me?" I said, excitedly.

She stared into the darkness, right at me. Sensing my presence, but unable to see.

"We don't have to be afraid," I said, again. "Never, *ever* afraid."

Somehow, in the warped laws of this dream world, she finally understood me. She stopped rocking and her hands stopped digging. She released her arms and rested them in her lap.

Her mouth, however, was still moving, even more urgently than before. It moved in the same motion, I realized, as I watched. The same motion, over and over. She was not mewling, but *speaking*.

"What are you saying?" I asked. I leaned in to peer at her lips. Over and over, the same thing. She was trying to tell me something. "What are you saying?"

I still heard the crowd outside, humming William's song. And, suddenly, I sensed the truth. She was not speaking, but *singing*. My eyes narrowed on her mouth. "Are you singing William's song? Do you know the words?"

I peered into her eyes, and saw that she did. She knew. I gasped—*I* knew—deep down inside. I knew William's song. And, deep down, I'd known it all along. He sang it back to me for weeks, but I sung it in the womb; I sprang forth with one song on my breath. *How did it go? How did it go?* I gazed in her eyes and, bit by bit, it came to me. Finally, we would sing as one. I took her hand and she took my waist and we rose up in song. Like ivy climbing the gibbet, we rose, and I remembered:

I am Arika of House Cobane.

Do not swaddle me.
I dare you
I dare you.

•

I awoke to the sting of Jones' hand connecting with my cheek.

"Good," she said, seeing I was awake. "Now I'll ask you again. Where is your essay?"

Ignoring her, I took stock. We were still in the testing suite. I was trapped against the wall. She'd tied my hands and feet as if she'd known, somehow, I would awaken ready to fight.

"Your paper!" she shouted. Her hand came down like a viper.

I heaved myself aright but, with my hands bound, her next three blows struck unmitigated, splitting my cheek, knocking a tooth out, filling my mouth with blood.

I surged with fury, twice as strong as the fear I'd cast aside. *Coward!* I thought, railing at her. *You coward!*

"Did you cheat?" she asked, breathing hard. "Did you give your essay away? Answer me, girl. Did you cheat?" *Slap slap slap!*

My temple hit the paneled wall, knocking me senseless for moment. She had a nerve, I'd give her that. Chastising me for cheating.

She shoved her face close to mine.

I bucked and butted her with my head, once, twice. I drew back and fired the filth in my mouth. Blood and spit landed with a splash across her hateful face.

She reeled back.

I spat again, hitting her feet. I sounded my battle cry— *hurrah.* "For Robin! For Kiwi, Sky, Fount! For William! For *William!*"

From the corner of my eye, I saw Jetson stand, ready to intervene. Hannibal, thank God, took hold of his arm. She could not stop him for long, I knew. Jetson, my comrade, would not be stopped. A new fear tickled my throat. I could not draw this battle out. For his sake, I had to finish it—and quick. I needed a way out.

With one good eye, I turned to study Jones at her desk. She wiped her soiled face and, unhurried, dropped the cloth in the trash. She opened a drawer and removed a chestnut box, too small to be a weapon. Almost gently, she plucked from it a ring, large and gilded. She slid the ring on her big finger, then returned to pluck another, even larger than the first. One by one, she covered her hands, two and three to a knuckle. She had a dutiful air, as if, by her logic, I'd signed my own death warrant. I wanted to die, needed to, *for the greater good*. She came forth, armed. I met her gaze. She stopped.

The corners of my swollen mouth turned up, gleefully. I bared my teeth, stifling a giggle. I imagine she thought I was out of my mind for smiling; I laughed all the more. In truth, dear reader, I *was* untethered. The Niagara Compromise remained the law for many more months. But on that day, I found my freedom. Trussed up in the corner of the Schoolhouse, my back against a wall, I roamed in plains as wide as my own heart.

Jones regained herself and pounced upon me. She wailed and I leered up, unafraid of pain and death—I was the very face of madness. Finally, her grip slipped and her next blow, a cut to my chin, drove me down to the ground.

"Do you need more?" she barked from above, shaking her fist.

To answer, I looked up, winked, exposed my bloody teeth.

"Have it your way, you stupid feral."

She was tired. Her breath labored and she braced her palms on the wall to steady her girth. I curled into a tight ball, willing her to do her worst—to *kick like a donkey*. Just as I hoped, she drew one black boot back, higher and higher. Her leg went back and her body tipped forward, one leg held her aright. I watched and waited. Up, up, it went. She tipped. Nearly there. Almost there—*there*.

With a guttural cry, I uncurled, jackknifing like a piston. My foot hit the knee of her standing leg. It bent backward with a sickening snap. Ligaments, tendons, bones gave way. Jones flew forward, airborne. Her crown hit the wall. Her left eye gouged on the wainscot. I rolled out of her way, just in time. With one last crunch she hit the ground, cold.

•

Silence reigned. My chest heaved. The others held their breath. I shifted aright. "Covington, untie my hands."

She backed away the moment I was free, her eyes locked on my face. I frowned. Perhaps she could see the storm of hate still raging inside me. I didn't care. I had a plan and I had to move fast. I would have to explain later. Reaching down, I untied my feet and took out the knife at my ankle. The rubies glinted victoriously.

I cut three strips of cloth from the hem of Jones' skirt, viciously ripping the fabric. With the strips in hand, I stood to address my peers.

"Hannibal," I pointed to the rope Jones had used to bind me. "Use that rope to tie Jones' hands and feet securely. Covington, find something to use as a weapon—something heavy. If she wakes up, crack her skull. Jetson, watch the door. If anyone comes, lie to them. No one comes into this room without me. East Keep, twist these strips into a braid and secure the ends." I tossed the trio of strips I'd taken from Jones' dress onto East Keep's desk. "Does everyone understand? No one comes in, no one goes out."

Their mouths gaped like a school of fish.

"Where are you going?" Covington breathed, breaking the silence.

There wasn't time to explain. "I have a plan and I'll be back. Wait for me—okay?"

Our eyes met. Hers sparked with rebellion, just as it had that first day of school. She glanced around the room. The others were frozen with fear. Covington's full mouth began to tremble.

I stepped forward and rested my hand on her shoulder. "Covington." The command in my voice was undeniable.

She looked back at me. Our eyes clashed.

Trust me, I said silently.

But what if—

Comrade, trust me, I repeated.

She took a deep breath, pulled in her lower lip and looked down at her sandals. When she looked up again, the spark was back, brighter than ever.

I squeezed her shoulder. I knew then that she would be my most loyal general in the war to come.

•

A few minutes later, I double-checked the hallway. It was empty. Everyone was in the arena for the Festival. Satisfied, I closed the door of my dormitory behind me. Wasting no time, I moved to the middle of the room and held out my hand. I did not doubt my ability to command the Double Helix. Having bested Jones, I knew the truth of my own vitality. Power surged inside me as undeniable as gravity. The Earth bound me by force of universal law. And I, with an irrefutable strength of will, called my Apex.

I opened my hand and reached out. It buzzed to life. It shook free of its *bambi* sheath and began spinning, flying from my bed. Faster and faster, it whirled. It circled left then right, testing the boundaries of the room. Finally, it wound its way to my grasp. It was warm with energy. I nodded, letting the substance of its weight reassure me of my own power. I gripped it, then for sport, flung it out again, aiming for my desk chair. It burst into dust on contact. I tossed it out again, destroying my desk, my bed, my basin and mirror.

When everything was destroyed, I looked down at my ruined *aura*. The tight nip of the hobble had ripped in my battle with Jones. Impulsively, I pushed two fingers in the gash and yanked it open, tearing the cloth from seam to seam and tossing it to the ground. Clothed in my *bambi* leggings, I shifted my pack onto my shoulder and, without looking back, I strode from my Schoolhouse dorm for the last time.

I walked quickly through the empty corridors and up the main stairs. Close to the Supply Room hall, I slowed. I measured my breathing so as not to make a sound. Inch by inch, I snuck up to the Chalk-Hand Guard—the one who called himself Jay.

I was close enough to see him. As always, his hands were powdery white. The ring finger on his left hand was bent just above the second knuckle. His other nine nails were congested with white crust.

I took a deep breath and shouted, "Condor!"

He jerked and jumped around—at the sound of his true name.

I stood to reveal myself.

"You!" he hissed.

I strode forward, triumphant, holding his naked gaze. Toe to toe, I stopped. "So, you are Condor," I said. "The muscle of Voltaire's Army."

"How did you know?" he said.

I took his wrist. My hand didn't span its girth. I lifted it so his chalk-white fingers fanned between us. "Your hands," I said. "We call you the Chalk-Hand Guard, but the whiteness isn't chalk; it's paint. When I realized that, I knew you were a White-Face soldier. Last night, I sensed you were lying about your name. The rest I guessed and, now, you've confirmed it. How clever of you to hide here at Cobane, the most tame of the Kongo Houses."

In clipped sentences, I told him how I had defeated Jones. I finished and crossed my arms high on my chest. He looked me over, skeptically. The cuts on my face and my right eye, swollen nearly shut, gave credence to my story. Slowly, a measure of reserved respect ripened in the air between us. He agreed to follow me back to the testing suite. Instead of taking the main stairs up to the next floor, I led him down to the first floor. We crossed the open colonnade, to the arched opening that led down to the Pit. I put my shoulder against the wood-and-iron door to open it.

Condor stopped me. "Do you lie, girl? Where are you

taking me?" His teeth clenched around the words—like a threat.

With a grunt, I shoved open the door and continued down a long flight of stairs. At the bottom, I turned and answered him. "We're going to free our brother, Martin. He is the brain behind your army, is he not?"

He stepped into the opening, closed the door and folded his arms. "Martin's life is finished. To free him is to forfeit my life and our cause! We must leave him be."

Before he'd uttered the last word, my Helix was in my hand. I bent my arm at the elbow and let it fly up the stairs, directly toward him. He ducked, saving his head as the weapon arced around him. Seeing he was terrified, I called it back. I leapt up, catching it with both hands. But I wasn't done. He needed to taste my strength.

In midair, I grunted and broke the Apex in two. As I fell, I willed the two broken ends to transform. I envisioned the shape I wanted and labored to give it life. Longer, wider, twisting and arching. I groaned as they pulled, sucking energy from my bones. Finally, it was finished. I landed on one knee, head bowed, chest heaving. In the air behind me, my Double Helix had taken its second form. The two halves of the boomerang were gone, transformed into a pair of curved swords with vicious, jagged edges. I looked up at Condor.

He crouched down, his mouth open, hands raised in surrender.

I got to my feet. "Stand," I commanded. "But I warn you, time is short and we must stand together."

He glanced up at me, "Together?" he asked.

"First and Second Brothers, Loyalist and Rebel, Hannibal,

Covington, West Keep, Bankhead and the like. Every Kongo must be united if we're to defeat our enemy."

"And who is our enemy?" he asked.

"Don't you see? Our enemy is the Niagara Compromise itself, and those whom the Compromise protects—the English." My tone reminded me of Voltaire. "Death to the *English!*" I shouted.

He shook his head. "You're mad!"

I lifted my chin, rejecting his assertion. "Not mad," I said. "I'm angry, as is my right—and yours. To hate hateful things is our liberation. Now, come. We will free Martin."

He was a proud man. I saw it galled him to follow my order, but he had no choice. He joined me at the bottom of the stairs.

The man standing guard over Martin's cell had witnessed my display. He looked terrified as he saw us coming and he backed away, surrendering his prisoner. We slid back the iron grate without incident. Condor hooked his powdery hands under Martin's arms and lifted the smaller man from the cell. Martin was unconscious and gagged.

"Needs water," the Pit Guard whispered to Condor. "Three days, no water."

Condor laid Martin on the cold stone ground and slapped his cheek. Except for the faint rise and fall of his chest, there was no sign of life in him. Condor looked up at me and confirmed, "He needs water and food."

I shook my head. "We can't wait. There's no time. Pick him up and follow me." I turned to the Pit Guard. "When they come for your prisoner, say nothing."

The Guard's beady eyes volleyed between Condor and me. He had a loose-lipped look and I suspected he would go on to spread the details of what he witnessed here.

Good, I thought. I wanted news of this burgeoning alliance— Record Keeper and Rebel—to spread throughout the twelve Houses. The quicker the better. It would pave the way for the united future I envisioned.

Martin was awake, but still immobile, when we reached the testing suite. The twins shrieked at our entrance and covered their faces. I strode to East Keep. "Do you have the braid?" I demanded.

She seemed unable to blink.

"East Keep, the braid," I commanded.

Fumbling, she held up the twisted length of Jones' dress.

I took it and turned away. The crystalights above me seemed to dim. The crowd of people around me and the others faded to the background as a smile formed on my bruised lips. I moved to stand over Jones. She lay on her back, her injured eye bulging obscenely. The skin around the globe was black and tender.

I bent for a closer look. Her fingers caught my eye. They were covered in rings. The same rings that had pounded me into submission. I shivered. Reaching out, I caressed the largest one then plucked it, gently, from her hand. I tried it on. It hung loose on my middle finger. I clenched my hand to secure it. Slowly, I pulled back my balled, bejeweled fist. I aimed the flashing ruby at her swollen eye.

When I was done, something red-tinged, like jelly stained with blood, oozed down her cheek. I wasn't satisfied. My breath came quickly as I picked up her right hand, her punching hand, and yanked the smallest finger to the side until a small *pop* reached my ears. She moaned. I bent down, holding my ear close to her chest. *Where was she? In her own dark Pit? Could she hear me?*

"Teacher?" I whispered.

She didn't respond.

Behind me, a voice called my name, as if from a distance. Jetson waved to get my attention. His motions were frantic with fear. I wrinkled my nose. Minus Voltaire, the people gathered in the testing suite represented the strength of the mighty Kongo, and still they were afraid of one slain English woman. *Not for long, comrades*, I vowed. *Together we will muster a power such that we will never be afraid again. To the contrary, we will banish the Assembly, abolish the Compromise and establish an independent Kongo nation. But first—*

Ignoring Jetson's waving motion, I drifted to the window overlooking the arena. I held up my hand and admired the ring in the sunlight. There was a faint trace of blood on the gold gilt—*hers or mine?*—there was no way of knowing. I removed the braided cloth from my pocket and took my time stringing the ring on the braid. I secured the braid around my nape, like a necklace. I adjusted the bauble so it quivered at the hollow of my throat. A greedy pleasure dilated my pupils, making me long to finish what I had started with Jones. I checked the feeling. I would not kill her—not today.

After years of torture, she didn't deserve the mercy of a quick death. I had taken one eye, for William. And one finger, for Fount. And that was enough, for today. Soon, when I consolidated the power of the Kongo, I would be back to take my revenge. I paused. I thought of Sky and Kiwi, Runner and Robin. I thought of my unnamed mother. Taking a deep breath, I adjusted the vow. When I had complete power, I'd be back to take not *my* revenge—but ours.

I turned to face the room. They whispered quietly now, worried and wondering. I took a moment to absorb their faces, a beautiful assortment of brown shades. Deep down, beneath my hatred for Jones, my heart throbbed with love for them. I sniffed and pushed that weaker sentiment aside. Then, with one hand on my Apex, I called them to order.

ABOUT THE AUTHOR

Agnes Gomillion is a speaker and writer based in Atlanta, Georgia, where she lives with her husband and son. Homegrown in the Sunshine State, Agnes studied English Literature at the University of Florida before transitioning to Levin College of Law, where she earned both a Juris Doctorate and Legal Master degree. She's a voracious reader of the African-American literary canon and a dedicated advocate for marginalized people everywhere.

ACKNOWLEDGMENTS

This story was quilted from four million souls, those that survived American chattel slavery, and those that didn't. Those that recorded their recollections, and those that died unsung, in graves without stones.

Their individual contributions found me in unusual ways as I wrote. A line of research, a gospel song or a look from a stranger would bring on inexplicable tears. And, filled with joy or pain, I would stop and listen for guidance. These moments were the old souls reaching out across space and time. They inspired *The Record Keeper*, shaped the plot and are entirely responsible for its success.

A particular debt is owned to Mr Frederick Douglass and Mr Fountain Hughes. Mr Douglass, your life and writings form the basis of Arika's narrative. Mr Hughes, your honesty and wit brought life to the Kongo Village. I'll forever remember the first time I heard your voice.

Thank you and thank you again for entrusting us with your stories.

In addition, I'd like to acknowledge Paul Stevens. Paul, your advice and support throughout the publishing process proved dependable. Thank you for seeing value in *The Record Keeper* when others didn't.

THE RIG
ROGER LEVY

Humanity has spread across the depths of space but is connected by AfterLife – a vote made by every member of humanity on the worth of a life. Bale, a disillusioned policeman on the planet Bleak, is brutally attacked, leading writer Raisa on to a story spanning centuries of corruption. On Gehenna, the last religious planet, a hyperintelligent boy, Alef, meets psychopath Pellon Hoq, and so begins a rivalry and friendship to last an epoch.

So many Lives, forever interlinked, and one structure at the center of it all: the rig.

"A triumph that is guaranteed to blow your mind."
Lavie Tidhar, author of *A Man Lies Dreaming*

"Roger Levy is SF's best kept secret, and *The Rig* is a tour de force: a darkly brilliant epic of life, death and huge drilling platforms. Read it and discover what you've been missing."
Adam Roberts

THE RIFT
NINA ALLAN

WINNER OF THE 2017 BSFA AWARD FOR BEST NOVEL
WINNER OF THE KITSCHIES RED TENTACLE 2017

Selena and Julie are sisters. As children they were close, but as they grow older, a rift develops between them. There are greater rifts, however. Julie goes missing aged seventeen. It will be twenty years before Selena sees her again. When Julie reappears, she tells Selena an incredible story about how she has spent time on another planet. Does Selena dismiss her sister as the victim of delusions, or believe her, and risk her own sanity?

"Astonishing and brilliant, the best thing this immensely gifted writer has yet done."
Adam Roberts, author of *The Thing Itself*

"A heart-rending novel about being believed, being trusted, and the temptation to hide the truth. Of people going missing, and their incomplete stories. A generous book, it leaves the reader looking at the world anew. Dizzying stuff."
Anne Charnock, author of *A Calculated Life*

EMBERS OF WAR
GARETH L. POWELL

WINNER OF THE 2018 BSFA AWARD FOR BEST NOVEL

The sentient warship *Trouble Dog* was built for violence, yet following a brutal war, she is disgusted by her role in a genocide. Stripped of her weaponry and seeking to atone, she joins the House of Reclamation, an organization dedicated to rescuing ships in distress. When a civilian ship goes missing in a disputed system, *Trouble Dog* and her new crew of loners, captained by Sal Konstanz, are sent on a rescue mission.

Trouble Dog, Konstanz and Childe find themselves at the center of a conflict that could engulf the entire galaxy. If she is to save her crew, *Trouble Dog* is going to have to remember how to fight…

"It's a smart, funny, tragic, galloping space opera that showcases Powell's wit, affection for his characters, world-building skills and unpredictable narrative inventions."
Locus

"An emotionally wrenching take on life in a war-torn far future."
Publishers Weekly

For more fantastic fiction, author events, exclusive
excerpts, competitions, limited editions and more

VISIT OUR WEBSITE
titanbooks.com

LIKE US ON FACEBOOK
facebook.com/titanbooks

FOLLOW US ON TWITTER
@TitanBooks

EMAIL US
readerfeedback@titanemail.com